FANTASY FICTION

Bloomsbury Writer's Guides and Anthologies

Bloomsbury Writer's Guides and Anthologies offer established and aspiring creative writers an introduction to the art and craft of writing in a variety of forms, from poetry to environmental and nature writing. Each books is part craft-guide with writing prompts and exercises, and part anthology, with relevant works by major authors.

Series Editors:
Sean Prentiss, Vermont College of Fine Arts, USA
Joe Wilkins, Linfield College, USA

Titles in the Series:
Environmental and Nature Writing, Sean Prentiss and Joe Wilkins
Poetry, Amorak Huey and W. Todd Kaneko
Short-Form Creative Writing, H. K. Hummel and Stephanie Lennox
Creating Comics, Chris Gavaler and Leigh Ann Beavers
Advanced Creative Nonfiction, Sean Prentiss and Jessica Hendry Nelson
The Art and Craft of Asian Stories, Xu Xi and Robin Hemley
Advanced Fiction, Amy E. Weldon

Forthcoming Titles:
Experimental Writing, William Cordeiro and Lawrence Lenhart
Poetry 2nd ed, Amorak Huey and W. Todd Kaneko
Environmental and Nature Writing 2nd ed, Sean Prentiss and Joe Wilkins
Advanced Poetry, Kathryn Nuernberger and Maya Jewell Zeller

FANTASY FICTION

A WRITER'S GUIDE AND ANTHOLOGY

Jennifer Pullen

BLOOMSBURY ACADEMIC
LONDON • NEW YORK • OXFORD • NEW DELHI • SYDNEY

BLOOMSBURY ACADEMIC
Bloomsbury Publishing Plc
50 Bedford Square, London, WC1B 3DP, UK
1385 Broadway, New York, NY 10018, USA
29 Earlsfort Terrace, Dublin 2, Ireland

BLOOMSBURY, BLOOMSBURY ACADEMIC and the Diana logo are trademarks of Bloomsbury
Publishing Plc

First published in Great Britain 2024

Cover design: Rebecca Heselton
Cover image: Planadviser by Tran Nguyen | mynameistran.com

Library of Congress Cataloging-in-Publication Data
Names: Pullen, Jennifer, 1986- author.
Title: Fantasy fiction : a writer's guide and anthology / Jennifer Pullen.
Description: London ; New York : Bloomsbury Academic, 2024. | Series: Bloomsbury writer's
guides and anthologies | Includes bibliographical references.
Identifiers: LCCN 2023025521 (print) | LCCN 2023025522 (ebook) | ISBN 9781350166936
(hardback) | ISBN 9781350166929 (paperback) | ISBN 9781350166943 (pdf) |
ISBN 9781350166950 (epub)
Subjects: LCSH: Fantasy fiction—Authorship. | Fantasy fiction—History and criticism. |
Fantasy fiction.
Classification: LCC PN3377.5.F34 P85 2024 (print) | LCC PN3377.5.F34 (ebook) | DDC
808.3/8766—dc23/eng/20230727
LC record available at https://lccn.loc.gov/2023025521
LC ebook record available at https://lccn.loc.gov/2023025522

A catalogue record for this book is available from the British Library.

ISBN: HB: 978-1-3501-6693-6
         PB: 978-1-3501-6692-9
         ePDF: 978-1-3501-6694-3
         eBook: 978-1-3501-6695-0

Series: Bloomsbury Writer's Guides and Anthologies

Typeset by RefineCatch Limited, Bungay, Suffolk
Printed and bound in Great Britain

To find out more about our authors and books visit www.bloomsbury.com
and sign up for our newsletters.

CONTENTS

SECTION 1
AN INTRODUCTION TO FANTASY WRITING

Introduction

As a lifelong enthusiast of fantasy fiction and an academic creative writer, I hear many opinions about fantasy. A man on a bus saw me reading a Peter S. Beagle book and said, "Is that some of that imaginary wizard shit? People used to read real books before Harry Potter. Like Beowulf." He went on to rant. Apparently, wizards in fiction leads to students wearing weird clothes, and summoning demons. Who knew?

This anecdote encapsulates a major misperception about the origins of fantasy fiction that I have found among the average person and many fellow writers and scholars. It is often believed that fantasy fiction is either a) a relatively recent phenomenon, often attributable to J. R. R. Tolkien or young adult fiction like the *Harry Potter* books, or b) has been around since the epic and folktales. The latter belief is usually espoused by fantasy apologists, and the former by its detractors. Both of these beliefs are simultaneously correct and incorrect. Fantasy fiction draws upon older traditions like folktales, fairy tales, and the epic, which are not technically fantasy. Neither Tolkien nor J. K. Rowling invented fantasy fiction, but both were, in their respective cultural moments, part of the crystallization and popularization of fantasy fiction. The beliefs I just described highlight the disputed nature of fantasy as a genre: passionately loved by some and bemoaned by others.

In reality, fantasy fiction begins not with the ancient world or medieval era, nor in the 20th century, but in the 18th and 19th centuries. To understand the history of fantasy, one must understand the contested nature of fiction itself. In this book I will begin with a history of fantasy fiction in the context of the development of the novel, specialized publishing, and academia. After setting the context, this book will focus on fantasy writing craft, an area highly underdiscussed in formal craft books. The entire orientation of this text derives from the knowledge that fantasy fiction has been and always will be political, and that the best writers of fantasy are aware of and deliberately use the sociopolitical tools available to them. After the chapters covering craft, there are instructions for accessing the online appendixes, and a anthology of fantasy short stories. As a reader or teacher, though you may jump around within this textbook, ideally you will cover the chapters in the order that they appear.

Note About English-language Emphasis

In the first chapter of this book, I will be focusing largely on fantasy in English. This focus derives from several factors. 1) Fantasy as a distinct and seperate genre grows out of the English-language novel tradition. Writers from other cultures did and do publish work that would now be called fantasy fiction, but the factors that lead to fantasy being pushed out of mainstream literature didn't occur in the same way.[1] As a result, the advent of specialized publishers and magazines for fantasy and science fiction outside of English-speaking countries occurred later, largely in response to an English-language influx. 2) Due to the successive imperial projects of Great Britain and the United States (not a situation that I condone) English-language literature was widely translated and disseminated. For example, in 1930s Mexico the pulp magazines that began to arise published translated American pulp science fiction and fantasy, with some work by Mexican authors.[2] In the 1950s, American genre mags flooded the market, displacing the Mexican pulp magazines. The reverse didn't occur. There is still a relative dearth of international fantasy being translated into English (this is beginning to shift, largely due to authors like Ken Liu advocating for translations).[3] In the late 1960s Mexican writers of science fiction and fantasy who *conceptualized themselves as such* emerged. Those writers often cited 19th-century science fiction and fantasy in English as their inspiration (especially H. G. Wells). Mexican science fiction and fantasy existed before, but largely without the genre labels. The subculture of science fiction and fantasy as genres apart wasn't embedded in the conversation. In Russia, traditional folktales remained widespread and science fiction that idealized Russia's technological prowess gained popularity in the USSR, but the subgenre of fantasy publishing didn't gain steam until the 1990s.[4] It was seen as subversive because of the prevalence of nostalgia for the monarchal past. Similar patterns of the formation of fantasy as a distinct genre in public conceptions can be found around the world, from Europe[5] to Latin America. 3) The dominance of English-language fantasy is beginning to wane, and more works of international fantasy are being translated, which is hugely important given that the "Big 5" publishers are headquartered in the US. Further, organizations to promote work by writers from outside of the US and the UK are gaining prominence, like the African Speculative Fiction Society. All of this is a welcome and much needed development. It is also relatively recent, and consequently the chapter about the history of fantasy as a distinct genre in the public conception will reflect the dominance of English-language fantasy in the 19th and 20th centuries. This not an endorsement of English-language dominance.

Note on Audience and Citation Choices

This book is intended for teachers who want to teach fantasy and for aspiring writers, including undergraduates. Thus, while it is based on a lifetime of reading and my scholarly work in fantasy and science fiction, as well as my doctoral work in 19th-century literature, it is not a scholarly monograph. My prose style and citation choices are guided by a desire to be simultaneously grounded in scholarship, and accessible to students. So my sources mix scholarly and academic texts with popular and online resources, so that students will feel empowered to look up my sources on their own. Additionally, much of fantasy is radically understudied in academia, resulting in limited scholarly sources. Consequently, I sometimes chose to use the sources of information generated by the fantasy and science fiction writing community in defining genres, etc.

Without further ado, let's dive in!

CHAPTER 1
FANTASY AND ITS EVOLUTION

The Wild-Wild Pre-20th Century

In the 18th century the novel was not the well-regarded literary form it is today. Poetry was the prestige genre. Novels that were praised were often praised in terms of whether they approached the level of poetry in the eyes of the reviewers. It was a "low" form for a variety of reasons, many of which had to do with gender and class. It was believed that novels could be read by the barely literate, and thus people of distinction (i.e., white educated men) should devote their leisure reading to poetry. More women were becoming novelists and were perceived as the primary market for novels. Concerns ran rampant: novel reading would lead to the death of poetry and loose morals among women! While reading alone, women could be thinking about *anything*. Similarly, there were concerns that the lower classes might become too aware of their own condition.[6] Novels like Samuel Richardson's *Pamela* were condemned for frankness about sexuality. Hordes of religious novels were written to counter the perceived moral depravity of the mainstream novel. Later, Nathaniel Hawthorne decried what he viewed as a takeover of fiction by a "horde of scribbling women."

The novel has always been a political and politicized genre, much like science fiction and fantasy. Because the novel was not a prestige genre nor an old one, it was essentially the mythical wild west of literature—nearly lawless. As the novel gained popularity and prestige in the 19th century, fiction writers weren't labeled by genre (fantasy, literary, etc.). Subgenres of the novel existed but were not treated (usually) as especially important distinctions. Many novelists in the traditional "canon" of English departments have been labeled as more "realistic" than they really are. For example, Charles Dickens's novels contain ghosts and spontaneous human combustion. Writers roamed all over the metaphorical frontier of fiction. Oscar Wilde wrote fairy tales, a gothic supernatural novel, and drama of manners. George Eliot, patron saint of 19th-century realism, wrote *The Lifted Veil*, a novella about a man who could read minds. Fiction writers who crossed what we would now see as genre boundaries between or within projects were the norm. Further, the 1830s saw massive increases in the ease of printing, leading to the proliferation of newspapers and periodicals.

Some of the cheapest periodicals, called *penny dreadful*s, contained sensational stories written for literal cheap thrills, appealing to the masses. Consequently, classism and sexism were entangled in cultural attitudes toward fiction.[7]

By the late-18th and 19th centuries the novel had developed the majority of the ancestors of the modern fantasy. The primary ancestors of fantasy fiction as we understand it today can be found in romance, gothic, mystery, adventure, and early science fiction and fantasy novels themselves.

Additionally, broader cultural shifts around Europe occurred concurrently, shifts that would be hugely important to the fantasy novel. Among them, the birth of folklore studies, rampant colonialism, women's liberation movements, changing family structures, the professionalization of science, spiritualism, industrialization, and mass publishing.

All of the above lead to a society in the midst of enormous change. Not unlike the 20th and 21st centuries, technologies shifted wildly, along with social mores, and information access.[8]

Seeds of Early Fantasy

A Changing World: Anthropology and Folklore

Folklore studies emerged from both colonialism and industrialization. People from the Grimm brothers in Germany (1780s–1860s) to Lady Gregory in Ireland (1850s–1930s) were worried that traditional culture would be lost to war, colonialism, and movement as people flocked to cities for factory work. Similarly, as Europeans encountered people from other parts of the world through trade and colonialism, an interest in understanding other cultures and their stories grew. Early anthropology is implicated in a lot of problems, from racism to eugenics. It also led to Europeans having access to global stories, from Japan to the vast territories of the then Ottoman Empire. The tales dubbed *The Arabian Nights* or *Tales of One Thousand and One Nights* was first translated into English in 1811. The first major translation of Grimm's fairy tales into English occurred in 1823. When you next read a fantasy novel in English and encounter a kelpie, selkie, jinni, or kitsune, you have the 19th century and folklore and anthropology to thank. This period also included high profile translations of *Gilgamesh*, the *Kalevala*, Greek mythology, *Beowulf*, and the Icelandic sagas.

Writers of proto-fantasy all over the world wrote short original fairy tales and retellings. Folklore is the lore/stories told by the "folk," primarily pre-literate and transmitted orally. Many tales were written down in the 19th century when industrialization made people (including the Grimm brothers) afraid that these stories would disappear. Many include outright magic or improbable circumstances. Written versions came to be called fairy tales. Folklorists wrote down the stories as they were told, thus, the earliest versions of the Grimm collections were violent and brutal, employing simplistic language, since they strove to change it as little as possible from the oral tale. When the tale is changed and/or elaborated upon it becomes a fairy tale. In the 19th century this meant adding Christianity and/or a moral, as well as eliding violence and sex. Retellings are new versions of existing tales. Original fairy tales remix characteristics of the genre to make something new. All of the above reached a pitch of popularity in the 19th century.[9]

Folklore collection was often political in nature, but so were fairy tales themselves. People used the magic and wonderous occurrences as a shield, allowing them to express taboo beliefs while reducing personal risk.

Oscar Wilde's collection of original fairy tales, *The Happy Prince and Other Tales* (1888), critiqued capitalism, heterosexual relationships, monarchy, and religion. Madame

D'Aulnoy (1652–1705) founded a salon for women to write fairy tales protesting their condition as second-class citizens. Her proto-feminist stories protested forced marriage, rape, and mandatory motherhood. Her story "The Green Serpent," a precursor to Beauty and the Beast, focuses on female agency, and the tyranny of beauty.

Full-length novels also borrowed from fairy tales. From Charlotte Brontë's *Jane Eyre* (a Cinderella story) to Robert Louis Stevenson's *Dr. Jekyll and Mr. Hyde* (combining early science fiction with the doppelgänger trope from fairy tales), or George MacDonald's *The Princess and the Goblin*, among many others.

Other Worlds, Medieval Literature, Faraway Places, and Challenging the Status Quo

In England, industrialization caused many progressive writers and thinkers to develop nostalgia for the Middle Ages. They created an imagined version of the past with pastoral fieldwork and benevolent nobles. While there are problems with this fantastical version of the medieval, it was a reaction to the destruction of the natural world, and the terrible suffering of the poor that occurred in cities unprepared to handle them. There's a reason that Tolkien, a medievalist, would write one of the defining fantasy novels of the 20th century. Nineteenth-century writers who wanted to preserve what they saw as good about the past used fantastical novels to make readers question their current smoke-clogged reality. In the late-18th and early-19th centuries, this had roots in Romanticism, a movement that sought to elevate the natural and the imaginative over the rational and modern. They saw rationalism as the source of the devastation of the natural world, and the loss of individual autonomy to the machine (literal and social).[10]

Seeds for early fantasy found in medieval and renaissance literature include Arthurian mythology, utopias (such as the proto-feminist 1666 utopia *The Blazing World* by Margaret Cavendish), epic poems, and hagiography.

William Morris wrote fantasies like *News from Nowhere* and *The Wood Beyond the World* in the late-19th century. Earlier, Sir Walter Scott's historical romances like *Ivanhoe* had similar themes. A Romance is a narrative with a large scope, intense feelings, and marvelous events. The medieval chivalric Romance influenced Morris and other writers who used nostalgia for social critique. The historical and the chivalric Romance are crucial sources for epic fantasy, without being fantasy themselves.

Writers also began to set stories in "lost" worlds, to create a blank slate for cultures of their own design. These adventures were precursors to modern science fiction and fantasy, nearly identical to planetary romance or space fantasy (like *Star Wars* or Frank Herbert's *Dune*). Sometimes there were elements of technology to bring readers to a fictional planet, but often it was just a made-up place "out there." Jonathan Swift's 18th-century novel *Gulliver's Travels*, a satire, falls within this category. Gulliver goes to lands that never were and never could be. *The Time Machine* (1895) by H. G. Wells also fits. The technology is an excuse to visit alternate versions of Earth which reflected the author's socialism.

H. Rider Haggard was one of the most popular 19th-century lost-world adventure writers. Gogol, from *She*, was acknowledged by Tolkien as the inspiration for Gollum. In these novels the "elsewhere" is Africa, and the main characters encounter cultures that blend aspects of Greek and Roman culture, with the (very poor) understanding the English had of indigenous African cultures. In *She*, the adventurers discover a kingdom in Africa governed by an immortal goddess queen with psychic powers. Haggard was a British civil servant. His depictions of colonized peoples are deeply problematic to modern eyes. The invented cultures within reflected Haggard's spiritualist beliefs and Bolshevism. His novels inspired *Indiana Jones*, and all of the Oxford Inklings through his elaborate attention to worldbuilding and high-stakes plots. Haggard provides a key example of how fantasy, even at its most swashbuckling and escapist, has always been politically situated. Fantasy fiction both reflects and comments on its time.

Made-up cultures in 19th-century fantastical works frequently resembled a real historical Earth culture, but with crucial changes in gender norms or social systems (often a version of socialism). Both other planets and faraway places acted as a way to posit alternatives to the status quo. While many of these writers had visions that we today may not find palatable, that doesn't mean they weren't pushing against the status quo of their moment. Twenty-first century accusations that "everything is political now" and longing for the days when stories were "just about adventure and imagination" derive from the fact that contemporary readers are regularly unaware of the political implications older texts had within their own times. To the Romantics, the very act of imagination was political. Even as the Romantic period passed (roughly 1798–1837), the ideas they espoused remained within the fantastical literary community.[11]

Science or Magic? The Gothic, the Supernatural, and the Birth of Science

You may have noticed that I have been referring to fantasy *and* science fiction in this history. This is not accidental. Fantasy and science fiction are not currently perfectly discrete categories, but before the 20th century, the differences were negligible. This is due to the state of science in the 18th and 19th centuries. Science largely wasn't taken on by professionals, but by gentleman intellectuals. Even among the professionals, the boundaries between disciplines weren't well established. Sir Arthur Conan Doyle was a medical doctor, botanist, and a prolific writer of mysteries and early fantasy. Research was sometimes motivated, like in Darwin's case, to display the glory of God. Darwin's *On the Origin of Species* (1859) was lauded by some in the scientific community and scoffed at by others. Spiritualism, which included talking to the dead, and the idea of a collective unconscious, was talked about in the same breath as early psychology. It was considered scientifically viable by some mainstream thinkers. The borders between science, religion, and the supernatural were porous. This flow of ideas across boundaries that seem firm to most 21st-century people is reflected in the literature of the time.

Gothic literature, an important seed for contemporary fantasy and horror, arose concurrently with the Romantics, and their interest in the *sublime*, in part as a reaction to the

Enlightenment. The words *awe* and *awesome* are tied, ecstatic joy barely separable from terror. The gothic novel used both the supernatural and nature to induce feelings of pleasurable fear. Contemporary dark fantasy and weird fiction are particularly indebted to the gothic novel. Stories with strange claustrophobic houses, animate machinery, mad scientists, brooding Byronic lovers (google the Byronic hero, you won't be disappointed), ghosts, maidens fleeing across the moors, and people dying of a broken heart, can thank the gothic novel.

The gothic feeds on big feelings and dramatic events. Sometimes this can lead to silly books (and my own teenage fascination with black lipstick), but it also leads to visceral stories that get under the reader's skin in a way that goes beyond logic. The intertwined joy/terror of the gothic showed up in early science fiction and fantasy novels (many of which are also gothic novels).[12]

Mary Wollstonecraft Shelley's *Frankenstein* (1818) explores the ways that science can go wrong, and how love can turn to hate. It is many kinds of books at once: gothic, science fiction (some consider it the first science fiction novel), and supernatural. Victor Frankenstein's monster, and his attendant horror at his creation, is akin to Dr. Faustus crying out, "I'll burn my books" after his deal with the devil. The novel is full of tragedy and sublime settings. Houses haunted by grief. An arctic journey. Mary Wollstonecraft Shelley would later write *The Last Man*, perhaps the first post-apocalyptic novel. Her work exemplifies the blending of science and the supernatural.

Mary Wollstonecraft Shelley's life highlights the political nature of fantasy. She was the daughter of Mary Wollstonecraft, the author of *The Vindication of the Rights of Women* (considered by many the mother of feminism) and was herself a boundary pusher. She ran off with Percy Shelley, had his child, and married him later. They faced social ostracization and poverty to be together. Their friend Lord Byron (famously "mad, bad, and dangerous to know") had both male and female lovers. The Byronic hero is named for him and his works. Most anti-heroes, the dark brooding men stalking around literature, owe something to him. Mary Shelley was an active writer, thinker, and philosopher who held her own among wild bohemian circles.

We also have the gothic novel to thank for vampires and many supernatural beings that heavily populate contemporary urban and paranormal fantasy. Bram Stoker's *Dracula* (1897), Joseph Sheridan Le Fanu's *Carmilla* (1872) are influential vampire novels. *Dracula* includes blood transfusion in a mental hospital (science), as well as the titular vampire (definitely not science). *Dracula* inaugurates the trope of the monster hunter (Van Helsing), and the brooding vampire lover. *Carmilla* doesn't have *Dracula's* scrim of science over magic, but it does have the emphasis on sexuality (lesbian tension) and atmosphere characteristic of the gothic.

The gothic novel was dominated by female writers, many of whom, sadly, spent a great deal of the 20th century being forgotten in favor of a male canon. Examples include Ann Radcliffe (one of the highest paid writers of her time), Louisa May Alcott (of *Little Women* fame), Mary Shelley, all of the Brontë sisters, and Charlotte Perkins Gilman (known for "The Yellow Wallpaper"). The gothic novel's extreme situations created the perfect canvas to explore darker sides of humanity and show women's oppression and capacity to fight back. The 19th century saw an increase of women questioning their confinement, agitating for political representation, rational dress, and more favorable marriage laws. Simultaneously, it saw a rise in reactive conservatism.

Charlotte Brontë's *Jane Eyre* (1847) exemplifies gender politics infusing the gothic. She used gothic stylistic elements to create a strong female character, who, in the midst of terrible circumstances, found herself. Emily Brontë's *Wuthering Heights* (1847) is a pure gothic novel, complete with Byronic Heathcliff, more a villain than a hero in this female-experience-centered novel. The influence of the Brontë sisters on fantasy hasn't been talked about enough and deserves whole books. They and their brother spent most of their childhood building a fictional world, complete with governance and geography, not unlike Tolkien, but it was never published. The work of the Brontë sisters is especially important to gaslamp fantasy.[13]

Contemporary dark fantasy commonly contains young women who must triumph against powerful monsters or monstrous men. While this is sometimes a sexist trope, it has also given us some of our most empowered heroines. Gothic fantasy often includes exploration of the edge of socially acceptable sexuality, questioning normative standards.[14] Storm Constantine's *Wraeththu*, a cult 1980s gothic fantasy, exemplifies this aspect of gothic-influenced fantasy. As do Anne Rice's vampire novels, and many within urban or paranormal fantasy. Urban fantasy in the 21st century is dominated by women, writing heroines who solve supernatural mysteries, both fighting and fucking the "monsters" they encounter. The gothic novel, in the past and in the present, pulls the veil away from characters by pushing them to their limits.

Other writers important to the gothic, though not contributing to the list of canonic monsters, include Edgar Allan Poe, Nathaniel Hawthorne, and E. T. A. Hoffman. Hoffman was a German Romantic writer of fantasy and horror, who influenced H. P. Lovecraft, and many contemporary writers. He is most known for his novella *The Nutcracker and the Mouse King* (1816) that became the inspiration for the ballet *The Nutcracker*. His work satirized the nobility through the guise of fantasy. The aforementioned novella includes a king who murders people for not properly stuffing his sausages, whose home is overrun by witchcraft-practicing mice.

Contemporary gothic fantasy (and urban fantasy) frequently incorporates a mystery. The role of mystery in the gothic and in much contemporary fantasy, especially the darker side of fantasy, is demonstrated in Sir Arthur Conan Doyle's work. While Sherlock Holmes is a genius polymath whose understanding of many scientific fields dwarfs even that of Doyle himself, many of the stories contain an undercurrent of the uncanny. Holmes spent a lot of time solving mysteries that at first appear to have supernatural causes, like ghostly dogs (*The Hound of the Baskervilles*). Doyle was both a man of science and fascinated by the occult. He was at different times a Freemason, a Spiritualist, and founder of a society to study psychic phenomena. He believed his children's nanny had psychic powers. This wasn't unusual: many people tried to turn science to studying psychic powers and ghosts, seeing it as no more fantastical than the idea that there were bones of great beasts from long ago buried under the earth (fossils!). Thus, in the gothic, as in much fantasy and science fiction, awe can come from the irrational and the rational.

As the 19th century wound down, the Decadents picked up some of the traits of the Romantics and of gothic literature. They sought to depict extreme experiences, often an exercise in seeking sensation, sometimes through drugs and sex. They believed in art for art's sake, a reaction to the Victorian obsession with meaning and utility. Oscar Wilde's *The Picture of Dorian Gray* (1890) is one of the most famous novels of the movement. It was used against him when he was put on trial for homosexuality. He was sentenced to hard labor, which broke his health and lead to his death. Wilde's novel is an example of how fantasy was (and is) often used as a way to get at social issues sideways, to push the buttons of the empowered. Sometimes the veiled rebellion protected the writer, and sometimes not.[15]

The Invention of Childhood: Here There Be Pixies and Monsters

In this wild-wild west of fiction, in addition to fiction itself being a point of contention (Could it be art? Or was it trash for the masses?), childhood and what children should read was another sticking point. At its heart was fantasy fiction and the role of imagination. This particular battle would be hugely influential for not only children's literature, but the status of fantasy fiction into the 20th and 21st centuries.

In the 19th century, Europeans, especially in England, began to construct the idea of childhood as most Western people understand it today. For much of human history, children had to work. Children's clothes were smaller versions of adult clothing. Children's literature didn't really exist—most stories (including fairy tales) were by adults and for adults. If children happened to hear them and like them, great. In the 18th and 19th centuries, change came for childhood. Child labor laws arose in response to the horrors of children in factories and mines, now up close and visible to the middle and upper classes in cities (industrialization, here you are again). The middle classes were growing, and one of the main markers of upward mobility was the ability to keep women idle. The consensus was that taking care of the home was women's rightful purpose, where they provided emotional succor to their men and raised children. Children began to be seen not as mini adults, but as innocents—childhood became a special pure time.

Some people thought children needed instructive books that taught morals and a realistic view of the world. This led to religious moralizing tomes, or stories about naughty children who died because they didn't listen to their parents. Endless quantities of this drivel were produced. Unless you are a scholar you probably haven't read these stories. I don't recommend them.

Other people argued that childhood was the time of whimsey and imagination, and that innocence was best protected through wonder. Lessons needed to go down with a spoonful of sugar. The children's stories of the 19th and early-20th centuries that have lasted are full of fantasy. Famous 19th-century examples include sanitized versions of fairy tales such as those found in Andrew Lang's fairy books, and original stories like Edward Lear's *The Owl and the Pussy Cat*, George MacDonald's *The Princess and the Curdie*, Lewis Carroll's *Alice's Adventures in Wonderland*, E. Nesbit's *The Story of the Treasure Seekers*, and Rudyard Kipling's *The Jungle Book*.[16]

Lewis Carroll's work exemplifies "nonsense" literature for children, influenced by 19th-century European absurdist traditions, like the Russian writer Gogol (his story

"The Nose" in particular). Absurdism and nonsense have a tradition of hiding political points. For instance, the aforementioned Gogol story pokes fun at his society's obsession with status.

The emphasis on nonsense and fantasy in the 19th century paved the way for 20th-century classics of children's literature including P. L. Travers's *Mary Poppins*, Frank L. Baum's *The Wonderful Wizard of Oz*, J. M. Barrie's *Peter and Wendy*, C. S. Lewis's *The Chronicles of Narnia*, and Madeline L'Engle's *A Wrinkle in Time*.

All of the authors above are widely read, remain in print, and have been adapted into other mediums. While it is good for children's literature that the didactic stories weren't the seed that grew to flower, as a result, toward the end of the 19th century (and into the 20th) authors like Henry James began to argue that fantasy was *only* for children, and the older and longer tradition of fantastical stories for adults was effaced. This has hugely impacted the way fantasy is published and read.

Early Fantasy and Science Fiction Itself

As you have seen from my discussion of the seeds of fantasy fiction in the wild time before the turn of the 20th century, most fiction that we now call fantasy has been retroactively categorized as such, since the publishing category of fantasy didn't exist. Prior to the 20th century, few writers self-consciously categorized their work as fantasies. It wasn't a genre so much as a mode, or a state of mind.

A few writers straddled the turn of the century, acting as pivot figures to the 20th and 21st. Lord Dunsany, W. B. Yeats, H. P. Lovecraft, and E. Nesbit were born in the 19th century, but published most of their work in the 20th. Tolkien and Lewis, and most other major 20th-century fantasy writers, would have devoured Dunsany, Lovecraft, Haggard, MacDonald, Shelley, Wells, Morris, and the Lang fairy books. The 19th century had a long tail.

The Fences Go Up: Fantasy in the 20th and 21st Centuries

If the 19th century was, metaphorically speaking, an open range, by the turn of the century, publishers, and other writers, were putting up fences, saying "you are a fantasy writer" or "you are a writer of realism." Fiction was no longer the scrappy underdog. Once you decide that some fiction *is* art, it becomes easier to decide that some fiction is *not*.

Henry James and William Forrester popularized the notion of literary realism as now understood by defining themselves against the fantasy and whimsey that dominated children's literature, as well as the adventure stories in penny dreadfuls and early pulps. That literature, they argued, was for children and unsophisticated poor people. Adults (by which they meant white educated men) needed to read *serious* books, defined by what they themselves wrote—books focused on the experience of the individual. Any large events should be the kind people experienced in real life: marriage, childbirth, loss of a loved one, etc.[17]

I do not mean to condone a divide between realism and fantasy literature. I love and read both, and you should, too. Narrow reading doesn't do anyone any good, least of all writers. But the opposition between fantasy and realism is still present in many publishing venues and creative writing programs. Therefore, it's important to understand where it came from, and how it has impacted fantasy fiction today.

As James, Forrester, and their ilk defined themselves against the fantastical, fantasy and science fiction began to define itself, through the creation of specialized publications.

The Early-20th Century

The Pulps, the Glossies, and the Lowly Masses

The pulp magazine began in the 19th century but took off in the 20th. They evolved out of the penny dreadful but were more professionalized. They were printed on cheap pulp paper and tended to have lurid covers. Detective fiction, fantasy, science fiction, and horror were the bulk of their contents. The first was *Argosy*, founded by an American named Frank Munsey (1882–1978). It featured original content and serialized reprints of Victorian adventure stories. *Argosy* and other pulps also featured stories about proto superheroes, like Flash Gordon. *Argosy* sold up to a million copies per issue, one of the largest circulations of any magazine in the world. It marketed itself primarily to young working-class men.

The pulp was primarily an American phenomenon, though there were some in Britain, notably *Tales of Wonder* (1937–42). In the 1920s, pulp magazines were so popular that publishers began magazines focused on single genres. With the advent of specialized venues of publication, editors, readers, and writers started seriously sorting work into categories. Many stories still didn't fit tidily in science fiction, fantasy, or horror, but writers began to see themselves (and be seen) as writers of a certain kind. With such definitions came the formulation of conventions.

Amazing Stories, founded by Hugo Gernsback in 1926, published the first stories by many stars of fantasy and science fiction including John W. Campbell, Isaac Asimov, Howard Fast, Ursula K. Le Guin, Roger Zelazny, Leigh Brackett, and Marion Zimmer Bradley. Gernsback's magazine was central to defining science fiction as a specialized publishing arena. The letters section where fans, writers, and editors corresponded with each other gestated fan culture. *Weird Tales* (1923), the first specialized magazine for fantasy and horror, debuted many well-known writers, including H. P. Lovecraft, Ray Bradbury, Edgar Rice Burroughs, Robert E. Howard, and Robert Heinlein.[18]

Men began to dominate fantasy more than in the 19th century. Women wrote for the pulps, but frequently under male pen names. Alice Bradley Sheldon wrote under the name James Tiptree, Jr., creating an entire second life. She maintained the on-paper identity of Tiptree until ten years before her death in 1987. Her public persona was that of both a macho male, and a male feminist. She was known for stories that explored the boundaries of gender norms and the ways society confined women.[19] Other women writers such as Leigh Brackett, Andre Norton, and Ursula K. Le Guin, who began in the pulps, would go on to be some of the biggest names in fantasy.

A few writers who began in the pulps gained broad public respect, though most did not. Le Guin and Ray Bradbury were exceptions. For every Le Guin and Tiptree with progressive ideas, there were writers like H. P. Lovecraft, whose world and phantasmagoric prose was hugely influential, but who was also deeply sexist and racist, even for his time.

In some respects, the pulps were too popular for their own good, and their covers didn't do them any favors (do an image search, you'll find men in space suits rescuing damsels with heaving breasts, or alien woman hybrids) in the public eye.[20] They were the largest markets for short fiction in the world. Side by side with the many authors who have endured were forgettable swashbuckling stories, the fiction equivalent of cotton candy. The mass popularity of the pulps meant that writers who desired to be seen as artistically serious wanted to publish in the slicks or glossies, highbrow magazines printed on high-quality paper. *The Atlantic Monthly* and *Harper's* were two of the biggest. They specifically marketed themselves as being for people of quality, in direct opposition to the pulps. These magazines sometimes printed stories that we would see as science fiction or fantasy, but the writers tended to strenuously deny that categorization.

The pulps and the paperback books that grew out of them led to the creation of specialized publishers, including DAW, the first publisher founded to publish fantasy and science fiction. Some have argued that this contributed to (or was a symptom of) the ways in which genre fiction was ghettoized. Others have argued that specialized publishing allowed fantasy and science fiction to develop as a genre and publish politically avant-garde fiction alongside the more overtly "pulpy" stories that the covers advertised so successfully. Both arguments have merit: specialized publishing venues were a double-edged sword. They allowed the genre to mature and gave it room to grow, while simultaneously giving credence to those who decided it was for the lowly.

Beyond the Pulps: Fairy Tales, Surrealism, and Men in Tweed

In the early-20th century, the trends of the previous century continued. Because the pulps were so prolific and had a reputation as being "low" writing, in America there were many writers creating work that would now be considered fantasy, but at the time wasn't, because it was perceived that serious writing couldn't be science fiction or fantasy.

Like the 19th century, in the 20th there were writers who engaged in folkloric research and other scholarly work alongside fiction writing. Zora Neal Thurston, an influential African American writer, was also a folklorist and sociologist. She published folklore collections and fantastical stories in which she retold African American oral tales, like her story "Uncle Monday" about a shapeshifter in Florida. She used her writing to talk about oppression and to save tales from erasure. Frank L. Baum, in addition to the *The Wizard of Oz*, wrote a collection of stories for adults made up of original fairy tales, called *American Fairy Tales*. Christine Quintasket, known by her pen name Mourning Dove, invested many years preserving tales told by the elders of her community. Her retellings of indigenous folktales, collected in the book *Coyote Stories*, are just one example of how folklore and retellings remained vital, and often one of the areas of the field where women and writers of color were able to find an audience in America and England, through scholarly or popular publishing.[21]

Many other writers wrote recognizably fantastical works in the 20th century outside of the pulps. W. E. B. Dubois wrote a story called "The Comet" which depicts a Black man and woman who appear to be the only two survivors of disaster which wiped out the rest of humanity, effectively making them a new Adam and Eve, until her family shows up and ruins their fresh start with racism. It is post-apocalyptic and an early gesture toward afro-futurism, but because of the venue of publication, and the perception that science fiction was written by and for white boys, it was ignored for most of the 20th century.

In addition to folk and fairy tales remaining important, in the early-20th century surrealism, fabulism, and magical realism in Europe and Latin America, as well as many parts of Asia, were crucial sources of fantastic literature. Latin American magical realism would become the dominant form of magical realism.[22] Surrealism, while not officially part of fantasy, would become one of the contributors to its development. While relatively few official members of the Surrealist movement were outright fantasists, they would inspire later writers like Angela Carter. A few, such as Franz Kafka, became foundational writers for fantastic fiction more broadly. Surrealism was most fertile in the visual arts, but its focus on overturning logical progression, and on image-driven narratives, would infuse 20th-century fantasy, especially by writers sympathetic to surrealism's anti-capitalist/anarchist orientation.[23] In the 19th century many major writers of early fantasy self-identified as socialists or communists. Surrealism fit with fantasy since it used nonrealistic depictions of the world to push against the mainstream. In surrealism it was primarily a matter of subjectivity and fragmented perception, yet many fantasy writers went on to use surrealist techniques. This influence is discernible retrospectively, based on fantasy writers describing their own personal canon.

In Britain, where the pulp tradition was less influential, fantasy took a different track. The prominence of some of the writers, scholars, and critics from the 19th century who wrote what we now call fantasy meant that it was seen as a more honorable tradition than in America. This led to the scientific romance, rather that science fiction, being the predominant British mode of the fantastic. The scientific romance has elements of both science fiction and fantasy. Their visions of the future were usually focused on social change instead of technology. As was the case with George Orwell, these writers were often public intellectuals.

There were prominent fantasy writers who occupied high social positions, which helped its respectability, and kept it from being as aligned with the lower classes as in America. A prime example is Lord Dunsany aka Edward Plunkett, 18th Baron of Dunsany. He held one of the oldest titles in the Anglo-Irish nobility and hobnobbed with important figures in the Irish literary renaissance. His most famous novel, *The King of Elfland's Daughter* (1924), is a tale of a king who marries the titular daughter. It was influential for Le Guin, Tolkien, Lewis, among other 20th-century fantasy writers. He also wrote another, stranger book, called *The Gods of Pegana,* where he developed a fictional pantheon. He's known for lyrical yet baroque prose which H. P. Lovecraft tried unsuccessfully to imitate.[24]

Hope Mirlees, British translator, critic, and modernist poet, born in 1887, lived to be nearly 100, and lent academic and scholarly credentials to her fantasy. She is known for her novel *Lud-in-the-Mist* (1926), about a town thrown into chaos by an influx of faerie fruit (an allusion to Christina Rosetti's "The Goblin Market"). Contemporary writers, from Kelly Link to Neil Gaiman, rave about the book and its importance to the fantasy genre. Her work showcases both the importance of fairy tales to fantasy, and the modernist preoccupation with art about art. E. Nesbit, known primarily as a children's writer, also wrote dark fantasy for adults. She, too, straddled the 19th and the 20th centuries; she and her husband were friends with William Morris, and they cofounded the Fabian society (dedicated to bringing socialist ideals into British society). She influenced 20th-century fantasy writers including C. S. Lewis and Michael Moorcock. These writers are foundational to high fantasy and secondary-world fantasy, genres that Tolkien would come to dominate.

In the early-20th century world of English literature, alongside the ever-growing prestige of realism, there existed a strong tradition of fantastical children's literature and high fantasy written by scholars and critics. Yet a bombshell was coming. While the pulps continued to create a specialized realm of publishing in America, in Britain the Inklings would change everything. While their writing was a continuation of what already existed, they would profoundly alter publishing and public perception.

Hobbits, Lions, Kings, and Castles, Oh My! The Mid to Late-20th Century and the Tolkien Takeover

In 1931, a group of scholars and writers in Oxford who loved fantasy formed a group and called themselves the Inklings. In 1933 Tolkien and Lewis began to lead the group, and it became a place where members would read unfinished compositions to each other.

Tolkien and Lewis were both influenced by medieval literature and impacted by the First World War. Their work emanated longing for a pastoral past, free of the horrors of modern war and industrialism. Both writers published popular works in the 1930s, but in the 50s and 60s their fame would explode.

The Lord of the Rings, Tolkien's most famous work, needs little introduction. If you are reading this book, you know of its existence; if you haven't read it, you have seen the films, or read some other book populated by elves, dwarves, and halflings. To this day writers of epic fantasy are compared to Tolkien in blurbs to indicate their importance. George R. R. Martin's *Song of Ice and Fire* novels were initially framed by blurbs calling him "the American Tolkien" even though their works bear almost no resemblance to each other. Tolkien, in the popular imagination, became synonymous with fantasy, and consequently, epic fantasy set in a secondary world of pseudo-medieval European origin became the main image of fantasy in public perception.

In America, *The Lord of the Rings* was popular with the hippie movement, because it was anti-war and anti-industry. Outside the hippie movement, many considered it a children's book, somewhat embarrassing for adults. It was also beloved by some Christians who sought parallels between elves and angels. Part of how such disparate groups as conservative Christians and hippies could take up Tolkien as a mascot is his lack of interest in character psychology. The books are written in a third-person objective point of view, and so we only know why characters do something if the narrator tells us directly. Tolkien wanted to write an alternate history for England. He modeled his work and his world after medieval and mythological stories, not modern novels. He made a deliberate authorial choice.[25] Unfortunately, because of Tolkien and a few literary descendants, people have claimed that fantasy isn't about characters.

C. S. Lewis's *The Chronicles of Narnia*, published in the 1950s, is an epic fantasy for children, and an early portal fantasy. Lewis was anti-war and nostalgic for the countryside. His work was fantasy and Christian allegory. The story was strong enough that it has influenced many writers, even if they don't share his religious views, like Philip Pullman.

With Tolkien and Lewis, who wrote for both children and adults, you can see how fantasy literature for adults (like *The Lord of the Rings* or Lewis's mythological retelling, *Till We Have Faces*) struggled to maintain the mantle of adult literature. Even so, because they were academics, in England their writing was able to maintain a respectability that fantasy writers in the US battled to achieve.[26] They did *not* invent fantasy; they merely became so popular that their versions of the genre dominated the mainstream.

Writing in England at the same time as Tolkien and Lewis were other fantasists whose work has been influential but who are often ignored in discussions about the creation of fantasy.

Once such writer was T. H. White. He published the books that would make up *The Once and Future King* in the 1930s. White turned down an invitation to join the Inklings, since he saw himself as more working class than the others. *The Once and Future King* was a modernist take on the Arthurian legend. It partook of the anti-war sentiments common to much fantasy, but it also strove for an underpinning of realism. It asked: what would it be like to be treated as a chosen king, when you'd grown up as an ordinary person? It takes seriously the psychology of the characters and the consequences of their actions. Martin and other fantasy writers interested in the darker corners of human psychology are more his descendants than Tolkien's.

Mervyn Peake was another important fantasist of the period. He was an illustrator first. When the Second World War broke out, he offered to create anti-fascist propaganda. He was turned down and conscripted into the army. He started his first *Gormenghast* novel, *Titus Groan*, during the war. The *Gormenghast* series was published in 1950. He also painted illustrations of 19th-century fantasy masterpieces. He was tormented by what he'd seen during the war. He was often compared to Tolkien, which irritated him. He saw himself in the tradition of the gothic novel and Charles Dickens. His dislike of the label of fantasy is ironic given that his sources of inspiration are so important to fantasy fiction itself. *Gormenghast* is the story of a fictional dukedom, in a castle of the same name, and a school also of the same name. The world of *Gormenghast* has little overt magic, but plenty of implied supernatural forces. It's a book about class, repression, and a rivalry between two young men. It has been cited as an influence by many fantasy writers, including Michael Moorcock. It is considered a cornerstone of modern fantasy—yet it isn't as famous as one might expect. It doesn't fit easily into the narratives of "fantasy is for children" or "fantasy is escapist." It is inconvenient for those who like to see Tolkien as the founder of fantasy, since it's contemporaneous, and Peake actively strove not to be aligned aesthetically with Tolkien.[27]

The extreme popularity of Tolkien and the character and world of Conan the Barbarian (by Robert E. Howard) contributed to the creation of specialized book publishers for fantasy and science fiction in the US, beginning in the 1950s, but really taking off in the 70s and 80s. As with the pulp magazines, specialized publishers were both a boon and a problem for writers. Writers who wanted literary acceptance tried to be published by mainstream presses instead. Kurt Vonnegut wrote novels that included super scientists and time travel but distanced himself from the genre. This problem was most pronounced in America, but it existed in the rest of the anglophone world as well. The dominance of Tolkien led many fantasies to be considered not fantasy because they were too different from the dominant books within the field. Consequently, understanding the history of fantasy necessitates retroactive unearthing.

Some of the most important science fiction and fantasy presses that were founded between the 1950s and 1980s include:

US: Ace (50s), DAW (70s), Tor (80s), and Baen (80s) UK: Del Rey (70s), Gollancz (20s, though not specializing in science fiction and fantasy until the 90s), Orbit (70s).

Some children's book presses gained fame for publishing important fantasy, even though they weren't specialized publishers, because many genre writers were forced to publish as children's authors. Parnassus (1960s) is one such press, most notable for publishing Ursula K. Le Guin's *A Wizard of Earthsea* (1968). This book is broadly considered one of the most important books in 20th-century fantasy literature and isn't really a children's book.

With the 60 and 70s, fantasy and science fiction exploded, especially in the United States and Britain. Tolkien, Lewis, White, and Howard dominated the public conception of the genre so much that, more and more, the most famous texts within the field took place within a pseudo-medieval, vaguely European secondary world. Content similarities were often surface level, but the predominance of white men wielding swords while wearing improbable armor on covers contributed to the public perception that the new publishers were an extension of the pulps.

Scores of Tolkien imitators arose, mostly forgettable, but some so widely read that the opinion that fantasy was derived from Tolkien was given more credence than it was due. Some writers who were vaguely Tolkienesque or Arthurian who contributed to this perception include David Eddings and Terry Brooks. Some criticism of Brooks's *Shannara* universe was so extreme that he was accused of plagiarizing Tolkien. Plagiarism is a bit of a stretch; the *Shannara* books take place 2,000 years after a nuclear war destroys the world as we know it. For some reason, nuclear fallout created elves, trolls, and halflings. *Shannara* is about one step removed from Tolkien fanfiction. I wrote fanfiction as a teen and into my early 20s. It is nothing to be ashamed of—but *Shannara* and its ilk have been very hard on the reputation of fantasy.

Another important Tolkien-inspired work came in the form of *Dungeons and Dragons*, created by Gary Gygax and Dave Arneson in 1974. *DnD* is a role-playing game, where one player, the Dungeon Master (DM), narrates the story and the mechanics, and other players create characters who then fight monsters and deal with obstacles set up by the DM. I am an avid player myself. The creators downplayed the importance of Tolkien, finally admitting it was one of "many" influences in the early 2000s, after a lawsuit from the Tolkien estate over the naming of some of their magical peoples. Its influence on fantasy should not be underestimated. It is a game founded on storytelling (even writers of realism like Junot Diaz have admitted to its influence on their writing). It led to a broad understanding of stock fantasy creatures. There are hundreds of tie-in books, as well as for the *Forgotten Realms* universe, a spinoff. *Dungeons and Dragons* was also influential for its systematized worldbuilding.[28]

The Tolkien clones that took up literal and metaphorical shelf space from the 1960s onward obscure the complex and diverse fantasy landscape that existed. Samuel R. Delaney, one of our most important fantasy and science fiction writers, a queer black man, won the Nebula Award in 1966 and 1967. His first novel, *The Jewels of Aptor* (1962), takes place on a world where disasters led to a regression to medieval technology. Delaney's work grapples with themes of language, mythology, perception, race, class, gender, and sexuality. He is an important critic, and a professor at universities including Cornell. Yet outside of the fantasy and science fiction community, he is little known, and when people talk about diversity in fantasy or sci-fi, his presence from the 60s onward is often ignored.[29]

Michael Moorcock, a writer, musician, political activist, and editor, is most known for his books focused on Elric of Melniboné, that he has been working on since the 1960s. Elric is an albino emperor of a dying civilization, with a magic talking sword. Moorcock's sword-wielding, sorcerous, anti-hero emperor is one of the most influential characters in fantasy fiction. Moorcock describes himself as an anarchist and lists Mervyn Peake as a primary influence. His activism includes convincing bookstores to not shelve books that glorify violence against women. He helped create the New Wave in science fiction, which emphasized the importance of prose in fantasy and science fiction. Despite barriers, many women published in the pulps and early specialized publishers. Leigh Brackett wrote from the 1940s through the 60s. She usually depicted agrarian societies and used the setting to explore issues including gender and the evils of colonialism. Notably, she wrote an influential draft of *The Empire Strikes Back*.

Brackett was a major influence for Marion Zimmer Bradley, an important early figure in feminist fantasy in the US. Long before becoming a professional writer, Bradley was active in fantasy and science fiction fandom. She invited other writers (including fanfiction writers) to contribute to her *Darkover* universe. She also wrote lesbian romance novels and edited the long running *Sword and Sorceress* anthologies. She solicited submissions from new writers, especially women writers and queer writers. She brought many influential female fantasy writers into the field through mentorship and publication. She wrote from the 1940s through the early 2000s, and was most famous for her feminist Arthurian novel, *The Mists of Avalon*. Her importance and her espoused principles made what happened in 2014 especially shocking. In 1990, her husband was arrested for child abuse and pedophilia. Then, in 2014, her daughter came forward to say that she had been abused by both parents but had been afraid to say anything because of her mother's reputation. It became clear that Bradley and her live-in female partner had covered up her husband's behavior and participated. Her writing and editorial importance is real, but her evil actions are, too.[30]

Another important fantasy and science fiction writer who got her start in the 1950s is Anne McCaffrey. Her *Pern* books are set on a world where humans have psychic bonds with dragons. She was the first woman to win a Hugo Award.

Octavia Butler, born in California, wrote science fiction and fantasy from the 1970s until her death in 2006. An African American writer, she was the first science fiction writer to win a McArthur Award, and a major contributor to afro-futurism. Her work was mostly science fiction, however, some novels, like the *Patternist* series, employ elements of both fantasy and science fiction. She explored social issues including race, class, gender, sexuality, and consent. She is one of our most important American writers, period.

Ursula K. Le Guin, the inspiration for the ethos of this book, wrote fantasy, science fiction, and criticism, from 1959 until her death in 2018. Her *Earthsea* books (1968–2001) introduced the idea of a school for wizards. Her work is characterized by a deep examination of ethics. She was influenced by anthropology, Taoism, anarchism, feminism, and environmentalism. Her prose is known for its beauty. She won nearly every award in the field. While for much of her early career she was mistakenly shelved in the children's section of libraries and bookstores, by her death she was a public intellectual, and achieved internet fame for her National Book Awards speech where she called out capitalism and Amazon.

I hope from the figures I have detailed here, their publishing history, intellectual and artistic preoccupations, as well as the wide range of stories that they wrote, you can see that Tolkien, while important, is overly credited for his impact on fantasy. His influence is most important not for content or style, but for drawing attention to the genre.

Fantasy and science fiction publishing, despite the presence of women writers and writers of color that are often left out of histories, was still very white and male. The influence of British fantasy and American pulps dominated the industry. Fantasy built upon European folklore was the majority. This can be attributed to how the 20th century was a world in which the globe had been dominated first by Britain, and then by the United States. Literature in the 19th century was used by English schools in India, for example, to try to "civilize" the populace. Further, in China after the Cultural Revolution, fantasy and science fiction was frowned upon, so specialized publishers for the fantastical didn't arise. The fantasy of the time that did get written in China has been severely undertranslated into English, though there has since been a boom in excellent Chinese science fiction.[31] Similar cases can be found around the world. Thus, the books that got the most mainstream attention create a sense of greater homogeneity than there actually was.

In the 1980s and 90s fantasy in English had been an established genre long enough that it began to fragment into subgenres. There had always been different types of fantasy fiction, but writers, editors, and readers began to name those types, and something approaching standardized expectations began to form. This process was accelerated and intensified by publishers striving to create clear marketing categories.

Epic fantasy, including its many subgenres like sword and sorcery, continued to be the most high-profile genre. Important authors of epic fantasy in the 1980s and 90s included Tad Williams, Robert Jordan, Terry Goodkind, Raymond Feist, Patricia McKillip, and Mercedes Lackey. Arthurian fantasy continued to be popular and was among the forms of fantasy likely to be published by mainstream presses in addition to genre presses. Important Arthurian fantasy authors of the 1980s include Mary Stewart, Guy Gavriel Kay, and Stephan Lawhead. Fantasy based on fairy tales remained popular, and relatively likely to cross into literary circles. Angela Carter, Jane Yolen, Terri Windling, and Tanith Lee were (and are) very influential.

Even within these relatively traditional fantasy categories, writers experimented in either form or content. Mercedes Lackey was noteworthy for her matter-of-fact inclusion of queer characters. Tad Williams took fantasy to dark and morally complicated places. Patricia Mckillip is known for the beauty of her prose and imagery. But the vaguely Tolkienesque work of Robert Jordan and Terry Goodkind were still overwhelming present in the 1980s and much of the 90s. With the 90s, more and more women began to get attention for high fantasy, including Sara Douglas and Robin Hobb. Robin Hobb's *Realms of the Elderlings* series, begun in 1995, and concluded in 2017, is arguably one of the most well-constructed, complete, and character-driven epic fantasy series ever written, following mostly one man, FitzChivalry Farseer, from youth until old age. Arthurian fantasy is a traditional genre that hid innovation within it. Patricia Kennealy blended Arthurian legend, science fiction, and her religious beliefs (she is a High Priestess in a Celtic Neo-Pagan order). Guy Gavriel Kay's first series *The Fionavar Tapestry*, blended portal, Arthurian, and contemporary fantasy.

Fantasy, always varied, became even more so, and some variations began to be codified, a process that shapes and is shaped by writers, readers, and editors.

At the same time the genre was exploding, publishing was contracting. There used to be the high-profile fantasy publishers that I have already alluded to, and also a lot of smaller presses. In the 1980s and 90s, more and more presses were absorbed into big ones, and many of the larger fantasy presses were purchased by international conglomerate publishing houses.

Simultaneously, in the 1990s, children's publishing underwent a revolution. Remember how the 19th century invented the notion of children's literature? For a long time after that there were picture books, and a few chapter books aimed at children learning to read to themselves. There were authors who wrote books for that mushy middle between childhood and adulthood, but no one was certain what age that was. What constituted "appropriate" content or reading level was inconsistent. Books would be shelved with the adult fiction in some bookstores, while in others they would shelve them with children's literature. Some fantasy would be published under a children's publishing label but be read largely by adults. Inversely, some books, like the first *Valdemar* trilogy by Mercedes Lackey, seem like Young Adult (YA), but were published as adult fantasy. Readers growing up in the 1980s and 90s would likely skip from kid's books to adult fiction.

Then, in 1997 (UK) and 1998 (US), a book about a boy named Harry Potter rocketed to the top of the *New York Times* bestseller list and remained there through 1999 and 2000. In 2001 the NYT split the list into children's and adult fiction because of *Harry Potter*'s dominance. Half of copies sold were sold to adults and older teens. Before *Harry Potter*, children's book sales were falling. By the end of the series, sales in children's books had risen by more than 50 percent. It caused an increase in longer books aimed at teens.[32] Then, it was controversial because conservative people were upset by the magic and progressive overtones. Now, it is controversial because of J. K. Rowling airing transphobic opinions. Regardless, *Harry Potter* was the driving force behind YA literature becoming the influence in publishing it is today.

As far as fantasy goes, in many respects, all of this has been for the good. Between *Harry Potter* in book and film form, *Twilight*, the *Lord of the Rings* films, the revival of *Star Wars*, and the new respectability of comic book movies, by the 2000s, fantasy and its adjacent genres spilled into the mainstream, and that meant more opportunities for fantasy writers and readers.[33]

But it also entrenched the belief that fantasy was for children or wasn't artistically serious. The books made into films cemented the perception that fantasy was mostly British and white.

Underneath the book to film phenomena, fantasy fiction itself began another huge expansion, not just in the genres of fantasy available, but who wrote it and what characters were depicted. Women and people of color, who had always written fantasy fiction, finally began to attract more attention, especially from around 2010 onward. The dominance of vaguely British or Celtic fantasy, patterned after Tolkien, was actively discussed. Fantasy set in universes populated by characters of color and inspired by African and Asian cultures began to win high-profile awards. Further, conversations about how to write people different from oneself rose in the broader conversation, shepherded by the inimitable Nisi Shawl, through their workshop series and book, *Writing the Other*, inspired by a conversation at Clarion West in 1992.[34]

Writers of color like Nisi Shawl, N. K. Jemisin, Sofia Samatar, Ken Liu, Ted Chiang, and others were nominated for and won major awards within the industry. There had always been high-profile writers of color in fantasy and science fiction, like Butler and Delaney, and more working invisibly, but the sheer number of writers who weren't white men gaining attention was new. More fantasy works were being set in the contemporary world, or places other than the United States or Europe, and female characters as well as queer characters took center stage more frequently. Writers like Jemisin and Shawl spoke openly about their experience entering the field, and about writing fantasy books that de-centered whiteness.[35] Much of the fantasy gaining renown was by women. Further, more writers in mainstream publishing began to write fantastical fiction, and more, like David Mitchell, were willing to admit it. Books like Mitchell's *Cloud Atlas* garnered acclaim both within the genre world and without.

Simultaneously, in 2011 HBO adapted George R. R. Martin's *Song of Ice and Fire* series. Martin's series was written as an answer to the stereotypical fantasies that featured the overthrow or defeat of an evil overlord. What happened when the heroes began to age and had to rule? It wasn't the first series to ask that question or depict fantasy political maneuvering. But nothing like it had been *filmed* before. It was gritty and had high production values. More people saw that fantasy could be for adults, and fantasy was pulled further out of the corners of culture.

The changes happening in fantasy publishing and fantasy fiction mirrored changes in broader culture. Much as in the 19th century, conversations about gender, sex, sexuality, race, and class gained traction. Barack Obama was elected president of the United States. Marriage equality became the law of the land in the US.

When change happens fast, or is perceived to have happened fast, inevitably some people push back. From 2013 to 2015, a group formed on the internet that called themselves the Sad Puppies (and the overlapping group Rabid Puppies). It was a right-wing, anti-diversity campaign intended to influence the Hugo Awards. It was started by Larry Correia in an attempt to get nominated. He said his work and other "popular" works like it were being ignored by the Hugo Awards in favor of more literary works with progressive themes. The Hugo Awards are determined (both the nominees and the winners) by *all* members of the World Science Fiction convention. It is based upon a *popular vote* by people who choose to become members. The argument made by the Sad Puppies that there was some elite group biased against popular works makes no sense. The structure of the awards meant that it was possible for someone to convince people to buy memberships specifically to try to fill the list of nominees with particular authors. Before the Sad Puppies, no one had tried. From 2013 to 2015, the Puppies attempted to spam the Hugo Awards. In 2015, they populated the list of nominees in several categories with the authors they had chosen. It had always been an option for voters to check "no award" if they thought no one on a list was worthy. In 2015, in the categories the Puppies spammed, voters did just that.

The Sad Puppies and Rabid Puppies were unsuccessful, and though they continued to exist, they lost cohesion, and list of people they wanted to nominate ceased to be radically different from nominations that were occurring anyway.[36]

It was ironic that the Puppies argued that fantasy and science fiction had changed radically, given that the field has consistently been peopled by writers with political agendas. The Puppies perceived the progressiveness of the winning works as new because they were ignorant of the original contexts of the stories they grew up with, and because the people who were winning awards weren't as homogenous as they used to be. In 2017, the third book in N. K. Jemisin's *Broken Earth* trilogy won the Hugo Award for best novel, making her the first author to win for each book in a trilogy, and the first to win best novel three years in a row.[37]

Fantasy as of this writing has arguably entered a golden age, receiving more cultural credibility than ever before, with more diversity of form, style, content, and authorship. With print-on-demand technology, and other innovations, there are abundant small presses publishing groundbreaking work, and helping to reduce homogeneity. Independents like Tachyon, Erewhon, Small Beer Press, Mythic Delirium, and Subterranean Press publish strange and wondrous fiction. Large publishers have imprints that prioritize diversity, such as Tor.com's novella line. Giants of the genre produce interesting books, and new writers with new visions appear constantly. Readers and writers push every day to make fantasy fiction more representative of the beautiful variety of people on this planet. The work isn't done, but the acknowledgment that the work must happen is widespread and gaining traction.

It is a good time to be a fantasy writer. Welcome.

Discussion Questions and Writing Activities

1. Why does it matter to know that writers who have been considered "canon" like George Eliot, Charles Dickens, and Charlotte Brontë weren't "realist" writers in the sense that people mean the term now?

2. How might it change the perception of fantasy if more fantasists before Tolkien, and contemporaneous to Tolkien, were well known?

3. Which aspects of the pre-20th-century history of fantasy were most surprising or interesting to you? Why?

4. What impact does the politics of 19th-century writers have on your perception of them, or of fantasy? Does it matter how many of them were countercultural within their time?

5. Were you assigned science fiction and fantasy titles as "classics" in high school or college before this? If so, which ones? If not, why do you think that was the case?

6. Pick an early to mid-20th-century author from this chapter who you don't know much about and do an internet search. What do you discover?

7. The chapter discusses the role of social change in fantasy, how the broader changes in society impacted the texts, from industrialization to feminism. Why do you think fantasy appeals to people during times of intense social change?

8. The anthology in this textbook includes two stories set in the 19th century, or the early 20th-century, one by Theodora Goss and one by Genevieve Valentine. Both combine history and fantasy. What techniques do they use?

9. It is important for readers to be able to see themselves in the fiction they read and the writers who write it. What impact do you think the visibility of writers like Ted Chiang or N. K. Jemisin will have on future writers?

10. The pulps are gone, but fantasy magazines remain. Look up *Uncanny*, *Lightspeed*, *Tor.com*, or *Beneath Ceaseless Skies*. What do you notice about the stories they publish? What type of work do they like, based upon the stories you can read there, and other factors, like visual design?

11. Look at the list of Hugo Award winners from the 1960s to the present. What changes or patterns do you notice? How do your observations connect to the chapter?

12. Jot down an idea for a story set in the 18th or 19th century. Then, jot down some things you need to know about the time period to do it properly. Finally, come up with three ways you would change the world to make it fantastical.

CHAPTER 2
FANTASY GENRES (A MOSTLY COMPREHENSIVE REVIEW)

In this chapter I will briefly survey and define most of the largest fantasy genres. The definitions will include a brief note about their origins, representative writers, and common characteristics. This list is necessarily incomplete since fantasy is a living and evolving genre. Further, because fantasy has not been as widely studied academically as realism, there is limited consensus; many genres overlap, intersect, or have conflicting definitions.

Genres

Secondary-World Fantasy

Any fantasy that is set in a world other than the "real" or primary world. It is a fictional world, not merely a modification of a real-world culture, though real-world cultures can be part of its inspiration. Some fantasy genres (like portal fantasy) can include both the real world and a secondary world.[1] Most high fantasy is secondary-world fantasy, so the history of the genre is very similar, though not identical to that of epic/high fantasy.[2] It also includes gothic secondary-world fantasy like *Gormenghast* in its genealogy.

Epic Fantasy / High Fantasy / Sword and Sorcery / Quest Fantasy

When people think of fantasy fiction, this series of overlapping genres is often the first that comes to mind. High fantasy and epic fantasy are sometimes seen as synonyms of each other. High fantasy is set in a secondary imagined world. Most, but not all, epic fantasy is also high fantasy. Early writers in the genre include William Morris, Lord Dunsany, and J. R. R. Tolkien.[3] Epic fantasy has roots in the classical epic and tends to focus on heroic characters who have extraordinary abilities or ordinary people who do extraordinary things. The stakes in epic fantasy are high, the fate of the world (or a nation) rests on the actions of the characters. The hero is often an orphan or younger son (paralleling fairy tales where the seventh son of a seventh son is significant or magical) or someone who comes from a mysterious or powerful lineage. Sometimes they are chosen by outside forces like gods or wizards. They frequently oppose forces of evil bent on domination and can overlap with quest fantasy. For example, *The Lord of the Rings* is a quest fantasy and an epic fantasy at the same time. Historically, the Eurocentric and male-centered Hero's Journey has driven the plot.[4] Sword and sorcery, like *Conan the Barbarian*, has high stakes, but more morally gray heroes. The white-male-centric focus is shifting, the moral certainty of early epic fantasy is giving way to greater ambiguity. Early tendencies to center plot over character have largely fallen away. Important contemporary writers include N. K. Jemisin, Robin Hobb, Brandon Sanderson, Guy Gavriel Kay, Patrick Rothfuss, Tamsyn Muir, Rebecca Roanhorse, S. A. Chakraborty, Jenn Lyons, Robert Jackson Bennett, Andrea Stewart, and Zen Cho.

Gaslamp Fantasy / Steampunk / Fantasy of Manners

Gaslamp fantasy is a subgenre of historical fantasy and alternate history fantasy, but so prolific that it contains within itself a series of further subgenres including fantasy of manners and steampunk. Gaslamp fantasy is set in a pseudo-Victorian, Regency, or adjacent time period, most often in England, America, or a secondary-world proxy[5]. Sometimes gaslamp fantasy mimics period novels in style, like Susanna Clarke's *Jonathan Strange & Mr. Norrell*. Sometimes gaslamp fantasy riffs on a specific aspect of period culture, like *A Natural History of Dragons* by Marie Brennan. Fantasy of manners novels are sometimes set in secondary worlds set in the past, such as Ellen Kushner's queer cult novel *Swordspoint* (often credited with inventing the fantasy of manners genre). A fantasy of manners uses/subverts tropes of the novel of manners, centering interpersonal or romantic relationships.[6] Not all fantasy of manners novels are romance novels, though there are gaslamp romances (like *Soulless* by Gail Carriger). They are usually focused on female identified characters and set out to highlight the problematic gender norms of the inspirational periods. Some are simultaneously gothic, such as *The Magicians and Mrs. Quent* by Mark Anthony. Steampunk is gaslamp fantasy with an emphasis on steam technology and the promises and perils of industrialization.[7] Gaslamp fantasy is increasingly used to critique colonialism. Genre mashups are common. Influential contemporary novels in this genre include Jo Walton's *Tooth and Claw*, Jeanette Ng's *Under the Pendulum Sun*, C. L. Polk's *The Midnight Bargain*, Mary Robinette Kowal's *Shades of Milk and Honey*, and Natasha Pulley's *The Watchmaker of Filigree Street*.

Silkpunk / Other Punk Genres

Silkpunk, like steampunk, blends science fiction and fantasy, and examines how technology can be simultaneously glorious and problematic. The term was coined by Ken Liu, one of our most important silkpunk writers, though novels that could qualify existed before (terms usually aren't created until a genre begins to coalesce). It is *not* just Asian-flavored steampunk. It takes its inspiration from the Romantic storytelling tradition (big R romantic, not bodice rippers) of East Asia, and classical East Asian antiquity.[8] Technology is often biomimetic, using materials indigenous to East Asian and Pacific Islander cultures. Like all *punk* genres, the punk signifies resistance, reappropriation, and defiance. This a rising genre. Key writers include Ken Liu, Nghi Vo, Zen Cho, J. Y. Yang, and Marjorie Liu. Note: there are *punk* fantasy subgenres for pretty much any historical time period or region. The thing they have in common is a desire to subvert, rebel, and defy authority, while blending fantasy with technology. Godpunk has been a recent place for writers of color to subvert white dominance in fantasy. Important writers include P. Djèlí Clark and Suyi Davies Okungbowa. Godpunk overlaps with mythic fantasy. Hopepunk, on the other hand, isn't really a genre, since it refers to a hopeful tone—any genre can be hopeful. Its inverse, grimdark, also isn't really a genre so much as tonal and worldview orientation.

Historical Fantasy

Broadly defined, this is fantasy set in the past. The genre is rapidly expanding and can be combined with other genres, like epic fantasy. It is usually set in a real place or a readily identifiable fantasy analog.[9] It is usually interested in treating its setting and time period realistically. It will often have limited magic, spending more page space on the political, social, and economic situations of the characters. It is more likely than epic fantasy to focus on ordinary people and de-emphasize destiny. The plots are usually large in scope but also character centered. The prose is frequently lyrical. This genre includes alternate history fantasy, which can be highly magically infused or contain no magic at all. The Netflix TV series *Bridgerton* is an example of this—it makes Queen Charlotte black and posits a changed social climate around race as a result. One of the most esteemed current practitioners of historical fantasy is Guy Gavriel Kay. The magical element in his fantasy is subtle but real. There are historical fantasy novels set in every imaginable time and place. Common subgenres include Wuxia fantasy, inspired by Chinese and Japanese warrior traditions, and Arabian fantasy, inspired by the *Arabian Nights*. Recent novels like *The Underground Railroad* by Colson Whitehead and *The Water Dancer* by Ta-Nehisi Coates add fantastical elements to American history to address racism.

Arthurian Fantasy

Patterned after the Arthurian chivalric Romance.[10] People have written Arthurian narratives long before fantasy was a genre. Famous examples from the 20th century include T. H. White's *The Once and Future King* and Guy Gavriel Kay's *The Fionavar Tapestry*. This genre has been blended with nearly every genre one could imagine, from science fiction, to horror, to romance. It has been a constant presence within fantasy, not particular trendy, but never entirely out of fashion. Themes of war, peace, destiny vs. freewill, and true love are common. Nicola Griffith's *Spear* is a recent standout example.

Romantic Fantasy

Romantic fantasy is a widespread subgenre of fantasy with diffuse boundaries. The stories focus on relationships, interpersonal, political, and romantic.[11] The love story is crucial to the broader plot, with sociopolitical implications. Romantic fantasy novels can also be epic fantasy novels, or any other genre. They usually center female-identified protagonists (although not always). There is usually a distinction made between a fantasy romance (a romance novel with fantasy elements) and romantic fantasy (a fantasy novel that includes a romance). The biggest difference between the two is tonal. A romantic fantasy novel doesn't need to end happily, while a fantasy romance must. Both tend to be compassionate regarding human nature. Diversity has been steadily increasing, with high-profile examples of works written by and about queer people and people of color. Well-known examples include Jacqueline Carey's *Kushiel's Dart*, Juliet Marillier's *Daughter of the Forest*, Naomi Novik's *Uprooted*, Katherine Arden's *The Bear and the Nightingale*, Kai Ashante Wilson's *A Taste of Honey*, and Tasha Suri's *The Jasmine Throne*.

Gothic Fantasy / Dark Fantasy

Gothic fantasy draws on the gothic novel. Characterized by extreme emotions (from pleasure to terror), eerie settings, and unsettling images. Similar to dark fantasy and horror, though it tends to contain less explicit violence than some horror. Magic/the supernatural must be the source of the uncanny.[12] The boundaries between gothic fantasy, dark fantasy, and horror are fuzzy. There are many texts that could easily fit all three categories. Dark fantasy and gothic fantasy are sometimes considered synonymous, though some argue that you can have dark epic fantasy, but not gothic epic fantasy. There are subgenres that have grown large enough to be considered related but distinct, like cosmic horror / Lovecraftian fantasy, and Weird Fiction. Gothic fantasy and its related genres draw upon the legacy of such writers as Nathaniel Hawthorne, Edgar Allan Poe, Mary Shelley, and Charlotte Brontë. Often used to discuss themes of oppression. Prominent contemporary writers include Silvia Moreno-Garcia, Cherie Priest, Victor LaValle, Anne Rice, and Stephen Graham Jones.

Weird Fiction / Cosmic Horror / Lovecraftian Fantasy

These overlapping genres are fertile enough to get their own sections, but difficult to separate. Lovecraftian fantasy draws upon the Lovecraft mythos. Much of it now uses the mythos in order to wrestle with Lovecraft's racism and sexism. Thus, writers like Ruthanna Emrys, Cherie Priest, and Victor LaValle have retold Lovecraft stories, or just borrowed elements, to write anti-racist, anti-sexist, and anti-homophobic works.[13] Any writer of this genre must deal with the reality that Lovecraft was simultaneously influential and hateful. Cosmic horror is adjacent, characterized by depicting humanity as small in the face of a vast uncaring universe. Weird fiction (or the New Weird) is typified by a combination of awe and horror using untraditional monsters or creatures.[14] The British fantasist China Miéville says that it is defined by a search for the "numinous." Its poster image is the tentacle. These interlocking genres tend to be image-driven, often with baroque or lyrical language. Important contemporary writers include China Miéville, Jeff VanderMeer, Kathe Koja, Victor LaValle, Sofia Samatar, Kelly Link, Carmen Maria Machado, Neil Gaiman, Elizabeth Hand, and Helen Oyeyemi.

Mythic Fantasy / Mythic Fiction

Mythic fantasy derives from the stories, creatures, and characters from mythology. Mythic fantasy can involve retellings, or mythology remixed to create a new magical world. Mythic fantasy connects to specific mythological systems explicitly. Seeing how a myth remains the same, or is changed for the new tale, is one of its pleasures. Feminist retellings like Ursula K. Le Guin's *Lavinia*, Margaret Atwood's *The Penelopiad*, or Madeline Miller's *Circe* are prominent. Retellings based upon Greek and Roman mythology have been especially common. Some stories mix myths to create large-scale fantasy universes, like Neil Gaiman's *American Gods* or Rick Riordan's YA novels. These books are sometimes published as fantasy, and sometimes as mainstream fiction. Writers like Louise Erdrich and Elizabeth Hand publish under mainstream presses. Myths beyond the Western canon have thankfully begun to gain greater prominence, like *Gods of Jade and Shadow* by Silvia Moreno-Garcia. The term is generally attributed to Charles de Lint and Terri Windling.[15]

Fairy Tale / Folkloric Fantasy

There is much debate about which stories belong in this category, and which in mythic fantasy. This ambiguity derives from the messy boundary between myths and fairy tales. For example, Ovid's "Cupid and Psyche" is also the first known Beauty and the Beast story. Generally, fairy tale fantasy retells fairy tales from traditions around the world in new ways, often as feminist retellings, or to draw attention to other issues.[16] Like mythic fantasy, part of the pleasure of this genre is the frisson of the familiar and the strange. Fairy tale and folkloric fantasy novels cross genre and mainstream literary publishing and predate the modern publishing system. Folkloric fantasy is connected to fairy tale fantasy, although a story can be folkloric fantasy without being a fairy tale retelling. Fairy tale and folkloric fantasy elements also show up in other genres. Important writers include Ellen Kushner, Angela Carter, Emma Donoghue, Charles de Lint, Terri Windling, Jane Yolen, Patricia McKillip, Juliet Marillier, Gregory Maguire, Kate Bernheimer, Helen Oyeyemi, Ken Liu, Sequoia Nagamatsu, Rebecca Roanhorse, Naomi Novik, Nalo Hopkinson, Salman Rushdie, and Alice Hoffman.

Faerie Fantasy

This subgenre is related to mythic fantasy and folkloric/fairy tale fantasy, although not identical. It consists of books that make the fae (or fay, they have many names) the source of magic. These stories usually synthesize the many stories of the fae folk from folklore, fairy tales, myths, etc., and make them into a coherent magical system. Sometimes these stories are portal fantasies or invasive fantasies. Sometimes magic is a given in the world. These stories can be contemporary or historical. Sometimes the fae are called elves. Tolkien's elves were largely inspired by a fusion of the sidhe and Icelandic elves.[17] Sometimes, especially in urban fantasy, the fae are placed alongside other magical beings, like werewolves and vampires. Laurel K. Hamilton's *Anita Blake* books include the fae, as do Patricia Brigg's *Mercy Thompson* novels. YA fantasy focused on the fae tends to be a bit erotic. Outside of urban fantasy, the fae are the source of magic in Guy Gavriel Kay's historical fantasy *The Last Light of the Sun*, as well as John Crowley's *Little Big*. Prose in this genre ranges stylistically from utilitarian (most urban fantasy) to lyrical. They tend to share a preoccupation with the ineffable and mysterious. The fae are not pleasant tidy faeries, nor the benevolent elves of Tolkien derivative fantasy. They are closer to their older forms. Compelling, inhuman, and dangerous. They have inhuman goals and desires. Their presence is frequently used to show that humans aren't the apex predators of the world. The fae are like nature, beautiful and potentially deadly.

Portal Fantasy / Invasive Fantasy (or Intrusive)

A portal fantasy occurs when characters are transported from a less magical world to a more magical one. Often this happens via an object or cataclysmic event. *The Chronicles of Narnia* and *Harry Potter* are two famous examples of portal fantasy. Portal fantasies for adults have been written by authors including Ursula K. Le Guin, Guy Gavriel Kay, Neil Gaiman, Alix E. Harrow, and S. A. Chakraborty. Seanan McGuire's *Wayward Children* series riffs on the long history of children's portal fantasy. Passage between worlds can be voluntary or involuntary. *Invasive fantasy* is the inverse of portal fantasy—the non-magical world is invaded by the magical.[18] Often not everyone in the world is aware of the change. Sometimes it's a state of affairs that has been constant but hidden, and the main character breaks through the illusion of ordinariness. Urban and dark fantasy are often invasive fantasies. There are mythic fantasies that dance on the line between portal and invasive fantasies, like Charles de Lint's *Newford* books. Both types tend to feature a protagonist or protagonists that are set apart or chosen for special knowledge of both worlds.

Magic School Fantasy / Academic Fantasy

Both academic fantasy and magical school fantasies take schools as their primary setting, often schools for learning magic, drawing upon the tradition of the novel of school, and the *Bildungsroman* (novel of education/growth). Diane Wynn Jones and Ursula K. Le Guin wrote early magic school fantasies.[19] A certain young wizard named Harry made this subgenre one of the most well-known forms of fantasy for children, though plenty is aimed at adults. Examples include Charlie Jane Ander's *All the Birds in the Sky*, Lev Grossman's *The Magicians*, and Leigh Bardugo's *The Ninth House*. Some novels include magical schools, but don't use the school as the sole focal setting. Academic fantasy centers a school but doesn't focus primarily on the students. Sometimes the academics are the center, and it's not a school for magic at all. For instance, Ellen Kushner and Delia Sherman's *The Fall of Kings* takes place at a university and concentrates on a professor and a graduate student who both study history. The novel is a secondary-world historical fantasy, and there's no magic—until suddenly there is. There are also novels that focus on academics who uncover something uncanny through research, like *Possession* by A. S.

Byatt, or *The Historian* by Elizabeth Kostova. Magic school novels are frequently coming-of-age stories with themes of finding, belonging, and discovering one's true self. Academic fantasy novels are usually focused on adults, and so not coming-of-age narratives, but they do focus on a sense of discovery. Academic fantasy can overlap with Dark Academia.

Paranormal Fantasy / Urban Fantasy / Contemporary Fantasy

This is a complicated series of interlocking genres that are still emerging and defining themselves. Contemporary fantasy is any fantasy set in roughly the present of the writer, altered to include fantasy elements. This can manifest as fabulism but can also be overtly fantastical. Highly fantastical contemporary fantasy is often categorized as urban or paranormal fantasy. Emma Bull's *War for the Oaks* and Charles De Lint's *Newford* novels are credited with crystalizing urban fantasy. These novels are set in cities, which at the time the first of them were written (1980s) was in direct contrast to the agrarian, rural, and historical settings of the majority of fantasy. Bull's novel included elements which would later become nearly obligatory in urban fantasy; magical beings disturbing the life of a relatively ordinary young woman causing her to believe in the supernatural and radically change her life. There is also a love story between her and one of the fae. In some urban fantasy few people know about the supernatural existing alongside the real world. In some, almost everyone knows, like works that emerged in the 1990s and early 2000s by Patricia Briggs, Laurel K. Hamilton, and Charlaine Harris. When a love story and sexuality become the primary narrative drive, the story is paranormal romance rather than urban fantasy. Both often involve characters who have historically been associated with horror, like vampires and werewolves. Many urban fantasies borrow from noir and detective fiction. The main characters frequently get pulled into crime solving, their expertise in the supernatural valuable to supernatural beings and human police departments alike. Sherlock Holmes and other 19th-century detective stories that include the occult or the appearance of the occult are influential. While this genre is dominated by female-identified writers, there are male writers who work within it, from Glen Cook to Jim Butcher, and Daniel Jose Older. Butcher's *Dresden Files* series is popular but became polarizing when they were part of the Sad Puppies campaign (not by the writer's choice). This is an active genre with new writers emerging all the time. Most books within it are series books. Any list of influential writers working within the genre, because it is a young one, includes writers from the early days alongside newer writers, from L. A. Banks to Kim Harrison, Marjorie Liu, and many others.[20]

Fabulism, Magical Realism, and Surrealism

These three genres are often confused. They are related, but not identical. Magical realism primarily refers to Latin American literature from the 20th century and beyond that depicts a realistic world infused with magical elements. These elements are natural, not invasive. Awareness of this genre burst upon the English-speaking world with Gabriel García Márquez's *One Hundred Years of Solitude*, though it predates this awareness. Jorge

Luis Borges was one of its early advocates. The decentering of the Western rationalistic worldview that occurs in these novels is a form of resistance to fascism and colonialism.[21] The term "magical realism" is sometimes applied to novels by English speakers like Alice Hoffman, but many argue that applying the term outside of Latin America or other colonized countries degrades the identity of the genre and is potentially appropriative. The term was also used in Germany to refer to Kafka's work, and other works by German writers who treated the extraordinary as matter of fact. The work of indigenous writers like Louise Erdrich are sometimes considered a form of magical realism since they frequently take for granted events and forces that are outside of Western notions of causality. Many European writers, like Italian writer Italo Calvino, have preferred the term "fabulist" to describe their work, which has in common with magical realism the tendency to describe the extraordinary in a matter-of-fact tone and draw upon oral narrative traditions to go beyond rationalist modes of thought, while infusing magical elements into an otherwise naturalistic or realistic setting. Surrealism uses these elements more metaphorically, rather than literally. While there are arguments about magical realism, the term has cultural implications that the term "fabulism" does not. Further, fabulism is more likely to draw upon well-known folkloric elements, instead of a general sense of magic. Novels and stories that fit within any of these traditions are likely to cross between mainstream, literary, and fantasy publishers. Many writers of fabulism identify as fantasy writers, some don't.[22] Writers like Kelly Link, Karen Russell, Helen Oyeyemi, and George Saunders are fabulist and fantasy writers. These genres are complicated to parse, and the ways in which they cross the publishing worlds has led to a lot of arguments about if they are fantasy, or just fantastical, which strikes this author as saying more about those who argue about it than the texts themselves, since all of them self-evidently include magic.

Space Fantasy / Science Fantasy

The lines between fantasy and science fiction have never been particularly thick. While high fantasy and hard science fiction are relatively distinct, there is a lot of wiggle room in between.[23] Planetary romance is secondary-world fantasy that uses another planet as the setting. Sharon Shinn's *Samaria* books are set on a world which was colonized by humans who set out to create an agrarian theologically driven utopia. Sheri S. Tepper, the ecoscience fantasy writer, writes novels that blend magic with the scientific. *Star Wars*, and similar works, are sometimes considered space fantasy since psychic powers are at the center of the narrative. Further, the themes of space fantasy, such as overthrowing an evil empire, are more common to fantasy narratives than science fiction narratives proper. N. K. Jemisin's *Broken Earth* series includes magic that is science to the characters within it. These are only a few of the endless examples of work that blends science fiction and fantasy.

Hybrid Fantasy

In addition to the specific hybrid genres I have described, you can find fantasy that blends any genres you can think of. There are steampunk mysteries and fantasy thrillers—

the options are endless. Genres and subgenres aren't rules so much as guidelines. Most successful fantasy uses conventions strategically but avoids being trope-ridden. "Rules" exist to be learned and broken. Countless novels are many genres simultaneously, or none in particular. Genres and subgenres evolve as quickly as humans can imagine. Consider this chapter a general sense of where fantasy has been and where it is going, a map that, like any map, is a relatively simple representation of something deeply complex.

Discussion Questions and Writing Activities

1. How many of these genres were you familiar with? Of those you already knew, did the definitions or history differ from what you expected? If so, how?

2. Of the genres and subgenres of fantasy you were unfamiliar with, which ones were most intriguing to you, and why?

3. Pick one of our anthology stories. Does it fit within a genre, or subvert one? Both?

4. Pick a favorite genre or subgenre, do an internet search, and find a story to read. Look at it in terms of its genre(s), as well as its unique features. How does the story use the genre but avoid being defined by it? Or does it?

5. Start a story that combines two or more genres. What are the challenges and opportunities created by this approach?

CHAPTER 3
FANTASY FICTION, PUBLISHING, AND CREATIVE WRITING IN THE ACADEMY[1]

Introduction

While fantasy fiction isn't new, the academic discipline of creative writing is. Further, the presence of both fantasy and science fiction within it is even newer. Creative writing in academia arose out of a specific cultural moment, which impacted which forms of fiction have historically been considered acceptable within MFAs and PhDs (and thus within the classrooms of teachers educated in those MFAs/PhDs). There is a long history of hostility toward so called "genre" fiction within academia. This hostility has started to wane, but it is still present in many places. It is the result of the circumstances that influenced creative writing's entrance to academia, as well as the historical and cultural forces that led to specialized genre publishing, as was discussed in Chapter 1. If you have been assigned this textbook, you are probably lucky enough to be in a creative writing program where fantasy is not heavily stigmatized. But you will encounter people within university systems and elsewhere disdainful toward "genre" fiction, as well as literary magazines that refuse to publish it. This chapter aims to help you understand the origin of this anti-genre bias, so you can understand that those who are biased against your chosen genre aren't out to get you, they are just tangled up with a broader cultural problem that they probably aren't even aware of. I wish for a future in which this chapter becomes unnecessary. The rise in prominence of fantasy writers within popular culture, and literary publishing, gives me hope.

The Current Contested State of "Genre" Fiction and What It Means for You

Even though the current moment is friendlier than the past, the sense of genre fiction as the ugly stepsister to literary fiction persists. The need to either deride genre fiction or defend it is rife in the press. The contentious conversation between the late Ursula K. Le Guin and Kazuo Ishiguro acts as a sort of case study. In March 2015, Kazuo Ishiguro published *The Buried Giant*. In an interview with the *New York Times*, Ishiguro said he was afraid that readers would think his latest novel was fantasy.[2] Le Guin, an ardent defender of science fiction and fantasy, fired back, calling Ishiguro's book fantasy, but not particularly good fantasy. Ishiguro later said that he was on the side of faeries and dragons, not against science fiction and fantasy at all, and that Le Guin misunderstood him.[3]

The press, from the *New York Times* to the *Atlantic*, continued the fight. Ishiguro's statement, regardless of intended meaning, displays the bias against genre fiction. Another example of a "literary" writer trying to write "genre" fiction, while refusing to claim the label, can be found in the upheaval surrounding Ian McEwan's *Machines Like Me*. When any writer writes a book that is obviously science fiction or fantasy, and then tries to claim it isn't such, because they are doing valuable thing x, they are committing a stacking the deck fallacy, excluding everything they think is good from genre fiction, thereby making it impossible for genre fiction to be good. However, they are not the problem so much as they are *symptoms* of it. Defining genre fiction through its least stellar examples would be similar to defining realistic fiction through Nicholas Sparks or (insert formulaic realistic book of your choice). While there is nothing wrong with books written to be consumed quickly and forgotten, they are the book equivalent of hotdogs— tasty, but not nutritional. While hotdogs, chicken cordon bleu, and sushi are all meat-based, one can't logically claim all meat-based foods are actually hotdogs.

As a result of the stacking the deck fallacy used against genre fiction, creative writing workshops and literary magazines have a long history of hostility toward it. SFWA (Science Fiction and Fantasy Writers of America) listed literary magazines friendly to genre fiction (not providing the longer list of those that aren't).[4] Even specialty MFA programs, which focus on genre fiction, are evidence of the stigma. There is no MFA specifically for realistic fiction because it is treated as the default. Many of the specialist MFA programs are in popular fiction, often seen as synonymous with genre fiction. Many so-called popular fiction novels are not popular, or trying to be, but are very dense and sell few copies, while many realistic literary novels, supposedly noncommercial, are bestsellers. In 2015, the bestseller lists included twenty-five "fiction, general" books and only seven science fiction and fantasy books.[5] High sales are exceptional for *any* book. This illusory divide between what we think of as artistic and what we think of as entertainment impacts what is taught in classrooms at all levels.

As a teacher, I comb through creative writing textbooks to check for anti-genre bias. Even the least hostile textbooks tend to feel the need to address the issue, sometimes saying that they are specifically about literary fiction, and that they will not be addressing genre fiction. Other times, these textbooks will attempt to describe the debate about the worthiness of genre fiction, usually in terms of genre fiction's ability to be used for social critique on the positive side, and on the negative side, its supposed reliance on cliches or tropes. It is fairly common in classrooms or textbooks for faculty to say something along the lines of "I have no problem with genre fiction, but I don't know anything about it, so I won't be teaching it." If I refused to teach realistic fiction because I "know nothing about it," I would be considered outlandish by my peers, yet declaring ignorance of fantasy or other forms of genre fiction is acceptable.

You can expect a certain number of your teachers, and books on writing, to seem as though they are ignoring or stigmatizing your genre of choice. You may have to apply lessons about creative writing, like dialogue use, or plot structure, that aren't addressed directly to you. Don't be discouraged. The tools your creative writing teachers teach you, even if they aren't fantasy writers, are just as relevant to you as they are to writers of realism (which many fantasy writers call "mimetic fiction" to explain how it is in its own way just as constructed as a fantasy world, since what seems "realistic" to a given writer or reader will depend on time period, class, national origin, race, gender, etc.). Don't fall victim to the logical trap of saying something like "fantasy fiction is all about the world, so I don't have to worry about character stuff." It isn't true. The majority of modern fantasy fiction is character-driven to one extent or another. Regardless, it's important to learn how to use all the tools in the fiction writer's toolbox. While not being addressed directly by craft books or teachers is annoying, it doesn't absolve you of responsibility to the class or your craft. I say this as a writer who has largely had to be the person who brought fantasy fiction into the classroom my entire career (from undergrad through PhD).

Additionally, your teachers may not know the nuances of publishing within genre fiction, like the existence of the SFWA. You may need to do your own research. But they will know information that crosses publishing communities, such as how to query an agent.

The state of affairs I am describing is the product of the ways in which publishing became fragmented, the cultural forces behind that fragmentation, and the way it was mirrored within academia. So, your struggles, and the fight in the popular press as exemplified by the Ishiguro/Le Guin battle, must be understood as the product of history.

Communism, Cornfields, and Publishers: The Founding of Creative Writing as an Academic Discipline

After the Second World War, American universities were flooded with ex-GIs, who might never have been able to go to college if not for the GI Bill. These students often didn't know the conventions of standard English. As a result, writing as a subject in and of itself first entered the college curriculum via composition. Simultaneously, creative writing sought to integrate itself into academia.[6] Creative writing tried to differentiate itself from composition which was primarily aimed at the new "interlopers." When GIs were integrated into creative writing, they had to ape the literary styles that were considered acceptable.

In *Workshops of Empire*, Eric Bennett describes the founding conditions of the Iowa Writer's Workshop (the first academic creative writing program). America was a nation afraid of cultural reform, utopianism, or collectivist ideas of any kind. Such ideas smacked of fascism and/or communism.[7] New tax regulations made it incumbent on the wealthy to find tax breaks. Resultingly, much of the funding for Iowa came from John D. Rockefeller. Crucial motivators for Rockefeller came from the argument that the new discipline would be housed in the Midwest, away from the liberal East Coast intelligentsia, untainted by communism, socialism, or collectivist reforms.[8] The founders of Iowa believed literature should focus on the growth of the individual. This was explicitly used as the definition of literary *high culture*, and a defense against the glorification of the common people seen in communism.[9] This fear, as well as the fear of decreasing class boundaries through the influx of GIs into universities and the influence of popular culture, created an incentive for founding and funding the Iowa Writer's Workshop[10] and solidified its foundational ideology.

What does all this have to do with genre fiction? The criticism of being idea- or ideology-driven is conventionally used to condemn genre fiction. It began as a critique based on a fear of communism but has been converted to an aesthetic criterion. Genre fiction is also devalued due to its supposed popular quality. What is that but a new guise for the anxiety of a ruling class as manifested in the arts?

Even though much genre fiction is not part of *low culture* (a loaded term, but the best one to describe the dominant literary community's perception at the time), to the post-war audience it seemed to be. Hugo Gernsback, one of the fathers of science fiction, founded *Amazing Stories* in 1926. One of the effects of *Amazing Stories* was the propagation of the pulps, an entire industry of cheaply printed and mass-produced magazines with lurid covers, primarily marketed at young men.[11] They came to be deeply associated with the Second World War GI.[12] The stigma of the pulps was so great that genre publishers struggled to expand into hardback or obtain a place on bookstore shelves that was not next to pornography. Ray Bradbury was one of the first writers who began in the pulps to get wider critical acceptance and a hardback edition in the US. This successful transition earned him the label "The Poet of the Pulps."[13] While intended as a compliment, it implies that he is an exception.

The fear of social agendas in genre fiction, as well as a fear of mass culture and a desire to separate high and low literature, began in the 19th century. Recall when we discussed the ways in which early fantasy and science fiction writers, as well as the seeds of the genre (folklore studies, the gothic) were intensely political, and frequently included subversive ideas, often related to socialism. Genre fiction has been politically engaged and artistically varied since its beginnings.

As explained in Chapter 1, the very notion of the fantastical was political in 19th-century England and tangled up with issues of class.[14] As mass-printed material became more available, class divisions within the novel began, mostly driven by ideas about *who* was reading *what*.[15] In the 20th century, the pulps contributed to the disparagement of genre fiction, while in the 19th century, it was the penny dreadful. They came to be associated with the working poor, and the dirtiness of city slums, loose sexuality, and alcoholism.[16]

As Britain, with its emergent middle class, tried to decide what being middle class looked like, the idea of childhood as a protected time began to take hold as a crucial divide between the classes.[17] As a result, the middle class began to decide what constituted children's literature.[18] By the late-19th century, fantasies belonged in the realm of children.[19] This attitude toward fantasy prefigures the debates surrounding books and fantasy novels in modern schools.

The 19th-century cultural concerns surrounding the novel and early genre fiction are directly connected to the way that creative writing is taught in America. Henry James, a transition figure between the 19th and 20th centuries, wrote "The Art of Fiction," still widely assigned in MFA programs. James claimed that novels rise above mere low-class entertainment and become only when realistic.[20] The 19th century followed by the GI Bill in the 20th century created the cultural conditions and aesthetic assumptions that have alienated the literary fiction and genre fiction communities within academia. When genre fiction writers are hostile to academia or the literary writing community, or vice versa, it is hostility and ignorance created by social forces, not a situation that should continue.

The legacy of the bias against genre fiction is visible in the way elements of the literary world fight over whether or not genre fiction can be art, or if certain pieces of art are genre fiction. We labor under the burden of the past. The arguments about the place of genre fiction in schools also show the influence of the 19th and 20th centuries.

As a specific example, *Harry Potter* is both defended and derided in schools. Detractors objected on religious grounds (before the upheaval surrounding Rowling's transphobia). Proponents said that fantasy helps kids enjoy reading, and *Harry Potter* encourages kindness and respect for others (not just anecdotally, a study in 2014 in the *Journal of Applied Psychology* concluded that reading *Harry Potter* made children more tolerant of difference).[21] Both sides assume that children will be seduced by fantasy and that fiction has the obligation to teach good or bad behavior. Mary Elizabeth Garcia argues that *Harry Potter* can be used to segue college students into serious adult literature.[22] This argument contains within it the idea that fantasy is for children and is *literature* appealing to mass culture, valuable only insofar as it can be used to get young people interested in *Literature*. This aesthetic heuristic has permeated publishing, MFA programs, undergraduate college classrooms, and K-12 education. It has also contributed to a near total ignoring, in many circles, of genre fiction written for adults.

Fantasy is *not* mostly written for children and young adults, far from it: young adult fiction (no shade intended, it is perfectly fine for it to be what it is) often reproduces trends that have been occurring in adult fiction for years. But the creation of YA as a publishing subset, and the extreme high profile of series that have been turned into film and television, contributed to the impression that fantasy is not primarily aimed at adults, and that writers like George R. R. Martin are an aberration, rather than part of a large and thriving tradition. All of which reinforces the stigma against genre fiction. You are likely to find teachers and writers who assume that serious fiction for adults can't be fantasy, and students who have mostly only been introduced to fantasy aimed at young adults and children, and thus find themselves ignorant of most of the genre they want to write within or read within, because it isn't being taught in the classroom much (if at all). This may or may not describe your experience, depending upon how lucky or unlucky you were in terms of your K-12 school system, how the library was stocked, or the experiences of your college professors. If you find yourself reading only young adult fantasy, it is in your best interest to also read fantasy for adults, a lot of it. Both for overcoming stigma and realizing what aspects of style are actually characteristic of fantasy fiction, and what aspects are merely conventional for young adult fantasy. This will help you connect the reading in your creative writing and literature courses more directly to your own writing, and help you advocate for the breadth and depth of the genre you have chosen to write within.

Luckily, bias against genre fiction is crumbling. As more writers like Jeff VanderMeer are published by both mainstream and genre presses, writers like George Saunders win the Booker Prize, and canonical genre fiction writers like Octavia Butler get film adaptations and popular press, the bias will continue to erode. But no change occurs all at once. So, as writers, teachers, readers, and students, if we understand the history behind the biases we encounter or hold, we can begin to break down those biases, and leave them behind. Leaving behind biases, be they social (like race, gender, class, or sexuality), or artistic, requires education and active effort. Frequently, as with the bias against genre fiction within academic creative writing, one bias is entangled with other biases, like class. It is our responsibility to learn from history and move forward, to broaden our aesthetic knowledge so our classrooms, publishing, and fiction itself can become more inclusive and open.

Discussion Questions and Writing Activities

1. Have you encountered people who dislike of fantasy or science fiction? If so, what was their justification? How did you respond? How might the information of this chapter change your response? If you haven't encountered bias against fantasy, why do you think that is?

2. How do the history of genre fiction and the history of the founding of creative writing as an academic discipline relate to each other?

3. What do you think the effect is when fantasy fiction, especially fantasy fiction written for adults, is rarely taught?

4. What changes can you bring to your reading, writing, or teaching practice as a result of reading this chapter?

5. Write a list of the fantasy writers who have inspired you. Did you encounter them in a classroom alongside other fantasy writers? How many were contemporary? How many were for adults? If you didn't read them in class, how did you discover them?

6. What are the implications of the divide between "high" and "low" literature? What do these terms mean to you? What patterns have you seen in how books are sorted?

7. What is implied when literary fiction is defined by being genre-less?

8. Google a few major publishers of fantasy and science fiction, and look at the covers of recent books, and then do the same for the covers of some mainstream realistic novels. What patterns do you see? What is communicated about style and audience expectations? Do an internet image search and look at the covers for David Mitchell's *Cloud Atlas* (a fantasy and sci-fi genre-bending book published by Random House) and *Harrow the Ninth* by Tamsyn Muir (an equally ambitious book which blends fantasy and science fiction, published by Tor). What can the covers tell you about marketing? Do the cultural divides that have been articulated in this chapter make their mark on the covers?

SECTION 2
THE CRAFT OF FANTASY WRITING

Introduction

Once you have learned about fantasy's evolution, you can place yourself within a writing tradition, learn from that tradition, and apply specific techniques. You can begin to think about how to craft socially engaged and artistically accomplished fiction.

These chapters are designed to help writers learn specific writing skills, with special attention to how those skills apply in fantasy fiction. Each of the major elements of fiction[1] craft will be covered, with an emphasis on concerns that are specific to fantasy fiction. Each chapter on craft includes examples to illustrate use. Chapters will include exercises and discussion questions. There are three worldbuilding chapters detailing process and the implications of one's worldbuilding choices. There is also a discussion on writing the Other in fantasy fiction.

CHAPTER 4
CHARACTER AND DIALOGUE

One key characteristic of fantasy fiction is that most fantasy fiction follows characters whose actions affect, or are affected by, the larger world. In other words, the importance of broader social pressures is central to the dilemmas faced by the characters.

In fantasy fiction, especially fantasy fiction that avoids tropes (elves hating orcs, for example), one cannot and should not depend on the reader understanding the social forces that pressure the characters. It is necessary to think through how to give readers the context they need to understand character motivations, without info dumping. In addition, larger social forces are often a central element of the plot, which is less frequently the case for Western realistic fiction. Using dialogue to convey information is something that fiction writers should be wary of. Fantasy writers, in particular, must be vigilant that they don't use characters as a mouthpiece to explain the world to the reader. How can character dialogue be used both to reveal character, explore conflict, and teach the reader, implicitly, about the world of the story? This chapter will cover these issues in detail.

Dialogue Broadly Considered

Dialogue

Regardless of what type of fiction you seek to write, dialogue and character are deeply important aspects of fiction writing craft. But the conventions of dialogue and character development that are considered acceptable are not consistent. Expectations change with time period and with culture; further, different genres will have slightly different expectations, even within the landscape of publishing in English. But, in the anglophone world, what does tend to remain consistent is the centrality of dialogue and character in fiction writing.

Generally (though this is not universally true) effective stories are driven by the motivations and desires of characters. You can develop them through *interiority* (their thoughts, feelings, and memories, as seen through a narrator, or directly), their *actions*, the *reactions* of others to them, and *dialogue*. Dialogue is unique because it is unfiltered. Narrators, even first-person narrators, are unreliable because they can't be objective. But dialogue in quotations is a direct representation of what is said by your characters. It has the potential to contribute deeply to the development of your characters, since *how* somebody speaks, and *what* they say, reveals a lot about who they are. This is as true of characters as real people, if not truer, since in fiction everything is premeditated.

Effective dialogue, unlike real speech, shouldn't be used merely to convey information. It should fulfill multiple purposes simultaneously. A line, including a line of dialogue, that only contributes to your story in one way is a wasted opportunity. In a novel, you can get away with some wasted opportunities, but in short stories there is no space to spare. So, how can you craft your dialogue to do the most work for your story? Here are a few tips and tricks:

1. *Avoid explanatory dialogue tags.* This is not a hard and fast rule, but it is a convention within fiction written for adults, especially fiction that intends to be artistic. Generally, "said" or "says" (depending upon your story's tense) is preferable to "exclaimed" or "interjected" or "snorted," or adverbial descriptions like "she said sadly." It can be useful to indicate volume, such as "whispered" or "shouted." When you limit your dialogue tags to mostly just "said" or "says" they become invisible, like punctuation. Descriptive dialogue tags often don't make sense as verbs. One doesn't "snort" words. Snorting and speaking are separate actions. When you use an adverbial phrase, or an explanatory dialogue tag, you take away the work of interpretation. The reader should be able to tell that the character is angry, sad, irritated, etc. by what is said and how. When I explain my dialogue, it is a sign that I am not giving my reader enough credit, or my dialogue is weak. It is common in young adult fiction and certain types of highly commercialized fiction within all genres to explain dialogue or vary tags. This is because all of the aforementioned fiction types are intended to be easy to read, either because of assumptions on the part of publishers regarding reading level, or because of the intent to be easily digestible. Perfectly fine in its place, but not suitable for all times and purposes. If you use descriptive tags, or adverbs to explain your dialogue, you are signaling that your writing is intended to be one of the aforementioned kinds.

2. *Think about the stakes of the conversation.* When characters interact, like people, they want something from the interaction. Their conversation is inflected by how they feel about the person and situation, their mood, and their biases or prejudices. Putting purely transactional conversations on the page (like ordering a cup of coffee from a random barista) is a waste. Evaluate the dialogue through the lens of the stakes for your characters. How can you convey their unstated desires? How can you show tension? People rarely say directly what they want, and characters do so even less. They may not know consciously what they want, though you the writer must. When you let character motivations steer dialogue, it makes it meaningful, and allows it to simultaneously characterize your characters and move the plot.

3. *Dialogue isn't real speech.* Real speech is full of fillers like "um," and hesitations. Real people say lots of meaningless things. Think of dialogue as speech distilled to its most interesting essence. This means that long monologues are not very useful most of the time. Nor is everyday interaction. If you just want to say that your character ordered coffee every morning, or always said goodbye to their mother before they went to school, say that in narration, save dialogue for moments that matter.

4. *Follow basic dialogue conventions.* Unless you are trying an artistic experiment where there is a reason to break dialogue conventions, clarity is your friend.

Dialogue goes in quotes and is usually in its own line. You can and often should intersperse thoughts and or actions between lines of dialogue from the point of view character.

In the story "Good Hunting" by Ken Liu, a young man whose father is charged with hunting down and killing kitsune, befriends one of the beings he is meant to kill. Keeping the secret from his father strains their relationship. He isn't sure how to interpret his own feelings toward the kitsune he has befriended. With industrialization and colonialism, the magical creatures that he and his father hunt for their living are disappearing.

She kept her voice unemotional and cool, like a placid pool of water in autumn, but her words rang true. I thought about my father's attempts to keep up a cheerful mien as fewer and fewer customers came to us. I wondered if the time I spent learning the chants and the sword dance moves was wasted.

"What will you do?" I asked, thinking about her, alone in the hills and unable to find the food that sustained her magic.

"There's only one thing I can do." Her voice broke for a second and became defiant, like a pebble tossed into the pool.

But then she looked at me, and her composure returned. "There's only one thing we can do: learn to survive."[2]

The entire scene is seen through the eyes of the first-person narrator. You can observe the tension between the characters and the disconnect between what is said and the unstated subtext. The conversation is boiled down to its most essential parts, which amps up the visibility of the emotional stakes. The tags are simple, and don't explain the tone of the dialogue. The indentations make clear where the dialogue for each character begins and ends. Dialogue and the physicality of the characters gives the reader the necessary information to interpret the scene.

Special Concerns for Fantasy Dialogue

Dialogue and Worldbuilding

Dialogue in fantasy fiction is just as important as dialogue in realistic fiction; however, the temptation to use dialogue to explain the world is hard to resist. But resist you should. Unless you have a scene with a tour guide for interdimensional travelers, or a particularly helpful person in a portal fantasy, there is usually no reason for one character to explain the world to another. Would you explain how grocery stores, public transit, or the US government works in regular conversation? If a date started spouting off about the electoral college or the mating habits of frogs, it would be very odd. The same is true for your characters. Except if they are meant to be odd, or it's in character (an academic who studies the electoral college might spout about it). Unless there is a good reason for one character to assume another doesn't understand the world, then there shouldn't be detailed explanations within dialogue. Your characters should think and talk about their world in the terms that are intrinsic to that world. The world will become clear gradually through context and will feel more natural if characters refer to events and experiences as casually as you refer to well-known events, experiences, and objects within your world.

Lexicon and Speech Patterns

In fantasy fiction character vocabulary will reflect the world. Avoid making up new words unnecessarily. It's okay, unless there is a compelling reason, for a cup to just be a cup. Lexicon choices should be meaningful and teach us about the characters and the world implicitly. This might include telling us something about technology, magic, class, social status, nationalism, race relations, and value systems.

People's language choices reflect their implicit biases and cultural assumptions. In the real world, the word that people from Japan use for themselves is different from the word that I as an English speaker would use. I would say they are *Japanese*. They would say they are *Nihonjin* (from the island of *Nihon*).[3] Imagine someone who works with international students at a university, who, when they talk to students from Japan, uses their word for themselves. Doing so is an intentional value statement because it is a departure from the norm for English speakers. An American GI from the Second World War would likely have another word for the Japanese, not one I want to repeat. The older woman who ran a boutique I worked at after college used to refer to people from Asian countries as "Orientals." This not politically correct now, but it was commonplace when she was young. These lexiconic examples show how you can draw conclusions about someone's value system, generation, nationality, and affect toward a country based upon what words they use to refer to people from that country. The same is true for fantasy cultures and the characters within them. N. K. Jemisin's award-winning *Broken Earth* trilogy is a great example of how the words characters use to refer to each other help the reader learn about the characters, their values, beliefs, and much more.[4] In C. S. E. Cooney's "Martyr's Gem,"[5] different households have particular names and varying social statuses. Stories set in patriarchal cultures will reflect the patriarchy in language. The more your fantasy world differs from the real world, the less your character's lexicon can remain unaltered. Secondary-world fantasy of any kind will consequently have more lexical differences than fantasy set in the real world with specific changes such as the introduction of wizards or vampires. Don't pepper every line of dialogue with specialized lexicon, be strategic. Conversely, don't mindlessly include slang and language from the real world (though fake swearwords are often very silly sounding; if you want your character to say "shit" it's mostly okay to simply use the word "shit").

In historical fantasy, one can employ vocabulary and speech patterns similar to that time period, within reason. If you are writing a gaslamp fantasy, borrowing language from Victorian England, or whatever culture of the time that is appropriate, would be useful. Formalized diction in some circumstances for your characters, and appropriate contractions (yes, people in the past did use contractions in English).[6] The Google Ngram Viewer lets you search the frequency of words in print, which can help with historically accurate vocabulary. However, you don't always have to go so far. If you are writing a novel like *Jonathan Strange & Mr. Norrell* by Susanna Clarke[7] that tries to mimic the style of novels published in the time it is set within, you should absolutely mimic the language and punctuation choices of the era as closely as you can. Otherwise, use archaic speech patterns and syntax strategically to signal time period. If going further back in time than the 19th century for inspiration for your historical fantasy, it is wise to be even more choosy. If you are writing a story set in a pseudo-medieval setting, à la Guy Gavriel Kay's stunning novel *The Last Light of the Sun*,[8] don't attempt to write dialogue that sounds like medieval literature. Instead, focus on having the lexicon from your characters be appropriate to the setting, and stick with largely contemporary syntax and speech patterns except for a few specific signals. However, avoid having your characters refer to things as "dope," unless you are deliberately being anachronistic (like the film *A Knight's Tale*).[9]

Character Development Generally Considered

As writers of fiction, regardless of genre, there are a range of tools available to you for developing your characters, in service of making characters that are "round" rather than "flat." "Round" characters give the impression of being multidimensional. Real people have feelings that motivate them: hopes, fears, dreams, desires, anxieties, regrets, vague cranky days, loves, hates, etc. Real people are shaped by their memories and experiences. They respond to situations based upon the mixture of conscious and unconscious drives that shape their personality and worldview. A "round" character can't actually be as complex as a real person, but they can give that impression. A "flat" character might be motivated by simple desires, have no memories, or be defined by a few easily discernable traits. Generally, in contemporary fiction in English people try for round characters, to one extend or another; however, there are limitations to this generalization, based upon time, context, story type (such as postmodern novels like Italo Calvino's *Invisible Cities*), and culture. Nevertheless, there are a range of writing tools that help to signal "roundness." A few of these tools are listed below:

1. *Interiority*. This is one of the most powerful tools in any fiction writer's toolkit, and the biggest thing that distinguishes fiction from other storytelling forms (like film or video games). Only in fiction does one routinely see directly into the mind of a character, allowing the reader to inhabit that person's mental, emotional, and physical experience. In first person, the reader experiences those things directly and unmediated by anyone but the first-person narrator. Depending upon how honest your character is with themselves, and how self-reflective, this unmediated experience may be more or less accurate. First-person narrators are intrinsically unreliable. Your reader grows to understand them through the intersection of their thoughts, actions, and how others react to them. With a third-person narrator, the reader will usually still see directly into the mind of one or more characters. When you are writing a close third point of

view, you can use *free indirect discourse*. This means that you can write a third that is almost as close as a first, though reflecting the language of the narrator. A third-person narrator can see into the minds of many characters, or just one, depending upon if the narrative point of view is omniscient, rotating, or a third person limited. One advantage of a third-person narrator is the capacity to zoom in and out, allowing the reader to know things the protagonist doesn't know. The narrator can move the reader through time, and give a sense of scope, without sacrificing the intimacy of interiority. Interiority is central to understanding what motivates your characters. Motivations can be thought of as occurring on a continuum, from what a character most wants to what they most fear.

2. *Narration* is when the narrator describes what is happening, like someone opening a door, tilting their head, taking a drink of water, etc. Narration occurs in time and is usually interspersed in scenes with dialogue and interiority. This allows the reader to see your character, characterizing them through behavior. Some stories, especially flash fiction, or short fairy tales, may occur almost entirely in narration. You can also narrate feelings. Emrys Donaldson's original fairy tale "The Albatrosses" is a great example of this. The storyteller tells the story, there is no dialogue, only a mixture of summary and exposition to quickly set the stage:

We warned the boys about the cliff, the one out there in the island cove. The story then summarizes that this cliff has the capacity, if jumped off, to turn boys into either albatrosses, or girls.[10]

The story moves from exposition to narration:

One day, three boys swam out to the island. Droplets glistened in the uncle's chest hair as he shook his finger at them, but again they ignored him. Finding footholds in the rock, the boys climbed, wet trunks sticking to their soft legs. It was hard going.

Exposition summarizes what is happening, interpreting it for the reader, covering a lot of time and information in a short space. Narration describes what is happening in close to real story time. As in a traditional fairy tale, Donaldson's characterization is minimalistic. Outside of such specific situations, narration is used in conjunction with dialogue, description, interiority, and exposition within scenes to characterize. For example, in C. S. E. Cooney's story "Martyr's Gem," the protagonist Shasta, before a journey to an arranged marriage, converses with his sister. The marriage is unexpected, and to a family of much higher status, and so both siblings are uneasy:

He patted his rucksack, which had the little lace purse she'd crocheted along with his own mesh-gift. **[narration]**

"Oohee, brother mine," said Sharrar. "By this time tomorrow you'll be a Blodestone, and no Sarth relation will be worthy to meet your eyes." **[dialogue]**

"Doubtless Hirrayi Blodestone will take one look at me and sunder the contract."

"She requested you." **[dialogue]**

Shursta shrugged, **[narration]** *sure it had been a mistake.* **[interiority]**

At that, there was one last hug, a vivid and mischievous and slightly desperate smile from Sharrar, followed by a grave look and a quick wink on Shursta's part. [**narration**] *Then he set off on the sea road that would take him to Droon.* [**exposition**]

As you can see with the above example, the narration is interwoven with the other elements of the scene and is crucial to our understanding of these two people as characters.

3. *Dialogue* is hugely important because it is the most direct method that we have of seeing a character's behaviors. I talked about dialogue in-depth earlier, so I won't belabor it.

4. *Memory* and *flashback* are important characterization tools. Much of our identity comes from our past experiences. It is the story we tell ourselves about who we are. People generally perceive themselves as the protagonist in their own story, and memories create an identity out of the chaos. Luckily, in fiction you get control, and the narrative of identity isn't an illusion. However, memory and flashback are *very* different from each other. Memory is when a character remembers something explicitly. Memory is conveyed in interiority or exposition, cut briefly into the present scene of the story. There must be a reason for the point of view character to remember a particular moment. Memory can be integrated into the scene quickly without disrupting the flow of the story. It can convey the character's conscious and unconscious thoughts and feelings. In contrast, a flashback is an entire scene set in the past, interrupting the present. This is a technique to be used with caution since it throws the reader out of the present moment. If you find yourself using flashbacks, it is worth asking if the story you are really interested in telling is the one in the past. Flashback is more useful in novels than short stories. It is not the same as a braided narrative where chapters alternate between the past and the present (like *The Handmaid's Tale*).[11] Both help the reader learn about your character's motivations, without the reader having to be told those motivations directly.

5. *Actions* are crucial for characterization. For non-point of view characters, action and dialogue are basically the only characterization methods available. Characters, like people, often behave in ways that contradict their words, or their self-concept. Character choices allow your readers to understand things that the characters don't understand about themselves. Your character's actions move the story forward and are intrinsically tied to their motivations. In Robin Hobb's *Assassin's Apprentice*[12] series, her protagonist and narrator Fitz Chivalry Farseer is a royal bastard being trained to be an assassin by another royal bastard. He resents his adopted father figures for not being his actual father. He doesn't consciously admit that resentment, nor does he understand that his loyalty to his king comes from reading every kind act as a sign of filial love. As readers we glean all of the above through his reactions and interactions. Rebecca Roanhorse's "Harvest"[13] highlights the importance of actions for character development, as her protagonist's killings drive the plot, and complicate

motivations and moral standing, even as the reader understands the righteousness of her rage. This underscores the importance of active characters (active in a way that is appropriate to their cultural context and the actions available to them).

There are limitations to generalizations about flat and round characters. Postmodern fiction, as well as traditionally told fairy tales, for example. Kate Bernheimer refers to the traditional oral fairy tale as "flat."[14] She doesn't mean this negatively. In an oral tale, the focus is on the narration and the narrator. The actions of the characters often follow dream logic, and the "why" of their behavior is implicit. Postmodern fiction, driven by intellectual games, like fairy tales, is often short. The reader isn't expected to read for a long time without characters to empathize with. Further, there are degrees of flatness and roundness. Characterization is a spectrum. From Hobb's *Farseer* saga at the extreme end of deep characterization (one first-person narrator followed through nine books and over fifty in-story years) to side characters that exist only to pour a cup of coffee and don't even get description at the other end. The most depth should be invested in the characters that are most important to the story.

Character Development in Fantasy Fiction

Some notes on mistaken beliefs held about fantasy fiction and character development

Everything covered about character development applies equally to fantasy and realism. It is a commonly held belief that fantasy fiction is usually less character-driven than realistic fiction. The number of times I've heard fantasy detractors explain their preference for literary realism based upon the supposed focus on character is beyond counting. If they are trying to placate fantasy and sci-fi lovers, they will say, "Fantasy and science fiction are more about the ideas." Similarly, I've heard many novice writers explain their fantasy writing choices (particularly, a lack of characterization, especially through interiority) as being because "fantasy is really about the world." Despite having completely different motivations for their statements, both groups of people are largely wrong, and their misconceptions have similar roots.

Both groups of people are usually speaking from ignorance. The anti-fantasy fiction folk have usually read little to no fantasy fiction, and their primary definition of fantasy often comes from Tolkien, and his imitators from the 1970s, 80s, and early 90s. Tolkien and his imitators, as well as the extreme visibility of YA fantasy like *Harry Potter* and *Twilight*, warp perceptions of fantasy fiction, especially in terms of characterization. *Harry Potter* and *Twilight* function like what they are, commercial young adult fiction. The norms for that kind of fiction don't translate well to fiction for adults. Tolkien was in fact focused on the world. His emphasis derived from a medievalist background, and his goal to create a secondary world that was an alternate history for England. His style drew from medieval epics and histories like *Le Morte d'Arthur*, more than from the tradition of the novel.[15]

The visibility and influence of Tolkien and his imitators has led to a situation where he and they are the most common early influential exposure to fantasy for generations of readers. I frequently encounter students who love fantasy who have never moved past YA fantasy or adult fantasy from the 1980s and 90s. There has always been character-driven fantasy fiction, even if it has gotten less attention. Since the 1990s, the Tolkien imitators, and the purely world-driven fantasy fiction subset has slipped ever further out of dominance. It would be near impossible, if one isn't already a famous author, or writing *Dungeons and Dragons, Forgotten Realms,* or *Dragonlance* tie-in fiction, to publish such fiction today. Both writers and readers are harmed by this misapprehension about fantasy fiction. Readers end up with an unreasonable prejudice not based on reality, which is especially problematic if they are teachers or editors. Even if the teacher of writing isn't prejudiced against fantasy because of their misapprehensions, they might avoid giving their students much-needed advice because of ignorance. Similarly, writers/students who are laboring under a similar misapprehension created by not reading contemporary fantasy fiction for adults might devote time and effort toward perfecting a style of writing that has a vanishingly small chance of ever seeing traditional publication.

Fantasy fiction that isn't character-driven (to one extent or another) published today is generally short stories written to mimic fairy tale or folktale forms, or postmodern experimental fiction. For example, Ursula K. Le Guin's "The Ones Who Walk Away from Omelas"[16] is essentially an ethical parable, and highly metafictional, with a narrator that comments on the probability or lack thereof of particular events. It is also brief. A novel in either of these modes is unusual (though not unheard of). Experimental novels that are abstract and idea-driven do happen of course, but they are not the predominant mode, and don't look like the world- or idea-driven fiction from the 1980s and 90s that people often reference when deriding fantasy.

All of this being said, there are concerns for character development and dialogue in fantasy fiction that are less of a concern in realistic or mimetic fiction.

Worldbuilding and Character Development

Worldbuilding and character development in fantasy fiction cannot be extricated. One key characteristic of fantasy fiction is that it has characters whose actions affect or are affected by the larger world. In this way, fantasy character development (and consequently, plots) frequently has elements in common with non-Western literatures, like African fiction, which Mathew Salesses, author of *Craft in the Real World*, says often includes less focus on individuality, and more on the "naked force of the world."[17] Similarly, fantasy fiction often focuses on the individuals caught up in events that they cannot control fully, no matter how much they strive. In other words, the importance of broader social pressures is frequently central to the dilemmas faced by the characters, beyond their individual agency.

If you are writing realism, and your main character is a 40-year-old auto worker in Detroit named Earl, there are a certain number of things that motivate him that your readers will probably understand without you having to explain the whole auto industry. However, in fantasy, you can't depend on the reader's understanding of the social forces that pressure the main character. Your readers will need more context to understand who your characters are and why they behave the way they do. That means you will need to understand how race, class, gender, socioeconomics, geography, etc. effect your characters. Simultaneously, you must avoid info dumping that information. Worldbuilding exposition given either through dialogue, the narrator, or the characters thinking about it for a long time usually slows down the story and feels artificial.

Characters should think about the world the way a real person thinks about their world. You think about it as it becomes relevant to your experience in the moment, but you don't think about it in detail most of the time. When I get catcalled on a run, I get scared, and I think about how much I hate the way I have to feel vulnerable in public places, but I don't go into a long digression in my head where I detail gender dynamics and rape culture in America. I already know what culture I live in; I'm not going to go into belaboring them in my mind unless I am writing about those issues and predrafting as I run. I wouldn't go into detail in conversation unless I am in an argument or teaching a gender studies class. Additionally, not every character will be equally knowledgeable about the world. As a college professor who teaches courses that often include a focus on gender, sexuality, and environmental studies within the humanities, I spend an above average amount of time thinking about why American society in the 21st century works the way it does, and how it impacts people. It would be more natural for me to think directly about social construction than your average CEO. Similarly, your characters won't possess identical tendencies toward self-reflection. Their life experiences and ideology will impact their understanding of the world. A noble might find their social system perfectly just and see their own status as a product of inborn worth, while a scribe might very well see the exact same world as intrinsically unjust. Your characters should think about the world, and talk about it, insofar as it is appropriate to the moment, to who they are, and to their worldview. The reader will simultaneously learn about the world and about the characters, without any clumsy info dumping or giant blocks of exposition.

Remember that section from C. S. E. Cooney's "Martyr's Gem" that we looked at when discussing narration? We learn a ton about the world from that whole scene, as well as about the main character. We learn, without anyone lecturing in their minds or in dialogue, that this is a very class-conscious world, and the Blodestones are of the highest status—higher than Shasta's. We learn that he and his sister are conscious of the mismatch in class. We also learn that women pick husbands, and husbands are sent off with marriage gifts. We learn that our protagonist doesn't find himself attractive. We also learn about geography when we discover the protagonist's anxiety about moving so far from his sister.

World and character are intertwined in the real world and in fiction, but fantasy fiction calls attention to that intertwining because the world is not the one that readers live in. The world cannot be a blank backdrop for the characters. Conversely, the characters must not be mere tour guides to a world, no matter how interesting the world is to the writer. While a fantasy novel will necessarily have a different ratio of worldbuilding to character development than contemporary realism (worldbuilding and the scope of many fantasy stories is why the average fantasy novel is much fatter than the average realistic novel). There isn't less character development, but there is a lot of other work that has to be done in a fantasy novel in addition to showing the arc of the characters. Consequently, it is to your advantage to build the world and the characters simultaneously.

Big Characters Big Stories, Small Characters Big Stories, and Small Stories and Big Characters

When writing fantasy fiction, it is easy to assume that the large scope of your story means that you also need large characters. Large in personality, status, or impact on the world. Fantasy frequently includes plots that have implications for the fate of entire worlds or civilizations. As a result, there is a long tradition of focusing on characters who are directly involved in the work to save the world or have their hands on the levers of power. Think King Arthur, Aragorn, Jon Snow, Daenerys Targaryen, or Harry Potter. These characters are all intimately connected with preexisting power structures through ability or blood. It is also common to have an ordinary person who ends up in a position of power or importance impact the fate of the world through coincidence or accident, like Frodo, or the children in the *Chronicles of Narnia*.[18] Even as fantasy has grown more diverse in terms of the worlds that are presented, writers, and characters (and grown more interesting as a result), many characters are still at the heart of whatever large-scale problem faces the world. But their motivations are generally more personal than in much older fantasy.

In Jemisin's *Broken Earth* trilogy, the main character Essen's choices impact the fate of the fragile world in which she lives. Crucially, Essen's choices, and those of her daughter Nassun, are driven by their personal experiences. Essen and the other main characters spend time trying to survive their oppressive society and apocalyptic environment, ultimately overturning the preexisting power structures, not simply because they believe those structures to be wrong, but because people they love are in danger, or people they hate could be destroyed. Jemisin's characters are magically powerful, and impact the entire fate of the world, yet driven by the intimate and personal.

Sometimes characters in fantasy who turn out to be crucial to the fate of the world as they know it aren't even seeking importance. Kvothe, in Patrick Rothfuss's *Kingkiller Chronicles*,[19] ends up entangled with virtually every major large-scale event in the world, from the return of magic and the invasion of the Chandrian. His family were traveling performers, and he's fascinated by tales of magic. When his family is murdered, he must fend for himself. His involvement with large-scale events is driven by his longing for knowledge, to understand what happened to his parents. His contribution to the fate of his world is an accident. His motivations don't become "to save the world" until deep into the story.

Even if a character is predestined by blood for power, like many of the characters in *The Daevabad Trilogy* by S. A. Chakraborty, their decisions derive from personal motivations. They have problems with their siblings, daddy issues, and sometimes don't even want the power the world thrusts upon them.[20]

As evident from these examples, big characters in plots with a large scope should still be motivated by the personal. This makes your characters feel multidimensional and ties the plot to their emotional lives.

Some writers, like Guy Gavriel Kay in recent years, have pushed back against the stereotypical storylines and characters of epic fantasy in different ways. Kay's historical fantasy has always had lyrical prose and an interest in the experience of ordinary people. But in recent books, like *A Brightness Long Ago*,[21] Kay directs the locus of attention almost entirely away from the big events and "important" people of the world (a fantastical version of Renaissance era Italy). Kay makes the context of wars and political maneuvering clear—but that's not what the story is about. It focuses nearly entirely on ordinary people who have no control whatsoever over the larger world. Villagers who live in the town that the army passes through. A young woman picked up in passing by a sadistic noble. This is a novel about the people ignored, forgotten, or not even included in traditional epic fantasy. It's a moving book by a master of the field.

Not all fantasy novels are epic fantasy. Many other genres of fantasy don't have fate-of-the-world plots at all.

Peter S. Beagle's *Summerlong* is a contemporary fantasy in which Persephone and Hades wander into a small island community and cause marriage disruption for one particular couple. The stakes are people's relationships.[22] Ellen Kushner's *Swordspoint*, an exquisite queer fantasy of manners, follows the experience of two lovers and their fates, but the world itself is never at risk. Nghi Vo's *Empress of Salt and Fortune* is the story of a monk discovering the true history of their recently deceased empress.[23] P. Djèlí Clark's *The Haunting of Tram Car 015*[24] is a detective story set in an alternate history Cairo. Mostly what is at stake is the narrator's job, and the danger presented by a possessed tram car (dangerous to those who try to enter the car, not to the city at large). Kat Howard's *Roses and Rot*[25] retells the Tam Lin ballad, and the only people in danger are the artists in a collision course with the fay. Marie Brennan's *A Natural History of Dragons*[26] is about a young woman's desire to be a naturalist in a pseudo-Victorian England.

When developing a fantasy character, be aware of the scope of your story, and how your character fits within that scope. They don't need to be the savior of the world, even if the world is at risk. If they are the savior of the world, or the one who will doom it, their motivations should be personal.

Beware the Trope

Fantasy fiction is sometimes accused of being prone to relying on tropes, an accusation frequently used to distinguish it from "literary" fiction. As someone who has read widely in both genres, worked at literary magazines, and been a teacher of writing for over thirteen years, I can confidently say that tropes don't belong to fantasy any more than bad marriages belong to literary realism. I can't even count how many stories I've seen revolving around a vaguely depressed young white guy working in a bar/restaurant who seeks meaning in drinking and women but fails. Or the middle-aged woman who finds her family insufficient and realizes she has wasted her life. All of which goes to say characters that are tropes show up everywhere. It's only more noticeable in fantasy because the worlds the characters operate within aren't real, and so any patterns are easier to discern. Literary realism gets away with being trope-heavy without people noticing because that which seems "normal" isn't questioned. It's less obvious when stories rely on dissatisfied housewives than it is when stories rely on predestined kings.

That said, how does one deal with the presence of character tropes in fantasy? Are you obligated to try for 100-percent original characters? Before you look at your manuscript in progress and panic, take a deep breath.

You are not obligated to be totally original. Originality is largely a myth. But, to make your story rich, and to avoid having your reader essentially skim it (tropes, like clichés, lose richness with repetition), focus not on what *type* of character you are writing, but *who* they are, on what is particular to them. Fitz may be a royal bastard (a character type as old as Mordred in Arthurian epics) and an assassin, but he's not like one you've seen before, because he's not just an assassin or a royal bastard, he's a man who wishes he had a father, who tends to resort to violence to avoid thinking things through, who loves animals deeply, and whose most beloved companion is the Fool, a gender-ambiguous jester. Fitz is Fitz, and nobody else. Nothing in your character's consciousness should be able to be copied and pasted into another story.

You can tell a fantasy story about anybody. Your point of view character doesn't have to be the predestined king, you could focus on his butler, or the baker living in the city under siege. You could tell the story, like Katherine Addison does in her novel *The Goblin Emperor*,[27] of the half-goblin son of an elven king in a racist society, who inherits the throne because everyone else in line before him dies in a terrible accident. He wants to make his kingdom better, but also struggles with insecurity.

Vandana Singh's story "A Handful of Rice"[28] follows a character sent to assassinate the ruler of an alternate history India, where they've ejected the British, but the ruler who saved them from the imperialists has become, in his own way, a tyrant. The protagonist discovers that the tyrant is his long-lost childhood friend. It manages to be a story where the character's choices have both epic implications, and profoundly personal impacts.

Read enough so you recognize when a character is a trope, and then go beyond it.

Discussion Questions and Writing Activities

1. How did the discussion of character tropes in fantasy and in realistic fiction make you feel? Was it surprising or uncomfortable to you? A relief? Why?

2. What character tropes, both from fantasy and realism, can you think of? List three from fantasy, and then list at least two ways that you could subvert each one.

3. What drives the characters in a fantasy you've read recently? What are their dreams and dreads? What details illustrated or revealed character motivations?

4. Think about your fantasy story in progress. What is the protagonist's position in the world? How are they empowered and/or disempowered? How does their social status impact their values, beliefs, and available choices? Do they strive against their place in society? Do they accept it? How does this influence their motivations and their actions?

5. Write a scene of dialogue for your story in progress or set in a fantasy world you know. Include two to four characters. Determine their stakes in the conversation, who they are, what they want from each other. Try to allow the reader to learn about the world through the conversation without direct explanation. Afterwards, reflect on the process.

6. Go through a fantasy story you've already written, and mark where you explain the world in exposition, as well as where you could insert interiority. Then, rewrite the story or a scene from the story, focusing on interiority and character, including worldbuilding only insofar as it is relevant to the characters in the moment. Reflect on the process.

7. Write a story about a monster with a problem. Maybe it's a werewolf with male pattern baldness. Or a siren who wants to sing opera. Take that problem seriously. Use the problem to create conflict and stakes.

CHAPTER 5
POINT OF VIEW

Introduction

In this chapter I will briefly define some of the most common point of view types, as well as the opportunities particular to each point of view. Then I will talk about point of view concerns particular to fantasy fiction. This chapter is close to my heart. As my students can attest, I believe that many difficulties writers face can be tied to problems with point of view. Point of view determines what information the reader will have, whose mind(s) and thoughts a reader will be given insight into, as well as the voice and prose style of a narrative. Point of view influences narrative distance, chronology, pacing, and more aspects of writing than I can possibly list. Malfunctions in point of view can lead to confusion on the part of the reader, slow pacing, dull or confusing information delivery, plot holes, and flat characters, among other issues. If you've ever read a story that, objectively speaking, nothing much happened, but the character's mind was so interesting that you kept reading anyway, you've seen the power of point of view. If you've ever read a story where you are bored by even the most sensational events, point of view gone wrong may be to blame.

Point of View Generally Considered

When deciding what point of view to put your story in, begin with deciding whose story you are telling, and what scope is most appropriate. The character or characters whose point of view you write from should, generally, be the character(s) with the most at stake. They should be the character or characters who will witness and experience the events that are central to the story you want to tell. While there have been fine novels written with observer narrators (like *The Great Gatsby*),[1] in general, if you find yourself writing a story from the point of view of a narrator whose is trying to tell us *about* a really interesting person, ask yourself, is this the best narrator? Or should my point of view character *be* the interesting person? That said, once you think about whose story you are writing, and why, then you need to choose a point of view. Below are brief definitions and explanations of different points of view:

- *First person* is a common point of view, in all forms of fiction, although it is more common in YA than in adult fantasy. First person means that the story is narrated directly by the protagonist in their own words. They will think about themselves and describe their actions in terms of "I." For this point of view you shouldn't have to write the phrase "I thought" because the story consists entirely of the thoughts and observations of the protagonist. With this point of view, every description, every detail, is colored by the beliefs, priorities, motivations, and feelings of the narrator protagonist. First person is the most highly subjective point of view. All narrators are unreliable, but first-person narrators are the most unreliable. Like a real person, they will be prone to blind spots, evasions, and biases. The reader can only know what the narrator knows, and so their view of the story, the world, and other characters will be limited by the knowledge of the narrator. Unreliable narrators are studies in subjectivity, and the reader must attempt to see around them in order to understand the world accurately. Some first-person narrators are more unreliable than others. If the narrator is highly perceptive and reflective, they will be relatively reliable. Kelly Link's short fiction is known for having highly unreliable narrators. Her story "The Faery Handbag"[2] as well as her story "The Wrong Grave"[3] are from the point of view of narrators whose honesty is suspect, both in terms of what they tell the reader, and what they admit to themselves. First person is an intimate point of view, but it does require the writer to write in the language that the narrator would use, and to only share information that the narrator would know, and so it has some limitations for stories of large scope. Occasionally, especially in fantasy short fiction, there will be first-person narrators who are unnamed, and are telling the reader a story for reasons unknown. These are usually very short, like Ursula K. Le Guin's "The Ones Who Walk Away from Omelas."

- *Third person* is one of the most common and most varied points of view. Third person, broadly defined, means that a narrator speaks about characters in the third person, i.e., "he," "she," or "they." What type of third-person narrator you are using determines how much information that narrator has access to.

1. *Close third or third person limited* is the predominant point of view for most adult fiction in the 21st century. This third-person narrator is largely invisible. They don't have a personality of their own, but rather convey the direct thoughts, feelings, and observations of one character at a time. When you hear the thoughts of a character in close third you don't have to label it "she thought" all the time, although sometimes you do. Nor do you have to put it in italics. Rather, it can be conveyed almost as though it is first person, but through the language of the narrator. Close third often has more lyrical prose than the first person and is more imagery-driven. The third-person narrator can zoom in and out, going from sharing the direct thoughts of the focal character, to describing what the room they are in looks like. Imagine this point of view like a camera that can zoom out enough to show the world around the characters, but also zoom into their minds. Free indirect discourse, when you hear direct thoughts through the third person narrator, can be seen in Cooney's short story in our anthology. When Shursta meets his intended for the first time, the reader can see both his thoughts, and his unconscious movements and mannerisms, because the third-person narrator zooms in and out within a paragraph:

"Shursta Sarth," she greeted him.

"Damisel Blodestone."

Shursta had wanted to say her name. Had wanted to say it casually, as she spoke his, with a cordial nod of the head. Instead his chin jutted up and away, as if a stray hook had caught it. Her name stopped in his throat and changed places at the last second with the formal honorific. He recalled Sharrar's nonsense about names having meaning. It no longer seemed absurd.

The narrator has access to what Shursta thinks, remembers, and does. As well as visual descriptions of his gestures that a person would never apply to themselves. A person would never talk about their chin moving "as if a stray hook had caught it." But a narrator can give the reader that striking visual.

Close third is common in both long and short fiction. Novels frequently have rotating points of view, either by section or by chapter, where a limited number of characters are rotated in and out as the focal character. Short stories commonly stick with a single focal character, but occasionally rotate. Rotating close third is often used to highlight subjectivity.

The reader mostly only knows what the chosen focal characters know or have known, but through the narrator the reader can also gain information about the past, the present, and the surroundings. In many respects this point of view is like having your cake and eating it: you get much of the intimacy of a first-person narrator, but with more flexibility.

2. *Third person objective* is an older and rarely used point of view. It allows no access to the thoughts of the characters, only their actions. It is like a camera pointed at the events of the story. This point of view is common in folktales, and Tolkien used it in his novels. Tolkien was trying to mimic medieval epics, so it was appropriate for his goals. But it is virtually never used in novels now. It forfeits almost every tool that is specific to fiction, like seeing inside the mind of the characters. Stories written in this point of view that I have encountered in classes or in the slush pile of magazine submissions look like the work of frustrated screen writers. If you want to write screenplays, write screenplays. Otherwise, why give up the ability to access the head of your characters, to let the reader feel *with* them, in a way they can't with any other narrative form? It's very hard to make a reader care about a story written in third person objective. It's also nearly impossible to publish. The exception is flash fiction. Flash fiction, due to brevity (1,000 words or less) often simply describes an event or series of events, in striking language.

3. *Third person omniscient* is another old point of view, and it can be hard to do right, but it is also used by many contemporary writers for its flexibility and the sheer joy of pulling it off. Third person omniscient is from the perspective of a third-person narrator who can see everything that is happening, and

everything that every character is thinking. The only limitation is what the writer decides is relevant. This point of view was widespread in 19th-century fiction. The narrator often commented on the characters, went on digressions, and inserted themselves into the story. Intrusive third-person omniscient narrators are in and of themselves a character. They can be named or unnamed. Sometimes they turn out to be part of the plot. Sometimes they are just an opinionated storyteller voice. In the most extreme instances, they will interject in the first person. You can also have a third-person omniscient narrator that isn't intrusive. Kelly Link has a lot of omniscient narrators, of both types, in her short story collection *Magic for Beginners*. In our anthology, Genevieve Valentine's short story "From the Catalog of the Pavilion of the Uncanny and Marvelous, Scheduled for Premiere at the Great Exhibition (Before the Fire)"[4] takes the form of an academic piece where a third-person narrator describes the pavilion of the title, the social context surrounding it, and catalogs artifacts, including programs and letters. The narrator knows more than any one person could know without a lot of research. This isn't a traditional omniscient narrator, though it is a type of omniscience. Modern novels with omniscient narrators come from both realism and fantasy. *Bel Canto* by Ann Patchett[5] has an omniscient narrator, but not an intrusive one. The narrator head hops from paragraph to paragraph, but never directly inserts their own viewpoint. They are not a character in and of themselves. Susanna Clarke's *Jonathan Strange & Mr. Norrell* has an intrusive omniscient narrator who comments in footnotes. The narrator even argues with characters within those footnotes and points out when the characters whose minds they can see into are factually incorrect about topics as diverse as the origin of magic or personal events. The advantage of omniscient narrator is that you can tell your readers anything you want to at any time. The danger of an omniscient narrator is that it can cause a lack of focus, and head hopping, if not handled carefully, can be hard to follow and confusing, lead to a lack of plot tension, or detachment from the characters.

4. *Second-person* narrators are rare except in experimental fiction but are interesting if done well. Second-person narrators come in essentially two forms. A disguised first-person narrator, essentially the narrator talking to themselves, such as in Lorrie Moore's short story collection *Self Help*. For example, in the short story "How to Be an Other Woman,"[6] the narrator gives instructions for how to be the "other woman" in an affair. But the instructions are incredibly specific, the narrator is describing what they themselves did. In N. K. Jemisin's *Broken Earth* trilogy, some of the sections are in second person. It becomes clear that those sections are from the point of view of a character who can only cope with telling the story in the second person because of trauma. Moore uses the second person to disguise the first-person narrator for comedy, and Jemisin for emotional impact. The other type of second-person narration is the kind that is actually addressing the reader. This is uncommon.

Third person without an intrusive narrator, or first person, can become invisible, and the reader can simply fall into the fictional dream. Second person draws attention to itself, rendering any story written in it at least a little bit metafictional.

5. *First person plural* is any story where the narrator speaks for a collective. Narrators of this type will say "we" rather than "I." Much like second person, this an experimental point of view. It is more common in short fiction than novels. It is commoner in short fiction because of the difficulty of sustaining it, and because of a lack of emotional intimacy. It can be used to emphasize a lack of individuality on the part of a group, group dynamics, or to create a kind of uncanny alienation. The plural point of view allows for a focus on group dynamics, on the kind of hive mind adolescents can get into. China Miéville's "The Condition of New Death"[7] uses a first person plural to create a sense of the uncanny. The narrator describes an event in which bodies upon death begin to rotate so that no matter where an observer stands, the corpse's feet point toward them. At first the story seems almost objective, the narrator describing when this change first occurred, giving information about the sociocultural reaction to New Death. Gradually it is revealed that the story that you have just read is the churning of a group mind. The first person plural, regardless of if it is used to create alienation, or to capture a group dynamic, is not a point of view that can become invisible.

There are points of view that don't fit tidily into these categories. But this encompasses the points of view that you will encounter most. All points of view create opportunities and liabilities; you should choose the one that works best for the story you want to tell. You may not be able to tell which point of view is best right away, so don't be afraid to experiment.

Point of View in Fantasy Fiction

Fantasy fiction comes in every point of view. However, there are certain points of view that lend themselves to certain types of stories. Considerations of scope are especially important when choosing a point of view for your fantasy story, as well as information delivery for worldbuilding. In this section I will focus mostly on first person and third person, and how the choice between the two can impact the type of fantasy story that you tell.

Short Form Fantasy Fiction

Short fiction ranges from the traditional to the experimental. Unconventional point of view choices such as second person or first person plural are common in fantasy short fiction.

While third person dominates fantasy novels, that dominance does not extend to short stories. If you look at our anthology, nearly half of the stories are in first person. Short stories use the closeness of first person to help keep the scope narrow, and to increase intensity. "Harvest" by Rebecca Roanhorse is a great example of how first-person short fantasy can have an almost claustrophobic intensity. A short story doesn't have the space for lots of worldbuilding, it must work through implication, otherwise you won't have space to develop your characters or tell a story. First-person narrators necessitate a narrow focus on what the character knows and cares about in terms of the specific events of the short story. This handily makes it impossible for your readers to reasonably demand a ton of background information. Further, short stories are rarely trying to tell a story of huge scope (though there are some epic fantasy short stories, they tend to stretch the page limits of the form). If the implied scope is large, the actual experience is generally narrowed to that of one character. Sticking to first person for a fantasy story can help to provide discipline and make certain that the character's voice drives the story. Which is not to say that third-person short stories can't be equally close to the main character's point of view. Short stories in close third are common, such as Rachael K. Jones's "The Night Bazaar for Women Becoming Reptiles."[8] Short fiction in omniscient third person tend to be more formally experimental, and even metafictional, like Angela Carter's fairy tales in *The Bloody Chamber*[9] or Kelly Link's "Magic for Beginners" from the collection of the same name.

Long Form Fantasy Fiction

Scope is a major concern in all novels, and in fantasy novels even more so. Fantasy novels often cover large swathes of time and space and include huge casts of characters. When trying to write a big story, make certain that you don't get overscoped and bite off more than you can chew. A well-chosen and effectively executed point of view can help. Because of scope concerns, epic fantasy is often written in the third person, past tense.

Third person has dominated epic fantasy for many reasons, one of which is that it lets the writer choose to give the readers almost any knowledge they want. If you choose a rotating close third, you can have point of view characters on multiple sides of war, in different social classes, etc. This creates opportunities for the reader to know more than any of the individual characters (i.e., dramatic irony). This can lend itself to nail-biting tension as the reader watches characters make decisions based upon incomplete information, until they want to scream at them through the page. I remember having that feeling reading the *Wayfarer Redemption*[10] by Australian fantasy writer Sara Douglass when I was in high school. I almost tore the cover off a paperback because I was gripping it so hard. Jenn Lyons's recent epic fantasy *The Ruin of Kings*[11] has a rotating third between the protagonist and one of his antagonists, as well as a narrator who likes to jump in and give his perspective through notes. In this way it also borrows heavily from intrusive omniscient third person, though in this case the intrusive narrator is a specific individual within the story. Ken Liu's *The Grace of Kings*[12] also has a rotating third point of view that allows the reader to gain knowledge that couldn't be encompassed by any single character.

George R. R. Martin's *A Game of Thrones*[13] and Andrea Hairston's *Master of Poisons*[14] also use this point of view. Done well, not only can a rotating close third increase plot tension, but it can also give your reader the pleasure of putting puzzle pieces together from a god's-eye perspective.

Through having point of view characters from opposing sides of a conflict, or from disparate race and/or class backgrounds, you can also make certain that no group of people in the story is villainized or dehumanized. A rotating point of view can highlight the importance of subjectivity, cultural specificity, and the ways in which characters are stuck in oppressive systems. Used effectively, a rotating close third can give you much of the intimacy of a first-person narrative, but with the scope to set your characters into a large sociopolitical context, while still centering character.

Done poorly, a rotating close third point of view can deprive a story of tension, or make your characters seem stupid. You want to be certain that your characters are making decisions based upon the best of their knowledge, not because you the writer have made them unrealistically obtuse to create misunderstanding. Basically, don't let a rotating close third and the large-scale knowledge of the reader make your fantasy novel feel like a sitcom where everything could be solved with one basic conversation. Also be careful that your reader's knowledge doesn't make everything that happens seem inevitable, since this deprives the narrative of tension and your characters of agency. Beware having too many point of view characters. Your narrative can end up bloated and overscoped, with too many threads, which can make it hard to pull the story together. I have a personal theory about why we have yet to see the end of Martin's *Song of Ice and Fire* series. Too many characters and too many threads make sticking the landing more difficult. Pick the point of view characters that are most relevant for the story you want to tell and stick with them. Generally, resist introducing a point of view character just for one scene, or just to kill them.

Third person omniscient is distinct from a rotating close third. A rotating close third means that character point of view rotates from section to section or chapter to chapter, and it is usually confined to just a handful of characters. Third-person omniscient narrators can see anything at any time, including inside the head of any character. An omniscient narrator can do anything a rotating close third perspective can do, plus a lot more. Structurally, because you don't have to pick a small handful of point of view characters and can just go into the mind of a character briefly, you can do things like explore the thoughts of a crowd who witness a duel, or the beliefs and opinions of a neighborhood upon hearing of a prominent person's disgrace. You can, as Guy Gavriel Kay does in his novel *The Last Light of the Sun* (a personal favorite that makes me weep every time I read it for sheer beauty) focus primarily on a few characters, but take a brief detour into the mind and life of an ordinary young woman who sees a man sneaking around the edge of the forest who clearly doesn't belong, recognizes that he's a threat, and runs to warn the local chieftain, dropping her bucket of milk. In many fantasy novels this event might happen, but it would be offstage. Kay not only goes into her point of view for about a page, he also then follows with a brief narrative, less than a page, of her life after this moment until she dies of old age. It's a moment of seeing the most ordinary person as important, and it wouldn't have been possible without the omniscient point of view. Kay's omniscient narrator is lyrical, but not intrusive, and isn't used to take the feeling of peril out of any given moment, or to have less intimacy with the characters, but rather to give Kay the ability to let the reader see the interconnected threads that bind all people.

An intrusive third-person omniscient narrator in fantasy fiction often resembles the narrator of a 19th-century novel like *Vanity Fair*,[15] commenting on characters, sometimes judgmentally or sarcastically, sometimes compassionately, and often explaining things they think the reader needs to know. An intrusive narrator has an element of metafictionality, since they usually know they are telling a story, and sometimes are even aware of the text you are reading. Susanna Clarke's debut novel *Jonathan Strange & Mr. Norrell* purports to be an academic text by a scholar of English magic. It has footnotes and contains stories within stories. The intrusive omniscient narrator, unlike an invisible one, has no pretensions of being nonpartisan. They may be all-knowing, but they are not unbiased. This type of narrator can be funny, and stylistically interesting to read. An intrusive narrator and footnotes allows the writer to include long digressions about the world, or stories related to the characters, without having to clumsily shove a monologue about the world or culture into the mouth of one of the characters. Done well, this technique can let the writer get away with all kinds of things that would normally be a violation of point of view.

Done poorly, the very freedom of an omniscient narrator can lead a writer down a tangled path full of thorny vines. In other words, the quantity of available choices can make you into your own worst enemy. It can be hard to know when you are including something that will actually add to the novel, and when you are including something that you enjoy that isn't going to be interesting to anyone else. Most novels with intrusive narrators tend to be long. Further, done poorly, the intrusions can slow down the narrative and make a writer lean far too heavily on telling instead of showing. Additionally, an intrusive narrator lends itself to the writer not getting close enough to characters.

An omniscient point of view novel of any type requires delicate control on the part of the writer to make certain that the reader can follow the point of view changes, and that they don't get lost, confused, or detached from the story. Think of writing a novel in an omniscient third as the equivalent of juggling two chainsaws, a torch, and a live meerkat. Thrilling to watch (read) but with the potential to go terribly wrong!

A close third that doesn't rotate but focuses entirely on one character has the closeness of first person, but with the ability to use prose and language that the character might not use. This point of view is common in all fantasy fiction, but especially in novels with a narrower scope.

Close third novels usually only focus on one or two characters. Getting overscoped is still a concern but having too many point of view characters is less likely. When telling a story with a smaller scope, picking the right point of view character is of even more importance, since the weight of the novel will rest on that character or characters. Recent fantasy novels that tell impactful stories with a narrow scope include Silvia Moreno-Garcia's *Mexican Gothic*,[16] Madeline Miller's *Circe*, P. Djèlí Clark's *A Master of Djinni*,

Charlie Jane Anders's *All the Birds in the Sky*,[17] Nghi Vo's *The Chosen and the Beautiful*,[18] Cherie Priest's *Maplecroft*,[19] and Alix E. Harrow's *Ten Thousand Doors of January*.[20]

Despite the relative dominance of third person in epic fantasy, there are still epic fantasy novels written in the first person and including among their ranks some of the finest fantasy novels written in the last fifty years. Robin Hobb's series is told in interlocking trilogies (and one four-book series), comprising a total of fifteen books, nine of which are from the first-person point of view of Fitz Chivalry Farseer. This series is epic fantasy, the fate of kingdoms rests upon the shoulders of Fitz and his compatriots, but aside from the two sets of books within the series that aren't from Fitz's point of view, the reader's knowledge is entirely confined to Fitz's experience, and he is far from omniscient; he's not even particularly wise. The story is written in a retrospective first person, so Fitz does have the capacity to reflect. The reader suffers the same limitations as Fitz. This builds tension in an entirely different way than the dramatic irony encouraged by the use of a rotating third-person point of view story. I don't think I've ever cared as deeply about a character as I cared about Fitz.

Patrick Rothfuss's *The Name of the Wind* is in first person from the point of view of Kvothe. Much like Fitz, Kvothe is highly fallible, and prone to making bad decisions based upon his feelings. The narrative is driven in both cases by the idiosyncrasies of the characters as they come up against the larger world and the forces arrayed against them. N. K. Jemisin's amazing debut novel *The Hundred Thousand Kingdoms*[21] is in the first person, from the point of view of a young woman named Yeine. The worldbuilding occurs seamlessly, integrated with Yeine's own struggle for knowledge and survival.

First-person narrators in fantasy fiction make bringing the reader close to the character easier. Unless you are doing first person radically wrong, the reader will know what the character knows and feel what they feel. As long as you avoid violating point of view, the danger of being too distant from your character is slight. Further, any time your character is in an oppressed position, or kept in ignorance by others, forcing the reader to experience those situations along with them can induce empathy. Yeine, Fitz, and Kvothe begin the stories disempowered; first-person narration, and the kind of claustrophobia that can come with it, works thematically.

First-person narrators in fantasy, especially epic fantasy, mean you as a writer have to be extra careful with worldbuilding. A character monologuing about the world they live in, or thinking about it for no apparent reason, feels especially awkward in a story with a first-person narrator. If you choose the wrong point of view character, someone who isn't central to the events you want to relate, or who isn't a complex or interesting person, you can derail the story and have no other character to fall back on. Hobb deals with the worldbuilding issue by having Fitz work on a research project about magic in his homeland, and so chapters often begin with an excerpt from his research project. Additionally, he's centrally located to witness a lot of important events without shoehorning. Kvothe is an obsessive researcher for personal and professional reasons. His drive for knowledge leads him to the middle of important events, and to travel all over the world. Yeine is deeply aware of how disadvantaged she is by her own ignorance, and so she strives to rectify it. She's in a palace surrounded by movers and shakers, so she's well placed to witness and discover important information without convoluted justification. A first-person narrator for epic fantasy who isn't well positioned, or inquisitive, would make showing the reader enough of the world to understand what is going on difficult.

While I have devoted the most time to first and third person here, issues of scope and information release are central to fantasy and the discussion of point of view, regardless of what point of view you choose. Be deliberate in your choices and be willing to experiment if your point of view choice appears to be going awry.

Discussion Questions and Writing Activities

1. What point of view do you prefer to write in? Why?

2. Read one of the stories referenced in this chapter from our anthology. Pay attention to how the point of view works. After reading the story, ask yourself what opportunities the point of view gave the story, and how it would be different if changed?

3. Look at the last three fantasy novels you have read. What points of view did they use? How could you apply the information you've learned to understanding how point of view works in those novels?

4. Return to your fantasy story in progress and rewrite the first scene in a different point of view. Compare the two versions. How did the change impact the tone of your story, the scope, or information release?

5. Pick one of the more difficult points of view from this chapter (like second person or third person omniscient) and start a story. Afterwards, reflect on the process.

6. Choose a story that you have a complete draft of and revise it with an eye toward making certain that you are close to your character's head. Is everything filtered through their eyes? Does the reader have access to their thoughts and feelings?

7. In your story in progress, how are you handling information release and worldbuilding? How is the point of view impacting your method?

CHAPTER 6
STRUCTURE AND PLOT

Introduction

It is a common misconception that fantasy fiction is primarily plot- rather than character-driven. This is no more accurate than if I asserted all realism is plot-driven because of the existence of John Grisham novels. However, it is true that fantasy tends to put characters into situations where their actions have the potential to cause large-scale change. The bigger the plot, the more chances for there to be issues of insufficiently connected causality, or plot holes. Thus, it is crucial that writers avoid following overly predictable plots and keep track of causality. In other words, in a story with a large scope, writers must be careful to have characters drive plot, not the other way around, and make certain that things happen for causal reasons, not just because the writer wants them to.

Structure and Plot Generally Considered

All stories have plots to one degree or another. The real question concerning plot is how much emphasis will it receive within the story? If the plot is small and quiet, the reader might hardly notice it. Large and complicated plots draw attention to themselves. If the plot is the skeleton on which one puts flesh, then stories that center plots have more bones interconnected in more complicated ways, which readers must track. To extend the metaphor, a plot-centered story is a dragon, a less plot-centered story is a snake. There are many kinds of plots and many kinds of structures, from the traditional to the experimental. First, some basic definitions:

Plot vs. Story

Story is a sequence of events told within time.

Plot is the reasoning, rational, and causality behind those events.

In other words, if you simply say, "the dragon ate the man," that is a story. If you say, "the dragon ate the man because he had trespassed on the dragon's territory," that is a plot.

Plot vs. Structure vs Form

While plot is the causality behind a story, structure is the shape into which you pour the plot and story. To extend the metaphor of a body, no living creature is complete as a skeleton, it has internal organs, muscle, blood, skin, etc. that determine how a creature looks and moves. Structures for narratives vary hugely, from traditional to experimental. Structure is a beautiful mythological bestiary. You want to make certain you choose the structure that is best for your particular narrative. Structure and form are less easily separated than plot and structure. The structure of your story can describe both the form (like choosing to have footnotes or take the shape of a letter) as well as deciding to write a coming-of-age tale, since the arc of a coming-of-age narrative will also impact the form. Form, in essence, is the type of text you are writing, and structure is the order and method chosen to present the narrative. Sometimes, in the case of experimental forms, like a text with footnotes, you can say that the form of the novel is a pseudo-academic narrative, but it is structured chronologically. However, if it is a story that is told backwards, that is both its form and its structure. Do you see the difficulty? *Form Is Meaning*

If you change the form, you'll end up changing the structure, and the entire reading experience and the meaning of what you have written. So, choose with care, and be willing to experiment. As I discuss structure and form, I'll discuss them in a more blended fashion than plot, simply because of the difficulty of disentanglement.

Some Plot Types

- Western narrative has often been described in terms of the Freytag Pyramid, named for Gustav Freytag (1816–95). He was a scholar of Greek drama, but his heuristic is widely used to analyze the structure of fiction. The story begins with an *introduction* (Act I) that lays out the time and place of the action, characters, sets the mood, and introduces a conflict or complication. It is followed by *rising action* (Act II) where conflict intensifies and leads to the climax. In the *climax* (Act III) the rising action comes to fruition, and the characters and events come to a point of no return. The *falling action* (Act IV) shows fallout from the events of the climax. The *catastrophe* is the conclusion (Act V) and shows a world and characters fundamentally altered by the events of the plot. Most modern novels don't follow a five-act structure and short stories don't have the time or space. Most fiction with chronological plots in the 21st-century Western tradition follow a modified Freytag Pyramid, where the story begins at the start of the *rising action* (conflict), hits the *climax*, and ends almost immediately, with brief *falling action*.[1] Many stories aren't fully chronological and don't follow even a modified Freytag Pyramid, particularly stories that are experimental or postmodern, or that come from non-Western traditions. The most useful thing about the Freytag Pyramid is as a reminder that the plot generally gains in intensity as it goes and ends in a place that feels like a completion of that which has come before.
- Interconnected complications: used for screenplays, but also applicable to fiction. Instead of the dramatic peaks and valleys of Freytag's Pyramid, it can be visualized as a series of interlocking circles, focusing on progression and

connections, adding up to a conclusion. This form of plot is especially conflict-driven.[2]

- A picaresque plot eschews progression, peaks and valleys, and standard notions of causality. Things happen, then more things happen, and then more and more until the story ends. Each event can have mini peaks and valleys, but the sense of rising action from the beginning to the end is minimal. *Don Quixote* (1605) by Miguel de Cervantes is the archetypal picaresque. Picaresque is often played for comedy. Many oral folk narratives use the picaresque. This is sometimes also called a "shaggy dog" story.[3]

- A style of plot that I like to call the roller coaster is one that is common to Hollywood action films, that consists of a series of large peaks, and ends with the hero on top at the end, and the status quo regained. Novels that follow this format are often series novels that are only semi-sequential, where the goal is to write as many of them as possible, and for the reader to be able to pick up a book from any point in the series.[4]

This is not a complete list of plot types by any stretch of the imagination. It is a basic survey. Plot is distinct from plot devices. *Plot devices* can lead to problematic causality. A few to watch out for:

- The *red herring*, a seeming answer, clue, or plot point that turns out to be misleading. Mystery novels sometimes use a red herring to distract the reader or detective, but it should be one that is reasonable to be distracted by. Outside of mysteries, red herrings are best avoided. Don't deliberately mislead, it breaks the reader/writer contract. If your character chases a red herring, it should be because they are working off of incomplete information, and it should make sense for their character.

- *Deus Ex Machina*, which means "God from the Machine." This plot device occurs when a character is extricated from trouble by a sudden and arbitrary, often coincidental event, object, or person. Frequently perceived as a violation of the rules of the story. If you find yourself introducing this device, go back and see if you are letting your character off too easily. Maybe their situation is unsolvable. Or maybe you put them into the wrong situation for the story you are trying to tell.

- A *Macguffin* is a plot device that involves a goal, sometimes an object, that the main character pursues. A Macguffin can be useful, but it crucial that characters have genuine motivation for chasing the Macguffin.

Structure is just as important as plot. Structure is the form that you put the plot into. There are so many potential story structures, trying to tell them all would be like trying to list and define every creature that ever lived or was imagined. Every *plot* can be told through a nearly infinite variety of *structures*. While many novels and short stories simply begin at the beginning of the action and go through the story in chronological order, many do not.

Tell your story in the way that is best for that particular story. As poets know, form and meaning are in many respects one and the same. The same story told chronologically in a nonintrusive structure will feel fundamentally different if told like *Jonathan Strange & Mr. Norrell*, in the form of an academic document, complete with footnotes.

Short stories lend themselves to experimentation. The brevity of short stories means that if the structure doesn't work, the time investment is lower for the reader and the writer. Our anthology contains a few innovatively structured stories. Sofia Samatar's "Meet Me in Iram"[5] is part definition, part encyclopedia entry, and part first-person reflection, in an effort to understand a lost city called Iram that is "unbuilt" and that both exists and does not exist. It is structured through fragments of prose, verse, and memories.

Genevieve Valentine's "From the Catalog of the Pavilion of the Uncanny and Marvelous, Scheduled for Premiere at the Great Exhibition (Before the Fire)" is structured through fictional letters, newspaper clippings, journal entries, and catalog excerpts from the Great Exhibition of 1851. This a variant on the epistolary story.

Outside our anthology, Angela Carter fused the gothic with the postmodern in baroque language. Her version of Little Red Riding Hood, "The Company of Wolves," is a spiral, circling down to the core narrative, the moment when the "Little Red" character tames the wolf (who is also a man) by becoming wilder herself.[6] Fairy tales are instructive for understanding form and structure, since a retelling highlights that the same basic story can be told an infinite number of ways.

Structurally innovative short stories that I have read recently:

- Kij Johnson, "The Apartment Dweller's Bestiary"[7] from *Clarkesworld Magazine* (second person in the form of a bestiary).
- Ana Blandiana, "The Phantom Church" in *The Phantom Church and Other Stories* (an attempt to trace, à la anthropology or folklore, tales of a phantom church).[8]
- Suyi Davies Okungbowa, "We Come as Gods" from *Tor.com* and *Fiyah* (flash fiction first-person-plural monologue).[9]

A few noteworthy books that sustain an unusual form or structure:

- Zachary Thomas Dodson's *Bats of the Republic* is an illuminated alternate history. It even includes a letter in an envelope.[10]
- Kai Ashante Wilson's novella *A Taste of Honey* has a fractured timeline, alternating between the past, present, and more than one possible future. In one future, Abiq and Lucrio (two men from feuding empires) sustain their romance; in another, it's doomed.[11]
- Amal El-Mothar and Max Gladstone's novella *This is How You Lose the Time War* is an epistolary love story of two rival agents in a time war. They write letters to each other that take the form of animals, plants, and scents on the wind.[12]

All of the books mentioned above make their experimental forms and structures intrinsic to the story. Form and structure are inextricably tied to content and meaning.

As a means test for experimenting with form and structure, ask yourself what is gained by telling the story this way. Is it necessary to the experience I am trying to create, for the story I am telling? Does the work it requires and the reward at the end feel symmetrical?

The last thing you want is a story that is difficult to read simply for the sake of being difficult. Most readers have probably experienced such a story. A text that is formally interesting, yet difficult to understand, and in the end, all you are left with is a shrug. You want to ask: I went to so much work for *that*? In sum, don't hesitate to experiment, but make certain that you are giving your reader a gift, rather than placing unnecessary obstacles in their path.

Some Common Structures

- Frame narrative. A story within a story, where one literally frames the other. You will recognize this from *The Princess Bride* (both the film and book). One should be careful that the frame actually adds to the story and isn't just a dangling narrative tentacle.[13]

- Metafiction. Metafiction reveals itself as fictive or addresses its textuality implicitly or explicitly. Examples include Italo Calvino's *If on Winter's Night a Traveler*, A. S. Byatt's *Possession*, Kurt Vonnegut's *Slaughterhouse-Five*, and Jasper Fforde's *The Eyre Affair*.[14]

- Milieu story. This type of story begins when the narrator arrives at the setting, the milieu, and ends when they leave. The setting and how it impacts the characters is a focal point. Ursula K. Le Guin's anthropological Hainish Cycle are milieu narratives.

- Journey narrative. Characters travel from one place to another, usually to achieve a major goal. The story often ends not long after they arrive and either achieve or significantly fail to achieve their goal. Sometimes journey narratives are road stories where there is no goal, but the characters are obliged to keep moving. Progression in the episodic journey is found inside the characters.

- Interactive narratives. Choose your own adventure-style books, or stories told through role-playing games. With the advent of the internet, interactive fiction began using techniques like hyperlinks, in which the story changes based upon reader choices.

- Comedy and tragedy. Traditional comedy and tragedy are defined by their structures. Comedy begins with the world going out of joint and ends in order. Tragedy ends in disorder.

- *Bildungsroman*. A story of education, or growth. The story ends when the protagonist gains maturity in some key area. Especially common in YA.

- Mystery. Not all novels with mysteries are "mystery" novels in the generic sense. Mysteries are often structured through an unpacking process, in which the character(s) are presented with a problem that grows in complexity before resolution. When it's just a novel *with* a mystery, the mystery doesn't have to be solved. This is distinct from a true mystery novel, which requires a solution.

- Claustrophobia story. In these stories, the characters are confined. Occasionally it is metaphoric, and they are socially confined (a feminist domestic novel, for example) rather than literally. Gothic fantasy novels are frequently claustrophobia narratives. These stories trade wide-ranging geographic locations for an in-depth examination of character and place. Characters often become of increasingly unsound mind. The story ends when they escape or die. Usually, the character has chances to escape that they can't or won't take before the end. Silvia Moreno-Garcia's *Mexican Gothic* is a stellar recent example.

- Out of sequence story. This began as an experimental structure but has become less experimental with use. Margaret Atwood's *The Handmaid's Tale* begins with Offred in Gilead. Some chapters take place in the present of the story while others take place in the past, showing how the present came to be.

Structure and Plot in Fantasy Fiction

Most of the examples I gave in the previous section on plot, structure, and form were drawn from fantasy, but everything I said could be applied to any genre of fiction. However, there are additional concerns that are most relevant to fantasy fiction (and science fiction).

Plot, Clichés, and Tropes

Contrary to popular opinion, fantasy isn't any more prone to tropes and clichés than other fiction. All fiction can overuse clichés and tropes. Unfortunately, plot tropes and clichés are more noticeable in fantasy fiction because they don't benefit from the invisibility of normalcy. For example, those who don't like fantasy fiction might mock the clichéd plot element of an orphan who is actually a prince in hiding. It's not actually more cliché than a story about a housewife who suddenly discovers that she's discontent.

What counts as "realistic" or "normal" enough to not be labeled a cliché is bound by time and culture. The ability to be home with children without financial difficulty, and then to suddenly find oneself plagued primarily by boredom, is specific to class. Someone from a lower socioeconomic background, or from a culture where this hasn't been a common phenomenon, might find this story's prevalence in American literary realism just as bizarre and clichéd as a fan of realism might find the predestined king. Similarly, plot elements that were not of note in the past might raise eyebrows in a contemporary novel.

The perception that fantasy novels are full of clichés isn't fair but must be confronted. You aren't obligated to avoid all clichéd plot elements. Still, you must read enough to realize when you employ a cliché, so that you can go beyond it. I've encountered countless people who want to write fantasy, but have read so little of it, they either a) don't realize their plot is full of clichés, or b) think that the clichéd elements are necessary to fantasy.

They are incorrect in both cases. These misapprehensions are easily dealt with by reading a lot of *contemporary* fantasy. Reading contemporary fantasy is of crucial importance to save the writer from accidentally doing something really dated. Everything cliché was original once.

Which is not to say that you can't have a predestined king in your story, but you must make him a specific individual, so the reader cares enough to not notice the cliché. In other words, make the character unique to balance out the plot tropes. Ask yourself, is this cliché really necessary, or am I just including it as a default, like a well-worn track for the brain?

That, at its heart, is the problem with clichés and trope-ridden plots: they are easy. Resultingly, the writer is likely to make unmindful choices, and be more prone to stereotyping characters, and other problematic storytelling elements. Further, a trope- or cliché-filled plot will be easier to predict, and the reader may not pay close attention. This makes your story less interesting and more forgettable.

However, there are reasons that certain tropes appear again and again. Humans find pleasure in recognizing patterns. That's part of why retellings of fairy tales and myths are so popular, and why the centuries-long fanfiction project of Arthurian storytelling is never over. But it's not just pattern recognition the human brain loves, it's the ability to recognize variations within the pattern. It can be powerful to take an old clichéd pattern that your reader might recognize, and then change it.

What if the predestined orphan king, when told he has to save the world says, "I'd prefer not to," and opts out, leaving the world to its mess? What if there are multiple young men, all of whom have been taught that they are predestined kings, with factions trying to put them into power; thus they ultimately realize that they can't all be predestined, and that maybe the whole notion of destiny is bullshit, and they band together? Take the old and make it new. Then you get to have your dragons and eat them.

Certain subgenres of fantasy thrive on having rules, like paranormal romance (romance novels require a happy ending), and there's nothing wrong with that. Be aware, these subgenres are not representative of fantasy as a whole. If there is a continuum upon which books fall, from the primarily artistic, to primarily commercial in intention, this type tends toward the commercial end (most books of any genre are somewhere in between). These is not intended to shame writers of books that have commercial intentions. I am merely pointing out that books intended to be read in this way have different rules and expectations that don't transfer well out of those subgenres into others. These types of books are also published in bulk. A few will rise to the top of the stack and remain wildly popular, most will not.

In sum, you don't have to avoid all clichés and tropes in your plots, but you should only use them purposefully, and carefully.

Overcomplications, Character Agency, and Scope

Fantasy books are often large in both scope and physical heftiness. A fat fantasy novel with a sprawling plot is its own great pleasure, which is why so many writers want to pen one. When doing so, beware making a plot so large and complicated that you can't execute it well. A common writer problem is starting a novel and realizing partway through that you are trying to cram two or three different books into one. That realization, though painful, is crucial. You must be willing to scale back so you can tell one story well, instead of several badly. Many an unfinished (or poorly finished) series suffers from this problem.

In *Collaborative Worldbuilding for Writers and Gamers*, Trent Hergenrader discusses the importance of control over the scope of your story. He articulates the peril of assuming that a fantasy narrative and its focal settings must sprawl. The scope of the story depends upon the story itself. Bigger isn't always better. Don't try to fit a novel's worth of plot into a short story. You could end up summarizing a novel instead of writing a story. Further, a large scope doesn't necessarily make for a better novel.[15]

For example, Katherine Addison's novel *The Goblin Emperor* follows the protagonist when he unexpectedly becomes king due to the sudden death of everyone else in line ahead of him. It follows him as he deals with the racism of the elven community as they find themselves with a half-goblin king, and with his own insecurities. The decisions he makes have large-scale implications, but the novel remains focused on his experience. Think of scope as that which is onstage vs. offstage.

Victor LaValle's novel *The Changeling* focuses on the protagonist and the loss of his child. Even as his story intersects with the broader story of a troll that steals children, and American racism, it doesn't detour from its chosen scope.[16]

Rebecca Roanhorse's novel *Black Sun* has a larger scope, and several focal characters, but she still doesn't try to tell the reader everything that is happening or everything that has ever happened in the world—only that which is relevant to the story that she is telling.[17]

Beware overemploying destiny, prophecies, or other plot elements that take agency away from your characters. Robin Hobb gets around the issue of agency and prophecy. In her world, prophets have to work to make the future they want. It is always contingent and in peril. There are even dueling prophets working to bring different futures into being.

Another way that you can end up depriving your characters of agency or stakes is by forcing them to follow a predetermined plot. Make certain your plot flows from your characters and their decisions, not the other way around.

Experimentation in Fantasy Structure and Plot

Fantasy is full of fascinating formal and structural experimentation. Because so much of what fantasy fiction does has to do with questioning preset expectations and positing alternate realities, it is common for writers to push reader expectations and experience through formal experimentation. Writers from Kelly Link to Sofia Samatar use formal experimentation in order to capture or highlight aspects of experience that couldn't be captured in realism or traditionally structured narratives. The fantasy community treats short stories seriously, writers get paid for them, make careers out of them, and treat them as an art form worthy of dedication. *Tor.com, Lightspeed, Uncanny Magazine,* and *Fiyah*, among many others, publish a lot of formally and structurally innovative short stories. Nontraditional forms and structures can be used to center marginalized communities and life experiences that can be difficult to convey in realism. There are countless essays describing how innovative form and structure, and fantasy or science fiction, have helped writers of color, immigrant writers, disabled writers, and writers from the LGBTQ+ community tell stories in ways that allow for representation beyond the hegemonic norm of the world that they live in. Further, fantasy fiction has a long history of association with mysticism and using form to invoke altered mental states.

It is generally a good idea, especially in novels, to make your work difficult in only a handful of ways. In other words, if your language, plot, structure/form, and content are all difficult, your reader might give up. I love difficult fiction, and I encourage you to write it if you want—but you should know what you are getting into. If your fantasy novel has a complicated plot, keeping some other elements straightforward to parse could be in your best interest.

When writing a complicated plot and/or formally innovative story, an outline (and/or a document where you keep track of your intentions for the story) is crucial. The bigger and more complicated the plot or structure, the more likely you will accidentally create a plot hole or make some other mistake. An outline or guidance document can be powerfully protective. A word of caution: leave yourself space for discovery as you write. Don't get so wrapped up in creating your guidance document that you don't actually write the story at all.

This discussion in no way covers every concern regarding plot and structure in fantasy fiction, but it covers major highlights that get neglected in creative writing textbooks.

Discussion Questions and Writing Activities

1. What are some differences between plot, story, and structure/form? Dissect and describe these elements in your story in progress.

2. Pick a favorite fantasy story. Did it avoid or subvert plot clichés? How?

3. Think of a clichéd fantasy plot element. Brainstorm ways to make it unique.

4. Read Genevieve Valentine's story from our anthology. How did the untraditional form impact your experience of the story? How did its form help create its meaning?

5. Have you ever read a story or novel in which the difficulty level of the structure or form did not equal the reward? If so, why do you think that was the case?

6. Try writing a fantasy story with footnotes, in the form of the list, or some other kind of document. What do you notice about the experience of writing in an unusual form?

7. How could you apply the advice about scope to your writing?

CHAPTER 7
WORLDBUILDING PART ONE: OVERVIEW

Introduction

Worldbuilding is a big word with even bigger baggage. Often the joy of fantasy and science fiction aficionados, used derisively by its detractors. The term is controversial even within the fantasy and science fiction community. Lincoln Michel, former lead editor of *Electric Literature*, weighed in with an essay "Against Worldbuilding" in which he claims that worldbuilding requires the writer to give exhaustive details about everything within a storyworld, and thus not leave any mystery. He argues for an alternative he calls "worldconjuring." He gives examples, assigning worldbuilding to Tolkien, and conjuring to myths and fairy tales. He specifically contests science fiction writer Chuck Wendig's statement that a world includes everything within it, from political structures to cuisine.[1] I respect both Wendig's and Michel's contributions to literature and criticism, but I am bemused by the dispute. They appear to actually agree with each other. In "25 Things You Should Know About Worldbuilding," Wendig argues that a fully known world is an uninteresting one, that mystery, along with conflict, is required to hook a reader. He urges writers to preserve some uncertainty, to leave blank places in the map, so the reader will want to know more.[2]

Both Wendig and Michel argued that mystery is essential and that too much information is death to storytelling. Their disagreement is just schematics. This exchange is emblematic of a debate I've seen many times before, usually (though not in this case) between so called "literary" fiction, and the so-called "genre" fiction spheres, where preconceived ideas about what the other does creates blindness.

Realists might think they don't worldbuild, when in reality they are writing within the "real" world, and so it comes prebuilt, its structures invisible due to familiarity. Yet, the best realist writers go beyond simply living in the house that was built for them (i.e., the world as it is). They realize that their experiences are not universal, and so they have put their character's experiences on the page in such a way that a reader whose experience doesn't mirror that of the character can inhabit it and feel with them. A good realist novel renders the invisible structures of the world visible.

Celeste Ng's novel *Little Fires Everywhere* is so compelling because her story's characters draw attention to the constructed nature of the world in which they live. They expose, through their actions and feelings, the fault lines of race, class, and gender, in Shaker Heights, Ohio. Through the characters' lived realities, the reader sees choices changed and constrained by Shaker Heights. Ng knows that the world is a *made* thing. She doesn't need to create an encyclopedia of her world, or to build it from scratch—she selects from the vast trove of information that is reality and chooses which parts are relevant and necessary to indicate the larger social structures the characters live within.

She didn't have to explain American racism, or the class issues in the American adoption system, rather, she wrote scenes that involved adoption with all of those things in mind, indicating, through the choice of relevant details, that race and class are at play.[3]

Fantasy writers do the same. The difference is that fantasy writers must also make their own encyclopedia, to one extent or another. Lincoln Michel and Chuck Wendig both point out a danger zone for writers. Sometimes writers, because they love the world they have built, feel compelled put it all on the page, and drown readers in largely irrelevant detail. It's great that you know how the transportation system in your world works but you don't have to explain it. You only need to explain the way the trains are powered if it *matters*. If you are writing a novel from the point of view of a civil engineer trying to convince his queen that it is antiquated and unethical to power a train off the souls of trees, the reader should know what he knows. If your main character is a wealthy socialite who doesn't even use public transit, then the train's power system probably isn't something she will know or care about. If trains aren't relevant to the story at all, you probably don't even need to know.

Really, what worldbuilding's detractors miss is that the type of worldbuilding they have a problem with is more the result of a novice or overly enthusiastic creator feeling like everything is equally important. The problem is *selection*, not worldbuilding itself. Fantasy fiction without effective worldbuilding can lead to vagueness, difficulties with establishing clear stakes, and clichéd generic stories. How much encyclopedia work a writer needs to go into before/as they write, depends upon what type of fantasy novel they are writing.

Are you writing a secondary-world fantasy? Then you probably need to write quite a few encyclopedia entries. Are you writing fabulism where the only major difference from 21st-century America is that people routinely speak to their dead relatives on the telephone? Then you probably only need to decide how the telephone works, and how it has changed society. The more your storyworld differs from the real world, the more you need to plan it out.

This chapter details the major ingredients of worldbuilding, such as religion, civic structures, natural environment, gender and race relations, economics, etc. Then, it discusses how to use the ingredients of worldbuilding to create worlds that will be productive and interesting places for characters. This chapter will also discuss the common pitfalls of worldbuilding. Other issues in worldbuilding will be covered in subsequent chapters.

Common Pitfalls

- *Planning everything and for too long.* Worldbuilding and storytelling are both pleasurable, but they are not the same. Writers are fantastic procrastinators. When writing gets hard, the dishes seem crucial. Or you decide you can't write another word without looking up exactly how many bars there were in downtown Seattle in the 19th century. I know many writers who have spent years of their lives building the encyclopedia of their world, and exhaustive backstories for their characters without having written much, if any, of the actual story. Anne, Charlotte, Emily, and Branwell Brontë spent much of their childhood and adolescence creating the fantasy kingdoms of Gondal, Angria, and Gaaldine. All three sisters went on to become novelists, but they didn't publish anything set in those kingdoms.[4] There is no shame in worldbuilding as an act of play. Worlds can expand infinitely. However, if you actually want to write a story set in the world you are building, at some point you just have to start. It shouldn't take you years to build your world. Save some mystery. Don't create so many rules and details binding the act of creation that there's no room for your characters to surprise you. It can be crushing to realize that you can't put every beautiful detail into the story. Plan your world enough that you understand the big things that will heavily influence the life of your characters, and then plan more as you find the need, but write!

- *Planning very little for not nearly long enough.* Not doing any worldbuilding is its own perilous mistake. If you are writing a secondary-world fantasy, and you don't plan, it is far too easy to reproduce assumptions from the real world or take for granted ideas from other fantasies. Without deliberate worldbuilding, you might have the patriarchy work exactly like it does in the world as it is without conscious decision on your part. Or you might default to that problematic vaguely European medieval world that used to dominate fantasy. Additionally, if you don't worldbuild effectively, you can easily find your character in a situation where you don't actually know what constraints exists, so you make them up on the fly.

C. L. Polk's *Kingston Cycle* novellas are an example of worldbuilding done just right. The setting echoes early-20th-century Britain (post-First World War), but it's not identical, and it differs in important ways. In this storyworld, the black residents of the country are marginally better off than the nonnobility white citizens, having better representation in government, and in the professional classes. The culture privileges heterosexual marriage, and relegates homosexual relationships, by custom, to adolescence. In doing so, Polk doesn't create a utopia, but does show how class, race, and gender boundaries aren't inevitable.[5] A writer who hadn't done enough worldbuilding could have created a world that simply copied the same type of racism and homophobia as real post-First World War Britain. Conversely, if you are going to write a historical fantasy actually set in post-First World War Britain, then you should reflect the mores of the time and place, especially if you want to draw attention to the problems rooted there. But if you don't know which of the aforementioned you actually want to do, then you can easily make mistakes that you later have to fix.

- *This isn't Tolkien, it's just a lot like Tolkien.* One big worldbuilding pitfall can be building a world that is too similar to one that already exists. If you want to include elves in your world, then you better do something interesting with them, and probably don't have every other Tolkienesque fantasy race as well. At some point, you are just writing fanfiction. Fanfiction is a blast—I wrote *Star Wars* fanfiction obsessively from middle school through college. I learned how to take feedback and got to see audience reactions in near real time on the *theforce.net* fanfiction message boards. I wouldn't be the writer or reader I am today without fanfiction. Fantasy and science fiction has a long history of writers moving from fanfiction to professional writing. But the fanfiction isn't what ultimately gets professionally published. Don't create a thinly veiled imitation of your favorite storyworld and expect to publish within it. If you haven't read widely enough in the genre, it can be easy to mistakenly believe that worldbuilding elements that are characteristic of a writer (or a particular shared storyworld, like *Dungeons and Dragons*) are characteristic of the genre itself. So, read widely, and make your world *particular*. If you are riffing on a classic fantasy world, it should involve significant changes that comment on the originals. For example, the *Orcs* series by Stan Nicholls features orcs, and other staple fantasy beings. But the entire story is centered on the orcs and told from their point of view.[6] It radically destabilizes the racial essentialism of stock fantasy peoples.

While I am sure there are other ways to go wrong with worldbuilding these are the main pitfalls that I have observed in the work of novice and practiced writers alike.

The Major Ingredients of Worldbuilding

There isn't uniform agreement on the absolutely essential ingredients that you need to know before you start writing in your storyworld. Further, the lexicon used to talk about worldbuilding varies from writer to writer, thinker to thinker. Two of my favorite texts that cover worldbuilding are Trent Hergenrader's *Collaborative Worldbuilding for Writers and Gamers*,[7] and Chapter 6 of Jeff VanderMeer's *The Wonderbook*.[8] Despite differences in lexicon, there are still consistent threads in the discussion on worldbuilding.

Trent Hergenrader's book (I highly recommend it for anyone interested in fantasy or science fiction writing) uses the terms "structures" and "substructures" to describe the most important ingredients in worldbuilding. He lists four structures: governance, economics, social relations, and cultural influences. Underneath each he places six substructures (under social relations those substructures include gender, race, class, and ability, among others). He's also created a fun and generative worldbuilding deck.

Jeff VanderMeer, in *The Wonderbook*, thinks of worldbuilding as being built on two basic pillars: the "worldview" and the "storyview." The former is what the writer knows and believes about the world, and the latter is what the characters within it know and believe. The characters won't be aware of all of their own biases and will hold values and beliefs that the writer knows aren't entirely accurate. The characters will also have a vantage point from which they view the culture in which they live. VanderMeer says characters are usually "natives of the culture," "tourists or visitors," or a "conqueror or colonizer."

Within the same story, characters, based upon their positionality and vantage point, will interpret the world differently. In Vandana Singh's "A Handful of Rice," the main character is a native of the culture, but oppressed given his status as a magic user, and so plans on assassinating a ruler he sees as tyrannical. But the ruler, whose point of view we get later through dialogue, views himself as the savior of his country, since he ejected the British.[9] Simultaneously, if the story had contained a visitor, depending upon where they were from, they would have different interpretations of the state of affairs in the country. Imagine how a representative of the East India Company, conducting trade with this liberated India, might react. He would probably have a lot of colonialist resentments, and racist ideas, like looking for signs that India was better off colonized. The storyview allows the writer to know and show that the characters have incomplete perspectives. Basically, VanderMeer, without enumerating specifics, tells the writer that all the things that make up a character's concept of themselves in relationship to the world should be known so that the writer can show the complexity of the world and the people within it. Consequently, you must think about the core aspects of personal and cultural identity that impact how characters view themselves and others.

Synthesizing both Hergenrader and VanderMeer, they are essentially describing worldbuilding as the intersection of the macro and the micro, the large aspects of the world as they impact the individual.

From now on, I will think about these ingredients of worldbuilding as either *opportunities* or *constraints* for the characters. Basically, how the realities of the world constrain or create opportunities for your characters, not only in their physical reality, but in the way they conceptualize the options available to themselves and others.

As you build a world, here are some basic questions you should answer for yourself:

- *How much does this storyworld differ from the real world?* It should differ from and reflect the real world in significant ways. Even a secondary-world fantasy isn't separate from the world that you live in, since your values, and the imagery and ideas available to you, come from the real world. Determine if you will be using preexisting constraints and opportunities, and to what extent.

- *What are the governmental, political, and civic structures of the country or countries of the story?* Is the country a monarchy? How benign, benevolent, or malevolent is the ruler(s)? If it's a democracy, is it representative or parliamentary? Or is it more of an oligarchy? If the country isn't a functioning democracy, how many of the citizens buy into cultural myths about the nation? Is the government communist, socialist, or fascist? (None of the aforementioned three are the same.) Perhaps it's a loose affiliation of city states or tribal groups? No matter what option you choose, including ones not detailed here, you need to think about not only how the government works, but how it impacts its citizens. Not everyone will view their government the same, nor will they all be equally served by it. Additionally, what is the relationship of the country or countries in which your story is set to others? Are they a big player, an empire or colonial power? Are they small but middle of the road in power? Are they abused and colonized? Within, what regional divides or tensions exist? These questions matter both for the nation at large, and for your characters. How does the law work within your storyworld? Is it intrusive? Is it believed to be just or unjust? How are your different characters afforded safety, or a lack thereof, by the legal systems? In Rachael K. Jones's "The Night Bazaar for Women Becoming Reptiles," selling the eggs that allow women to become reptiles is illegal, but enforcement of the prohibition is poor.[10] In Theodora Goss's "England Under the White Witch,"[11] the surveillance state is so intrusive that possessing a banned book can lead to death.

- *What are the distinctive features of the landscape and climate?* No nation or planet is made up of one landscape or ecosystem. So, while the nation(s) in your story will probably have particular ecological characteristics, your story isn't set in an entire country. Most of it will take place in a handful of focal locales. If your story takes place in a city, is it a coastal city? Coastal cities are usually more diverse than inland cities; this impacts everything from architecture to cuisine. If your story is set in a desert community, then the relationship of the characters to water will be different than in a rainforest. Similarly, any story set in London that ignored the impact of the Thames on the city would be incomplete. Think about the relationship the characters and their culture have with the landscape. Do they value it? Do they view it as hostile? Do they churn up the natural landscape with near impunity, covering it with corn? Or do they exist in an uneasy balance, where the economy rests in many respects on natural exploitation (logging) but yet most citizens are avid hikers, and Christianity is often tinged with near nature worship? The identities of your characters and the structures of their society will be highly influenced by the landscape and their relationship to it.

- *What are the main economic and socioeconomic structures of the society or societies in which your story is set?* You should consider not only the literal economic systems but also a slew of other factors. How is wealth distributed? Is there relative equity? Or is wealth concentrated in the hands of a few? If so, who are those few? How do people feel about wealth distribution in the country? In America, we have a lot of wealth stratification, but many people still believe, counter to data, that we are a meritocracy. How does gender, race, class, national origin, or ability impact participation in the economy? Are particular types of jobs either customarily (or by law) closed to certain people? How mutable are class boundaries? Avoid writing a story where there are only nobles and peasants. Even though a large middle class isn't a feature of every nation, there are always degrees of poverty and wealth. Even in Ursula K. Le Guin's great novel *The Dispossessed*, the utopian anarchist society of Anarres still has inequities, though those inequities are less structural than in the real world.[12] One person's idea of a utopia might sound like another's idea of a dystopia. Ursula K. Le Guin's story "The Ones Who Walk Away from Omelas," focuses on this very idea—a "utopia" is usually built upon someone's suffering. Humans know this on an unconscious level and thus tend to find stories that claim total equity lacking in verisimilitude.[13]

- *What is the racial and cultural makeup of the world?* Race and culture influence the constraints and opportunities for real people in the real world. Similarly, race and culture will be important in any well-constructed fantasy world. Don't create a homogenous culture. Homogeny in fantasy has historically had (purposeful or accidental, but either way, real) white supremacist overtones. Humans in all parts of the world won't look identical to each other, that isn't how evolution works. Further, cultures will develop differently around the world, which then acquire connections to race and ethnicity. The degree of diversity and multiculturalism will differ from place to place, but diversity always exists. When inventing cultures and racial or ethnic groups, avoid stereotyping or essentializing. But that doesn't mean your characters will avoid stereotyping each other. There is an important difference between you the writer (and the story) engaging in stereotyping and characters within the story doing so. Humans are prone to in-group out-group difficulties; it's unrealistic to pretend otherwise. Even *Star Trek*'s universe, arguably one of the most optimistic visions of humanity's trajectory, still has issues of prejudice. But rather than humans being bigoted against each other, they've moved on to bigotry against some aliens, based upon cultural interactions, such as in *Star Trek: The Next Generation*'s "The Wounded."[14] Juliet Marillier's historical fantasy series *Sevenwaters* depicts real-world cultural divides between the Irish characters and the characters from the European mainland and England.[15] They often stereotype or fear each other. No reasonable reader could think that Marillier condones any of their prejudices. She lets the characters reflect the blind spots that real people would have. This is the difference between the storyview and the worldview of individual characters. As you write, think about the racial and cultural makeup of your world, and the power dynamics involved within and between groups. In Chapter 10 we will talk more about how to do this well, while avoiding appropriation or whitewashing. A story that pretends that there is total equality among difference robs the world of the story of texture, tension, and verisimilitude. Depicting and condoning are *not* the same thing. Fantasy critiques real social ills by highlighting problems and positing alternatives.

- *What are the norms surrounding sex, sexuality, and gender?* Sex, sexuality, and gender are important parts of worldbuilding because they are pivotal modes of societal organization. Is your storyworld one with only two culturally recognized genders, or are there three or more? What are the social implications for the sex and/or gender identity of the characters? What is the state of gender equity? Is it a matriarchal society, patriarchal, or built upon an invented gender-based power structure? How is sex, sexuality, and marriage viewed? Is the society rigid or flexible in its social mores? If the rules are rigid, what the consequences for breaking them? In Rachael K. Jones's "The Night Bazaar for Women Becoming Reptiles," everyone has a sunside lover and a moonside lover. The two are never allowed to meet. Everyone has one male and one female lover. The taboos of this world are different than the ones of the real world, but taboos still exist. There is a reason that the word "utopia" literally means no place or no time—they can't exist. Utopias tend to lack plot tension. Also avoid mindlessly reproducing the sex and gender dynamics of your real-world culture. If you do so, it should be on purpose. Don't forget to think about how the norms of the setting of your story impact your main characters, as well as how they view those norms.

- *How does the society in which your character(s) live understand the concept of disability?* Who is considered "disabled" in your storyworld, and how are their choices constrained? Be mindful of your depictions. Race, class, gender, and disability are all social constructs. Disability is coded and viewed differently in different societies. Physical differences are considered disabilities when a society has not accommodated for them. Before the availability of glasses, vision problems were severely disabling, now they aren't. Like with gender or race, constraints for those with physical disabilities can be *de facto* (normative culturally) or *de jure* (enforced by law). People who are nonneurotypical or have an invisible disability face issues distinct from those with visible disabilities. Experiences will differ based upon individual psychological or cognitive characteristics, and how society views their ability to participate economically and socially. This has little to do with actual capacities, and more to do with how much a given society has accommodated for or accepted differences. Avoid using disabilities to Otherize your characters. There is a long dishonorable history of villains marked by physical disabilities. On the other hand, fantasy can also allow for a centering of disability in ways that realism usually doesn't.[16]

- *What is the role of religion in the culture(s) of your storyworld?* Avoid having only one religion. There can be a dominant religion, but there shouldn't be only one. There can be subsets or schisms within the dominant religion, and other religions can be licit or illicit, but avoid homogeneity in belief systems. Is it a largely secular society? Or are most people fairly religious? Is religion for most people a matter of true faith, or is it more cultural? What is it like to be a religious minority in this storyworld? To what extent is church and state separate or connected by either custom or law? How do the answers to these questions impact your characters?

- *How does magic work?* Your reader should be able to glean the possibilities and constraints of magic in your storyworld. Your reader's knowledge comes from your point of view character(s). There are a variety of questions you should answer for yourself. Is magic ordinary or extraordinary in this world? Is it seen as magic or science? In "A Handful of Rice" magic is forbidden but viewed by practitioners as a part of their faith. In V. E. Schwab's *Shades of Magic* trilogy there are multiple Londons in different dimensions. One of them (Gray London) is mostly the real 19th-century London. Another (Red London) is full of magic, to the degree that someone who can't perform magic is an aberration.[17] If magic is rare, who is allowed to wield it? Are those who wield it revered or feared? Is there more than one kind? Does magic come in the form of magic wielders, or magical beings? Guy Gavriel Kay's *The Last Light of the Sun* has magic, but no human magic workers. Rather, there are magical beings who most humans don't believe in or interact with directly, but nonetheless impact the plot and characters.[18] In Marie Brennan's *A Natural History of Dragons*, dragons are just extraordinary natural creatures, like polar bears.[19] Be it magical beings (like faeries) or magical creatures (like dragons), or people performing magic, you need to develop rules for the magical aspects of the narrative. An aspect of the story is magical if it doesn't or can't exist in the real world. Magic in stories can come from preexisting fantasy beings like faeries or deities (be careful, especially with living religions), or you can make up your own. Similarly, your magical creatures can come from folklore and myth, like dragons, or kelpie, or be made up. Either way, be systematic, and consistent, even if the rules are left implicit.

- *What is the role of science and technology in your storyworld?* Even in a fantasy universe, science and technology still play a role. Knowing the level of technology present in your storyworld, as well as the function it plays within your focal society or societies, is important to understanding the constraints and opportunities that your characters encounter, as well as logistics. Transportation, for example, will impact how far and fast characters travel. If long-distance communication isn't reliable or present, then moving across the country becomes much more high stakes. If there are weapons of mass destruction, war changes. Domestic technologies like heating and cooking will often impact gender dynamics. Is clothing custom made, or mass produced? This influences how easy it is to "pass" as a wealthy person. In Patrick Rothfuss's *The Name of the Wind*, Kvothe struggles to afford books, because books are expensive and time-consuming to produce in his world.[20] Different types of fantasy have different norms regarding technology. Steampunk has one particular aesthetic, and space fantasy (à la Tamsyn Muir's *Gideon the Ninth*), has another.[21] The technology within your fantasy story signals many things, including time period equivalency, place, and genre. Technology impacts your characters, and hence, the plot.

Discussion Questions and Writing Activities

1. Pick a favorite fantasy novel or short story and dissect how each of the major ingredients of worldbuilding play into the experiences of the characters. How does the main character's race, gender, or class offer them opportunities, or constrain their choices?
2. Which worldbuilding pitfalls most stuck out to you, and why?
3. What is the difference between depicting a social ill for the sake of social critique, and condoning it? How can you tell the difference?

4. Check your story in progress for worldbuilding pitfalls. If you find one, how might modifying your story to avoid it increase the particularity of your story? How would it change the stakes for your characters?

5. What does it mean to think of worldbuilding in terms of opportunities and constraints for characters? Is this different from how you thought about worldbuilding before?

6. Analyze a story from our anthology using the tools from this chapter. List your observations about the world, its major ingredients, and how those ingredients impact the characters.

7. Write a profile of the main character for your story in progress. Describe their worldview. Does their worldview match or diverge from the storyview?

8. Start a short story set in country where water is scarce, the society is matriarchal, and your main character lives in the capital city next to the only large freshwater lake. Your main character is either a local farmer or a diplomat from another country. Write a scene or two with these factors in mind.

CHAPTER 8
WORLDBUILDING PART TWO: SETTING AND DETAIL

Introduction

Fantasy fiction has a paradoxical relationship to setting. Fantasy novels, on average, tend to be much longer than realistic novels. Invented places require more details to feel fully imagined. Yet too many details can bog down the narrative. It can be difficult striking the balance between offering too little detail (resulting in dull unoriginal fantasy settings) or too much (the writer tries to tell the reader *everything*. In these situations, lots of information that isn't actually important masks crucial details). Fantasy fiction is often mood-driven; thus, the selection of relevant detail is of utmost importance.

How far a fantasy setting differs from the real world determines the amount and type of detail needed. For example, in contemporary or urban fantasy, the story is often set in the real world, but with one or two important things changed—like faeries owning most of the real estate in New York City. Or the existence and recent legal personhood of vampires. In a real- world or real-world-adjacent story, if one of your characters goes to the doctor, you can skip giving many details of what a doctor's waiting room looks like— instead mention that the medical forms contain boxes to check *living* or *undead*. In a secondary-world fantasy, all kinds of details become necessary. For example, what does medical practice look like if medicine is primarily practiced by women in religious orders? These types of questions must be addressed for every major setting within your storyworld. You will know more about the setting than what will (or should) appear on the page.

Which details will enliven the setting? Which ones are unnecessary? How does a writer determine which details are significant?

Been to That Galaxy, Done That Ring: The Perils of Vague or Cliché Settings

When constructing settings, beware descriptions that make your settings seem like copies of settings from other books. For example, as a teen I loved Peter S. Beagle's *The Last Unicorn* (my affection is undimmed).[1] I wrote a story set in a castle by the sea. Afterwards, I realized that I had populated the details of my castle with the details of King Haggard's castle. From the windswept battlements overlooking the water, to a dungeon full of angry beasts. The plot bore no resemblance to Beagle's, but I'd unconsciously echoed his setting.

While no detail will ever be fully original, scrutinize your choices. Especially for resemblances to books whose settings have been copied endlessly. A halfling village with turf roofs and round doors was once original. No longer. If you are going to write about a bucolic village, populate it with your own details. A village built with every house facing the stream because local superstition dictates that facing running water wards your house against demons. With hillsides that turn yellow in the spring as the wild mustard blooms.

Beyond accidentally using stock or cliché setting details, a lack of details is a problem as well, especially in your focal setting(s). Most stories will have a handful of settings within the world where most of the story is staged. These settings are *focal settings*. Sometimes focal settings and set pieces are the same, and sometimes not (a *set piece* can be the location of the climax of the story, but not where the majority of the story occurs).

Even large novels have focal settings that reappear frequently and must be invested with more detail that the surrounding world. For example, in Robin Hobb's *Farseer* trilogy, Chade (a royal bastard and assassin) has a lair within the walls of Buckkeep Castle.[2] Chade's lair is where FitzChivalry Farseer spends most of his adolescence training, and so the level of detail it receives is greater than the castle as a whole. Details like the smell of Chade's ferret, and niches overflowing with parchment. Fitz spends less time in the main environs of the castle, and so they get comparatively little detail. Spend the most energy on the focal settings that matter to your main character(s). Buckkeep is rendered unique by focusing on the personal and sensory experiences of Fitz.

Other settings in Hobb's storyworld need even more emphasis. The Rain Wilds is a marshy area with a river that expands erratically. Sometimes it flows white and acidic. The economy of the Rain Wilds is built upon ransacking the ruins of the Elderling civilization. Nothing is in danger of being generic, but vagueness in setting (such as the logistics of living in a place where the water can turn abruptly acidic) would make it confusing in the hands of a lesser writer.[3]

Daniel Jose Older's urban fantasy novel *Half Resurrection Blues* is set in New York City, so he can dispense with describing well-known details (like the Empire State Building). Instead, he spends details on the focal settings that are important to the protagonist, Carlos. Such as the house haunted by Mama Esther, a spirit who can sometimes encompass an entire building, and at other times huddles in the corner of her library. Other focal places include a particular bar, and the Underworld. Older, through Carlos's eyes, focuses on unique aspects of each setting within New York.[4]

Patrick Rothfuss's novel *The Name of the Wind* is huge. Only a fraction of its locales can be focal settings. The main focal settings include the slums of Tarbean where Kvothe lives on the street, and later, after he's admitted, the University. On an even closer level of detail, Kvothe spends enormous amounts of time in the Archives of the University, as well as a musical bar called The Eolian. Rothfuss inflects every focal setting through Kvothe's emotions. The Eolian is a place that Kvothe loves, and so the prose lingers on its visuals, smells, and sensations. The Eolian is a *specific* bar, occupied by a *specific* people.

Particularity in setting can save a world that might otherwise be cliché. There are a lot of fantasy novels set in pseudo-medieval Europe (usually England) or the Celtic Twilight (a reference to the W. B. Yeats collection of the same name), a premodern era shaped by ungrounded ideas about pre-Christian Europe.[5] Specificity of focal setting and character is usually the only thing that saves such books from vagueness/problematic ideas about the past. A world that draws upon a more diverse array of time periods and cultures will make it much easier to avoid clichéd settings or whitewashing. While pulling inspiration from around the world can help create interesting fantasy worlds, take care not to write a story that replicates cultural and ethnic stereotypes through details. If you write a story that draws inspiration from the Shogunate era of Japan, and crowd it with samurai and cherry blossoms, you are reiterating clichés about the culture, not reflecting the actual culture. This makes you vulnerable to cultural appropriation. Do your research, and make your details concrete, from the construction of the buildings to the way food is cooked. Concreteness and accuracy help give credit where it is due, and respect.

In short stories there are usually only one or two settings. Each must implicitly teach the reader about the storyworld. For example, Rebecca Roanhorse's short story "Harvest" is from the point of view of a young indigenous woman from New Mexico who is a chef in training at a prestigious school in New York. Her lover, a deer woman, seduces her into helping with revenge killings. The story juxtaposes a bucolic college campus, a brutal high-end restaurant kitchen, and a half-world where the protagonist cuts out hearts. Setting is delineated quickly. Each detail bears the weight of the entire narrative, acting as a stand end for the world. When the narrator first meets her lover, Roanhorse simultaneously evokes setting, and its meaning:

We did not meet in a chance encounter in a moonlit wood, in the way of fairytales. I did not chase her fleeing shadow through a dappled grove of ancient trees to the banks of an enchanted pool. I was not lured away, as is the way of hunters who have, on a solstice eve, somehow become the prey themselves.

I met my lover in a bar on a weekend trip to Manhattan, an impetuous late train from my upstate culinary school down to the city, a solo escape from a mind-numbing week spent on gastronomy etiquette. Spirit dulled by the proper way to sit at a table, the hand to use for the seafood fork, the ordering of stemware. I am lost in this white man's world, drowning in a sea of their buttery sauces and unfamiliar histories, wishing for something known, something to remind me of home. I overhear a boy in class mention a food truck somewhere on the Lower East Side that serves oven bread and prune pastelitos. It feels like a sign.[6]

Observe the delivery of details that are relevant to the speaker. What those places are like, what they lack, and her emotions about them. A different character describing the same location would result in a different series of details.

Beyond the Fields We Know: How To Choose Details That Matter

Now that we have discussed clichés, vagueness, and the problems thereof, as well as stories that successfully avoid these pitfalls, it's time to devote more space to how to choose details that matter:

- Know what you want each scene to accomplish, and how the setting functions within the plot and the world. If you want a scene to feel ominous, then choose setting details that contribute to ominousness. If the protagonist loves the place, choose accordingly. The desired function of a scene also impacts how your chosen details should be described. In "Harvest" the high-end restaurant scene is depicted as uncomfortable. Yet if the speaker grew up with a French grandmother, the buttery sauces would remind them of childhood. If you don't know what you want a scene to do, or what the place means to the character, you will have a hard time knowing which details are significant.

- Use your senses. When you walk into a place, think of the flood of sensory perceptions that you get. Now, select a few that to you evoke the place you've stepped into. Sofia Samatar's "Meet Me in Iram" is a Borgesian description of a lost city briefly mentioned in the Qur'an. In the story, the lostness of the city stands in for personal losses, a kind of overwhelming melancholy and loneliness:

  > Because we are familiar with gold and we are familiar with mountains. Because we are familiar with pillows and spoons. Because we are familiar, we can imagine. Is that true? Look, here I am, at my desk on the highest roof of the city. I sit up here at night so that you can find me if you come. I am listening to my father's cassettes. You will have noticed that there is sound in Iram, and this is why I come back, I think, to these blank and shrouded streets. I am trying to imagine sound as an object. As soon as I press play the light comes on, that white ceramic glare, and cigarette ashes lift away from the tape recorder and disappear in the air of Iram, where it is always night. Light pins me to my seat. When my father was in the basement listening to poetry, we knew we mustn't disturb him. The door was edged with grainy fluorescent light, the stairs coated with black rubber. It was a terrible, terrible place.[7]

  Samatar's speaker sits on a roof in the lost city, its ever-disappearing nature evoked through "blank and shrouded streets," and the sound of the cassette player transforming into cigarette ashes, and a memory of her father. Samatar conjures a rooftop in a lost city, the streets as seen from above, and a childhood basement where her father used to disappear. Poetry and music = sound. Cigarette ashes = smell, sight, and touch. A space is the sensory impressions the speaker of a story receives. A world is largely an accumulation of settings, and the details therein.

- When picking evocative details, pick a few that will reappear, accumulating meaning. Duchess Tremontaine, in Ellen Kushner's *Swordspoint*, drinks chocolate nearly every morning in opulent Tremontaine House. Kushner doesn't describe Tremontaine House exhaustively every time, but once the opulence of the setting is established, details like the Tremontaine crest on everything, or the taste of the chocolate, pull earlier descriptions and scenes into conscious memory. Alec and Richard in Riverside, a bohemian slum, live in cramped apartments cluttered with tattered luxuries. A huge carved bed, and a fireplace that was once ornamental when their rooms were part of a great house. The fireplace and bed are mentioned enough that they become a shorthand that calls up the sensations of Alec and Richard's rooms. Don't repeat descriptions ad nauseam. Reuse details *as they become relevant.* Alec might kick a bedpost in the night, or overuse firewood. Make setting come to life by having your characters live in it. The contrast between the lives of Richard and Alec and that of Duchess Tremontaine helps the reader understand the world.[8]

- Do your research. Having a wealth of potential details at your disposal that are particular helps you create a textured setting. Your forest shouldn't just be made up of trees, but of the types of trees that would be correct for the ecosystem. If you draw inspiration from real periods or places, research can save you from doing something foolish or offensive. The house of a peasant in the European Middle Ages would be made out of different materials depending upon location. But it would *not* be made out of wood or bricks: both were expensive. Homes might be stone, turf, or wattle and daub, depending upon region and degree of poverty. If you put an American log cabin in a story set in a pseudo–Renaissance Italy, you will look silly. In a piece for *The Center for Fiction* called "Research Your Life," Alexander Chee recalls taking a class with Annie Dillard, who asked her students how much they truly knew about where they lived. Did they know its geological features? Its major industries? Chee realized that he knew almost nothing about his hometown—familiarity had rendered his lack of knowledge invisible. Chee argues that if you are drawing upon a familiar place for writing, research will allow you to see it anew.[9] For secondary-world fantasy, even if you make up entirely fictional plants, research will help you invent plants that are biologically logical.

- Know how the setting relates to the larger world. The reader of "The Night Bazaar for Women Becoming Reptiles" by Rachael K. Jones needs to understand how the focal setting of the titular bazaar functions in the city. In other words, the bazaar doesn't operate in isolation.

What you must remember above all is that settings should be created deliberately, with details that help the reader understand the larger storyworld, and the point of view character's experience of that world. This means avoiding the temptation of thinking that a lack of specificity results in universality. A well-realized setting is almost a character in and of itself. No reader of *Gormenghast* will ever forget the titular castle. There is a reason that people will pay thousands of dollars to go to a version of Hogsmeade village. Setting, done well, helps bring the entire story to life.

Discussion Questions and Writing Activities

1. What are some distinctions between a story's world, and setting?

2. What is meant by the term "focal setting"? How would you as a writer treat a focal setting differently than the broader storyworld?

3. Which tips seem most useful for avoiding vagueness, and why?

4. Have you ever read a story where the setting seemed almost like a character? How did the writer do it?

5. Pick a story from the anthology and analyze the setting. What details does the writer include? What makes those details significant?

6. Apply at least one of this chapter's tips for creating a vivid setting to your story in progress. What happens as a result?

7. Pick a particular time and place to research. Write a scene in a fantasy world that draws upon that research. What details were most useful for creating a sense of place?

8. Write a scene set in a cafeteria somewhere in the United States (you pick), in which your point of view character is afraid, and they sense something uncanny. How do you make this seemingly ordinary setting particular, and creepy?

CHAPTER 9
WORLDBUILDING PART THREE:
IDEOLOGY AND CULTURE

Introduction

Writers are responsible for the worlds they make. No story is ideologically neutral. In many respects, fantasy fiction (and its adjacent genres) increases writer responsibility, since at no point will the writer have the excuse of "I don't make the world, I just write about it." Additionally, fantasy fiction has a long history of being written to make sociopolitical points about the real world. In the first chapter of this book, I demonstrated how fantasy writers from the past to the present have used their fiction to highlight social problems, or to posit an alternative worldview. From William Morris's 19th-century anti-industrial medieval fantasies[1] to Angela Carter's 20th-century feminist fairy tales,[2] fantasy writers have created stories that are both works of art, and ideologically motivated. Even writers who aren't trying to make social statements still reveal their worldview in the way they depict or create a world.

The internet controversy factory (social media) has been filled in the last decades with people who decry the ways in which film, television, and books have "become political." All of these folks are under a misapprehension about the nature of storytelling. Storytelling has been and always will be political. The most famous of these controversies is the "Sad Puppies" and "Rabid Puppies" (based primarily on Reddit, starting in 2013 and ending in 2016) who argued that the Hugo Awards were unfairly slanted toward more literary fantasy fiction with progressive themes and ignoring books that were "popular" and ideology-free. All books that win Hugo Awards are popular; the list and the winners are determined by the members of the World Science Fiction Association (WSFA). Anyone with 75 US dollars can buy a membership.[3] The Puppies attempted unsuccessfully to sweep the awards. Some of the books they advocated for were by Vox Day (pen name of Theodore Robert Beale), known for his white supremacist ties and vocal hostility toward anyone with values different from his own. He was expelled from the WSFA. Other books they advocated for were by authors unassociated with the movement, who asked for people to vote "No Award" on any category that the Sad Puppies succeeded in stacking with their nominees.[4]

As one can see with the above story, when people argue for fantasy and science fiction that "isn't ideology-driven," really what they mean is they want stories that match *their* ideology. It is common for people to view their own worldview as normal and necessary, as "neutral" and everyone else's as abnormal and/or as ideologically slanted or "biased." When someone comes from a normative position, the ideological nature of their worldview can feel invisible, but it's present all the same.

Additionally, books written before the reader was born can also appear to be ideology-free because the reader isn't privy to the cultural context. For example, in her important scholarly work *Tolkien, Race, and Cultural History: From Faeries to Hobbits*, Dimitri Fimi looks at how Tolkien's writing was influenced by the Edwardian and Victorian intellectual currents in which he moved. How the climate of nationalism, and fears of invasion and change, though not explicitly the purpose of his writing, still shaped it. Why, for example, does he create a hierarchy among the races of Middle Earth? Why are the orcs so frequently described as "swarthy" and "slant-eyed?" Fimi argues that as a medievalist, Tolkien employed and replicated racial stereotypes from medieval literature by using physical descriptions to indicate the moral status of characters and races within the story.[5] While Tolkien would never have endorsed fascism and white supremacy[6] (he was far too close to the Second World War and the bombardment of his home country to forget what Nazis really are), his work still contains ideas that bear the fingerprints of white supremacy. It was surely accidental, but also still real. It's possible to miss these problems within *Lord of the Rings* if you aren't familiar with the racist tropes used within. Similarly, it is easy for writers, Tolkien included, to be blind to the fingerprints of their culture on their work, including but not limited to white supremacism.

Thus, as writers of fantasy fiction, engaging in the act that Tolkien called "sub-creation," (i.e., the building of a fictional world)[7] we must realize that our fantasy worlds, even if we aren't specifically setting out to make a sociopolitical point, aren't neutral. As writers, we need to engage and improve our cultural sensitivity so that all of our ideological and cultural choices in worldbuilding are on purpose, rather than on accident.

This isn't intended to terrify you, but rather, to help you avoid accidentally causing hurt, or making mistakes that you might pay for later, and to give you tools to create worlds that are complex and nuanced. Beyond avoiding accidentally creating a world with the marks of prejudice upon it, many writers of fantasy want to tell great stories while simultaneously critiquing some aspect of the real world. For writers who have a point to make, it's crucial to contemplate how to avoid didacticism. Didacticism tends to make stories boring and put the reader on the defensive.

Writers seeking to critique Eurocentrism and other aspects of white supremacy in their fiction must avoiding whitewashing their writing. Simultaneously, writers must be careful when writing about characters different from themselves or borrowing from a real-world culture (especially if they are a Western writer borrowing from a non-Western culture).

The rest of this chapter will cover ways to catch cultural and ideological assumptions in your worldbuilding, and how to make a point without being didactic. It will also cover the thorny subject of cultural appropriation from a variety of angles.

Some Thoughts on Cultural Appropriation, Diversity, and Worldbuilding

No conversation on culture and worldbuilding can escape the question of cultural appropriation. If you are active on social media, you have witnessed the internet fervor over films, fashion, books (or any other part of culture) that has been accused of cultural appropriation. You are probably worried about getting caught up in the internet anger cycle. You are right to be concerned. Not only because it would be personally upsetting and traumatic, but because as a person who wants to do the right thing, you would never want to harm another person or group of people with your writing.

Cultural appropriation, briefly defined, is the adoption of an element or elements of a culture or identity by a person or entity from another culture or identity, without giving credit, acknowledging original context, or sharing the profit of the usage. Further, it is especially controversial when the culture being borrowed from is a historically or contemporarily marginalized culture or identity, and the borrower is from a more dominant culture or identity. Cultural appropriation can contribute to stereotypes, and to the cultural erasure and exploitation of the cultural resources of marginalized peoples. All of the above is not only harmful on a micro level but on a macro level. For example, every time someone writes a stereotyped depiction of immigrants from Mexico, it contributes to the mindset that has led to racialized fear-driven anti-immigrant sentiment in the US, which has very real consequences.[8]

Now that I've scared you, here's another wrinkle. You, as a writer, are also contributing to a problem if you write books that are culturally homogenous, especially if you write books full only of white people and in fantasy worlds drawing exclusively upon Western culture.[9] This can lead to the sense that fantasy is by heterosexual cis-gendered white people for more of the same. Writing as though people of color or the queer community didn't exist in the past or in the present normalizes homogenous spaces and stories. The person of difference becomes the marked person, the Other, and the normative person or character natural, good, and unmarked. As in stories, in life. If people are taught by culture to see white spaces and diverse spaces as separate, they will expect it, and think it is okay. Every time someone gets mad when a historically white comic book character in a film is played by a black actor, you are seeing the results of homogeneity. Not only does homogeneity have real-world consequences, but it can also open writers to trouble. Such as the criticism about Laurel K. Hamilton's conspicuous dearth of characters of color in both the Meredith Gentry urban fantasy books, and the Anita Blake books. Hamilton is using vampires and werewolves as a proxy to talk about racism, but yet the whiteness of the narrative is still noteworthy. She has said in the past she didn't include many characters of color because she was afraid of doing it wrong.[10]

Which comes to the crux of the issue. If a writer is afraid of cultural appropriation, so they write only characters and worlds that mirror their own identity, they are going to end up whitewashing their work, or making it homogenous in some other way, which is its own problem. It can feel like a bit of a double bind. This feeling isn't without justification. In 2018, YA author Amelie Wen Zhao pulled her debut fantasy novel *Blood Heir* before publication, because of accusations of cultural appropriation (the decision to pull the novel was eventually reversed). In her novel, people referred to as Affinites, who can control parts of the world around them, are reviled and forced into indentured labor and slavery. A few pre-release reviews accused her of racism because she was depicting a form of slavery, yet wasn't talking about the experience of Africans, nor was she herself part of the African diaspora. Zhao, an immigrant from China, drew upon the history and present of human trafficking in Asia. It was unjust to accuse her of appropriation. The accusations themselves were rather racist, since they assumed that slavery has exclusively happened to people of African descent.[11]

I bring up this story to point out that no reasonable person would have objected to Zhao's story on the grounds of cultural appropriation. She drew upon a phenomenon from the region of her birth, and she was trying to call attention to human trafficking. While there are many cases where the accusations of cultural appropriation are justified, there are also many cases where it isn't. So as an author, you must realize that homogeneity in your fantasy culture won't protect you, and even people (like Zhao) who you would assume would be safe to write a story of the kind she did are not always so. The internet has no mercy.

Given that there is no real way to be "safe," it is best to realize that writing itself *isn't safe*. When you write, you are putting something deeply personal out in the world for others to read. Once published, it leaves your command. You can't control how people will respond to it, or what the social conversation will be around it. If you are read (which is what writers who want to publish hope for), there will be divergent opinions about your work. Some people will love it. Others will hate it. A huge number of people will be indifferent. You are going to be vulnerable no matter what you do![12]

There are people who think you shouldn't write characters or worlds that aren't based upon your home culture; I am not one of those people. Telling people that they can only write about their own experience is a form of essentialism, which is one of the building blocks of stereotypes of all kinds, and a form of bigotry itself. Simultaneously, I also know that writing outside of your experience is more of a risk that sticking within what is familiar. In her interview with the *Paris Review*, Toni Morrison said that great artists must look outside their own experience, in order to write the best, most compassionate, truest story they can. The job of the writer is to try to access that which is universal about being human, but also, what is particular. If you write outside your experience, according to Morrison, you are taking a risk of people getting mad at you if you do it poorly. So do it well.[13] If you create compassionate stories, and write the Other well, and people are still mad at you, well, you can't worry about unreasonable people, it's a waste of energy and time. In another interview with the *NEA Arts Magazine* in 2014, Morrison said:

When I taught creative writing at Princeton, [my students] had been told all of their lives to write what they knew. I always began the course by saying, "Don't pay any attention to that." First, because you don't know anything and second, because I don't want to hear about your true love and your mama and your papa and your friends. Think of somebody you don't know. What about a Mexican waitress in the Rio Grande who can barely speak English? Or what about a Grande Madame in Paris? Things way outside their camp. Imagine it, create it. Don't record and editorialize on some event that you've already lived through. I was always amazed at how effective that was. They were always out of the box when they were given license to imagine something wholly outside their existence. I thought it was a good training for them. Even if they ended up just writing an autobiography, at least they could relate to themselves as strangers.[14]

What I believe is that you can and should make your stories as diverse as the real world, but you must do so with great care. There is so much to be gained, not only for you as a writer, but for the world, if stories contain characters as varied and vibrant as the real world. Fantasy is in a golden age, largely because more people from a greater range of identities are writing and publishing fantasy fiction. Further, writers from all backgrounds are beginning to include more diverse representation in their fantasy. This is all to the good.

People want to see characters like themselves in literature, to see themselves as normal, as acceptable, as the heroes of stories, as the center of the narrative. This not only makes your readers feel included, but also broadens your audience. If done well, everyone wins.

How To Write Diverse Fantasy Well?

The gold standard for the above question is Nisi Shawl and Cynthia Ward's book, *Writing the Other: A Practical Approach,* and their *Writing the Other* workshops that they hold regularly online and in person. They were inspired to do this work in response to a conversation they had at a Clarion workshop in 1992, where they discovered many writers were too terrified of writing diverse characters to even try. Shawl saw that response as taking "the easy way out." The now venerable *Writing the Other* workshop and book came out of that response. Shawl and Ward discuss how and why to write outside your race, orientation, ability, age, religion, or sex. In one essay entitled, "Appropriate Cultural Appropriation," Shawl references a panel on the issue she attended by Diantha Day Sprouse at WisCon38, who categorized those who borrow from other cultures as "Invaders," "Tourists," or "Guests."

According to Sprouse, invaders arrive without invitation and without fair warning, take what they want, use what they take however they please, and give nothing in return. Tourists are expected, and pay their way, though they can range from annoying and rude, to curious and educable. Guests are invited, and their relationships with their hosts are or become long-term, and their relations, rather than being one-sided, are reciprocal. They give as well as take. Shawl argues that the writers who haven't had true contact with another culture must act like good tourists, and not confuse themselves with guests. Tourists must be alert for their own biases, the dangerous and harmful nonsense that can come from the unconscious where implicit biases live, and not pretend to be other than what they are. A good tourist does lots of research and understands that research and firsthand experience are not the same. A tourist, according to Shawl, can become a guest, "if the locals like what they see and ask her to return." But, as Shawl points out, rarely is there a single entity, or official person, that one can approach and get a signed and stamped permission that says that you are a guest and have the right to your creative use of their culture. So, while you should ask for help, and be prepared to admit to your own ignorance, you should also be prepared to pay your way like a tourist, and to realize that acceptance or rejection of your work will happen on an individual level. You cannot gain blanket acceptance from an entire people group.[15]

Shawl and Ward argue that not only *can* you write fantasy about characters and cultures different from your own, you *should*, since homogeneity narrows your fiction and misrepresents the experience of being a person, but you must be careful to avoid major pitfalls.

Shawl and Ward are wonderful teachers and writers, known in the fantasy and science fiction writing community for their generosity and insight. Read *Writing the Other* (published by Aqueduct Press, and widely available for purchase online) and take one of the online seminars (there are scholarships for attendance available) for specific techniques.

Other writers have different answers. Charlie Jane Anders, in her series of essays on writing for *Tor.com*, "Never Say You Can't Survive," wrote one focused on the topic of writing outside your own experiences. She describes her early desire to write an Asian-inspired fantasy. She'd been an Asian Studies major in college, and was fluent in both Mandarin and Japanese, and she'd lived and worked all over Asia. So, by many people's standards, she was certainly a good tourist, maybe even a guest. But, as she was working on the book, Anders describes feeling a sick sensation in her stomach. She remembered the way her Asian friends reacted to *Memoirs of a Geisha*, and the flood of books about various Asian cultures, written by a white person, but from an Asian perspective, that made it easy and palatable for a white audience. Essentially, these writers were acting like tour guides through a construct of a place and culture. But what about books about Asian culture, or fantasy books inspired by Asian cultures written by people from Asia? Were books like *Memoirs of a Geisha* taking over that part of the marketplace, and silencing books by Japanese writers? In the end, Anders tossed her Asian-inspired fantasy, and focused on writing work that represented her experience as a transwoman. Anders decided to write characters from all kinds of backgrounds, representing human diversity (to the best of her ability with the full weight of history, culture, and lived experience), but not trying to speak directly from those perspectives:

> But I've never tried to write stories that center uniquely Asian cultures or experiences. Like, I wouldn't try to write a story that's all about what it means to grow up in a Taiwanese family. Or a story about the experience of living through the Hong Kong protests from the point of view of a Hong Kong native. Or a deep dive into Chinese history. There are other people who could write those stories way better than I could.
>
> That's where I decided to draw the line for myself, but everybody has to figure this out themselves. (And Hiromi Goto's WisCon guest-of-honor speech includes a very helpful checklist of questions to ask yourself before writing a story about a culture outside your own.) But I feel like this is always going to be messy, and ever-shifting, and contain exactly no straight lines, because we're talking about human beings, and the complexities of history. You never get to be done trying to figure this stuff out.

Anders goes on to say that as a writer, if you are drawing upon cultures other than your own, you are under an obligation to promote work by writers of that culture, to buy their books, and even donate to relevant causes.[16]

In the speech referenced by Anders, Hiromi Goto says:

It matters who and what is being focused upon in fiction. It matters who is creating a fictional account of these tellings. I don't think the "burden of representation" rests upon the shoulders of those who are positioned as under-represented. If this were the case we would fall into an essentialist trap that will serve no one well. However, I'm okay with saying that it is my hope that white writers who are interested in writing about cultures and subjectivities outside of their own consider very carefully: 1) how many writers from the culture you wish to represent have been published in your country writing in the same language you will use (i.e. English) to write the story, 2) why do you think you're the best person to write this story? 3) who will benefit if you write this story? 4) why are you writing this story? 5) who is your intended audience? 6) if the people/culture you are selecting to write about has not had enough time, historically and structurally, to tell their story first, on their own terms, should you be occupying this space?

Stories are wondrous devices. They can serve as time travel modules as well as being the most perfect empathy generating operations with holographic capabilities. Stories can create imaginary simulations of experience so rich and dense they can feel like they are your own. We can live and die, mourn and rejoice; we can feel affinity for a fictional character in a more intimate way than we can feel for our dearest friends and lovers, because we are allowed access to a character's mind. Fiction can sometimes feel more real than our lived lives. If only in that moment of intense connection, when our physical world slides away, and the words casts [sic] another before your mind's eye.

This magic is not a bubble world that exists in a neutral space. The magic was wrought by the author who has a connection to the world she was born into, and she consciously and subconsciously carries those relationships into the story.[17]

Goto's profound speech, which I highly encourage you to read (the references for this chapter include the link to the whole speech on Goto's website), and the questions she asks in the above excerpt, lead Anders to choose not to write her Asian-inspired fantasy.

Jeannette Ng, in her essay on *Medium*, "Cultural Appropriation for Worried Writers: Some Practical Advice," and her follow-up essay, "Cultural Appropriation: Some More Practical Advice," also references Goto's speech. She asks writers from a dominant culture to ask themselves a series of questions. Among them: "Examine your motives. Why do you want to write about this?" as well as "Are you looking to write a story about that identity?" She argues that a writer from a dominant culture shouldn't try to write a story to "save" a marginalized group. That you as a writer from a dominant culture are unlikely to do the marginalized group justice, and that if you write a story about, for example, slavery in America, you are still going to force African American readers to sit through a story by a white person in which people who look like them experience terrible things for many pages. Any mistakes you make (or lack of nuance that exists) only exacerbates the pain and discomfort. In other words, don't try to speak *for* someone else. She says:

> It is fine and good to write a story with gay characters if you are straight. I would strongly advise against writing a story that centres [*sic*] on the specific struggles of being gay in a oppressive society if you are straight.
>
> It is excellent and representative of reality to have black characters, but if you're a white American writer, I urge you not to try and write the next *Hate U Give*.[18]

Which is not to say that you can't write fiction that deals with racism—but Ng would argue that you shouldn't try to write *for* African Americans if you aren't African American. So, why not write about racism in some other way? In her second essay, Ng argues that you should ask yourself what about another culture, specifically, is fascinating to you? She uses the example of a British person fascinated with Japan. If, as a British fantasy writer, you find yourself drawn to writing a fantasy inspired by Japan, what is it about Japan that makes you want to do that? Is the hierarchy and formality present in historical Japanese society interesting to you because it highlights your own experiences with hierarchies? Couldn't you write a fantasy story with a highly formalized society and strict hierarchy that isn't based on Japan?

If you still want to draw upon another culture after examining your motives, Ng argues for research, and constant self-questioning, but also awareness of your own biases and the biases within your sources.

Ng is the author of *Under the Pendulum Sun*, a gothic gaslamp fantasy novel that grapples with colonialism, missionary culture, and sexuality. She was born in Hong Kong and lives in Britain. When she accepted her British Fantasy Association Award for her novel, she used that time to talk about John W. Campbell's fascism (the award was named after him at that time) and racism. She is no stranger to writing from and toward liminal spaces, as is evident in her novel.[19]

In the end, she says that there are no rules, and no one will ever give you permission, but striving is the only way to improve.

These writers, and countless others, all have different perspectives. Some say you *can* create a fantasy world inspired by culture(s) not your own, but only with great caution. Others say you can and should, as long as you don't act like an invader. Yet others assert that you should have diverse characters, but not create entire worlds derived from a culture not your own. They all advocate for fantasy worlds as diverse and varied as the real world.

In the end, only you can answer where the line falls for you. I highly recommend a great deal of self-reflection on your part, so that you make your decisions consciously. In addition, read the full essays that I summarize and quote here, and *Writing the Other* by Nisi Shawl and Cynthia Ward.

Now, based upon the assumption that you should write diverse characters, and that you may decide to write fantasy worlds at least partially inspired by something other than Western European history, how do you avoid offense and harm?

How To Catch Yourself Before You Create an Orc Problem

If you are reading this book and have made it this far, you don't want to create prejudiced fiction accidentally or on purpose. The following list is a synthesis of everything I have read about writing diverse fantasy (including the articles and books I mentioned earlier) as well as my observations from my own reading and experiences as a writer, teacher, and scholar:

1. You *will* make mistakes. It isn't possible to make everyone happy, or to be all-seeing and all-knowing. Just as typos somehow creep into professional manuscripts no matter how many eyeballs look at them, so you can accidentally play into a stereotype, and fail to catch it. Even if you somehow manage to make everyone happy and make no mistakes, time itself will inevitably render something you say socially unacceptable. Language and human society are ever-changing and evolving. So, if you make a mistake, take a page out of the book of the late great Ursula K. Le Guin, who looked back at her choice in the 1960s to use he/him pronouns as gender neutral in *The Left Hand of Darkness*, and realized that her perspective at the time was limited and flawed. Be willing to admit to mistakes, and if necessary, apologize. Don't beat yourself up, do the best you can.[20]

2. Depicting and condoning are not the same thing. I repeat: *depicting and condoning are not the same thing*. Oftentimes to critique a social ill, you have to depict it. Margaret Atwood is anything but pro-theocracy or women losing control over their bodies, but she depicts lost agency in a theocracy in *The Handmaid's Tale* to highlight the ways in which the real world tries to deprive women of the right to choose, using religion as a cover. As my grandmother used to say, there is more than one way to skin a cat. (Don't worry, I would never skin a cat.) You can make social critiques both through depicting a problem to draw attention to it, and through creating a world without a particular problem in order to show that it is not inevitable. Both are valid writerly techniques that have their own strengths.

3. There is an enormous quantity of resources out there on how to worldbuild, and how to worldbuild in a socially conscious way. For every possible issue, there are countless perspectives. People don't all agree on how to worldbuild, or on how to do so without replicating or adding to social problems. There is a lack of agreement because the issues are so complex. No single person can possibly cover or understand everything. Disagreement is natural and valuable; it's how ideas are tested and improved.

4. Implicit and explicit biases are not the same. We all have both kinds to some extent. An explicit racial bias in fantasy (i.e., outright racism) is like Vox Day (of Sad Puppies), implicit bias is like Tolkien and the way he described orcs. Implicit bias is unconscious, and often horrifies the person who holds it if it is pointed out. A conscious belief that you are not racist does not prevent you from having racist ideas, and implicit racial biases. This applies not to just to race, but to gender, class, sex, sexuality, region of origin—you name it. Thus, you can't tell yourself, "I'm not racist, so I don't have to worry about how I will depict people in my writing." No one is exempt, and no one gets to opt out. Thus, be willing to accept when someone notices bias in your writing, and instead of getting defensive, take it as an opportunity to reflect. For an excellent and important book on implicit bias, I recommend *Biased: Uncovering the Hidden Prejudice That Shapes What We See, Think, and Do* by Jennifer Eberhardt.[21]

Those basic principles out of the way, lets dive in to how to do your best to avoid creating an orc problem:

- *Be aware of your own biases.* If you are aware of your biases, you are more likely to catch yourself when you write or react in a biased fashion. The Harvard Implicit Associations test is a great place to start. Try to be as literate as possible in the social problems endemic to your country and your region. No one can entirely escape their upbringing, and if a particular viewpoint is common where you are from, even one you consciously abhor, it has more likely than not influenced you. For example, America, as a culture, broadly speaking, has bought into the myth of the meritocracy. Thus, Americans generally have closely held myths about how class works. America has very *low* rates of social mobility, yet most Americans believe we have *high* rates of social mobility, and so tend to blame poor people for being poor.[22] Even though I teach about this issue, and know that we don't live in a meritocracy, that doesn't mean that I haven't unconsciously internalized American ideas about class. Thus, I must be alert for this American form of classism in my writing.

- *Avoid essentialism.* When writing about people groups real or fictional, don't create hard and fast characteristics. Even positive essentialism is still reductive and harmful. For example, while I enjoyed the *Forgotten Realms* books when I was a teen, a central idea in the *Forgotten Realms* universe at that time was the idea that all drow but Drizzt were evil.[23] Come on, really? You create dark-skinned elves and make them all evil? No group of people is entirely evil. Arguably, barely any people can be characterized as evil as individuals. Mostly people are just humans who sometimes do good and sometimes bad. Aligning darkness with evilness is white supremacy embedded within language that folks have been calling attention to at least since Malcolm X. Even if all of your fantasy people groups are light-skinned, or all brown or black, creating simplistic essentialized ways of looking at those people groups contributes to the idea that there are social and personality characteristics inherent to genders, cultures, or ethnic groups, which there are not. Race, gender, and culture are all constructs, and no people group is a monolith. Which is not to say that you won't have characters who falsely believe in essential cultural or racial characteristic. In S. A. Chakraborty's *Daevabad* trilogy, many of the characters hold bigoted views about each other. But through multiple perspectives, Chakraborty uses the biases of these characters to show how flawed such essentialist perspectives are, and that they only lead to pain and division.[24] So, don't essentialize based upon race, gender, sex, sexuality, etc. Make each character and people group nuanced and complicated, neither all good nor all bad.

- *Be aware of and avoid tropes that promote stereotypical ideas about race, sex, gender, sexuality, etc.* Be leery of the damsel in distress, or the white savior. Don't have the dark hordes invade the castle. To be aware of these and other tropes, read widely, and deeply, with eyes wide open.

- *Avoid using physical appearance as a shorthand for character's inner state or moral being.* There is a long history in fantasy and science fiction (as well as other types of fiction) of having villains or antagonists that are in some way physically warped (like a scar) or disabled. Using disability as a shorthand for the evil or uncanny contributes to ableism. Similarly, don't equate beauty with goodness. The halo effect is a real psychological phenomenon; people perceive those they find attractive as smarter, kinder, and all around better than those they don't. Resultingly, people who fit normative standards of attractiveness are likely to earn more than those that society deems less attractive. You can have beautiful characters who are good people, but don't make causal connections between appearance and goodness or badness.

- *Don't create homogenous worlds or cultures.* The real world is a diverse place, your fictional world should be, too. Even if the peoples of your universe bear little to no resemblance to the peoples of the real world, diversity is still vital. China Miéville, author of our anthology story "The Condition of New Death," created a world called Bas-Lag.[25] This world is like nothing else you've ever read. There are cactus people, mosquito people, humans, and, and, and … The diversity of peoples makes the world feel real, even though cactus people bear no resemblance to any sentient life form we know. Everyone in N. K. Jemisin's *Broken Earth* series is human or humanoid, but there are many different people groups coexisting (some in relative peace, some not) on the same continent, even though her fantasy world isn't based on a real-world analog.[26]

- *Do your research.* And then do more. Be alert for biases not only within yourself, but within your sources. Jeanette Ng, author of *Under the Pendulum Sun*, said, in an article for *Medium*, that writers seeking to draw from cultures other than their own must understand that research isn't a panacea, and that sources will have their own biases. She gives an example, asserting that if you want to write a story based on Norse mythology, awesome. But Nazis also really loved Norse mythology, and there are a ton of white supremacist groups online that write about it. There's nothing wrong with Norse mythology (blame the user, not the myths, which predate modern notions of race), but lots of contemporary and historical fans of the myths were white supremacists, and it shows in how they interpret the stories. Lots of research will give you ideas to choose between, and assist in avoiding cherry-picking cultural touchstones, and or essentializing cultures. Research can come in the form of nonfiction books and articles, museums, interviews, travel, art of all kinds created by people from the culture you are interested in, and much more. Doing honor with research isn't just about accuracy, but about not contributing to harmful stereotypes or clichés, and not exploiting. Fantasy stories can and do make changes, especially secondary-world fantasy, but make certain that the boundary between the real and the imagined is clear, and that your changes are to make your story more fantastical, not to create a warped essentialized version of a place or time.

- *Remember that even in a fantasy world, everything you write has implications for real people.* Give credit where credit is due. Support and lift up artists from marginalized groups. Buy their books. Donate to appropriate causes. Don't try to argue with people about their own personal experiences.

- *Ask for help.* All human beings have limitations. No one can catch every possible error, stereotype, etc. Your own closeness to the manuscript can keep you from seeing problems. If you can afford it, there are professional sensitivity readers. For the love of all that is good, especially if you are from a normative identifying group, don't ask your friends or relatives of difference to be sensitivity readers, unless they offer without prompting. Exploiting unpaid labor from historically marginalized populations is problematic. If you can't afford to compensate a sensitivity reader, do a manuscript exchange with a writer or two you trust. Ask them to read for cultural sensitivity. If there is something in particular you are worried about, be sure to articulate that.

- *Dialogue is a danger zone.* Be leery of dialects and accents. They almost always end up being offensive. Don't try to appropriate the language rhythms of a dialect or subculture that is not your own. Represent differences in language through selective lexical choices. Marie Brennan's series that began with *A Natural History of Dragons* focuses on a scientist in an imaginary version of the 19th century who travels around the world studying dragons. She encounters many cultures along the way, but their dialogue isn't written in stilted English, or in any way that Otherizes those characters. Rather, Brennan sprinkles in occasional local words such as the names of fruit, or places.

- *Don't exoticize non-Western characters.* Don't focus on making a non-Western or non-Western-inspired culture and characters radically alien. Conversely, don't minimize real differences. Cultures will have different norms around marriage, for example, or proper table etiquette, but everyone gets hungry, everyone is capable of grief and loneliness. Nisi Shawl's novel *Everfair* is a great example of how you can use multiple point of view characters to showcase simultaneously that which is unique and that which is universal, avoiding both exoticizing, and overuniversalizing.[27]

- *Remember constraints and opportunities within worldbuilding.* Be aware of the power dynamics operating within your storyworld. Who has power? Who doesn't? What does it mean to be a woman in this society? A man? A non-binary person? What role does religion play? What tensions exist between religious or ethnic groups within and between societies?

- *Your fantasy worlds don't have to map onto any single real place.* Ursula K. Le Guin's *Earthsea* novels have dragons and wizards, and other elements that seem Western European. Yet much of the food and other aspects of culture within the stories seems very Mediterranean. Subtly, without focusing on race, Le Guin makes clear that the majority of the inhabitants of her storyworld are brown. There are white people, but they are from far away, and seen as rather strange-looking by the locals. When you read the *Earthsea* books, you can find inspiration for Le Guin's world in real-world cultures, but sufficiently transformed that the story reads like a true secondary world. Rachael K. Jones's "The Night Bazaar for Women Becoming Reptiles" is set in a desert, and there are elements of it that evoke the Middle East, but it is also clearly an invented world, no aspect feels lifted directly from reality.

- *You can undermine injustices, or show oppression, such as racism, without writing about racism.* In V. E. Schwab's *Shades of Magic* series, Red London, where most of the action of the story takes place, the most magical and prosperous London, is also primarily a state of black and brown people. The story isn't about race—the skin pigmentation of the characters is mentioned offhand. Schwab decenters whiteness in fantasy by making the most prosperous, magical, and central London not primarily white. The protagonist of Alix E. Harrow's *Ten Thousand Doors of January* is multiracial and so experiences the difficulty of being a brown girl in upper-class 19th-century America. The difficulty of her situation is part of her story, but the story isn't about racism, it's about her self-actualization. It's dishonest to depict America without racism, or to have the world of the story be so homogenous that racism never even comes up, but it's not the topic of Harrow's story.[28]

- *Be curious.* The strange and the wonderous can be found anywhere. There are fantasy stories that draw upon the present and the past in endless variety. Scott Lynch's *The Lies of Locke Lamora* riffs on the Italian city states.[29] Stories like the world of Ellen Kushner's *Swordspoint* gets inspiration from 18th-century France, but also includes interactions with other cultures. In her world, the pseudo-European culture hasn't figured out how to navigate long distances at sea, and so are the subservient trading partner with parts of South America in order to obtain the chocolate they love so deeply. Read widely, find something interesting everywhere. I really enjoy the website and book *Atlas Obscura*, which helps you find the unusual all over the world, including right out your back door. The whole website is a story seed. Use real historical events to help you learn how humans and city states and nations have interacted, to give your invented culture verisimilitude.

- *Cultures are made up of many ingredients, no culture is a monolith.* Food, architecture, history, gender relations, geography, religion . . . cultures are created by all these ingredients working together. Within every culture there are many subcultures. And within each subculture there will be variation between people. No one is a perfect representative of their culture or subculture. Humans don't fit into boxes. Neither should characters, or the cultures they live within.

- *Don't take your own experience or worldview as the default.* Write characters who believe differently from you and make them just as complex as you are.

In addition to issues of representing cultures other than your own, when worldbuilding, being didactic can also be a problem.

How To Avoid Being Didactic (aka How Not To Hit Your Reader over the Head with the Theme-Hammer)

- When worldbuilding, avoid making characters or peoples who are just representative of ideas, or a mouthpiece for a particular point.

- Don't set out to teach your characters a lesson. Characters can (and should) grow, change, and learn, like real people, not like a cartoon where the characters learn about sharing and sum it up in the final scene.

- The problems the characters face must be important to them, not just abstractions. Ursula K. Le Guin's *The Dispossessed* works even though it is set up to show the difference between anarchism and oligarchy, because the idea of seeking truly free choice is central to the main character's experience. A loss of will manifests differently for him in each society. In one, it is covert, through social pressure which leads to suppression of his research, in the other, overt. Shevek, the main character, demonstrates the novel's point by striving for his desires, not by being a puppet.

- Avoid simplicity. Binaries, like good and evil, right and wrong, rarely apply well to people. Complicated characters, even the most unpleasant ones, are still people. Don't turn someone into a villain or a saint for the sake of your argument. This helps nobody and is also boring.

- Theme. That thing your high-school teachers probably hammered into you to look for in fiction. Stories do have themes, but if you spend too much time worrying about it, and not enough time on characters and pacing, your story will feel wooden, and probably didactic. Themes usually emerge in revisions, not in first drafts, and generally come from patterns and resonances across the narrative, not explicit statements. Rebecca Roanhorse's "Harvest" has themes of identity, power, and loss. The narrator is engaged to a man and also has a female-identified lover. The narrator is both an indigenous person, and someone trying to make a place for herself in Western high-end cuisine. She never says: "Holy shit my identities and life choices are in conflict, this really sucks!" She just experiences her life and its pains. If she was a young white woman trying to become a chef, gender might still be salient (prestige cuisine is still male-dominated) but there would be less conflict between life choices and identity, and so identity would probably be a less dominant theme. My dissertation advisor, Joan Connor, often said about repetition in fiction, that once might not mean anything, twice might be a coincidence, but three times is a pattern. Repetition gains power through accretion. Multiple instances help theme rise to the surface without you ever having to be explicit. You don't want your themes to be reductive and easy to discern. Ursula K. Le Guin doesn't tell you what "The Ones Who Walk Away from Omelas" is about. The ethical stance of the story has been a source of debate for decades, a sign of a truly interesting story!

In summation, when it comes to making a point, be it through thematic elements of your story, or through outright social critique, trust your reader enough to not tell them how to read your story but don't expect them to be mind-readers. Use repetition of ideas, images, character struggles, etc. to let your points rise naturally to the surface.

A Note on Short Stories

Due to their brevity, short stories don't allow for detailed explicit worldbuilding. However, you should still know the answers to the basic questions about the world, and the culture within which your characters live. Most of it can't and won't make it onto the page; but it should inform how your characters act, and what they believe. Because you will only be able to include a few details, your choices for your worldbuilding will receive more attention. Read or reread the stories in our anthology, especially the ones with more complicated worlds, with an eye for what is included, and what isn't. Find places where you can tell there is more behind the characters' interactions, yet you only know the information through implication. C. S. E. Cooney, Ken Liu, Vandana Singh, Rebecca Roanhorse, Yxta Maya Murray, and Theodora Goss all have stories that are particularly useful for this task.

No matter what you are writing, don't go for the easy answers, keep trying, keep getting better, and remember the constraints and opportunities in the world you create.

Discussion Questions and Writing Activities

1. Examine a story in our anthology for cultural influences. What culture or cultures does the writer draw upon? How do you know? How did they avoid the pitfalls discussed in this chapter?

2. Are there any aspects of this chapter that made you uncomfortable? If so, why? What previous experiences contributed to that discomfort?

3. How do you feel about writing characters different from yourself? Why do you feel the way you feel?

4. Which techniques for creating complex and interesting cultures from this chapter were most useful to you, and why?

5. Where have you seen writers make some of the mistakes mentioned in this chapter? How did those mistakes impact the narrative?

6. Why is the relationship of empowerment and disempowerment so important in the conversation of about writing the Other?

7. How does the world and culture of your in-progress story create constraints and opportunities for your characters?

8. Pick a story from the anthology and write an internal monologue from the point of view of one of the characters who is different from you. Reflect on the experience.

9. Write a scene from the point of view of a character that is disempowered, interacting with someone from an empowered group. Then, rewrite the same scene from the opposite point of view. How do these characters experience the moment differently?

10. Research a time or place that fascinates you. Try to find information that you've never seen before. Look for information from people actually from that time and/or place. Compare it to information or texts written by outsiders. How is it different?

11. Examine a character in your story in progress. List their characteristics from the ROAARS list from Shawl and Ward's *Writing the Other* (race, orientation, ability, age, religion, and sex). Contemplate how that character's experiences and worldview would vary if any aspect of their identity changed.

12. How do you ethically write from a perspective not your own, or draw from a culture not your own, for a fantasy world? Write notes on how you would do so, if you were going to, and why.

CHAPTER 10
STYLE AND REVISION

Introduction

This chapter covers two deeply intertwined topics: style and revision. *Style* refers to prose style, the rhythm and music of language, as well as the form of the narrative itself. Revision refers to the act of writing past the first draft, from major structural changes to final line edits. These two topics, although not usually covered simultaneously, are inextricably tied. *Style develops through revision.* Style is rarely fully mature in a first draft. Additionally, writers find their style as they develop their skills. In sum, style and revision are process-driven.

Both style and revision are underdiscussed topics in writing generally, as well as fantasy writing in particular. One of the major misconceptions that those outside the fantasy writing community often have is that fantasy fiction is purely commercial or "popular" and thus not concerned with style. This identification of fantasy with the popular is a classist assumption derived from the days of the pulp magazines. It was never entirely accurate and is definitely not accurate today. All types of fiction have their commercially *intended* books (no one can tell if a given work will be popular or a commercial success beforehand) as well as those whose intention is primarily artistic. What an artistically or commercially intended book will look like varies by genre, time period, and culture. The style of a given narrative will be influenced by its intended audience, as well as genre, theme, and tone.

While some writers change style from story to story, many settle into patterns as they develop their craft. An identifiable style doesn't come from writing what you think and feel, unfiltered by editors, or revision. It comes from time, effort, careful thought, and a willingness to change anything and everything if it will make a story more wholly whatever it is becoming.

Prose Style and Genre

Let's think of prose style as a continuum. On one end, you have minimalism, and on the other, the baroque. Most writers fall somewhere in between. To use the metaphor of furniture, Scandinavian minimalism is about smooth lines, comfortable but pared down to its most basic function with few adornments. The baroque is both a style and a time period (starting in Europe around 1700, flourishing for about forty years, though continuing until the early 1800s) with an emphasis on the ornate, highly detailed, and luxurious.[1] The word has evolved in usage to refer to any crafted object (from furniture to literature) that uses exuberant detail, color, and ornamentation to produce an intense reaction in the person engaging with the object.

When thinking about prose rather than furniture, the basic distinctions still remain. Minimalism boils down language to its most essential parts to create its effects. The baroque employs lots of details, often heavily visual and sensory, to create an intense impression on the reader.

From our anthology, "Red" by Jessie Ulmer:

Red. Grandmother. Namesake. Leader of wolves. Baker of bread. She called for you. Spoke of communion. Consume body. Consume blood. Details are important. There are reasons widows move to wolf-infested woods, build a house, call it home.

Minimalist language is sparse, relying on shorter sentences, nouns, verbs, and very few (if any) adjectives or adverbs. One detail instead of two. One descriptive sentence instead of three. In realism, minimalism is exemplified by Ernest Hemmingway and Raymond Carver.[2] Advocates for minimalism often describe it in opposition to "purple" prose (a term I honestly hate!). There are relatively few truly minimalist fantasy writers, mostly because minimalism relies on the reader being able to fill in the blanks, and in secondary-world fantasy that would lead to confusion. However, fantasy minimalists do exist, often in fabulism or some fairy-tale retellings.[3] Fabulism, if you will remember, is fantasy that is mostly set in the real world, but with some specific strangeness or alterations. Consequently, as a writer, you don't have to worry about the basics of, say, transportation or geography. Fairy-tale retellings, on the other hand, while they can be told in a baroque style, are not always so, since if you are retelling a very well-known tale, the reader's preexisting knowledge is scaffolding you can hang details on. Oral tales as they were first written down by folklorists used flat minimalist language—a style often chosen by those who want to echo the oral roots of fairy tales. Japanese fabulist Haruki Murakami is a great example of a fantastical writer with minimalist prose.[4] Emma Donoghue's fairy tale "The Tale of the Shoe," a queer retelling of Cinderella, is also minimalist in its style.[5] Minimalist narratives are often (though not always) on the short end. Characterization tends to rely on negative space, on the pressure of the unsaid. Done well, this style causes every detail to take on a significance akin to poetry. One or two striking images can carry a story and induce ambiguity fertile for discussion and dissection. Done poorly, this style can be vague and uninteresting, with generic characters, and setting, etc.

From our anthology, "Meet Me in Iram" by Sofia Samatar:

When I say that Iram is lacking in domestic objects, I mean that we haven't gathered enough. I try to bring something with me every time. Last time it was a collection of my father's audiotapes, crammed into a pair of black plastic bags. The tapes are dusty with cigarette ash and poetry. It is only possible to listen to them in the worst light. A white, ugly, institutional light that, despite its harshness, is too weak to travel more than a couple of feet.

Baroque (or maximalist, if you will) prose is sometimes though not always freer with its use of adjectives and adverbs. Baroque writers generally try to overwhelm their readers, to create a sense of sumptuousness, or intensity through the quantity and quality of details. These are stories where the reader is often totally immersed in the sensory experience of the characters, or stories with intrusive narrators that share their obsessions and fixations. Baroque writing uses lots of visual details, as well as taste, touch, smell, etc. Baroque writers often include literary allusions, and other forms of densely nested references. Long sentences are common. So are poetic techniques such as alliteration and self-conscious metafictional techniques and extended wordplay. Characterization can occur through reverie, stream of consciousness, or deliberate exaggeration. These stories create an intense visceral reaction in the reader, from awe to unease. It frequently appears in gothic fantasy, Lovecraftian/weird fiction, as well historical fantasy. The neo-Victorian novel will often be written in baroque prose, such as Michael Faber's *The Crimson Petal and the White*.[6] This is also true of many neo-Victorian fantasy stories or novels, such as Genevieve Valentine's story from our anthology,[7] or Susanna Clarke's *Jonathan Strange & Mr. Norrell*.[8] Baroque stories and novels are usually longer. Done well, this style is intensely felt, and leads to unforgettable stories that people return to again and again. Done poorly, it can be needlessly confusing or emotionally alienating. Some noteworthy baroque fantasy writers include Tanith Lee, Angela Carter, Jeanette Ng, David Mitchell, C. S. E. Cooney, Sofia Samatar,[9] Gabriel García Márquez, and Jonathan Carroll.

Both baroque and minimalist prose styles ask a fair amount of the reader. In one, the reader must read *into* the text with relatively few clues for interpretation. The other asks the reader to parse through details, to untangle many threads. If prose style is a continuum, both of these far extremes can be thought of as stylized, and common to texts with more artistic intentions. At both extremes, language draws attention to itself, asking the readers to pay attention not just to *what* is said, but *how* it is said. Minimalism and maximalism require attention to the connection between form and meaning.

Most writers are not pure minimalists or maximalists, but merely tend more in one direction or another.

On our continuum, closer to minimalism is transparent prose.

From our anthology, "Harvest" by Rebecca Roanhorse:

"Tansi, Tansi," my lover whispers my name. "Is it time to harvest the hearts?"

The horror of her question is always fresh, always a shock. I suppose in the daylight hours when she is not here, I am able to tell myself that it never happened. That her words are other than what I know them to be. As long as I don't look at what we keep in the old cooler on the fire escape, as long as I ignore her bloody breath.

Transparent prose doesn't draw attention to itself. Depending upon the story there may be a lot of details given or relatively few if they aren't necessary (depending upon genre, for example). Regardless, transparent prose is a conduit for the story, and usually strives to avoid making the reader work. This is the most common style in fiction, especially in its most commercial variants.[10] Done well, there are selectively chosen sensory details, and a careful balance between scene, narration, and occasional summary. These narratives often intend to be immersive in the sense that you can forget you are actually reading. Books with extremely complicated plots are commonly written in this style, since asking the reader to track complicated prose *and* a complicated plot is not always ideal. Writers with complicated ideas that they want you to be able to parse very clearly often write this way as well. Long sentences are used sparingly in this style. Done poorly, this style feels mediocre, and is the source of a lot of really terrible prose. Done well, this style lends itself to the kind of book you can devour quickly. A lot of epic fantasy is in this style (due to the involved plots) as well as much urban fantasy. Frankly, you will find a lot of every type of writing in this style. It is the dominant mode of fiction in English in the 21st century. Noteworthy fantasy writers who do this style well: Rebecca Roanhorse,[11] Benjamin Percy, Naomi Novik, Katherine Arden, and Victor LaValle.

Closer to the baroque, but not quite there, is the lyrical or conspicuous.

From our anthology, "England Under the White Witch" by Theodora Goss:

You have seen our beloved Empress from far away, from below while she stands on a balcony, or from a sidewalk as she is drawn through the city streets in her sleigh. But I have met her. I have kissed her hand. It was white and cold, with the blue veins visible. Her grip was strong, stronger than any man's, as she was taller than any man. Her face was so pale I could only look at it for a moment without pain.

The lyrical or conspicuous is quite common in contemporary fiction writing of all stripes, though not as common as the invisible style. It is generally seen in narratives possessing intentions of combining artistic sensibilities with general readability. This prose style often feels poetic and uses more visuals and sensory descriptions than invisible prose, but less than the baroque. Extended metaphor and poetic technique can occur. Sentence structure is often relatively complex, with a mixture of scene, half scene, summary, and narration. This allows the writer to manipulate time more easily (and so frequently not purely forward moving sequential narration). Character point of view changes will often result in content and style changes. Frequent use of free indirect discourse. More voice-driven. Character interiority is central and informs word choice. Done well, it is both immersive, and sufficiently nuanced to sustain interpretation and discussion. Often deeply felt. Done poorly, it can be confusing, or slow down plot. This style is frequently used in fairy-tale retellings, mythic fantasy, historical fantasy, fabulism, and gothic fantasy, secondary-world fantasy . . . honestly, you can write any genre in this style. Doing so generally signals to the publisher and reader that your work has artistic aspirations, in addition to any commercial aspirations you may have. I will admit to a bias toward this style, the majority of my favorite writers tend in this direction. Noteworthy fantasy writers who write in this style: Ursula K. Le Guin, Kelly Link, Karen Russel, Elizabeth Hand, Ken Liu, Guy Gavriel Kay, N. K. Jemisin, Madeline Miller, Theodora Goss,[12] Brenda Peynado, Sequoia Nagamatsu, Sofia Samatar, and Ellen Kushner.

Style and Genre

Every genre of fantasy has prose stylists from all over the continuum. Secondary world and epic fantasy have writers who write in transparent prose, and writers who write in lyrical prose. Often prose style will be related to how traditional or experimental a story is, as well as its intended audience. However, despite the presence of all styles across all genres, there are genres in which certain styles are more common than others.

For example, some fantasy fiction, particularly that which is more plot-focused, often has transparent utilitarian prose, versus gothic or Lovecraftian fantasy, which tends toward using dense language and imagery in order to create a sense of fear, claustrophobia, or unease. Angela Carter and China Miéville are great examples of this.[13] Inversely, fantasy noir, which often includes a mystery, will frequently signal its aesthetic roots by using minimalist clipped sentences that mirror the prose in hardboiled detective novels. None of this is an indication that if you want to write gothic fantasy you must have baroque prose, or that if you write urban fantasy you must write in minimalist or invisible prose. These are broad trends that come from practical considerations.

Combining epic fantasy and baroque prose would likely lead to a novel of even longer than average length for epic fantasy. It doesn't mean that these novels don't exist, it just means they are less common. However, there are plenty of lyrical writers of epic fantasy from Patrick Rothfuss to Guy Gavriel Kay, and Ursula K. Le Guin. Conversely, as stated earlier, you are unlikely to find secondary-world or epic fantasy that is written in a minimalist style, simply because of the difficulty of worldbuilding and being minimalist at the same time.

Dark fantasy and horror tend to thrive at either extreme of the style spectrum, both the baroque and the minimalist being useful for making a reader read carefully, and for inducing a sense of alienation. Minimalist dark fantasy edging toward horror can be found in the work of Shirley Jackson, and some Joan Aiken. Baroque writers of darker fantasy include Angela Carter and China Miéville. Appropriately, the two big awards in dark fantasy/horror (it is hard to draw a firm line between these two) are the Shirley Jackson Award[14] and the Bram Stoker Award.[15]

Short stories are frequently the site of stylistic experimentation. There are plenty of experimental fantasy novels, but short stories are where the boundaries of style, from prose to form, are pushed. One, because they aren't as expensive to publish, for the writer (in time) or for the publisher (pages, dollars, and space). If the experiment fails, the writer probably hasn't spent ten years working on it, and the publisher probably hasn't spent tens of thousands of dollars. Two, it's easier for the reader and the writer to pay the requisite amount of attention to stylistic experimentation for a page to twenty-five pages, than for five hundred pages.

In addition to practical considerations, style in fantasy is shaped by the genres that influenced it. Many genres of fantasy are riffs on other types of stories. Urban fantasy is often (though not always) focused on a main character who solves mysteries. Gothic fantasy (shocking no one) draws upon the gothic novel. The fantasy of manners is a novel of manners plus magic. Consequently, many writers use the source genre as a stylistic inspiration. Fairy-tale retellings sometimes (though not always) attempt to mimic the minimalist flat style of folktales, or the oral storyteller voice (like some of Jane Yolen's work).[16] Part of what makes fairy tales so recognizable is stylistic cues. For instance, use of certain colors, like red, black, and white. Or the prevalence of certain types of settings or characters (witches, the woods, talking animals). Even certain types of events (physical transformation, loss of a parent). All of the above helps to signal to the reader that they are reading a fairy tale. A fantasy of manners is likely to have a witty narrator and be driven by voice to one extent or another, with an interest in issues of class, gender, and marriage. If you have read Jane Austen, read a fantasy of manners novel, like *The Magicians and Mrs. Quent* by Galen Beckett,[17] *The Midnight Bargain* by C. L. Polk,[18] or *Swordspoint* by Ellen Kushner,[19] and pay attention to similarities in the prose style. If you want to write a particular genre, you should also be at least marginally well read in the roots of that genre, so you are aware the range of possibilities, and where certain stylistic tendencies arose.

Revision, and the Myth of the Inspired Writer

One of the most pernicious myths about writing is the idea of inspiration. As much as I swooned over *Shakespeare in Love*[20] in high school, the image of the bearded white man scribbling madly, while inspired by some woman's breasts, and coming up with an immortal work of art within a few days, weeks, or months—it's utter nonsense!

All of the stories about writers writing a book in a month or two, or even a week, leave out the information that those are examples of writing a *first draft*, and *not* how long it takes to write the version of a book that appears in the bookstore.

On the Road by Jack Kerouac is often cited as a book that took a month or less (three weeks) to write.[21] Kerouac did type it on a 120-foot piece of paper he'd taped together over a three-week period. However, it was based on seven years of notes from his travels. Further, his famous three-week typing spree took place in 1951. It was published in 1957. His writing process for *On the Road* could more accurately be described as taking ten to fifteen years.[22]

National Novel Writing Month (NaNoWriMo) is a community event and organization. Every November, participants are given benchmarks and goal posts. The idea is to write 50,000 words (roughly the minimum for a novel) in thirty days.[23] Many novels written with them have gone on to be traditionally published (i.e., not self-published) including Sara Gruen's *Water for Elephants*, Erin Morgenstern's *The Night Circus*, Hugh Howey's *Wool*, Rainbow Rowell's *Fangirl*, Jason Hough's *The Darwin Elevator*, and Marissa Meyer's *Cinder*.[24]

The organization can help people create writing habits and set aside time to write. However, the attention paid to the organization, and the way it is discussed, ignores the fact that what it actually does is help people get a *first draft* written in thirty days. *Not* a polished and ready-to-hit-the-shelves book.

I bring all of this up, not to criticize NaNoWriMo, or anyone else who has drafted a book quickly, but rather to undercut the myth of inspiration. I can't count the number of students I've had who believe they can only write well (or at all) when they feel inspired, or peers I've met who struggle for years under a sense of failure because the words don't flow from their fingers like a gift from heaven. They wonder, is something wrong with them, are they not real writers, real artists?

Most people who write have experienced, at least once or twice, the story that won't let go. The one that springs into their brain nearly fully formed. Sitting down in front of the page, it feels more like you are the conduit for a message from the gods than writing. It's a glorious feeling. Those who study creativity now call this a "flow state." You are creatively in the zone, and the work feels easy.[25]

This is a wonderful feeling, but it can contribute to the sense that all creation that isn't part of the flow state is worse, or that you should be able to reach the flow state on command.

In reality, the flow state is the result of immersion and a lack of distraction. You can increase the likelihood of getting into the flow state by being very practiced at your art. Sometimes all of your thinking, practice, and mood come together in just the right mix. It's a gift, but it can't and won't happen all the time. It also doesn't mean that whatever you create in the flow state won't need revision. This is probably what happened to Jack Kerouac. He wrote *On the Road* after thinking about it for years. His practice, habits, and percolation time lead to an extended period of the flow state.

I once saw a comic (I've never been able to find it again) about the writing process. It showed a writer in the flow state. She typed in a spree of joy, and thought, "I am a god king, I am a gift to humankind, my art is amazing." The next day, she looked at the screen and thought, "I am shit. This is stupid. This is worse than stupid, it is trash, I will never make anything good ever!" Finally, a day or two later, she decided, "This is actually pretty decent, and with work, it will be truly good!"

Drafting, especially when in the flow state, is exhilarating and feels amazing, yet what you create almost never lives up to that feeling, and so the next day it looks like garbage. That crash, the dive into the valley from the peak of the flow state, isn't the truth either. In reality, with reflection, the work will look interesting, but there will be room for improvement. That, right there, is usually the truth.

So, set aside the idea that writing your book will be fast. If you are lucky, and you have the time, means, and solitude to write a draft in a month (or three months, as Stephen King recommends in his memoir *On Writing*), great, but realize that the first draft isn't the only draft.[26] The more complicated your novel is, on the level of prose style, plot, or form, the more revision will be involved. Think of it like juggling. The more balls you have in the air, the more likely you are to drop one, and thus, the more practice (revision) you will need.

The Writing Process

Composition scholars talk about writing as being comprised of multiple steps, beginning with prewriting, then drafting, then revising.[27] These steps can be recursive. Prewriting is everything before you start a draft. Thinking in the shower about your story. Scribbling notes and character ideas. Worldbuilding. Research. Traveling (à la Kerouac). Outlining.

Some writers prewrite extensively, which can make the drafting process faster. In his book on fiction writing, *Thrill Me*, Benjamin Percy describes the process of his first novel as exhausting; he wrote, rewrote, and rewrote some more, largely because he was resistant, at that time, to an outline.[28]

Similarly, I have historically hated the idea of outlining (I stand by my opinion for short stories, but not for novels), but with my own novel in progress, I ended up working with my agent to create an outline after I'd already written and messed with a first draft. I don't think I will ever write a novel without an outline again. The draft that came after the outline was enormously better. I wish I could go back in time to the moment I started that first draft, and whisper in my own ear, "Write an outline; really, it will save you a lot of time and pain."

Anne Lamott famously refers to her first draft as a "shitty first draft." She says admitting to yourself that it will be "shitty" is freeing. Other writers have described writing their drafts slowly and deliberately, even the first one, revising as they go.

The revision process itself has many stages even after the first draft has been achieved. Revision exists on a global and local level. Global revisions are the kind developmental editors help with. Plot, character development, structure, etc. Local revision is on the line level, where you are thinking about each sentence, each word. Not only making certain that you are saying what you meant to say, but that you are saying it in the best possible way. Is it clear? Is it beautiful? If your prose style is anything other than "normal" prose, you will need to spend extra time thinking about how you say what you say. Transparent or normal prose, while not easier to write, does tend to lead to a focus on clarity rather than artistic affect, and so the considerations for the local revisions will be different. Generally, it is best to work from the global to the local. Agonizing over the exact wording of a sentence that you might very well end up cutting can lead to wasted effort and time. Given that most of us are not rich in time, this is an important consideration.

Not every writer will have the same rhythms for their process. One common distinction that is made is between the "plotter" and the "panster." Often it is discussed as though writers are one or the other. I suspect most people neither write everything totally by the seat of their pants, or plot everything out. Total planning can take away the joy of discovery. Living the pure "pantster" life can mean writing a whole book to discern what the story is about. Most writers, especially for novels, should do a bit of both. Leave room for discovery but do a basic outline of the high points in the narrative, and major character motivations.[29]

Different writers work at different paces. Sometimes the differences have to do with their lifestyle (Are they a full-time writer? Do they have children?) and sometimes with the type of fiction they write.

The more complicated the task you have set yourself, the longer it will likely take you to complete it. Is it an epic novel with lyrical prose and a complicated plot? If you aspire to the epic scope and complicated style of David Mitchell's *Cloud Atlas*[30] or N. K. Jemisin's *The Fifth Season*,[31] be prepared to have your writing process be slower, and to revise many times.

Some genres or subgenres tend to have prolific authors. For example, mysteries, romances, and thrillers. This has to do with reader expectations and the style expected from many mystery and romance publishers. For instance, different lines of romance novels by Harlequin have specific requirements such as length, heroine types, and amount of explicit sex.[32] A reader who picks up a Harlequin medical romance, for example, will have certain expectations and desires they expect to be fulfilled by each book. This is the equivalent of a chain restaurant. Its value is in its consistency. There is nothing wrong with this. Sometimes, just as Starbucks Caramel Frappuccino is exactly what you want that day, you may want to be able to go to a bookstore and pick out a book from a particular shelf.

Because these books are often written to be consumed in this way, that means that readers who read these books can go through *a lot* of them in a short period of time. Consequently, they are set up to be produced quickly. Not all romance works this way; this is what is referred to as series romance. Many writers of urban fantasy/paranormal romance, like Patricia Briggs, aren't particularly speedy or fulfilling required formulaic elements.[33]

Some writers, like fairy-tale writer and scholar Jane Yolen, are prolific because, as far as I can tell, they are incredibly disciplined (and potentially made a deal with a faerie spirit!).

In Jeff VanderMeer's *The Wonderbook*, famous writers talk about how long it took them to write their breakout book. Writers describe their revision process, and how many drafts it took before their book was accepted by a publisher. The low number of drafts seems to be about three (Alliette de Bodard, Daniel Abraham, and Carrie Vaugh) and the highest 200+ (Patrick Rothfuss). The average was about six to ten drafts.[34] Most writers also have abandoned books stashed away before their breakout book. After a publisher accepts your book, there will be various editors who will ask you to make changes. From copyeditors to continuity editors and developmental editors.

In the end, writing is a long process, and those 200+ drafts (horrifying, I know) that Patrick Rothfuss describes came from taking care over every word, the process of discovery, having many beta readers and taking their advice, and just generally writing an ambitious book. Few books will take 200+ drafts to be ready for a publisher; conversely, few books will take only one, and if any writer says their only wrote one draft, assuming they are telling the truth (fiction writers lie, you know), then they probably did extensive prewriting, and rewrote as they went.

However long your book takes to write, it's okay, it will take how long it takes! You won't find your style, or employ it consistently and well, unless you accept that.

Some general tips for revision and style:

1. Try to make a rough outline for your novel (major plot points, what your characters want or desire in each chapter).

2. Work from the macro to the micro.

3. Set yourself revision tasks. Don't try to deal with every problem at once. Choose to focus on clarity of character motivation during one round of revision, then plot tension the next. Another day, on the micro level, look for what writer Matt Bell calls "weasel words" (the words that you overuse). Two of my weasel words are "vast" and "dark."

4. Set aside time for revision and writing. Close your internet browser while you write. Make notes of things to look up later if you need to.

5. Pay attention to the writer(s) whose style seems closest to the kind you want. Reread their works. Pay attention to prose. Imitate a passage. It should stretch your writing muscles and give you a sense of what it feels like to employ particular techniques. Painters have long copied the works of masters, to learn the brushstrokes those masters made. Choose your own masters and reread them mindfully.

6. Read widely and deeply. Don't confine yourself to one genre or style. You will come into your style through a diverse array of influences, and lots of practice.

7. If you are stuck on a task, such as creating a gripping first chapter, reread first chapters of books you find gripping, and dissect them. Figure out how they did it and try to apply those lessons to your work. For short stories, do the same thing with first pages.

8. Find readers you trust. The ideal reader gives you real suggestions, and catches your mistakes, but they will also be a fan of the kind of work you do.

Discussion Questions and Writing Activities

1. What was the biggest takeaway for you from the discussion of prose style? Why? How will you apply it to your work?

2. What writers do you most admire? What prose styles do they incline toward?

3. Examine a piece of fiction that you've written and are proud of. What prose style do you see yourself leaning toward? How might you further develop and enhance that style?

4. Pick a story from our anthology. How would you characterize the author's style? How do you know? If you were to imitate this author's style, what characteristics of their writing would you use to create a similar effect?

5. Do you see yourself primarily as a "plotter" or "panster"? How does this self-conceptualization affect your writing choices? Try, for the length of one story, or a chapter of a novel, to do the opposite of what you normally do.

6. What does prewriting, drafting, and revision usually look like for you? Try to draw it. Do you feel like your current process is working, or not working?

7. Create a revision plan for your work in progress.

8. How is this chapter's description of the role of revision different or similar from how you've thought about it before?

9. Why do you think this chapter spends time breaking down the myth of the inspired writer? What might it do to our ideas about art if we realize that the inspired writer is a myth? How would it impact you and your writing?

SECTION 3
GENRES AND STYLES OF FANTASY WRITING

Overview

This section exists to guide writers and students through the interconnected nature of genre and style in fantasy fiction. This chapter will apply our knowledge of craft, genre, and style from the previous section(s) to particularly prominent genres of fantasy fiction. The implications of style on genre and vice versa will be discussed. Within fantasy fiction, "genre" refers to different types of fantasy that have specific expectations for form, content, and style. For example, in a fantasy of manners, the book will often fulfill many expectations for a novel of manners à la Jane Austen, but then add a fantastical element, such as dragons, or witchcraft, that is intrinsic to the social fabric of the world, and thus, to the social status of the characters. This chapter will reference the techniques from the craft section to guide students in the intentional development of style, and thus building directly upon the skills previously learned.

It has been my experience, as a reader, writer, and teacher, that the differences in style and craft for the various genres of fantasy fiction are rarely, if ever, discussed in print. Fantasy writers talk about it among themselves, but critics have barely scratched the surface, and craft books by fantasy writers have generally spoken from their own writing experience, not differentiating between their genre(s) and other genres of fantasy when giving craft advice. As a result, people make generalizations which barely apply to one genre let alone the whole of fantasy. This section is an attempt to begin to rectify the lack of explicit discussion on the history, craft, and styles of common fantasy genres. I will not be covering every fantasy genre, since the list is ever-expanding. I will cover six of the most prolific genres that are related to or influence most others. While Chapter 2 gave an overview of the history and characteristics of the genres in question, now I will focus on how to apply it to your own writing, and to understanding the writing of others. This will help you be a better writer and a better reader for your peers.

CHAPTER 11
EPIC FANTASY, HIGH HANTASY, AND SWORD AND SORCERY FANTASY

Dominating Public Perceptions

Epic fantasy, high fantasy, and sword and sorcery fantasy are hard to distinguish from each other. Most of what the general population thinks of when fantasy is mentioned falls within these interrelated genres. *Lord of the Rings, Game of Thrones, Harry Potter,* the *Chronicles of Narnia,* and many more. Much of the early fantasy "canon" (a contested idea, to say the least) is epic fantasy, high fantasy, or sword and sorcery fantasy.

High fantasy and epic fantasy are essentially synonymous.[1] High fantasy as a term has mostly fallen out of favor because it implies that other genres are low fantasy, and somehow lesser. Both terms refer primarily to the scale and scope of the narratives. Both generally include a struggle between good and evil, where the fate of an entire world/culture/nation is at stake. The hero is usually chosen or predestined. Historically, they have been analyzed according to Joseph Campbell's hero's journey trope (a trope as problematic as the man who coined it, given its extremely masculine and conflict-driven nature). Traditionally, high and epic fantasy are secondary-world fantasies (set in a made-up world, not an altered version of the real or primary world).[2] But many fantasies like *Harry Potter, The Chronicles of Narnia,* or Philip Pullman's *His Dark Materials* series are both epic fantasies and portal fantasies. These series have all of the characteristics commonly associated with epic fantasy, except for the pure secondary-world setting. Note that all of the books listed have been adapted for film or television.

This is part of *why* this genre is the one most associated with the term "fantasy," and a symptom. Its ascendancy, aside from the attention draw via film and television, is also due to the pervasiveness of Tolkien in the early-20th century, and the prolific Tolkien-inspired fantasies from the 1970s through 90s. Additionally, a lot of 19th-century fantasy, as well as much Arthurian literature, would be considered high fantasy now. The genre is in part inspired by the epic, which predates the novel itself as a form. Sword and sorcery, though similar, doesn't usually have the firm good and evil distinctions: the hero is more likely to be an anti-hero, or morally gray. Sword and sorcery fantasy is otherwise similar to epic fantasy. The *Elric* novels are a classic example.[3]

You may have noticed the dominance of white male writers and my use of the term "hero" in this description so far. This genre and its related genres are the ones that have been most associated with male writers and Western traditions of the epic. This very masculine and Western orientation has led to a lot of early and famous examples of these novels showcasing few female characters, and even fewer characters of color. Those female characters who are present are usually motivation for male characters—damsels to rescue, or beloveds to return to. The exceptions have been powerful sorceress or witch characters (Galadriel in *Lord of the Rings* or Morgaine from Arthurian mythology),[4] often depicted as evil or kept mostly out of the direct action. In much early epic fantasy, non-white characters were associated with invading hordes, villains, or subordinate helper characters. Disability was often used to represent evil (like Grima Wormtongue in the *Lord of the Rings*).[5]

While the above description has never covered all of epic fantasy, it does describe the form of epic fantasy and its related genres that used to dominate. Epics have been written all over the world, beginning in oral tradition, eventually written down by one or more people. Epics are usually foundational stories for the cultures from which they arise, the source of archetypal narratives, character types, etc.[6] While in the English-speaking world, people have historically only been taught a handful of epics from Western cultures, including *The Aeneid*, *The Odyssey*, *Beowulf*, and one or more of the Arthurian epics. However, this is an extremely limited picture of the epic, and the lack of exposure most English speakers have to world epics is mirrored by the ways in which epic fantasy has been largely a one-way transmission.[7] Epic fantasy written in English has been translated into numerous world languages, but relatively little fantasy has been translated into English and promoted. Translations of world epics are widely available, but their reading in English is confined mostly to scholars. The popularization of more world epics, and translated epic fantasy, is an important growth area.[8] I highly encourage everyone to investigate epics from around the world, as well as translated epic fantasy. More will be translated into English only if English speakers show that they will read translated fantasy literature.[9] Some of the more high-profile translations of epic fantasy or sword and sorcery fantasy into English have been from Slavic countries (the most famous example being *The Witcher* series by Andrzej Sapkowski), helping to encourage a trend in Slavic fantasy written in English.[10]

Modern epic fantasy, for decades now, has been working against the dominance of monolithic ideas about epic fiction. This has taken many forms, including undermining the hero's journey narrative in novels and popular discussion.

Ursula K. Le Guin's *Earthsea* series is a great example of how epic fantasy doesn't have to be so white, masculine, or focused on power. The world is populated mostly by black and brown people, including the protagonist Ged. While his quest has epic consequences, he is searching for knowledge, not dominance. With later works in the series, Le Guin called out her own failure to imagine epic fantasy without a male hero and wrote two novels focused on heroines.[11]

The task of a contemporary epic fantasy / sword and sorcery / high fantasy author is to discern how to write an epic tale that fits the genre while subverting the problematic elements.

How We Write Epic Fantasy Now

In the 21st century, the stakes of epic fantasy stories are still large, and the protagonist(s) (regardless of gender identity) have to make choices that impact the larger world, not just their own life or immediate surroundings.

However, how that scope is presented varies widely, as do the pivotal protagonists. Epic fantasy doesn't always have the firm good and evil boundaries that used to characterize it. Even if the protagonist(s) are fighting evil, they might make decisions that are morally ambiguous. While use of prophecies and other methods of predestination still appear, they are usually undercut, or not present at all. Often it is mere circumstances, such as being in the wrong place at the wrong time, which pulls protagonists into large-scale events. Sometimes the protagonists are from the upper classes, and sometimes they rise from low beginnings. Though the doings of the powerful still frequently have a strong influence on most epic fantasy, simply because of scope (generals and monarchs make national decisions, not bakers).

Increasingly, female-identified protagonists and writers are centered in epic fantasy. From N. K. Jemisin (the *Hundred Thousand Kingdoms*)[12] to Juliet Marillier (the *Sevenwaters* series),[13] Jacqueline Carey (the *Phèdre Trilogy*),[14] Lois McMaster Bujold (*The Paladin of Souls*),[15] Robin McKinley (*The Blue Sword*),[16] and Neon Yang (*The Red Threads of Fortune*).[17] Ista from *The Paladin of Souls* is not only a woman, but middle aged.

Further, queer characters (and authors) have an increased presence, as well as epic stories focused on characters of color, by authors of color, in non-Eurocentric worlds. Like *Black Sun* by Rebecca Roanhorse[18] and *Black Leopard Red Wolf* by Marlon James,[19] among many others.

Even within books set in worlds that may feel more like traditional English-language fantasy, there are still so many ways that the epic fantasy writing ecosystem has grown more complex and varied. From the metafictional calling out of tropes in Jenn Lyons's work,[20] to the intimate and lifelong portrait of Fitz over multiple series by Robin Hobb,[21] to the way Kvothe, in the *The Name of the Wind* by Patrick Rothfuss,[22] far from being "chosen" repeatedly thrusts himself into important events through sheer persistence and a refusal to live in ignorance.

Now, most epic fantasy novels are written on a more psychologically intimate scale. A distant third-person objective point of view doesn't fly. Character motivation is centered. First-person narratives have become common, as well as close third-person perspectives. The use of a true omniscient point of view, like in Guy Gavriel Kay's novels,[23] is used to give a more intimate portrait of the world, rather than less, showcasing the importance of even the most seemingly minor individual, as well as the personhood of people on all sides of a conflict.

The unseen and impersonal "dark hordes" of old are no longer mainstream or acceptable in fantasy fiction. Whole series, like Glen Cook's *The Black Company*, are even centered on characters who were formerly faceless or vilified.[24]

Don't try to write another version of something you loved as a child. Be bold. Innovate. The claim that epic fantasies are about the world, not the characters, is simply false. You wouldn't be able to publish something like that now, which is a good thing. A world that is complex and interesting, populated by characters with beating hearts, conflicted minds, and internal conflict—just like us—enriches fantasy rather than impoverishes it.

Characterization and plot in epic fantasy, as with most aspects of craft, is culturally dependent. What counts as an event, or as an "active" character, will vary from place to place, time to time. In *Craft in the Real World*, Matthew Salesses describes the ways in which much East Asian fiction is structured not in three acts, but four, and change in the narrative often occurs, not in the characters, but in the way the reader is meant to conceptualize the characters or events. As a result, many Western readers have seen East Asian fiction as "plotless." In reality, its plots are written for a different audience, with different expectations for plots. Salesses describes how different cultures have distinct expectations or attitudes toward character agency. How much coincidence is acceptable, how much a character is allowed to surrender to circumstances, etc.[25]

Interestingly, a lot of fantasy fiction, even modern fantasy written focused on the intimate experience of characters, has an orientation toward individual agency that stands out from that of much Western literature (and may be part of why some literary circles have looked down upon it). Most epic fantasy turns upon the idea that while the small individual can have an impact, it is usually because they have help. Additionally, the turns of the broader world greatly impact the ability of characters to have agency. Fantasy fiction, especially epic fantasy, in that way, is more likely to recognize the constraints society places on the individual than most realism written by white male cis-gendered English speakers. Characters often struggle against those constraints. But not always.

As a writer of epic fantasy, as with all writers, what counts as "good" plot, character development, or any other aspect of craft, is culturally and contextually dependent. My advice is dependent upon context. It describes the expectations of readers and editors in the 21st century in the mainstream publishing in the English-speaking world.

Within this context, writers are expected to not only create an interesting world, a compelling plot within it, but also nuanced characters. Thus, epic novels tend to be *long*. From 350 to 1,000 pages is not unheard of. Consequently, a good epic fantasy takes a long time to write.

To keep track of all of the moving parts (who is backstabbing who, who wants to have sex with who, who has power, who wants it ...) you will definitely want an outline. A character family tree, as well as some method of keeping track of how each character is related to every other character (not just blood relation, but how their actions, as well as their dreams and dreads, coincide with, conflict with, or impact other characters), will be especially useful. Pay extra careful attention to causality. Beware letting your plot control your characters.

With the kind of worldbuilding needed in these narratives, it is tempting to have characters explain things in order for the reader to learn them. While occasionally this is reasonable (like librarians explaining the rules of the library to Kvothe in *The Name of the Wind* when he gets to the University, information that will be crucial to the plot, but also something Kvothe cares about and that the librarians would reasonably tell someone), most of the time it feels artificial. People rarely lecture at each other. Find other ways to integrate worldbuilding and information as needed. A protagonist who is searching for knowledge (like Kvothe) is helpful. Many authors include tiny excerpts from texts at the start of chapters that leave worldbuilding breadcrumbs for readers. It's also permissible to let the reader piece a lot together from context. Maps can help the reader with spatial relationships but aren't obligatory.

Additionally, epic fantasy and its related genres often feature physical conflict, army, sword, or wizard battles, etc. There are a range of ways to handle battles. One way (my preferred method) is to focus on the perspective of your protagonists during the battle, and let the reader learn about how the whole thing went in the aftermath, just like how it would work in real life. If you must give a bird's-eye view, do it through a *brief* narrative zoom out, or through multiple perspectives à la Kay's work. With one-on-one fights pay careful attention to blocking and physicality. If someone is swinging a sword, you should learn how that type of sword would actually work. Read up on real swordplay and watch videos.

Further, not all problems or conflicts need to be solved through physical conflict. While there is war in Jacqueline Carey's *Kushiel's Dart*, the main character is a priestess of a goddess focused, at least partially, on sex, and she solves problems through cleverness, guile, and her sexuality. She impacts the fate of the world without raising a weapon.

All of which goes to say, look beyond the battle as the climax of epic fantasy. It can be the climax, but it doesn't have to be.

Prose style can vary greatly, from the lyrical to the invisible, though the baroque is rare in this genre, simply due to the level of complication already present. But that doesn't mean you can't give it a go!

Finally, read gobs of contemporary epic fantasy, as well as nonfiction about history, and sociological works, to get a real sense of how societies work on a grand scale, and how to translate that inspiration into fiction.

A Note on Short Stories

Epic short fiction does exist. It generally focuses on a single character and begins right before the traditional climax. It compresses epic fantasy into the most intense final moments, and the decisions that lead to them. *A Handful of Rice* by Vandana Singh is the epic fantasy in our anthology.[26] *Beneath Ceaseless Skies* is an award-winning online fantasy magazine that focuses on secondary-world fantasy where you will find a greater proportion than average of epic fantasy short stories. I highly recommend perusing it!

Discussion Questions and Writing Activities

1. What are your favorite epic fantasies, and why? What do you like about this genre and why? If you don't enjoy it, why?

2. List a few common patterns or tropes in epic fantasy and brainstorm how you might subvert or reverse those tropes.

3. Pick an epic fantasy you know and imagine ways that the conflicts in the story might be solved other than a battle. Are there any? Why, or why not? What would

happen if you changed the final focal conflict to something other than a physical confrontation?

4. Why does it matter that epic fantasy is pushing back against the white-male-dominated narratives of the past?

5. If you have an epic fantasy in progress, look for exposition or explanatory worldbuilding. How might you integrate that information in another way?

6. What was most useful to you about this chapter, and why?

7. Pick your favorite epic fantasy and analyze the point of view. How does the chosen point of view impact the way the story is told?

CHAPTER 12
HISTORICAL FANTASY

The Past Is Never Past

This genre is one of the most diverse and productive genres of fantasy, overlapping with or leading to the creation of many other genres and subgenres, like gaslamp fantasy, fantasy of manners, and alternate history fantasy. The historical fantasy genre is frequently used for the purposes of social critique, à la Colson Whitehead's *The Underground Railroad*,[1] to create a socially rich fantasy world, or to give life to a time period little thought about or studied. This form can be highly fantastical or a secondary world without a single bit of magic. Most readers of fantasy fiction have probably read historical fantasy without realizing they were doing so. The very diversity of this genre has made it diffuse and somewhat hard to quantify. Historical fantasy is rarely used as a marketing technique or category, unlike epic fantasy. Additionally, many works of historical fantasy are published by mainstream rather than genre publishers and marketed as simply "literary fiction" or "magical realism" (though the two are not the same thing). Many are published by genre publishers as well. Historical fantasy consequently can be found in both expected and unexpected places. Broadly speaking, it is defined as fantasy set in a period other than the present or recent present. If a similar mimetic or realistic piece of fiction set in that period could be categorized as period piece or historical fiction, then you are writing historical fantasy. Historical fantasy can either be fantastical fiction set in a real and specific time and place, or in a secondary world that is meant to be a barely disguised fantastical analog to a specific time and place.[2]

Historical fantasy consequently overlaps with other genres or subgenres within fantasy, such as epic fantasy, fantasy romance, or a fantasy of manners. Historical fantasy bleeds into many related subgenres. Gaslamp fantasy, for example, is historical fantasy set in mostly Victorian- or Edwardian-era England (or sometimes America). Steampunk usually shares with gaslamp fantasy the time period and setting, but instead of magic, it focuses on a retro-futuristic aesthetic, where steam technology remains dominant, and takes on fantastical forms. In that way, steampunk is a form of alternate history fantasy.

An epic fantasy novel is generally considered historical fantasy rather than epic fantasy (as its primary genre) when the realistic application of the real cultural constraints of the historical period are taken seriously, with the research required being nearly equivalent to what it would take to write a historical fiction novel.

Hopefully, from this little digression on gaslamp fantasy, steampunk, and alternate history fantasy, epic fantasy, and their relationships to each other, you can see why historical fantasy is simultaneously simple and difficult to define.

This genre's growing popularity and prolific publishing profile comes from its diversity, its emphasis on verisimilitude, and the ways in which using real historical time periods lends the genre to making critiques of dominant culture. It is often used to emphasize aspects of history that have been ignored or deliberately repressed in the hegemonic historical narrative.

Why Choose Historical Fantasy? Possibilities and Perils

For writers, historical fantasy offers some compelling advantages. It doesn't require you to build an entire world from scratch. While secondary-world fantasy necessarily draws upon the real world, the writer must employ invention in order to make a lived-in and convincing world full of the social tension, stratification, and complexities that the real world has. Rather than inventing the gender norms of the upper classes, if you are writing a story set in 17th-century India, you can look it up. Instead of inventing the power dynamics between peoples in your story, you can depict the real power dynamics that existed. This is not to say that research is easier than invention. It is a different kind of challenge that some writers find preferable.

Research requires curiosity, patience, and then a careful selection of details. With the richness of the real world and its vast array of time periods and cultures to choose from for historical fantasy settings comes a responsibility on the part of the writer to represent the chosen period and culture with accuracy and fairness. You will have to be extra alert to your own biases, as well as the biases in your sources. The need to be aware of bias in yourself and your sources is also true when you are inventing a culture, but in the case of historical fantasy, you are writing about real cultures and real peoples. Additionally, much like with historical fiction, unless what you depict is overtly fantastical or an obvious deliberate change from historical reality, your readers might assume that you are depicting the truth. This is especially true when writing historical fantasy that is extremely close to the historical record as it is currently understood.

For example, if you decided to write a historical fantasy about Marie Curie, or another female-identified scientist in the early-20th century, and simply ignored or erased the real barriers, difficulties, and sexism that she and other women in science experienced, you are in effect lying to your readers, and propping up the mythology that the scientific world is a meritocracy where one's gender, sex, or race has no bearing.[3] Even if you changed the story so that radium came from faerieland, and its toxicity derived from its otherworldly origin, you still wouldn't get to ignore the issue of sexism in the early-20th century. Let's say you wanted to write an alternate version of history, where in the 19th century a terrible epidemic killed 80 percent of adult men, the inversion of gender norms could be part of the story, but it would be a deliberate and noticeable change, rather than a historical inaccuracy.

Similarly, you would be doing a terrible thing if you set a historical fantasy novel in 17th-century India and depicted an India totally cool with being colonized. On the other hand, if you wrote a story where the British were ejected from India sooner than they were in real life (as did Vandana Singh in *A Handful of Rice*), then you are writing alternate history, not propping up white supremacy.

Nisi Shawl's majestic alternate historical fantasy novel, *Everfair*, asks what if, in Belgian-occupied Congo, the native population developed steam power before their oppressors?[4]

In other words, when you write historical fantasy, changes from the historical record should be deliberate, and have a purpose. The closer your fantasy world is to the real historical period and real place, the more deliberate you must be.

A thoughtful change can defamiliarize the past, and help the reader see the ways in which our narratives about history (history is itself, after all, a story) are constructed, and that historical and contemporary power dynamics were not and are not inevitable, or the result of inherent superiority or inferiority.

Some historical fantasy changes little about the historical setting. Ta-Nehisi Coates's debut novel, *The Water Dancer*, takes the genre of the escaped slave narrative, and merges it with fantasy, by giving his protagonist, Hiram, as well as a few others (including Harriet Tubman), the ability to physically transport themselves through memory. The broader arc of history isn't changed in this novel, but the power given to Hiram allows for a profound investigation of the power of memory, identity, and the terrible harms of slavery.[5]

Novels like *The Water Dancer* are often published outside of the genre fiction publishing ecosystem (though they are also published within it, see Octavia Butler's *Kindred*)[6] and overlap with fabulism and magical realism. The magic element allows the writer to emphasize certain aspects of the narrative more than they could in a straightforwardly realistic novel.

Alice Hoffman's Second World War novel, *The World That We Knew*, uses Jewish folk beliefs about golems, and has one woman create a golem to protect her daughter. The novel follows a range of characters, including the golem, and a heron that carries messages between characters. The magical elements defamiliarize a story that the reader might otherwise have been numbed to.[7]

In addition to the ability to highlight the experiences of the vulnerable and oppressed, or question dominant narratives about people and history, historical fantasy can be used for purposes other than social critique. It also allows a writer to play in a historical period, or a period that is a close analog to a real one, like a sandbox, in the way one couldn't in a true historical fiction novel.

Guy Gavriel Kay's historical fantasies recognize that to write a history is to write a fantasy. We can't fully know the past. What we do is tell stories about the past, and the stories we tell about particular periods and places, and call history, tell us as much about ourselves as those times. Which is not to say that there are no such things as verifiable historical realities, but rather, that all of our knowledge of history is imperfect, and when we write historical stories, we are imagining a lot more than we like to admit.

Kay's novels create mirror worlds to tell stories that ask questions about the narrative of history itself. *The Lions of Al-Rassan* depicts the destruction of a culture through war. Through its varying perspectives, Kay shows the impossibility of reconstructing a culture from fragments (destruction cannot be undone, only changed) and how the victor in a conflict will create a story, called "history," that is fraught with ideology. By creating a mirror world with Al-Rassan (a thinly disguised version of Al-Andalus, the historical term for the Muslim-ruled area of the Iberian peninsula between 711 CE and 1492), Kay can ask questions about the erasure of the past without being beholden to strict historical accuracy. *The Lions of Al-Rassan* has nearly zero magic, but it is a fantasy because of the secondary-world setting.[8]

Similarly, though with less serious intent, Marie Brennan's historical fantasy, *A Natural History of Dragons*, is set in a pseudo-19th-century England inspired by the history of gentleman scientists. The novel follows a woman who against all odds becomes the foremost naturalist studying dragons.[9] Brennan's and Kay's works both arise from a deep interest in the periods and places that inspired their works. But by creating looking-glass versions of those times and places, they can ask questions or posit potential realities, playing around, but with more freedom to create than in more literal historical fantasy. However, in both cases, if they have intents to make social critiques, readers who are unaware of the real history could possibly miss the historical analogs. Thus, the more you want to critique the real history, or make the reader see how our current world and its problems are influenced by history, direct historical fantasy might be more appropriate. On the other hand, the approach of Kay and Brennan also has less chance of triggering defensiveness against social critique.

There is also plenty of historical fantasy that just wants to have fun in the time period, and ask, what if? What if a portal between the magical world and the human were opened in Egypt (*The Haunting of Tram Car 015* by P. Djèlí Clark)?[10] What if Sherlock Holmes, Dr. Moreau, and other 18th and 19th-century English characters were real, had families, and knew each other (*The Strange Case of the Alchemist's Daughter* by Theodora Goss)?[11] What if you rewrote *The Great Gatsby*, but with a female-adopted, queer, immigrant protagonist and added ghosts (*The Chosen and the Beautiful* by Nghi Vo)?[12]

No matter what type you want to write, historical fantasy offers the opportunity to take what is most interesting to you about the real world, and cover it with ghosts, glitter, and dragons.

So, You Want To Write Historical Fantasy, Now What?

We've broadly defined historical fantasy, referred to a few of its many genres and subgenres, and discussed its pleasures, perils, and opportunities.

Beyond the writing concerns discussed already in this chapter, what do you need to think about as you begin writing historical fantasy?

That question is slightly more complicated to answer than in our earlier chapter discussing epic fantasy, since historical fantasy can take so many different forms. You can write an epic historical fantasy. You can write a historical fantasy romance, an alternate history fantasy, a steampunk fantasy, a silk-punk historical fantasy, a historical fantasy mystery, or . . .

Each of these variants will have their own writing concerns. If you are writing a historical fantasy mystery, you not only need to think about historical fantasy and historical fiction[13] (which can teach you a lot about how to write historical fantasy), you need to think about what makes a good mystery novel, too.

Historical fantasy is intrinsically a hybrid genre, such an abundant one that it deserves its own category. Additionally, all concerns about writing characters that aren't stereotypes, as well as the culturally contextual notion of craft, and history, apply. To avoid simply repeating things I've said before, here I will cover a few writing tips that will apply across historical fantasy subgenres:

- *Historical dialogue is tricky.* Unless you are being deliberately anachronistic (like *The Knight's Tale*),[14] you don't want your 12th-century Spanish princess saying things like, "I'm for sure down with going to the ball." Nor do you want to force your reader to read people actually speaking like someone from the 12th century. You would need a great deal of expertise to write that well, and your readers would likely find it needlessly difficult. Much as with accents, generally avoid warping your character's dialogue so that they sound like stereotypes, or sprinkling in "thee," "thine," and "thou," as though to signal, "This is old timey, you know, the *past.*" Writers also tend to drop contractions in dialogue to indicate a historical setting, but in fact the contraction has been around for a long time. Old English as far back as 450 CE had some forms of contractions. The goal with historical dialogue is to capture the feel of the time period and how people would talk, without religious accuracy. One method is to have characters use small amounts of time-period-appropriate slang. Another is to use words they would have known, but with modern spelling. Use the correct lexicon. Would someone from 1920 say "phone" or "telephone," for example? If you don't know, look it up. The Google Ngram Viewer lets you search for the historical occurrence of words. The Oxford English Dictionary (full version) gives you the history of words in the English language, back to first known occurrence and usage. Read literature written during the time period you are writing in and pay attention to how people speak. Use the internet, museums, and libraries to read old letters written by ordinary people. Don't sprinkle dated slang, or historical references, in every line of dialogue. Use enough to signal period without being hokey. For example, my grandma would call someone who drank too much a "lush" rather than an "alcoholic." Additionally, don't impose contemporary norms and language onto your characters. In the 1980s, the term "African American" began to be preferred by many within the American black community to earlier terms like "Afro-American." The Black Power movement in the 1960s successfully changed the contemporary acceptable terminology from "negro" to "black."[15] Now, as of 2021, people will often use the term "person of color" instead. All of which goes to say, if you had a man of color in the 1920s refer to himself as such, or as "African American," you would be imposing contemporary language on the past.[16] Language evolves over time, and it does no one any good if you pretend that that isn't the case, and that our values and language are natural, inevitable, and have always existed. Older language can be uncomfortable, but sanitizing the past for contemporary values and beliefs is ahistorical and harmful. So, be judicious with your use of historical language in dialogue, but don't be actively a-historical either. If your characters are meant to be progressive for their time, then they should have a worldview and language that reflects what that meant in their own time and place, not ours.[17]

- *The worldview of your characters will be shaped by their time and place.* The show *Peaky Blinders* is a great example of this. The protagonist Thomas Shelby and his brothers were in the First World War, and their status as veterans of a war that killed nearly a generation of British men inflects their worldview, how people interact with them, and how they respond to men who managed to get out of serving.[18] In Silvia Moreno-Garcia's novel *Mexican Gothic*, the main character, Noemi, is a daughter of the wealthy elite in Mexico City. While she pushes against the boundaries of her class and gender in some ways, she is still a product of her time and place.[19] What counts as radical or boundary-pushing varies based upon time and culture. In the popular historical fantasy series *Outlander* by Diana Gabaldon, the transition to the past for Claire when she accidentally time travels from 1945 to 1743 is not seamless.[20] Jaime, who she marries in the past and comes to love, has beliefs about gender that Claire (and we, even more so) find abhorrent, but we aren't meant to see him as a bad man, just a product of his time and culture. He couldn't possibly have the same worldview as Claire, let alone a 21st-century reader.

- *Find that which is essentially human.* I hate the term "relatability" to the depths of my soul. If I could, I would light that term on fire and throw it off a cliff! It is so often used to justify a belief that readers can or should only care about people who believe what they believe, or who are like themselves. It represents a profound failure of imagination and empathy. Additionally, it has historically (and contemporarily) been used by dominant groups and people as a justification for failing to care about the experiences of characters from nondominant backgrounds, or to declare their experiences somehow niche or specialized, and the experience of the dominant group (straight, white, cis-gendered, male) universal.[21] So, I won't use that term here. Readers don't need to "relate" to your characters. But you do want your readers to see the humanity in your characters, to feel it thrum off of their own humanity. Fiction can help readers see the personhood of those who are radically different from themselves. People (human and nonhuman since fantasy can have nonhuman persons) still have basic things in common. People want to be able to live safely, to not be alone, to actualize their selfhood, whatever that means for them. Grief, love, and fear are universal. What a character fears will change based upon their context, but they will have fears. People have family drama, even if their families come in shapes that are different than the normative Western nuclear family. I had a professor once who said that most stories can be boiled down to: "I don't want to be alone, and mortality fucking sucks." While he was partially being facetious, I think he was also partly right. Historical fiction or historical fantasy can go awry if the characters are made too familiar or contemporary. It can also go awry if it depicts the people of the past as radically alien. The power of Hilary Mantel's *Wolf Hall* is that she takes Thomas Cromwell, and while remaining historically accurate, lets us feel his wounded human heart, traumatized by an abusive father, and his own daughter's death by the plague.[22] He is terribly different from me, a woman in the 21st century. I'm not even a parent. I can still feel his grief with him.

- *Take seriously the effects of material history on the realities of the characters.* If your story is set in a time when long-distance communication was only conducted by letter, and there is no transportation faster than a horse or horse equivalent, then a loved one moving far away is a different experience than it is for someone now. Not only might you not see your mother, sister, daughter, brother, father, etc. ever again (or rarely), communication would be sporadic and difficult. This is just one example of how you need to consider the ways material realities of the world impact the plot, and the character's emotional experiences. Marriage that took you geographically away from your family in a world with slow transportation and communication was for most young women a loss akin to death. Does the historical time period your fantasy is set in, or its analog if you are doing what Kay does and creating a looking-glass world, have contraception? If so, does it work well? Is it widely accessible? If there isn't reliable accessible contraception, women would spend most of their lives pregnant, and in near-constant danger from childbirth. They would probably also have a lot of dead children, and many children would have a dead mother. The only way, through much of history, to not have children would be to be celibate. But if a married woman had a husband who would allow her that option, how would it impact their marriage? These types of questions are important in all fiction, including secondary-world fantasy, but in historical fantasy, you have a historical starting point that helps you discern these types of constraints. Constraints of the basics—sex, death, birth, marriage, food, transportation, home, etc.—are especially important to consider as you write.

- *Style in historical fantasy is as flexible as the genre itself.* Some writers use transparent or "normal" prose. Others use lyrical or baroque prose, much more so than within epic fantasy. While historical fantasy frequently matches epic fantasy in length and complication of plot, it also comes in shorter lengths. The issue of length usually depends upon the scope of the plot, or the length of time covered within the text. Pam C. Zhang's historical fantasy *How Much of These Hills is Gold* covers two siblings over about a decade in the desert Western United States during the late-19th century, though the bulk takes place during a handful of months.[23] Because there are two focal characters, limited magic, and the scope of the novel is confined to their lives, not the fate of an entire country or world, the novel is relatively short. However, *Little Big: Or the Fairies' Parliament* by John Crowley[24] is an intergenerational novel, with a greater emphasis on magic than Zhang's, and consequently is much longer. Both, however, are prose forward. If you are writing about a time period and place that is relatively recent, or relatively well known to your audience (like Second World War-era America), you would need to do less detailed worldbuilding than you would for a historical fantasy set in, for example, 10th-century Spain.

A Note on Short Stories

Historical fantasy is common in short fiction, more common than epic fantasy. We have historical fantasy stories in our collection by Vandana Singh, Genevieve Valentine, Theodora Goss, and Ken Liu. Knowledge available to readers extrinsic to the story is part of the greater prominence. In Theodora Goss's "England Under the White Witch," it is assumed that the reader knows what the Second World War was. If the story was a secondary-world epic fantasy, Goss would have to find a way to explain what the war was about within the short story. Short historical fantasy commonly explores experimental forms. Valentine's short story in fragments of letters, and a catalog from a fictional pavilion of the Great Exhibition, is a prime example.

Historical fantasy can be powerful, fun, or just engrossing. It has so many possibilities that an entire book could be devoted to it. Take this chapter as a starting point for your investigation of this fantasy genre, as both a writer and a reader.

Discussion Questions and Writing Activities

1. Read one or more of the historical fantasy stories in our anthology. What writing choices does the writer make that seem to you to be characteristic of historical fantasy? What is the effect of setting the story in a particular time and place?

2. What is the most recent historical fantasy novel you have read? Were you aware that it was historical fantasy, or was it categorized it differently? Does the genre distinction matter?

3. What excites you about historical fantasy? What frightens you? Why?

4. What are the strengths and weaknesses of historical fantasy for social critique? Explain your answer.

5. Write a historical fantasy short story in an unusual form. Reflect on the experience. What did you learn? What was difficult about using a nontraditional form? Did the historical period as a guide make it easier or harder?

6. Pick a time and place in history that interests you. What interests you about it? Why? How much magic or fantastical elements would you add to make it historical fantasy? What purpose does the addition of the fantastic serve? How does the addition of magic impact the type of stories you can tell?

7. Go to the website *Atlas Obscura* and look up some of their entries on places or historical events/persons. Read until you find something that seems like a historical fantasy story seed. Start the story, finish it if you want. Then reflect on the process.

CHAPTER 13
WEIRD FICTION, LOVECRAFTIAN FANTASY, GOTHIC FANTASY, AND COSMIC HORROR

These overlapping genres are increasing in popularity. It encompasses huge amounts of fantasy that borders on horror fiction. At its heart is an influx of writers trying to grapple with the complicated and tainted legacy of H. P. Lovecraft. There is an entire cohort of women writers, LGBTQ+ writers, and writers of color revising and reclaiming Lovecraft and his mythos.[1] Weird fiction overlaps with Lovecraftian fantasy, though not all weird fiction is Lovecraftian. Dark fantasy and gothic fantasy also belong to this cluster of genres. All of the aforementioned fantasy genres and subgenres draw heavily upon the history of gothic fiction.

Once you try to define a fantasy genre, you realize it's a giant spiderweb of interrelated genres that can't be separated and are most usefully defined in relation to each other. In the case of weird fiction and its cousins, the image of a giant spiderweb is thematically appropriate. Gothic fantasy evolves from the gothic tradition but makes the supernatural and fantastic an intrinsic part of the story. Dark fantasy is any fantasy that puts more emphasis on the disturbing elements of the fantastic and has a more cynical or nihilistic worldview. Weird, Lovecraftian, and gothic fantasy are all forms of dark fantasy, but not all dark fantasy is one of the above. Some books, like *Mexican Gothic* by Silvia Moreno-Garcia, are arguably both gothic and weird.[2] Dark, weird, gothic, and Lovecraftian fantasy can be difficult to distinguish from some horror.

Fantasy fiction deals in wonder, but within wonder is also terror. As the word "awful" contains the idea of being full of awe (awe-full),[3] the sublime can turn into the horrific and uncanny. Even the most whimsical fantasy stories contain traces of this element. Fairy tales may mostly reward protagonists with a happy ending, but along the way there is great danger. Fairy tales include transformations into other creatures, bargains with the supernatural, and great bodily harm, from dancing in red-hot shoes to being impaled by nails in a barrel. Myths from around the world inflict fates on characters that are reminiscent of body horror. One can't read Greek mythology and come away with the impression that the gods care about mortals. Even Tolkien, who saw fantasy as an escape from the meaninglessness of the modern world, still had Shelob. Darkness and grotesquery are part of fantasy.[4]

In weird fiction and its cousins, darkness predominates. While much fantasy seeks order and meaning and ends with the world in a better place, weird fiction ends with the world worse, or the same as before. These genres tend to decenter the human to show the vast indifference of the universe. If the life of a protagonist improves, it is result of luck or suffering.

The term "weird fiction" originated in the 1930s, driven by the magazine *Weird Tales*,[5] an American fantasy and horror pulp founded by J. C. Henneberger and J. M. Lansinger. It published early work by H. P. Lovecraft, Seabury Quinn, and Clark Ashton Smith.[6] The term reappeared in the 1980s and was newly popularized in the 90s and early 2000s by writers like China Miéville and Jeff VanderMeer.

Jeff and Ann VanderMeer's influential anthology *The New Weird* described it as more of a mode than a genre, since one of its distinguishing features is a tendency toward a heterogeneity of sources and inspiration, and a deliberate turn against romanticism.[7] Miéville, in *The Routledge Companion to Science Fiction,* describes weird fiction as "usually, roughly, conceived of as a rather breathless and generically slippery macabre fiction, a dark fantastic ('horror' plus 'fantasy') often featuring nontraditional alien monsters (thus plus 'science fiction')." Traditional monsters like vampires and werewolves rarely appear in this genre (part of what distinguishes it from the gothic) and are radically altered if they do.[8]

This genre and its cousins are characterized by unease, and by a sense that there are things in the world beyond the control of humanity.

But weird fiction has some rotting tentacles in the closet. It has historically been so identified with H. P. Lovecraft that Lovecraftian fantasy, though part of the weird, is a distinct subgenre. There is a cottage industry of writers and other media producers who make texts derived from the Lovecraft mythos (most of Lovecraft is public domain). While Lovecraft's influence is undeniable (the World Fantasy Award was a bust of Lovecraft until 2015, when he was rightfully removed), so, too, is his racism and sexism irrefutable. He held outright white supremacist and anti-Semitic views, and a highly misogynistic fear of women. He wrote essays about a secret conspiracy of Jews to overthrow the government and defended the lynching of African Americans in the South in service of anti-miscegenation. Women, if present at all in his world, were cruel, stupid, shallow, or channels for eldritch entities beyond time.[9]

His fiction used imagery that evoked the Other to align those who aren't white men with entities from other dimensions that want to destroy civilization. His story "The Horror of Redhook" is a reaction to the Great Migration of African Americans northward. He saw Brooklyn as being invaded by immigrants and black Americans.

His problematic beliefs are nothing to take lightly. His imagery is startling enough that it has been profoundly influential, and unfortunately his ideas still speak to the dark heart of America, as can be seen by anti-immigrant sentiment, and the lies about the Black Lives Matter movement that have been perpetuated by American conservative politics and media.

Some writers take on the racism and sexism of Lovecraft directly, to cope with the terrible reality that an author who has influenced their chosen genre so heavily was so hateful.[10] Many have penned works that reappropriate his racist imagery to confront contemporary racism. Victor LaValle's stunning novella, *The Ballad of Black Tom,* rewrites "The Horror of Redhook" from the point of view of a young black man in early-20th-century New York whose father is murdered by police, and who takes his revenge.[11] In this important novella it is not the Old Gods who are the greatest worry of the protagonist, but white society. That a vast alien intelligence from another dimension doesn't care about you is hardly surprising—it's far worse to realize that other humans don't see you as a person. The TV show *Lovecraft Country* (based on the 2016 novel by Matt Ruff) is part of this broader effort within the fantasy writing community.[12]

Similarly, Ruthanna Emrys[13] and Cherie Priest wrote novels that confront Lovecraft's sexism. In Priest's *Maplecroft*, Lizzie Borden devoted her life to keeping humanity safe from other such interlopers, despite getting no thanks, and being treated like a monster herself.[14] Some writers, rather than revising Lovecraft, avoid Lovecraft's oeuvre, and draw inspiration from other writers associated with early weird fiction, or that predate the label, like Edgar Allan Poe, E. T. A. Hoffmann, Charlotte Perkins Gilman, or Lord Dunsany.[15] China Miéville and Jeff VanderMeer belong to this group. Other writers, like Angela Carter and Storm Constantine, have written work retroactively identified with weird fiction.[16] Miéville is best known for his Bas-Lag universe. Bas-Lag is a secondary world that eschews traditional fantasy peoples or technology and is filled with fantasy cultures and peoples of Miéville's own creation, most of who are humanoid nonhuman hybrids, like insect (khepri) or bird (garuda).[17] Hybridity is not the source of horror, it is governmental and corporate systems that exploit people, forcing body modifications, such as replacing legs with wheels. While Miéville is focused on the ways in which people are exploited by systems, Jeff VanderMeer uses the weird to show how humans exploit and harm nature.

Fantasy fiction that dances with horror is growing. *Tor.com* has an ongoing column called *Reading the Weird* in which "Ruthanna Emrys and Anne M. Pillsworth get girl cooties all over weird fiction, cosmic horror, and Lovecraftiana—"

What counts as weird fiction, gothic fiction, horror, and dark fantasy is often up for debate. The hard to contain nature of these genres is part of what makes them so interesting.

Writing the Weird

Weird Fiction Tends to be Very Language-focused

Writers who work within it frequently employ stylized language, often the baroque or the lyrical. This is partially tradition (the writers who are considered founders of these genres were maximalists) but also a matter of how one creates the desired effect of discomfort. Weird fiction is usually image- and sense-driven because the human brain responds to images and sensory language at a visceral level.

Alienation either through sensory overload, the unreliability of a narrator, or through distance that deprives the reader of the interpretative tools a narrator usually provides, while quite different techniques, accomplish similar ends. Alienation and discomfort are key moods and modes of the weird and its cousins.

Miéville's story from our anthology uses distance to create discomfort, describing the titular problem, "The Condition of New Death." The first recorded case of New Death and its discovery is described thus:

With great alarm, Mr. Morris began to walk around the body, but he stopped when, in his words, "those feet wouldn't stop pointing at me." Ms. Morris's body appeared to him to be swiveling like a needle on a compass, her feet always facing him.

He remained frozen, his wife's feet a few inches from his own shoes. He was unwilling to move and thereby provoke that smooth and perfectly silent motion. That was how the paramedics found him by his dead wife.

At one point in the highly confused moments that followed, a medic demanded that Mr. Morris be careful not to tread on his wife's hair. Which was, however, from Mr. Morris's perspective, on the other side of her body from him.

Thus the specificity of New Death began to emerge.[18]

The story is written in a pastiche of incidents, reports given by paramedics, witnesses, and scientists, among others. The lack of a standard narrator to interpret events, as well as the clinical tone, make the story feel simultaneously real and surreal.

Some writers who have latterly been identified with the weird, like Angela Carter or Storm Constantine, have phantasmagoric and lush prose, reminiscent of Edgar Allan Poe. In the short story "The Masque of the Red Death" (1847), you can see the roots of the lush and grotesque imagery of weird fiction:

> "But these other apartments were densely crowded, and in them beat feverishly the heart of life. And the revel went whirlingly on, until at length there commenced the sounding of midnight upon the clock. And then the music ceased, as I have told; and the evolutions of the waltzers were quieted; and there was an uneasy cessation of all things as before. But now there were twelve strokes to be sounded by the bell of the clock; and thus it happened, perhaps that more of thought crept, with more of time into the meditations of the thoughtful among those who revelled. And thus too, it happened, that before the last echoes of the last chime had utterly sunk into silence, there were many individuals in the crowd who had found leisure to become aware of the presence of a masked figure which had arrested the attention of no single individual before. And the rumor of this new presence having spread itself whisperingly around, there arose at length from the whole company a buzz, or murmur, of horror, and of disgust.[19]

Storm Constantine's *Wraethu* trilogy was described by Locus reviews as verging on gothic "with a decadence just short of the frenzied works of Poe."[20] Her novel's descriptions, while they use contemporary language, echo Poe in their lushness and terror.

Language that is both beautiful and grotesque usually employs complex sentence structure. Imagery that focuses on the body, the setting, and forceful sensations predominates. This kind of intensity can be used to make a range of points, to render almost anything either beautiful, terrible, or both at the same time.[21]

Experiments in Structure and Point of View are Frequent in Weird Fiction and Its Cousins

Because the goal is often to disturb the reader to make a point, weird fiction frequently incorporates experiments in form and structure.

Victor LaValle's *The Ballad of Black Tom* abandons the titular character's point of view halfway through the novella for a policeman. An unconventional choice that forces the reader to see how the policeman's perspective on Tom and the events of the narrative are radically warped by his worldview.

N. K. Jemisin's *The City We Became* begins in the point of view character to which the novel will never return, but who is central to the story all the same.[22]

Cherie Priest's *Maplecroft* is composed of documents by characters whose minds are unraveling. It is difficult to establish stability for the reader and increases unreliability.

Short stories can take the form of documents, often reports, or fragments of letters. Kelly Link's short story "Lull" from *Magic for Beginners* (one of my favorite collections) is a nesting narrative: storytellers relate tales to each other, which get incorporated into other tales. By the end it's hard to tell *story* from *reality*, or if there is even a meaningful distinction between the two.[23]

While formal experimentation is not obligatory, it is a well-utilized tool by writers of the weird and its cousins to make the reader experience discomfort.

Some Tips and Tricks

- Images that are stereotypically horrifying become invisible. A giant spider is creepy, but a giant spider covered in human baby mouths is worse. If you can make readers feel simultaneously compelled and repelled, you induce extra layers of complication to the narrative. Complications can make readers stop and think in order to understand their own reactions, which is useful when you are trying to make a point.

- When using body horror, take extra care not to turn images of people with disabilities, or people of color, into the source of the horrific. This is how writers, including Lovecraft, have pushed white supremacist ideologies, and one of the ways that writers, even accidentally, can contribute to ableist or white supremacist narratives.

- When going for phantasmagoric prose, it is okay to overwrite, and then cut back. You aren't obligated to keep every sentence; in fact you almost never will.

- Point of view is crucial in all fiction. In fiction, in which uncertainty is so central, your awareness of what your point of view character(s) knows and doesn't know is especially key. Your reader doesn't need a tidy understanding of the world. *You* should still understand how your world works, but an inability to fully encompass or rationally process the story is a big part of what makes these genre(s) run.

- If you are 100-percent chill with all your content and imagery, if none of it makes your stomach writhe, you probably aren't writing weird enough. Discomfort forces your reader to pay attention, to wrestle with your text, and if you do a good job, ask themselves *why* they are uncomfortable.

- The characteristics of the genre conducive to Lovecraft perpetuating his bigoted worldview also make it useful for talking about bigotry of all kinds, because it deals with the way that people respond to the Other. Who or what you depict as Other in the story is under your control. As Matthew Salesses says in *Craft in the Real World,* you can't control who reads your story, but you can control who you write for.[24]

- A crucial distinctions between weird fiction and other genres like epic fantasy isn't scope (*The Scar* by China Miéville is quite epic),[25] it is the orientation of the story toward the power and significance of individual characters. The individual is ultimately insignificant in the face of the raw force of the universe. That doesn't mean people don't matter or are dehumanized. People matter to each other, but not to the gods, the weather, or giant squid. Sometimes you get eaten by a squid god, and it doesn't mean anything. You were just there at the wrong time.

- As always, read widely within the genre(s) you are trying to participate in.

Discussion Questions and Writing Activities

1. Had you heard of weird fiction and its related genres? If not, what sticks out to you? If you had, how is this chapter similar and/or different from your previous understanding?

2. Why is it important to comprehend the influence of H. P. Lovecraft on weird fiction? What does it mean for a writer to be influential, yet also problematic? Why do you think LaValle and other writers like him choose to use Lovecraft's oeuvre to point out his problems?

3. Do you feel drawn to trying out weird fiction and/or its cousins? Why, or why not?

4. Do an internet search and explore some of the writers, past or present, associated with weird fiction. What are your impressions?

5. Read the Miéville story from our anthology. How does it make you feel? How would it be different if written from the point of view of a single character?

6. Write a weird story from the point of view of a narrator whose perceptions are unreliable. Afterwards, describe how and why you made the choices you did.

7. Read Edgar Allan Poe's "The Masque of the Red Death" or E. T. A. Hoffmann's "The Sandman" (in the public domain and online). Take notes about characteristics of style, etc. Then, rewrite one of these stories as a modern weird fiction tale.

8. *Weird Tales* was recently revived. Go to their website and explore. Analyze it. What types of images are presented, both visually, and in texts? How do you see it positioning itself as a publication, and in relationship to the genre?

9. Describe some disquieting images, of either a creature, or a place. How can you make it seem alien and avoid clichéd descriptions? Afterwards, analyze your descriptions. What works and what doesn't?

CHAPTER 14
CONTEMPORARY AND URBAN FANTASY

This genre is relatively young but growing. It draws primarily upon 19th-century literature, most specifically the gothic novel, detective novel, and the monsters of 19th-century literature, from Frankenstein's monster to Dracula. It also riffs on folklore and fairy tales. It contains subgenres, such as the paranormal detective novel, and the paranormal romance. In general, contemporary/urban fantasy takes place in or close to the present of the writer. It is mostly set in real places. Sometimes a real city within a real country, or an invented city in a real country such as Charles de Lint's Newford. The real world is altered to include the fantastical. Sometimes the fantasy elements are well known to the human population in the story, sometimes to a select few. Much urban fantasy and contemporary fantasy is also intrusive/invasive fantasy (where the magic intrudes into the real world, the opposite of portal fantasy). Urban fantasy is a subgenre of the broader category of contemporary fantasy, but the latter is so broad that it doesn't require much specific definitional work to understand.

The 19th-century roots of the genre are straightforward. Early detective fiction, like Sherlock Holmes, usually takes place in cities and depicts detectives encountering something seemingly inexplicable. Unlike in Doyle's stories, the supernatural isn't explained away with scientific rationalism. If *The Hound of the Baskervilles* was an urban fantasy novel, the hound might be a shapeshifter displaced by real estate development.[1] Many of the supernatural beings common to urban fantasy first rose to popularity in the 19th century.[2]

There are Broad and Narrow Definitions of Urban Fantasy

While there have nearly always been contemporary fantasy novels, urban fantasy is more recent. Urban fantasy gained its name initially because of the way such contemporary fantasy took cities as their primary setting.[3] This was worthy of note because fantasy has historically been dominated by rural or feudal preurban settings.[4] Using the urban landscape as a source of the fantastical was rare and innovative. Some people will argue for maintaining the broader definition of urban fantasy; however, I believe it has ceased to be useful because urban settings have become so common that virtually every fantasy genre now has many books that take cities as their primary location. Just as no one feels the need to specify rural fantasy as a genre because of its pervasiveness, so, too, has the city setting become ubiquitous.

Urban fantasy narrowly defined is more useful to describe a set of shared expectations. Urban fantasy is now primarily a term used to describe contemporary fantasy fiction that borrows from mystery, noir, and romance. It doesn't seem to require a major urban setting anymore, sometimes the setting is a smaller metro area, like the Tri-Cities, as in the works of Patricia Briggs. Urban fantasy in its narrower definition sometimes blurs into paranormal romance when the love story submerges the mystery, noir, or gothic elements. The two authors generally credited with the crystallization of urban fantasy as its own genre are Charles De Lint and Emma Bull. Both are part of the first wave of urban fantasy.

Charles De Lint sets many of his novels in Newford, a fictional Canadian city. He published twenty-four Newford books between 1993 and 2017. DeLint's characters are usually artists who encounter the Otherworld (a mixture of traditional magical creatures or gods, as well as endless spirit Elvises—magical beings in his world arise from human belief). Tonally, his novels focus on hope despite adversity, and the human capacity to grow. De Lint's fantasy, if published now, probably wouldn't be marketed as urban fantasy, but as contemporary or mythic fantasy. But it was crucial to popularizing fantasy set in a modern city.[5]

Emma Bull's *War for the Oaks* (1987)[6] is one of the first novels that looks like urban fantasy as we know it.[7] A rock musician named Eddi McCandry unwillingly gets pulled into a supernatural conflict between the Seelie and Un-Seelie faerie courts. At her side, first as her reluctant recruiter, then as her friend and love interest, is Phouka, a trickster faerie shapeshifter. Eddi is useful to the faerie courts because, as a human, she is considered not intrinsically on one side or another, and because her musical gifts contain magical potential.

Bull's novel originates many of the tropes that now characterize urban fantasy:

1. A female-identified protagonist (there are male protagonist urban fantasies, but they are the minority, and I have yet to encounter one with a non-binary protagonist).

2. A love story, usually between a human or partly human protagonist, and a magical being.

3. A mystery.

4. The human protagonist helpful to one or more factions of the magical world, either because of some semi-magic ability, or because of their position (a cop, a lawyer, etc.).

5. The protagonist gets drawn progressively deeper into the magical world. It creates conflicts between their "normal" life and their magical one. Sometimes the magic is known to the world at large, and sometimes it is a secret. This inflects the conflict that occurs. In Laurel K. Hamilton's *Anita Blake Vampire Hunter* books, as Anita's relationship to the vampire and other magical community grows, so, too, do the human bigots become suspicious of her. This contrasts with Karen Chance's *Cassie Palmer* books, where the magical world is hidden, and so Cassie must deal with magical conflicts while keeping nonmagical people ignorant.

When urban fantasy emphasizes the romance more than the mystery or magical elements, it becomes paranormal romance. When it *contains* romance but isn't *focused* on sex or romance, its urban fantasy.

Urban fantasy often combines a range of different magical beings into one storyworld, from vampires to faeries, shapeshifters, and others. Often the protagonist acts as a go-between for these factions. Or is part of a human organization tasked with liaising between humans and the magical world.

The model created by Emma Bull has proliferated. There are more urban fantasies that come out on a year-to-year basis than I can count. Writers have made a career out of it. Other writers who primarily write other kinds of fantasy have ventured into urban fantasy, such as Jacqueline Carey.[8] There are men who write urban fantasy, most famously Jim Butcher, but it remains a field dominated by women, and by female-identified protagonists.[9]

The field has lately become more diverse. It was predominantly white for a long time, more so than many other genres of fantasy. Writers of color are writing excellent urban fantasy books including Daniel Jose Older, Marjorie Liu, L. A. Banks, and many more.[10]

Stylistic Characteristics, Possibilities and Perils

Series Length, Episodic vs. Nonepisodic Structures

Urban fantasy, like the genres it draws upon, frequently becomes long-running series. Patricia Brigg's Mercy Thompson books are at twelve and counting. Laurel K. Hamilton has as of this moment published twenty-seven Anita Blake books. Charlaine Harris published thirteen Sookie Stackhouse novels. Others have limited their series to trilogies. C. E. Murphy's *Negotiator* trilogy follows a young woman of color in New York who works as a public defender. She becomes a lawyer for oppressed magical beings, from selkie to gargoyles. Daniel Jose Older finished his *Bone Street Rhumba* series in three books.[11]

Long-running series tend to be more episodic, so readers don't get lost if they skip a book. Not unlike the early seasons of the TV show *Grimm*[12] where each episode is a mostly self-contained supernatural mystery, so, too, do the longer-running series tend to center the plot of each book on a mystery that will resolve in a single book. The relationships between characters develop from book to book, as well as the world. Shorter series tend to follow a more traditional trilogy structure, where starting in the middle would lead to deep confusion.

If you write an episodic urban fantasy series, it's useful to find ways to insert explanations quickly and unobtrusively toward the beginning of the novel. In each Mercy Thompson book, Patricia Briggs gives Mercy a reason to think about her relationship to the local werewolf pack, as well as her own powers. Even if a reader picks up the books out of order, they'll understand the basic facts about Mercy.

Popular long-running series have the potential to keep an author employed on the same project for a long time. Publishers often appreciate the reliability of readership. However, a long-running series runs into danger when a) it becomes too repetitive, or b) it evolves into something that the majority of the original readership doesn't like. Much like a long-running TV show, at some point the writer(s) exhaust the original premise and long lines of tension. At that point, the writer(s) must either end the series or find a way to evolve. Sometimes that evolution is gradual over a few books, sometimes its abrupt, through skipping forward in time. The Anita Blake books started out as noirish mysteries with a romantic garnish. Around book ten the romantic elements increased. I stopped reading after book fifteen, even though I enjoyed the early novels—my interest was in the world and its mysteries. However, it has run to twenty-seven novels, plus comics, so there are plenty of people who weren't put off by the change. A long-running series must evolve which means the writer always runs the risks of losing some readers.

Nonepisodic urban fantasy series still usually have a mystery element, but it's not always as central, or it will stretch across multiple books, instead of resolving in one. Further, they are more often focused on a specific character arc. Change in an episodic series usually occurs slowly. Consistency is valued, readers come to a long-running series because they want more of what they had before. Like getting chocolate ice cream with different toppings. Additions that add novelty, but don't change the base.

To Trope or Not to Trope

Urban fantasy tends to use tropes more prominently than other fantasy genres, due to a variety of factors. One, it isn't usually considered a prestige genre. Which is not to say these are bad books—they are just usually marketed as and considered closer to entertainment than high art. Though this does not preclude compelling stories or great writing (even the great Octavia Butler took a swing at an urban fantasy novel with *Fledgling* because she enjoyed the early Anita Blake books so much).[13] Two, like the detective fiction from which it borrows, part of the pleasure of an urban fantasy novel is seeing familiar patterns used differently. Variations on a theme incite simultaneously the pleasures of familiarity and novelty.

The worst of urban fantasy takes the basic ingredients (kick ass heroine, romance, magic, and a murder), shakes it up a bit, and then pours it out. Easy to consume and forget.

The best of urban fantasy innovates, finds ways to comment on the formula, to question it, or to make it richer and more complex. What distinguishes the best urban fantasy from the worst is not if tropes exist or not, but if they are used in interesting and unusual ways, and the protagonist feels fully realized.

Prose and Other Stylistic Concerns

Urban fantasy is usually written in the first person. There are third-person urban fantasy novels, but first person is most common. These books succeed based upon how compelling the protagonist is, and if their voice/point of view is one that readers want to stick with. The prose in urban fantasy ranges from the invisible/utilitarian to minimalist. Minimalist prose is likely in novels that borrow from the hard-boiled detective genre.[14] I have yet to encounter an urban fantasy with baroque prose.

These novels tend to emphasize plot over prose. Consequently, the plot and the voice of the narrator are crucially important. Is the voice spastic and snarky like Karen Chance's Cassie Palmer?[15] Is the voice brooding and full of anger like Laurel K. Hamilton's Anita Blake? Or sardonic but secretly warm hearted like Daniel Jose Older's Carlos Delacruz? The voice of the protagonist influences the feel of the book. I recommend reading mystery novels to get a sense of how mystery plots work if you want to write urban fantasy. The clues to solve the mystery must be present in the story. When the protagonist solves the mystery, the reader should be able to look back and see all the pieces. A mystery that exists just because the writer withholds information the protagonist has is essentially lying to the reader.

Urban fantasies are usually shorter. They range from 190 to 350 pages. The average is in the 200s.

Because urban fantasy novels drop magic into a world that is close to the real one, the worldbuilding is different than in secondary-world or historical fantasy. The writer doesn't have to explain basic technology, the structure of the American government, or Victorian gender norms, for instance. Worldbuilding comes into play where the writer makes alterations to the real world and to distinguish the rules of their magical beings in relationship to other versions of those magical beings. If you are going to have vampires, devote time to making up specific rules for how vampire society works, what it means to be a vampire, and how they interact with humans. Jacqueline Carey, Octavia Butler, Laurel K. Hamilton, L. A. Banks, Charlaine Harris, Patricia Briggs, Karen Chance, and C. E. Murphey all write urban fantasy with vampires. None share the same rules. Variety within the pattern is key with worldbuilding as within anything else in urban fantasy.

Urban Fantasy and Social Justice

Fantasy novels often tackle issues of social justice and oppression—urban fantasy is no exception. Many of the most commercially successful series have dealt with social justice to one extent or another. Worldbuilding highlights the artificiality of social structures because writers emphasize certain aspects of society, undermining perceived inevitabilities of social relations. Urban and contemporary fantasy usually makes points about social ills by selectively altering the real world. In Charlaine Harris's Sookie Stackhouse books, the American reaction to vampires is parallel to homophobia. Bigots carry signs that say "God hates fangs" (alluding to the Westboro Baptist Church and its real-life propagation of homophobia with signs that say "God hates fags"). In the Anita Blake books, the cultural pushback to vampires becoming legal persons is a surrogate for racism, even to the extent to which supernatural beings are subject to police violence. The bloodborne disease of shapeshifting functions as an analog to the AIDS panic. In the Mercy Thompson books, the main character Mercy is Native American. She has to deal with complicated emotions regarding her heritage, especially when the fay are forced into reservations. Daniel Jose Older's urban fantasy books deal with social issues from gentrification to racial profiling, through the experiences of the supernatural community. Marjorie Liu's *Hunter Kiss* series follows Maxine Kiss, who is from a family of women who have fought to save humanity from invading demons for generations. Maxine faces racism and spends time living at the edges of society, often among the homeless.

Not all books effectively handle difficult themes. How successful Hamilton is at talking about racism depends upon who you ask. On the one hand, Hamilton definitely shows the ways in which those who are different can be marginalized by structural bigotry. On the other, her novels contain few people of color.

One common factor in most urban fantasy novels interested in social justice is that the protagonist usually occupies a liminal position within the magical world, the human world, or both. Their precarity offers a vehicle to examine the precarity of anyone who doesn't fit into the normative expectations of their society.

Last Reminders

- Urban fantasy, broadly defined, is any fantasy that takes place in a city, in any time period. In terms of marketing and publishing, it is usually more narrowly defined toward being fantasy set in roughly contemporary times with a dash of mystery and/or romance.

- Urban fantasies are mostly contemporary fantasy, but not all contemporary fantasy is urban fantasy. Contemporary fantasy is any fantasy set in the late-20th and 21st centuries, usually within the lifetime of the writer. Most contemporary fantasies are also another kind of fantasy, such as mythic, epic, or urban.

- Read widely in the genre you are trying to write in, as well as in the genres that have influenced it. This includes contemporary and classic novels. Contemporary novels ground you in how people are writing the genre now. Classic novels help you understand the source of genre traditions.

- If you want to distinguish yourself in this genre, innovate, don't just reproduce what you have read elsewhere. Also, as a reader of fantasy who enjoys urban fantasy, but is picky, if you give some attention to your prose, you will make this reader (and others of my ilk) happy.

- Narrative voice is of crucial importance.

- Plan your plot.

- Have fun! Urban fantasy is not the heaviest of fantasy genres, and that is okay!

Discussion Questions and Writing Activities

1. What was your level of familiarity with urban fantasy and contemporary fantasy before this chapter? Did this chapter's description of the genre match up with your understanding? Why, or why not?

2. If you've read an urban fantasy novel, how would you characterize the voice of the narrator and protagonist? How did that voice impact your reading experience?

What characteristics of language or affect lead to the overall feel of the voice you experienced?

3. Why do you think urban fantasy is generally considered a more commercial genre? Does the influence of romance and mystery contribute to that perception? Does the perception matter? Is it fair? Explain your answers.

4. Find a noir novel, or a hard-boiled detective novel. Raymond Chandler is a good place to start.[16] Read the first few pages and analyze the prose and voice. Then, write the first few paragraphs of a story that feels like hard-boiled or noir detective fiction, with a fantasy element. What is this experience like? What writing choices did you find yourself making?

5. Why do you think women writers have dominated this field? What are the impacts of the gender dynamics of the genre?

6. How many of the fantasy novels you've read have a mystery at their center, even ones that aren't strictly about solving the mystery? How does the presence of a mystery to drive the plot impact storytelling?

7. What is the difference between urban fantasy and paranormal romance? Why does the distinction matter? Or does it?

8. Pick a city you are familiar with and imagine how it might be impacted by the presence of the magical/supernatural. Once you come up with some basic premises for how the city could be altered by the magical and supernatural, invent a character who could sit at the crux of the magical and mundane divide. How might her position help make her a compelling character? How do the characteristics of the original city impact the story? How is using a real city different than inventing one?

9. Read "Harvest" by Rebecca Roanhorse from our anthology. How does the contemporary setting impact the storytelling? In what way does it fit or not fit within urban fantasy? How does the story depict marginalization?

CHAPTER 15
FABULISM AND MAGICAL REALISM

Introduction

These are growing and interrelated genres, though the relationship between them is complicated. Magical realism, in particular, is a frequently misused term. It was first used in the English-speaking literary world in the 1940s to refer to Latin American writers who sought to reject European social realism and revive traditions that weren't linked with their colonizers.[1] Thus, magical realism is associated with postcolonialism. Magical realism is a narrative strategy in which fantastic elements are included in a matter-of-fact manner within fiction that otherwise reads like realism. The inclusion of the fantastic elements undermines oppressive rationalism and can be used to disrupt accepted categories and normative structures. It is sometimes seen as a more inclusive form of reality; it gives equal credence to the religious worldview, and the magical worldview, not just Western scientific rationalism. The term "magical realism" was applied in the 1920s to a school of German painting, but other than the fact that both included the strange within the ordinary, they really have nothing in common, and shouldn't be conflated.

The term "magical realism" became widespread in America and other English-speaking countries with the popularization of Jorge Luis Borges, Gabriel García Márquez, and Isabel Allende. It has been extended to include other writers working in a postcolonial tradition, even those not from Latin America, such as Salman Rushdie.[2]

It is problematic to separate magical realism from its postcolonial origins. Generally, when people try, it is because they are confusing fabulism with magical realism. Further, those who are subject to anti-fantasy bias often attempt to exclude magical realism and fabulism from fantasy because they are under the mistaken impression that fantasy only takes places in secondary worlds and never contains elements of social realism. Saying magical realism/fabulism isn't fantasy also reveals an implicit assumption that fantasy is a white genre. This perspective is wrongheaded and demonstrates an ignorance of fantasy fiction.[3]

Fabulism is easy to confuse with magical realism because of stylistic similarity.[4] Fabulism, however, doesn't have a direct relationship to postcolonialism, nor does it have explicit ties to a single culture. Fabulism takes place in a world mostly recognizable to readers, but twisted slightly, the real world reflected through a glass darkly. George Saunders and Karen Russell are two writers well known for their fabulist fiction, as is Steven Millhauser. Fabulist novels are increasing in popularity and prominence. Historically, the term has mostly been applied to short fiction with fantastical elements that is heavily invested in language and striking imagery. Fabulist fiction writers move between the so called "literary" and "genre" publishing communities, getting published in both literary and genre magazines. Fabulism is further distinguished from magical realism because while it often treats the fantastical in a matter-of-fact manner, it also sometimes treats it as extraordinary, such as in Haruki Murakami's "Super Frog Saves Tokyo," in which a man dreams that a frog tells him that they have to fight a monster to stop an earthquake in Tokyo.[5] The reality or unreality of the frog is questioned once the man wakes, though the quake they mostly avert is real. Alice Hoffman is one of the most well-known America fabulists, though people often mistakenly call her work magical realism.

Occasionally the misinformed will also confuse fabulism and magical realism with contemporary fantasy. While fabulism is often contemporary fantasy, all contemporary fantasy isn't fabulism. Fabulism can draw upon myths and fairy tales, like mythic or fairy-tale fantasy, but it's not identical. The matter-of-fact treatment of magic in magical realism or fabulism is different than in secondary-world fantasy where the magical is a natural part of the world. Magical realism treats the wonderous matter-of-factly within the context of the real world, even when the magical might otherwise be considered an aberration.[6]

Stylistic Characteristics, Possibilities and Perils

Fabulism, Magical Realism, and Identity

I am going to focus on aspects of style that apply to both fabulism and magical realism. Essentially, stylistic tools that you can use to add the fantastic into the real, in a way that creates a friction between multiple realities rubbing up against each other. While there are exceptions, you will notice that most of the well-known writers of this form aren't white men. Brenda Peynado, in her essay "Is Fabulism the New Sincerity?" for *Lit Hub*, posits that fabulism and magical realism appeal to writers who have found themselves constantly gas-lit by the accepted consensus reality of the world in which they live (generally Western patriarchal capitalism). In magical realism, the way in which the fantastic is presented fights back against that gas-lighting. It is a way to unbury that which the powerful want to leave buried.[7]

In Peynado's story "Thoughts and Prayers" from her collection *The Rock Eaters*, angels sit on the roofs of houses.[8] When children are murdered in a school shooting, the presence of the angels and the ritualized shouting of "thoughts and prayers" reveals how American culture constantly works to undermine the reality of school shootings, especially when those killed are black or brown. The magical elements of Peynado's story reveal the horror of reality that people try frantically to deny.

Writers like Alice Hoffman have used fabulism to reveal how women's experiences are erased and silenced. Her famous *Practical Magic* uses magic to get at the experiences of women that are frequently treated as trivial or abject.[9] Childbirth, love, menstruation, escaping from abuse. The terrible vulnerability of girlhood is redeemed by giving girls and women power through community togetherness, and the potions they mix.

Toni Morrison, in *Beloved,* uses the haunting of the protagonist Sethe to remind the reader of the ongoing reality of the trauma of slavery on the minds and bodies of black people. By including the ghost of Sethe's dead child, the story refuses to take part in the forgetting that America tries so desperately to engage in.[10]

Emrys Donaldson's "The Albatrosses" (see our anthology) describes, in the simple yet lyrical language of a fairy tale, a cliff where young men and boys can jump into the sea and transform, sometimes into girls, and sometimes into albatrosses—as long as they survive. This gets at the trans and nonbinary experience by showing how one might jump off a cliff if by doing so one could shed a body that doesn't reflect one's true identity.[11]

In fabulism and magical realism, much like folktales and fairy tales, the ordinary world can and does have magic, and the people who it saves, or plagues, are usually the marginalized. In fairy tales it is usually women, orphans, or youngest sons. In fabulism it can be anyone who has been left out of the dominant narrative, whose experiences have been erased and effaced.

Technique and Language

Fabulism and magical realism share a series of common techniques to make the ignored unignorable, to poke holes in dominant narratives of reality. One is that some object, natural feature, place, or person becomes ungovernable, breaks the bonds of accepted reality, and forces the characters and/or reader to acknowledge something hidden.

Gabriel García Márquez's landmark novel, *One Hundred Years of Solitude,*[12] turns a town into a microcosm of the horror colonialism wrecked on Columbia. A massacre is ignored and denied (based on the Banana Massacre of 1928). The only survivor can't get anyone to believe him. In this multigenerational novel, history and time trap characters in destructive patterns. While this vast novel has many symbols used to bend reality, from colors, to creatures like ants, the town of Macondo itself is the locus of the story. In Alice Hoffman's interconnected short story collection *Blackbird House,*[13] the house grows increasingly haunted by grief and trauma, manifested in the reappearance of the color red, and a ghost blackbird.

Short stories, unlike novels or linked collections, often pick just one source of the fantastical. Aimee Bender's work is emblematic of this. Her stories frequently include women giving birth to children altered in some specific way, like keys for fingers, or an iron for a head. This is used to show how people who don't fit into what is considered "normal" can end up isolated and alone.[14] In Sequoia Nagamatsu's "Rokurokubi" (named for a demon from Japanese folklore), a man who can stretch his neck to incredible lengths uses his ability to spy on his wife.[15] This story tackles the ways in which having to hide an aspect of one's identity impedes human connection.

Within fabulism, picking the place, object, person, etc. that is the source of the fantastical allows the reader to invest the ordinary with magic and meaning beyond the surface. The breaking of reality is at once both literal and symbolic. Hoffman's turnips are simultaneously real turnips and a physical embodiment of everyone lost, buried, and forgotten.

Pick your choice of the fantastic carefully, avoid having too many. Your choice accrues significance and emotional heft with repetition and context. Once you tie turnips to grief, every instance of a turnip in the story waves its hand and says, "Hey you, pay attention! Grief is important here." It renders the ordinary extraordinary.

A second technique common to fabulism and magical realism is the use of folklore, myth, and fairy-tale patterns. Fairy-tale retellings are their own genre and aren't necessarily fabulism but fabulism and magical realism borrow from the fairy tale and folktale the flat and unquestioning way in which the magical or unreal makes itself part of the real. Further, fabulism and magical realism will often use fairy-tale logic. Things happen because they happen. Associate leaps of narrative logic, rather than straightforward causality expected in Western rationalism. The boundaries between humans, plants, animals, and objects are fuzzy and prone to violation.

A third stylistic characteristic is lyrical language. Fabulism and magical realism share an attention to language, to *how* something is written as much as *what*. A writer can make something feel strange and invested with meaning, be it a house, or a rosebush, just by how it is described. In Kelly Link's "Stone Animals," a house and the objects within it become progressively more and more haunted, but the "haunting" emanates from the objects, it's a feeling, not straightforward like a poltergeist. The magic rests, for most of the story, in how Link's characters perceive the space around them.[16]

If the language isn't lyrical, it will sometimes be written in the style that Kate Bernheimer has called the "flat" language of oral folktales.[17] This, much like the clipped minimalism of noir, is highly stylized when used for contemporary fiction, and it gives heightened significance to each word and image.

Perils and Possibilities

Fabulism and magical realism can both be used to undermine power structures and make the lived realities of the marginalized more visible. If you write fabulism or magical realism, you also have a greater likelihood of avoiding some pushback from the realist literary establishment, while still having credentials within the fantasy writing community. But you are also in a boundary zone, neither this nor that, which has its own dangers.

Avoid calling your work magical realism if you are a white writer. Using the term "fabulism," which doesn't have specific cultural associations, will save you pain and bypass the ongoing argument about whether anything that isn't postcolonial in orientation can be magical realism. I am on the side that it can't and find the other side ahistorical. Further, fabulism, while it can be used for liberatory purposes, can also simply be used to create wonder.

Fabulism can be set in any time period. But, because of its tendency toward fairy-tale logic, it distinguishes itself from other types of fantasy, in that the magical elements aren't systematized or explained.[18] When done well, it feels beautiful, meaningful, and *right* in a way that transcends logic or description. But be careful to at least make it follow the internal logic of the story, don't just fling in strangeness to no purpose. Fabulism done poorly is unsystematic magic devoid of meaning, which can make it feel like nothing more than sloppy worldbuilding. This is particularly a problem in contemporary fantasy that tries to borrow the techniques of fabulism without the emotional heft or overall ethos.

Fabulism and magical realism are growing in popularity and in artistic and literary respect. Done well, it's chock full of beautiful language, stunning images, and well-developed characters.

A few noteworthy authors:

Kelly Link, Carmen Maria Machado, Gabriel García Márquez, Toni Morrison, Sequoia Nagamatsu, Haruki Murakami, Isabel Allende, Laura Esquivel, Brenda Peynado, Aimee Bender, Karen Russell, George Saunders, C. Pam Zhang, Salman Rushdie, and Louise Erdrich.

Discussion Questions and Writing Activities

1. Read "Meet Me in Iram" by Sofia Samatar in our anthology. Then, google "Iram" and see what you discover. Is this story fabulism, magical realism, or something else? What leads you to your conclusions?

2. Compare the language of Sofia Samatar's "Meet Me in Iram" and Emrys Donaldson's "The Albatrosses." What differences do you notice between the lyricism of Samatar and the minimalism of Donaldson? How do these very different stylistic choices change the way the magical elements of the story function?

3. Imagine a story from your family history, or your hometown. Imagine all the domestic or social traumas and dramas it might contain if it were a realistic story. Then, think of what emotional or social tensions that you might want to amplify. After you pick one or two of these, brainstorm objects, places, or animals that might be rendered magical in order turn up the volume of those ideas or moments you want to have heightened significance. Try to write the story!

4. How did this chapter impact your understanding of fabulism and magical realism? Did it change the way you'd heard these genres discussed previously?

5. What's the most important thing to understand about the connection between magical realism and postcolonialism? Explain your answer.

6. Google some of the writers discussed in this chapter. Pick one or two whose works you'd like to read, and then pick a book or story from that writer to read. Consider sharing with the class after you read it.

CHAPTER 16
MYTHIC, FAIRY-TALE, FOLKLORIC, AND FAIRY FANTASY

A widely popular set of interconnected genres and subgenres of fantasy built from folktales, fairy tales, and mythology. These interlinked genres are often combined with others, such as epic, urban, or gaslamp fantasy. Retelling old stories to fit one's own ideas is an ancient human habit. For example, Apuleius' "Cupid and Psyche" is often considered the first Beauty and the Beast story.[1] Madame D'Aulnoy riffed on it in the 17th century with "The Green Serpent" (which she used to critique forced marriage and the tyranny of beauty standards),[2] and again later, by Marie Beaumont, who changed the tale to reflect her idea of proper feminine behavior.

Writers in these genres sometimes retell specific old stories, from Greek mythology to fairy tales, or borrow from folk traditions from around the world (from Irish mythology and the *sidhe,* to Christian mythology, or pre-Columbian North American civilizations and belief systems) to create wholly new tales. Such fantasies can be set in the past or present, in the real world or an invented one.

A quick note on definitions. The term "myth" is fraught because it is often applied by Western people to stories from any religious tradition outside of Christianity. Myth is thus used to describe stories from dead religions, or religions that one doesn't ascribe to. This is a bit problematic. Yet saying "religious stories," or some other combination of words, confuses people. Consequently, in terms of this chapter, when I use the word "myth," or "mythic fantasy," I include *all* stories based upon religious tradition, including stories that draw upon the Judeo-Christian Islamic tradition. A folktale is any story traditionally told orally by ordinary people, often containing unusual, magical, or miraculous events. The literary versions are called fairy tales.

Direct retellings of old stories use global oral traditions. Folktales, fairy tales, and mythologies aren't owned by particular individuals and so will appear in different times and places in different guises. Because stories from oral and religious traditions predate widespread literacy, the knowledge we have of these stories is complicated. Writers frequently riff off the first version they encountered, rather than the "original" version. Often, it's not even possible to determine which version *is* the original. Usually all that can be said is that a particular version is the first written version, to the best of our knowledge.[3] Many oral traditions were first encountered by Western cultures in versions written by other Westerners, and so the older stories in their original languages have been displaced or lost. Often, older versions aren't available in English. Most early collections of folktales available in English come from 19th-century collectors. In the case of the Grimm brothers, the original versions of the German folktales they collected in 1812 weren't translated into English until 2016. Previously, English speakers only had access to the later editions. Changes occurred in each edition; the tales were progressively sanitized and Christianized. Even the first edition, made as the Grimm brothers transcribed, can't be said to be the "real" or "original" versions of the ancient tales they collected.[4] To complicate the notion of source material even further, many collections of oral tales from non-Western cultures available to us are tainted by colonialism; stories of colonized peoples written down by colonizers. Even if the writers intended to capture the stories accurately, human bias means their own worldview would influence the process. Translation can't help but impact meaning. Worse, sometimes the Europeans collecting folktales around the world did so condescendingly.

The collection of tales commonly called *The Arabian Nights* or *Tales of a Thousand and One Nights* is a key example of the complications of cross-cultural folktale collection. It was translated into French in 1706 by Antoine Galland from partial manuscripts and conversations with a Syrian writer living in Paris named Hanna Diyab. It was translated into English anonymously shortly after. It didn't pervade the consciousness of the English-speaking world until Sir Richard Francis Burton's 1885 translation. Burton is an example of the paradox of 19th-century translation. In some respects, he was an excellent translator, drawing upon thirty years of research. He wrote and spoke twenty-nine European, Asian, and African languages. He was openly critical of British colonial policy and found much to admire in many non-Western cultures. Yet, as an explorer and employee of the East Indian Company, he engaged in flagrantly disrespectful actions, such as sneaking into Mecca. So, while his translation was probably the best that could be hoped for at the time, it is also deeply embedded in his white, male, British perspective.[5]

Written versions of folk narratives predate the fantasy genre, and continue unabated, from novels and stories marketed as fantasy, to those published as mainstream literary fiction (still fantasy). I could write an entire book about feminist and queered retellings of *The Odyssey* and *The Iliad*, from Pat Barker's *The Silence of the Girls*, Maya Deane's *Wrath Goddess Sing*, to Madeline Miller's *Song of Achilles*.[6] The same goes for fairy tales, from Angela Carter's *The Bloody Chamber* and Emma Donoghue's *Kissing the Witch*, to selections from Ken Liu's *The Paper Menagerie*.[7] Terri Windling's fairy-tale anthologies, the literary journal *The Fairy Tale Review*, and the web magazine *Corvid Queen* are devoted to retellings and original fairy tales/myths. Novel retellings range from Ellen Kushner's award-winning *Thomas the Rhymer* to Kat Howard's *Roses and Rot*, or Helen Oyeyemi's *Boy, Snow, Bird*.[8]

Writers also remix folk traditions into new stories, like S. L. Huang's *Burning Roses*, Victor LaValle's *The Changeling*, Silvia Moreno-Garcia's *Gods of Jade and Shadow*, Nnedi Okorafor's *Akata Witch*, and Rebecca Roanhorse's *Trail of Lightening*.[9] Writers use what Marina Warner refers to as the fairy-tale grammar to create original tales.[10] The narrative grammar of fairy tales includes motifs like the transformation of a human into an animal, apples, the color red, three wishes ... the list goes on. Not unlike the famous definition of pornography given by Supreme Court Justice Stewart ("I know it when I see it"), when you see a fairy tale, you know!

Fairy fantasy is similar to mythic fantasy, but also distinct. Fairy fantasy uses the fairy folk, the fay, faeries, fae, sidhe, or the Good Neighbors (they have many names) as the source of magic. Often the fairy folk derive from the sidhe, mixed with other European fay. More non-Western fay beings have begun to appear. The main difference between fairy fantasy and mythic/folkloric fantasy is that usually the basic idea for the fay beings influences the story, not a particular tale. Folklore supplies seeds: the magic system and culture that grows from those seeds differs so significantly that it can't be seen as a retelling. One commonality in these novels is a pushback against the idea of fairies as small twee beings. These stories lean into the strangeness of the fay, their alienness, their ability to be both beautiful and cruel.[11] Important novels include Zen Cho's *Sorcerer to the Crown*, Jeannette Ng's *Under the Pendulum Sun*, Marie Brennan's *Midnight Never Come*, Keith Donoghue's *The Stolen Child*, Hope Mirlees's *Lud-In-The-Mist*, Lord Dunsany's *The King of Elfland's Daughter*, Daniel Heath Justice's *The Way of Thorn and Thunder*, and Garth Stein's *Raven Stole the Moon*.[12]

The fairy folk are commonly included in many other kinds of fantasy from urban to secondary-world fantasy.

It's difficult to separate folkloric, fairy-tale, fairy, and mythic fantasy since the gods and magic beings of the universe hop back and forth between narratives and story types. They all pull from an exceptionally long tradition of oral stories to one extent or another. They are, especially retellings, published in both mainstream and genre venues.

Stylistic Characteristics, Possibilities and Perils

You Can Do Anything. . .Carefully

This complicated and interconnected series of genres is delightfully fertile, but consequently difficult to fully encompass. Humans are a storytelling animal. As Marina Warner aptly describes in her book *Once Upon a Time: A Brief History of Fairy Tale*, humans will tell stories to anyone who listens—stories don't respect borders. Stories from oral traditions bounce from mouth to ear, hand to page, and back again. Thus, you can find Cinderella-like narratives from Germany to China.

Similarly, humans explain their world through storytelling. Scholars have long noted how many religious systems have stories about a giant flood, for example.

Certain stories are mimetic because they resonate with basics of human experience. Who will I marry? What happens when my parents die? When I leave home? Many folktales cater to wish fulfillment. The powerless youngest son or abandoned daughter becomes royalty. There is a reason that comics have included so many gods from various religious traditions as superheroes. What is the difference, really, between Thor and a superhero?

As a result of this aura of universality, it can feel as though these stories belong to all of us. In a way they do, and in a way they don't. No one holds a copyright on stories from oral tradition. They travel around and change over time. There isn't a single "true" version, so writing your own is a way of expressing your appreciation of, rage at, or obsession with a particular tale or character. Stories live when told and die when untold. But, writing a story that uses traditions of disempowered people, when you are someone from an empowered group, can go *very* wrong. Refer to our chapter on worldbuilding and writing the Other. Don't be an invader or tourist, be a guest. Do your research and be aware of your biases.

Writers read between the lines and rewrite tales for their own purposes. Folk traditions and the characters and beings that populate them don't have just one meaning, but many, and are constantly being retold, reappropriated, and reinterpreted. This can happen in wonderful and negative ways. You can retell a myth to highlight gender inequity or to propagate hate. Such as what the Nazis did with some of the Grimm brothers' stories (particularly the tales focused on young men like "The Story of the Youth Who Went Forth to Learn What Fear Was"). They made comic folktales about adventure into white supremacist propaganda films for the Hitler Youth.[13] There is nothing intrinsically white supremacist about those stories, but the wonder and terror of folktales that comprise their bare bones can be covered with almost any flesh, and be recognizable, yet deeply altered. You can write a feminist version of the story or an anti-racist version, but you can also purposefully or accidentally take a folktale and make it racist.

As a result of this propensity for folk narratives to shift based upon who tells them, when doing research, take care to read more than one version of a story, and be aware of potential biases within your source material to avoid accidentally passing on problematic tropes or images. Cross-reference and find not only outsider versions of stories, but insider versions. Translators and transcribers aren't neutral parties any more than other storytellers.

Another example of this can be found in depictions of goblins. "Goblin" is a generic term for a tiny fay being, usually prone to mischief, that appears across many European folk traditions, from English, to Scots, French, German, and Russian. Each has several different versions of goblins. Lately, there have been people who have argued that goblins are inherently anti-Semitic. This perspective has largely evolved from a conversation on social media about the *Harry Potter* films, and the way they depict goblins as hook-nosed and obsessed with gold. This particular depiction does indeed smack of anti-Semitism. However, what this ahistorical conversation on social media misses is that the film's depiction of goblins isn't representative. In fact, Hebrew folklore has a tradition of telling stories using goblins as the troublesome Other. A famous example: "Hershel and the Hannukah Goblins."[14] Attempting to declare one version of a piece of folklore definitive ignores the way folklore actually works. Be wary of any simple interpretations of a character, story, or being from folklore. There isn't a single version, but many versions told many different ways.

In sum, when writing your own story employing preexisting traditions, do your research purposefully and with awareness to your biases and the biases of the version that you read. Find joy in the nearly endless sources of material. Even if you focused on one story or tradition for the rest of your life, you wouldn't run out of versions to read or ways to reshape the story.

Common Techniques and Stylistic Choices

When you retell a well-known story, you are intrinsically telling it in relationship to and against the versions that your readers already know. The likelihood of you writing a Beauty and the Beast story and your reader not having any experience with the tale is slim. When

Emma Donoghue retells Cinderella in "Tale of the Shoe," and Cinderella runs off with the fairy godmother, the reader will likely realize what Donoghue is doing because they know what normally happens. The lesbian retelling becomes a statement about the heteronormativity of the most common versions of the story. A retelling of a well-known story is intrinsically metafictional because of the extrinsic knowledge the writer and reader bring to the tale. When Helen Oyeyemi retells Snow White in *Boy, Snow, Bird*, and uses the story to talk about racism and colorism, using Snow White adds to the social critique because of the traditional fixation on the color of Snow White's skin. If a reader with no knowledge of Snow White comes to the retelling, they will miss out on the metafiction. Additionally, not all readers will have the same version of the story in their minds, even if they know the basic tale. Many American readers will have Disney versions as their first or primary version of a tale, even if the writer is writing in conversation with an older version.[15]

In addition to implicit metafiction, many retellings are explicitly metafictional. They draw attention to their fictive quality in the prose itself. If any writer begins a story with "Once upon a time," they are saying "Don't fall into the fictional dream, think about the story as a story." Many retellings go even further. Margaret Atwood's novella *The Penelopiad* has Penelope's maids (who are murdered by Odysseus for sleeping with his enemies) acting as a Greek chorus between chapters.[16] They comment on the story using scholarly language, discussing story tropes, feminism, etc. Jesse Ulmer's flash fiction story "Red" retells Little Red Riding Hood in second person, using archetypal images associated with the tale, like wolves, blood, baskets, and the forest.[17] The language is fragmented, and image-focused, like a poem. It calls attention to its status as a tale constantly reinterpreted.

Allusion and explicit metafiction are rampant in retellings, they are necessary to it. The pleasure given with a retelling is that of both recognition and novelty. Patterns met and subverted.

This is still true of fairy fantasy, or novels that use myths without retelling specific ones, like Neil Gaiman and Terry Pratchett's *Good Omens*. It uses Christian mythology about angels and demons to tell a story of the apocalypse averted. Much of the humor of the novel depends upon the idea that an angel and a demon might, over time, become friends and decide they like Earth better than Heaven or Hell. The fact that this isn't how Christian culture conceptualizes angels or demons is a big part of the joke.[18]

Rebecca Roanhorse's postapocalyptic urban fantasy novel, *Trail of Lightening*, draws upon the beliefs of the Navajo Nation. Coyote and other important figures show up, but she modifies the existing belief system to tell a tale about new characters in a post-climate-disaster world. She doesn't expect the reader to share her in-depth knowledge of traditional Navajo belief systems, so she builds in explanations. Most Americans are not going to be as familiar with indigenous stories as they are with European folktales, because of our history of indigenous genocide and erasure. Her tale is still metafictional and intertextual but doesn't rest upon metafictionality as its primary device in the way of *Good Omens* or Jessie Ulmer's "Red." Jessie Ulmer's story is experimental and written for a specialized literary magazine. Roanhorse's novel and Gaiman's are written for larger mass market audiences, and so are written differently. This doesn't mean any of these novels or stories are better or worse; they are written differently because of dissimilar assumed audiences.

Roanhorse's "Harvest," because it is a short story, does much less explaining than her novel. It doesn't explain the place of deer women within indigenous folk traditions—if you don't know how those stories normally go, you won't understand that the revenge fantasy is in direct conversation with the violence perpetrated upon deer women in most narratives.

Mythic, folkloric, fairy-tale, and fairy fantasy run the gamut in prose style. They are written in invisible or "normal" prose, flat and minimalistic prose, or elaborate baroque prose. Generally, the more metafictional or experimental the writer intends to be, the more likely the narrative will be in lyrical or baroque prose. If written in "normal" prose, they stories are often more focused on plot. Either extreme of the spectrum, or anywhere in between, is possible. Retellings tend toward the lyrical or baroque, but fantasy that remixes without retelling is more likely to be plot-focused. This may be attributable to how the reader can be assumed to have the basic plot architecture of say, Cinderella, in their minds already, and so the writer can play with language more without causing confusion.

Discussion Questions and Writing Activities

1. What is the first fairy tale you encountered? What sticks in your mind about this story and why?

2. Fairy tales aren't originally for children, it was really only in the late-19th and 20th centuries that people began to conceptualize them as children's stories. What does the resulting sanitization do to the stories? Why do you think so many writers work to undo that sanitization?

3. Have you ever read mythic fantasy, fairy fantasy, or fairy-tale retellings? How does this chapter add to or change your understanding?

4. Why does this chapter put so much emphasis on doing research, and being aware of your biases, and the biases of sources? How do you know when you have done enough research? Is it different if you are retelling a story that is from your own culture? Explain your answers.

5. What images, objects, characters, or events make up the grammar of a fairy tale? What signals to you that you are reading a fairy tale? How can you use it to your advantage as a writer?

6. Write an original fairy tale using the grammar of fairy tales.

7. Write a myth or fairy-tale retelling, but radically change it to make a point.

8. Read one of the anthology stories referenced in this chapter. Make a list of writing tools you can gain from it, and what genre or genres it seems to fit within.

9. Do an internet search of a piece of folklore, from a particular story to a creature type, and follow the rabbit trail. Keep a research log. What do you notice about the permutations of the story or creature? How could you use it for a short story?

CHAPTER 17
HYBRID FANTASY

A great deal of fantasy fuses multiple genres to create something surprising or new. Hybrid fantasy is a way for fantasy writers to both subvert and employ traditions of their chosen genre(s), which can act as a commentary on the genre(s) and their thematic preoccupations.

Because the fantastic narrative predates written literature itself, arguably all fantasy is hybridized. It blends ideas, images, creatures, and impulses from oral culture with literary culture. Perhaps because of this transformation at the heart of fantasy fiction, fantasy writers hybridize with abandon.

Many of the genres covered earlier in this book are, at their roots, hybrid fantasy. From the fantasy of manners (the novel of manners plus fantasy) to historical fantasy (historical fiction plus fantasy), mythic fantasy (myths plus the modern fantasy novel), dark fantasy (horror plus fantasy), and so on. There are more examples, but these hybrids have become so common that they have developed their own mores and patterns and preoccupations within themselves. So, for the purposes of this chapter, I will primarily be thinking about unexpected hybrids, or hybrids that remain noticeable and/or contested in some way.

Fantasy and Science Fiction

I'm a member of an online group of fantasy and science fiction writers. It encompasses experienced writers to aspiring writers. I find it surprising is how often someone asks some version of this question:

"I'm thinking of combining some elements of science fiction and fantasy, is that okay, has anyone done it before, will it make people mad?"

I find this question surprising because combining fantasy and science fiction has a long and honorable tradition.

In the early-20th century, writers began writing *planetary romance* novels.[1] These novels were stories set on alien planets, but the exact nature of the alien planet was unimportant. The alien planet was essentially an excuse to make up a culture and have characters swashbuckle around. It was in the tradition of the Romance, i.e., a story focused on large-scale sweeping events with a heroic central character, as well as intense feeling. Think adventure stories of chases, escapes, and quests. The planet is usually technologically primitive. Sometimes people get to and from planets (if they travel between planets at all) through nontechnological means, like magic carpets, or psychic powers. This genre is a fusion of science fiction with sword and sorcery fantasy. Marion

Zimmer Bradley's *Darkover* books,[2] as well as some of Frank Herbert's works, would be considered planetary romance.[3] Many early examples of science fiction in the anthology *The Future is Female!* edited by Lisa Yaszek are planetary romance.[4]

Planetary romance is similar to space fantasy/science fantasy (used interchangeably). Oftentimes science space fantasy is marketed as just one or the other, for the sake of ease. Sharon Shinn's *Archangel* novels are marketed as fantasy despite being science fantasy.[5] They center love stories, are set on a planet called Samaria, a planet with primitive technology, except for a few leftovers that have been integrated into their religious system, like audio recorders that contain recordings of hymns. They have legends that their deity brought them to Samaria. Their oracles use a device that the reader would recognize as a computer. The angels sing to their god, medicine rains from the sky, or a weather pattern changes, depending upon the song. As the story goes on, you learn that their civilization comes from a group of humans who left Earth with the intention of returning to a primitive level of technology, but they wanted to keep antibiotics and a few other things, so they left their highly sophisticated ship up in space. They genetically modified a few people to have wings and voices that could carry to the ship in the upper atmosphere and allow them to ask it to perform actions.

Sheri S. Tepper's ecofeminist science fantasy novels are less likely to center a love story, but they often take place on planets that humans colonized and forgot their technology. Or on planet where magic and futuristic technology coexist. For example: *Singer from the Sea.*[6]

Anne McCaffrey's *Pern* universe is a famous science fantasy series. Humans travel to another planet, and create a civilization based upon psychic bonds with dragons.[7]

Many argue that *Star Wars* should be considered space fantasy. The technology in *Star Wars* doesn't even attempt to base itself on real science, and the Jedi are essentially magic users. In *A New Hope*, Luke Skywalker even calls Obi Wan a wizard. In the prequels, George Lucas tried to retroactively add a fake science skin over the source of the Jedi's powers. Overall fan disdain toward the idea of midichlorians shows that folks know the truth—it's magic.

Tamsyn Muir's debut novel, *Gideon the Ninth*, is also arguably a space fantasy. It takes place in a culture with spaceships, and on two different planets. They have advanced technology, but the story is centered on necromancy.[8]

On the flip side, there are novels that turn magic into a science—fantasy with a scientific edge.

Fantasy and science fiction is a sliding scale, with pure fantasy on one end, "hard" science fiction on the other, and a whole lot in between.

Tips for Writing Fantasy and Science Fiction Hybrids

- Be deliberate about where on the sliding scale you fall. Use the elements of technology and magic purposefully.

If you were Sharon Shinn planning the Samaria books, you would have had to ask yourself: what do I gain as a writer by having humans go to another planet and deliberately forget their technology to build a pseudo-Christian culture centered around genetically modified humans? The answer: the ability to make points about the social construction of religion and the role of belief. A secondary-world fantasy universe where the angels are magic, and they really pray to a deity when they sing, would entirely change the meaning of the story.

Additionally, what counts as magic or science is partially in the eye of the beholder. Arthur C. Clarke famously said, "Any sufficiently advanced technology is indistinguishable from magic."

- Combining science and magic lends itself to questions about epistemology and worldview.

'Worldview" is a philosophical term that refers to the comprehensive orientation of an individual and/or society toward the world. Their beliefs about ethics, about identity, about human nature, etc. In essence, it means the cluster of beliefs that determine how cultures and individuals interpret and respond to the world.

Epistemology is a branch of philosophy that studies knowledge. It asks, how do we know what we know? Human ways of knowing are often divided into *a priori* (knowledge held independent of experience, gained through reason, authority, or intuition) and *a posteriori* (gained through experience, usually empiricism).

In many science fantasy novels, there is tension between knowledge gained through intuition and tradition, and knowledge gained through scientific experimentation. How one believes that one gains legitimate knowledge shapes and is shaped by worldview.

Charlie Jane Anders's *All the Birds in the Sky* includes witches *and* super-scientists, forcing the reader to reconcile two very different ways of knowing.[9]

This tension is at the heart of a lot of contemporary sociopolitical debates. Climate change denial in large part comes from a refusal to recognize the legitimacy of knowledge gained through scientific observation and an insistence that knowledge gained intuitively or given to them by a figure whose authority they recognize is superior to scientific knowledge. This is a question of worldview and epistemology, in which different cohorts of humans don't recognize or accept the legitimacy of each other's ways of knowing. It's hard to persuade someone with science if that person doesn't accept the validity of science as a way of knowing.

Stories that combine science and fantasy grapple with different ways of knowing through characters. Many ecofeminist stories try to resolve the conflict, showing science as a source of both solutions and danger (through destruction of the natural world). Tepper's stories are often centered on women who, through intuition and a magical connection to the land, pull together faith and reason to solve social and environmental problems. Ursula K. Le Guin's novels frequently wrestle with similar tensions, showing through characters the push and pull of different ways of knowing.

So, when writing these kinds of works, be conscious of the epistemology and worldviews of your characters and cultures. This is an issue of worldbuilding and point of view, since your main character's orientation toward the world should be part of how they act, react, and think.

It can be dangerously easy to have your characters monologue about their belief systems. Resist this urge. Most people don't spend a lot of time consciously thinking about their worldviews or explaining them. People hold worldviews so deeply that they see their own perspective as natural and right, and conversely, everyone else's behavior/worldview inexplicable and wrong.

Some Unusual Hybrids

Science fiction plus fantasy may be the most common example of hybrid fantasy, but there are nearly endless possibilities. Here are a few recent examples to kickstart your ideas:

- *Utopia Avenue* by David Mitchell[10]

Mitchell combines the 20th-century period piece, the band novel (the rise of a hippie rock group), and fantasy. Reality gradually gets bendy. One character hears voices. Other people hop from body to body, mind to mind, trying to live forever.

- *Boneshaker* by Cherie Priest[11]

  Priest blends steampunk, the western, a mad scientist, and zombies.

- *Kafka on the Shore* by Haruki Murakami[12]

This novel combines a coming-of-age story with ghosts, talking cats, and interdimensional communication. The level of hybridity here makes it hard to untangle one thread from another.

- *A Brief History of the Dead* by Kevin Brockheimer[13]

  Brockheimer's novel goes back and forth between the world as we know it, in the grips of a scientifically caused apocalypse, and the afterlife, where people are slowly disappearing.

- *Jade City* by Fonda Lee[14]

The author has described this innovative novel as *The Godfather* meets wuxia fantasy (like *Crouching Tiger Hidden Dragon*)[15] and kung-fu movies.

- *The Lies of Locke Lamora* by Scott Lynch[16]

A secondary-world fantasy inspired by Renaissance Italy that fuses *Oliver Twist*, a coming-of-age tale, and a heist narrative.

- *The Girl in Red* by Christina Henry[17]

A loose fairy-tale retelling in a postapocalyptic setting.

- *Appleseed* by Matt Bell[18]

A novel that combines historical fiction, myth, science fiction, postapocalyptic fiction, and ecofiction to irreducibly powerful effect. Following Johnny Appleseed as a faun, throughout spacetime.

Some Final Thoughts on Hybrid Fantasy and Craft

In his substack, *CounterCraft* author Lincoln Michel wrote about genre after the release of his novel, *The Body Scout*, in 2021. He writes about the power of genre to be generative, a source of both inspiration and productive restraint. He describes his root inspiration for his novel that he wrote on the very top of the first draft was: "a science fiction body horror baseball novel noir."[19] Those genres were the conversations and traditions he wanted to take part in. As in the artistic movement Oulipo (started in 1960s France), by giving yourself a guideline, you force yourself to make decisions that you might not otherwise. A productive constraint makes the writer innovate by narrowing options. Michel said making these genres feel natural together helped him revise toward a thematically dense and structurally interesting book.

The way Michel describes his process is a good way to think about hybridity. Hybrid fantasy at its best is highly generative, pushing writers to find new ways of storytelling. The act of trying to resolve tensions between genres, and the worldviews embedded within, can create thematic layers through ideological friction.

I encourage you to play with hybridizing genres. It's not necessary to write a hybrid story novel to write interesting and innovative fiction. But the potentiality of hybrid fantasy is a good reminder that genres aren't rules but rather patterns that can be used and broken. Hybrid fantasy highlights that fantasy fiction is a chimera genre made of many different beasts.

Discussion Questions and Writing Activities

1. Have you read any hybrid fantasy stories recently? If so, hybrids of what? What opportunities were created for the writer by combining genres?

2. When this chapter described *Star Wars* as a form of space fantasy, did you find yourself rejecting the idea, or did it resonate with you? Why?

3. What do worldview and epistemology have to do with hybrid fantasy? Explain.

4. What worldviews or epistemologies are implicit in fantasy you've read? How do you know?

5. Try combining two more genres in a short story. Some prompts to get you started:

   - Put Cinderella into space.
   - Combine a romantic comedy with orcs or some other not traditionally romantic or attractive fantasy being. What tensions or possibilities does this create?

- Combine sword and sorcery fantasy with a reality TV contest show. What types of contests would a sword and sorcery universe have? What can it demonstrate about their world?
- Sprinkle a pinch of academic mystery with body horror.
- Retell a Shakespeare play with dragons.
- What if a super-scientist fell in love with a faerie, but she doesn't believe faeries exist?

6. What intrigues you about hybrid fantasy? What can go wrong combining science fiction and fantasy? Are you excited or nervous to try it?

7. What are the implications of the idea that all fantasy is hybridized to some extent?

CONCLUSION

Thank you for reading my book about fantasy fiction, its history, its present, and how to write it. I love fantasy fiction and have spent most of my life trying to bring it into academia. This book represents my research into genre fiction, my experiences as an educator, my experience as a writer, and a lifelong obsession with promoting the value of fantasy fiction, celebrating its glorious diversity and strangeness. A book this size can't be fully comprehensive, even if I could encompass all the knowledge in the universe. Since I'm not a cosmic super-being, I can't even come close. Fantasy is always evolving and shapeshifting, to its great glory. The website to go with this book will periodically contain updated information, as well as a range of ancillary elements for the book, useful for students and teachers, from information about publishing, to book lists, activities, and sample syllabi. An anthology of short fiction is included in this book. If we ever meet each other, I hope to share a long and interesting conversation with you about the fantasy that you love and write.

See companion website for ancillary materials, including the below appendices: https://www.bloomsburyonlineresources.com/fantasy-fiction

Appendix A: Fantasy Fiction Outside the Classroom: Writing, Publishing, and Activism

This appendix offers students and teachers advice on writing and publishing fantasy, from different sizes/varieties of magazines and presses, as well as a discussion on the role of activism in the fantasy writing community.

Appendix B: Teaching and Learning Materials

Appendix B contains resources to supplement teaching and learning. Also activities and lesson plans to facilitate effective fantasy writing, sample syllabi, suggestions for using the book, and for further reading on the history and craft of fantasy fiction.

ANTHOLOGY

C. S. E. Cooney "Martyr's Gem" from *Bone Swans* (Mythic Delirium Books)

Biography (from her website and other online sources)

C. S. E. Cooney is a fiction writer, poet, and performer, who grew up in Arizona, but now lives and writes in Queens. She holds a degree in creative writing and theater from Columbia College. Cooney is the author of the World Fantasy Award Winning *Bone Swans: Stories* (Mythic Delirium, 2015), an audiobook narrator, and a singer/songwriter. In 2022, her novel *Saint Death's Daughter* debuted with Solaris, as well as her collection *Dark Breakers* (all stories taking place in the world of *Desdemona and the Deep*, published by Tor.com in 2019), forthcoming from Mythic Delirium. *The Twice-Drowned Saint* appears in Mythic Delirium's *A Sinister Quartet*, which made the 2020 Locus Recommended Reading List for Best Anthology. Her 2021 short work includes stories in *Uncanny Magazine* and *Mermaids Monthly*, both inspired by story prompts from *Negocios Infernales*, a TTRPG designed by Cooney and her husband Carlos Hernandez, forthcoming from Outland Entertainment. Find her online at csecooney.com, @ csecooney on Twitter and IG, and facebook.com/cscooney.

Literary Introduction

C. S. E. Cooney's short story "Martyr's Gem" is fascinating. It is a secondary-world feminist romantic fantasy, yet also postapocalyptic. It inverts gender norms to ask productive questions about marriage, love, and the way we organize our social relationships. "Martyr's Gem" is part of a long tradition of romantic fantasy, and fantasy that inverts and rearranges social relationships to highlight the arbitrariness of contemporary norms. Ursula K. Le Guin's short story "The Matter of Seggri" and Sheri S. Tepper's novel *The Gate to Women's Country* could be seen as literary ancestors of this tradition.

Martyr's Gem

Of the woman he was to wed on the morrow, Shursta Sarth knew little. He knew she hailed from Droon. He knew her name was Hyrryai.

"...Which means, The Gleaming One," his sister piped in, the evening before he left their village. She was crocheting by the fire and he was staring into it.

Lifting his chin from his hand, Shursta grinned at her. "Ayup? And where'd you light upon that lore, Nugget?"

Sharrar kicked him on the ankle for using the loathed nickname. "I work with the grayheads. They remember everything."

"Except how to chew their food."

"What they've lost in teeth, they've gained in wisdom," she announced with some pomposity. "Besides, that's what they have *me* for." Her smile went wry at one corner, but was no less proud for that. "I chew their food, I change their cloths, and they tell me about the old days. Some of them had parents who were alive back then."

Her voice went rich and rolling. Her crochet hook glinted on the little lace purse she was making. The driftwood flames flickered, orange with tongues of blue.

"They remember the days before the Nine Cities drowned and the Nine Islands with them. Before our people forsook us to live below the waters, and we were stranded here on the Last Isle. Before we changed our name to Glennemgarra, the Unchosen." Sharrar sighed. "In *those* days, names were more than mere proxy for, *Hey, you!*"

"So, Hyrryai means, *Hey, you, Gleamy*?"

"You have no soul, Shursta."

"Nugget, when your inner poet is ascendant, you have more than enough soul for both of us. If the whitecaps of your whimsy rise any higher, we'll have a second Drowning at hand, make no mistake."

Sharrar rolled her brown-bright eyes at him and grunted something. He laughed, and the anxious knots in his stomach loosened some.

When Shursta took his leave the next morning at dawn, he lingered in the threshold. The hut had plenty of wood in the stack outside the door. He'd smoked or salted any extra catch for a week, so Sharrar would not soon go hungry. If she encountered trouble, they would take her in at the Hall of Ages where she worked, and there she'd be fed and sheltered, though she wouldn't have much privacy or respite.

He looked at his sister now. She'd dragged herself from bed to make him breakfast, even though he was perfectly capable of frying up an egg himself. Her short dark hair stuck up every which way and her eyes were bleary. Her limp was more pronounced in the morning.

"Wish you could come with me," he offered.

"What? Me, with one game leg and a passel of grayheads to feed? No, thank you!" But her eyes looked wistful. Neither of them had ever been to Droon, capital of the Last Isle, the seat of the Astrion Council.

"Hey," he said, surprised to find his own eyes stinging.

"Hey," she said right back. "After the mesh-rite, after you've settled down a bit and met some folks, invite me up. You know I want to meet my mesh-sister. You have my gift?"

He patted his rucksack, which had the little lace purse she'd crocheted along with his own mesh-gift.

"Oohee, brother mine," said Sharrar. "By this time tomorrow you'll be a Blodestone, and no Sarth relation will be worthy to meet your eyes."

"Doubtless Hirryai Blodestone will take one look at me and sunder the contract."

"*She* requested *you*."

Shursta shrugged, sure it had been a mistake.

After that, there was one last hug, a vivid and mischievous and slightly desperate smile from Sharrar, followed by a grave look and quick wink on Shursta's part. Then he set off on the searoad that would take him to Droon.

Of the eight great remaining kinlines, the Blodestones were the wealthiest. Their mines were rich in ore and gems. Their fields were fertile and wide, concentrated in the highland interior of the Last Isle. After a Blodestone female was croned at age fifty, she would hold her place on the Astrion Council, which governed all the Glennemgarra.

Even a fisherman like Shursta Sarth (of the lesser branch of Sarths), from a poor village like Sif on the edge of Rath Sea, with no parents of note and only a single sister for kin, knew about the Blodestones.

He had no idea why Hyrryai had chosen him for mesh-mate. If it had not been an error, then it was a singular honor. For his life he knew not how he deserved it.

He was of an age to wed. Mesh-rite was his duty to the Glennemgarra and he would perform it, that the world might once again be peopled. To be childless–unless granted special dispensation by the Astrion Council–was to be reviled. Even with the dispensation, there were those who were tormented or shunned for their barrenness.

Due to a lack of girls in Sif, to his own graceless body, which, though fit for work, tended to carry extra weight, and to the slowness of his tongue in the company of strangers, Shursta had not yet been bred out. He had planned to attend this year's muster and win a mesh-mate at games (the idea of being won himself had never occurred to him), but then the Council's letter from Droon came.

The letter told him that Hyrryai Blodestone had requested him for mesh-mate. It told him that Hyrryai had not yet herself been bred. That though she was twenty one, a full year past the age of meshing, she had been granted a reprieve when her little sister was murdered.

Shursta had read that last sentence in shock. The murder of a child was the highest crime but one, and that was the murder of a girl child. Hyrryai had been given full grieving rights.

Other than this scant information, the letter had left detailed directions to Droon, with the day and time his first assignation with Hirryai had been set, and reminded him that it was customary for a first-meshed couple to exchange a gift.

On Sharrar's advice, Shursta had taken pains. He had strung for Hyrryai a long necklace of ammonite, shark teeth and dark pearls the color of thunderclouds. Ammonite for antiquity, teeth for ferocity, and pearls for sorrow. A fearsome gift and perhaps presumptuous, but Sharrar had approved.

"Girls like sharp things," she'd said, "so the teeth are just right. As for the pearls, they're practically a poem."

"I should have stuck with white ones," he'd said ruefully. "The regular round kind."

"Bah!" said Sharrar, her pointy face with its incongruously long, strong jaw set stubbornly. "If she doesn't see you're a prize, I'll descend upon Droon and roast her organs on the tines of my trident, just see if I don't!"

Whereupon Shursta had flicked his strand of stone, teeth and pearl at her. She'd caught it with a giggle, wrapping it with great care in the fine lace purse she'd made.

Hyrryai Blodestone awaited him. More tidepool than beach, the small assignation spot had been used for this purpose before. Boulders had been carved into steps leading from searoad to cove, but these were ancient and crumbling into marram grass.

In this sheltered spot, a natural rock formation had been worked gently into the double curve of a lovers' bench. His intended bride sat at the far end. Any further and she would topple off.

From the smudges beneath her eyes and the harried filaments flying out from her wing-black braid, she looked as if she had been sitting there all night. Her head turned as he approached. Perhaps it was the heaviness of his breath she heard. It labored after the ten miles he'd trudged that morning, from the steepness of the steps, at his astonishment at the color of her hair. The breezy sweetness of dawn had long since burned away. It was noon.

Probably, Shursta thought, falling back a step back as her gaze met his, she could smell him where she sat.

"Shursta Sarth," she greeted him.

"Damisel Blodestone."

Shursta had wanted to say her name. Had wanted to say it casually, as she spoke his, with a cordial nod of the head. Instead his chin jutted up and awry, as if a stray hook had caught it. Her name stopped in his throat and changed places at the last second with the formal honorific. He recalled Sharrar's nonsense about names having meaning. It no longer seemed absurd.

Hyrryai the Gleaming One. Had she been so called for the long shining lines in her hair? The fire at the bottom of her eyes, like lava trapped in obsidian? Was it the clear bold glow of her skin, just browner than blushing coral, just more golden than sand?

Since his tongue would not work, as it rarely did for strangers, Shursta shrugged off his rucksack. The shoulder straps were damp in his grip. He fished out the lace purse with its mesh-gift and held it out to her, stretching his arm to the limit so that he would not have to step nearer.

She glanced from his flushed face to the purse. With a short sigh, as if to brace herself, she stood abruptly, plucked the purse from his hand and dumped the contents into her palm.

Shursta's arm dropped.

Hyrryai Blodestone examined the necklace closely. Every tooth, every pearl, every fossilized ridge of ammonite. Then, with another breath, this one quick and indrawn as the other had been exhaled, she poured the contents back and thrust the purse at him.

"Go home, man of Sif," she said. "I was mistaken. I apologize that you came all this way."

Not knowing whether he were about to protest or cozen or merely ask why, Shursta opened his mouth. Felt that click in the back of his throat where too many words welled in too narrow a funnel. Swallowed them all.

His hand closed over the purse Sharrar had made.

After all, it was no worse than he had expected. Better, for she had not laughed at him. Her face, though cold, expressed genuine sorrow. He suspected the sorrow was with her always. He would not stay to exacerbate it.

This time, he managed a creditable bow, arms crossed over his chest in a gesture of deepest respect. Again he took up his rucksack, though it seemed a hundred times heavier now. He turned away from her, letting his rough hair swing into his face.

"Wait."

Her hand was on his arm. He wondered if they had named her Hyrryai because she left streaks of light upon whatever she touched.

"Wait. Please. Come and sit. I think I must explain. If it pleases you to hear me, I will talk awhile. After that you may tell me what you think. What you want. From this." She spread her hands.

Shursta did not remove his rucksack again, but he sat with her. Not on the bench, but on the sand, with their backs against the stone seat. He drew in the sand with a broken shell and did not look at her except indirectly, for fear he would stare. For a while, only the waves spoke.

When Hyrryai Blodestone began, her tones were polite but informal, like a lecturer of small children. Like Sharrar with her grayheads. As if she did not expect Shursta to hear her, or hearing, listen.

"The crones of the Astrion Council know the names of all the Glennemgarra youth yet unmeshed. All their stories. Who tumbled which merry widow in which sea cave. Who broke his drunken head on which barman's club. Who comes from the largest family of mesh-kin, and what her portions are. You must understand," the tone of her voice changed, and Shursta glanced up in time to see the fleetingest quirk of a corner smile, "the secrets of the council do not stay in the council. In my home, at least, it is the salt of every feast, the gossip over tea leaves and coffee grinds, the center of our politics and our hearths. With a mother, grandmother, several aunts and great aunts and three cousins on the council, I cannot escape it. When we were young, we did not want to. We thought of little else than which dashing, handsome man we would . . ."

She stopped. Averted her face. Then she asked lightly, "Shall I tell you your story as the Blodestones know it?"

When he answered, after clearing his throat, it was in the slow measured sentences that made most people suck their teeth and stamp the ground with impatience. Hyrryai Blodestone merely watched with her flickering eyes.

"Shursta Sarth is not yet twenty five. He has one sibling, born lame. A fisherman by trade. Not a very successful one. Big as a whale. Stupid as a jellyfish. Known to his friends, if you can call them that, as 'Sharkbait.'"

Hyrryai was nodding, slowly. His heart sank like a severed anchor. He had hoped, of course, that the story told of Shursta Sarth in the Astrion Council might be different. That somehow they had known more of him, even, than he knew of himself. Seeing his crestfallen expression, Hyrryai took up the tale.

"Shursta Sarth is expected either to win a one-year bride at games, do his duty by her and watch her leave the moment her contract ends, or to take under his wing a past-primer lately put aside for a younger womb. However, as his sister will likely be his dependent for life, this will deter many of the latter, who might have taken him on for the sake of holding their own household. It is judged improbable that Shursta Sarth will follow the common practice of having his sister removed to the Beggar's Quarter and thus improve his own lot."

Shursta must have made an abrupt noise or movement, for she glanced at him curiously. He realized his hands had clenched. Again, she almost smiled.

"Your sister made the purse?"

He nodded once.

"Then she is clever. And kind." She paused. The foam hissed just beyond the edges of their toes. A cormorant called.

"Did you know I had a sister?" she asked him.

Shursta nodded, more carefully this time. Her voice, like her face, was remote and cold. But at the bottom of it, buried in the ice, an inferno.

"She was clubbed to death on this beach. I found her. We had come here often to play—well, to spy on mesh-mates meeting for the first time. Sometimes we came here when the moon was full—to bathe and dance and pretend that the sea people would swim up to surface from the Nine Drowned Cities to sing songs with us. I had gone to a party that night with a group of just the sort of dashing handsome young men we would daydream about meshing with, but she was too young yet for such things. When she was found missing from her bed the next morning, I thought perhaps she had come here and fallen asleep. I thought if I found her, I could pretend to our mother I had already scolded her—Kuista was very good at hanging her head like a puppy and looking chastised; sometimes I think she practiced in the mirror—and she might be let off a little easier. So I went here first and told nobody. But even from the cliff, when I saw her lying there, I knew she wasn't sleeping."

Shursta began to shiver. He thought of Sharrar, tangled in bladderwrack, a nimbus of bloody sand spreading out around her head.

"She was fully clothed, except for her shoes. But she often went barefoot. Said even sandals strangled her. The few coins in her pocket were still there, but her gemmaja was gone. I know she had been wearing it, because she rarely took it off. And it's not among her things."

A dark curiosity moved in him. Unable to stop himself, Shursta asked, "What is a gemmaja?"

Hyrryai untangled a thin silver chain from her hair. If she had not been so mussed, if the gemmaja had been properly secured, it would have lain across her forehead in a gentle V. A small green stone speckled with red came to rest between her eyes like a raindrop.

"The high households of the eight kinlines wear them. Ours is green chalcedony, of course. You Sarths," she added, "wear the red carnelian."

Shursta touched the small nob of polished coral he wore on a cord under his shirt. His mother had always just called it a *touchstone*. His branch of Sarths had never been able to afford carnelian.

"Later, after the pyre, I searched the sand, but I could not find Kuista's gemmaja. I was so..." She hesitated. "Angry."

Shursta understood the pause. Hyrryai had meant something entirely else, of course. As when calling the wall of water that destroyed your village a word so common as "wave" was not enough.

"...So angry that I had not thought to check her head more closely. To see if the gemmaja had been driven into... into what was left her of skull. To see if a patch of her hair had been ripped out with the removal of the gemmaja–which I reason more likely. But I only thought of that later, when... when I could think again. Someone took the gemmaja from her, I know it." She shook her head. "But for what reason? A lover, perhaps, crazed by her refusal of him? She was young for a lover, but some men are strange. Did he beat her down and then take a piece of her for himself? Was it an enemy? For the Blodestones are powerful, Shursta Sarth, and have had enemies for as long as we have held house. Did he bring back her gemmaja to his own people, as proof of loyalty to his kinline? Was he celebrated? Was he elected leader for his bold act? I do not know. I wish I had been a year ago what I am now... But mark me."

She turned to him and set her strong hands about his wrists.

"Mark me when I say I shall not rest until I find Kuista's murderer. Every night she comes to me in my sleep and asks where her gemmaja is. In my dreams she is not dead or broken, only sad, so sad that she begins to weep, asking me why it was taken from her. Her tears are not tears but blood. All I want is to avenge her. It is all I can think about. It is the only reason I am alive. *Do you understand?*"

Shursta's own big, brown, blunt-fingered hands rested quietly within the tense shackles of hers. His skin was on fire where she touched him, but his stomach felt like stone. He said slowly, "You do not wish–you never wished–to wed."

"No."

"But your grieving time is used up and the Astrion Council–your family–is insisting."

"Yes."

"So you chose a husband who... Who would be..." He breathed out. "Easy." She nodded once, slowly. "A stupid man, a poor man, a man who would be grateful for a place among the Blodestones. So grateful he would not question the actions of his wife. His wife who... who would not be a true wife."

Her hands fell from his. "You do understand."

"Yes."

She nodded again, her expression almost exultant. "I knew you would! The moment I held your mesh-gift. It was as if you knew me before we met. As if you made my sorrow and my vengeance and my blood debt to my sister into a necklace. I knew at once that you would never do. Because I need a husband who would *not* understand. Who would not care if I could not love him. Who never suspected that the thought of bringing a child into this murderous world is so repellent that to dwell on it makes me vomit, even when I have eaten nothing. I mean to find my sister's killer, Shursta Sarth. And then I mean to kill him and eat his heart by moonlight."

Shursta looked up, startled. The eating of a man's flesh was taboo–but he did not blurt the obvious aloud. Had not her sister–a child, a girl child–been murdered on this beach? Taboos meant nothing to Hyrryai Blodestone. He wondered that she had not yet filed her teeth and declared herself *windwyddiam*, a wind widow, nameless, kinless, outside the law. But then, he thought, how could she hunt amongst the high houses if she revoked her right of entry into them?

"*But.*"

He looked up at that word and knew a disgustingly naked monster shone in his eyes. But he could not help it. Shursta could not help his hope.

"But you are not a stupid man, Shursta Sarth. And you do not deserve to be sent away in disgrace, as if you were a dog that displeased me. You must tell me what you want, now that you know what I am."

Shursta sat up to remove his rucksack again. Again he removed the lace purse, the necklace. And though his fingers trembled, he looped the long strand around her neck, twice and then thrice, before letting the hooks catch. The teeth jutted out about her flesh, warning away chaste kisses, chance gestures of affection. Hyrryai did not move beneath his hands.

"I am everything the Astrion Council says," Shursta said, sinking back to the sand. "But if I wed you tomorrow, I will be a Blodestone, and thus be more useful to my sister. Is that not enough to keep me here? I am not so stupid as to leave, when you give me the choice to stay. But I shall respect your grief. I shall not touch you. When you have found your sister's killer and have had your revenge, come to me. I will declare myself publically dissatisfied that you have not given me children. I will return to Sif. If my sister does not mesh, you will settle upon her a portion worthy of a Blodestone, that she will never be put away in the Beggar's Quarter. And we shall be quit of each other. Does this suit you, Damisel Blodestone?"

Whatever longing she heard in his voice or saw in his eyes, she did not flinch from it. She took his face between her palms and kissed him right on the forehead, right between the eyes, where her sister's gemmaja had rested, where her skull had been staved in.

"Call me Hyrryai, husband."

When she offered her hand, he set his own upon it. Hyrryai did not clasp it close. Instead, she furled open his fingers and placed her mesh-gift into his palm. It was a black shell blade, honed to a dazzle and set into a delicately scrimshawed hilt of whale ivory.

"Cherished Nugget," Shursta began his missive:

It is for charity's sake that I sit and scribble this to you on this morning of all mornings, in the sure knowledge that if I do not, your churlishness will have you feeding burnt porridge to all the grayheads under your care. To protect them, I will relate to you the tale of my meshing. Brace yourself.

The bride wore red, as brides do–but you have never seen such a red as the cloth they make in Droon. Had she worn it near shore, sharks would have beached themselves, mistaking her for food. It was soft too, to the touch. What was it like? Plummage. No, pelt. Like Damis Ungerline's seal pelt, except not as ratty and well-chewed. How is the old lady anyway? Has she lost her last tooth yet? Give her my regards.

The bride's brothers, six giants whose prowess in athletics, economics, politics and music makes them the boast of the Blodestones, converged on me the night I arrived in Droon and insisted I burn the clothes I came in and wear something worthy of my forthcoming station.

"Except," said one–forgive me; I have not bothered to learn all their names–"we have nothing ready made in his size."

"Perhaps a sailcloth?"

"Damis Valdessparrim has some very fine curtains."

And more to this effect. A droll scene. Hold it fast in your mind's eye. Me, nodding and agreeing to all their pronouncements with a fine ingratiation of manner. Couldn't speak a word, of course. Sweating, red as a boiled lobster–you know how I get–I suppose I seemed choice prey while they poked and prodded, loomed and laughed. I felt about three feet tall and four years old again.

Alas, low as they made me, I could not bring myself to let them cut the clothes from my back. I batted at their hands. However, they were quicker than I, as are most everybody. They outnumbered me and their knives came out. My knife–newly gifted and handsomer than anything I've ever owned–was taken from me. My fate was sealed.

Then their sister came to my rescue. Think not she had been standing idly by, enjoying the welcome her brothers made me. No, as soon as we'd stepped foot under the Blodestone roof, she had been enveloped in a malapertness of matrons, and had only just emerged from their fond embraces.

She has a way of silencing even the most garrulous of men, which the Blodestone boys, I assure you, are.

When they were all thoroughly cowed and scuffling their feet, she took me by the hand and led me to the room I am currently occupying. My mesh-rite suit was laid out for me, fine ivory linens embroidered by, she assured me, her mother's own hand. They fit like I had been born to them. The Astrion Council, they say, has eyes everywhere. And measuring tapes too, apparently.

Yes, yes, I stray from my subject, O antsiest (and onliest) sister. The meshing.

Imagine a balmy afternoon. Warm, with a wind. (You probably had the same kind of afternoon in Sif, so it shouldn't be too hard.) Meat had been roasting since the night before in vast pits. The air smelled of burnt animal flesh, by turns appetizing and nauseating.

We two stood inside the crone circle. The Blodestones stood in a wider circle around the crones. After that, a circle of secondary kin. After that, the rest of the guests.

We spoke our vows. Or rather, the bride did. Your brother, dear Nugget, I am sorry to say, was his usual laconic self and could not find his way around his own tongue. Shocking! Nevertheless, the bride crowned him in lilies, and cuffed to his ear a gemmaja of green chalcedony, set in a tangle of silver. This, to declare him a Blodestone by mesh-rite.

You see, I enclose a gemmaja of your own. You are no longer Sharrar Sarth, but Damisel Sharrar Blodestone, mesh-sister to the Gleaming One. When you come of croning, you too, shall take your seat on the Astrion Council. Power, wealth, glory. Command of the kinlines. Fixer of fates.

There. Never say I never did anything for you.

Do me one favor, Sharrar. Do not wear your gemmaja upon your forehead, or in any place too obvious. Do not wear it where any stranger who might covet it might think to take it from you by force. Please.

A note of observation. For all they dress so fine and speak with fancy voices, I cannot say that people in Droon are much different than people in Sif. Sit back in your chair and imagine me rapturous in the arms of instant friends.

I write too hastily. Sharrar, I'm sorry. The ink comes out as gall. I know for a fact that you are scowling at the page and biting your nails. My fault.

I will slow down, as if I were speaking, and tell you something to set your heart at ease.

Other than the bride–who is what she is–I have perhaps discovered one friend. At least, he is friendlier than anyone else I have met in Droon. I even bothered remembering his name for you.

He is some kind of fifth or sixth cousin to the bride–though not a Blodestone. One of the ubiquitous Spectroxes. (Why are they ubiquitous, you ask? I am not entirely sure. I was told they are ubiquitous, so ubiquitous I paint them for you now. Miners and craftsmen, mostly, having holdings in the mountains. Poor but on the whole respectable.) This particular Spectrox is called Laric Spectrox. Let me tell you how I met him.

I was lingering near the banquet table after the brunt of the ceremony had passed from my shoulders.

Imagine me a mite famished. I had not eaten yet that day, my meshing day, and it was nearing sunset. I was afraid to serve myself even a morsel for the comments my new mesh-brothers might make. They had already made several to the end that, should I ever find myself adrift at sea, I might sustain myself solely *on* myself until rescue came, and still be man enough for three husbands to their sister!

I thought it safe, perhaps, to partake of some fruit. All eyes were on a sacred dance the bride was performing. This involved several lit torches swinging from the ends of chains and what I can only describe as alarming acrobatics. I had managed to eat half a strawberry when a shadow dwarfed the dying sun. A creature precisely three times the height of any of the bride's brothers–though much skinnier–and black as the sharp shell of my new blade–laughed down at me.

"Bored with the fire spinning already? Hyrryai's won contests, you know. Although she can't–ah–*couldn't* hold a candle to little Kuista."

I squinted up at this living beanstalk of a man, wondering if he ever toppled in a frisky wind. To my surprise, when I opened my mouth to speak, the sentence came out easily– in the order I had planned it, no less.

(I still find it strange how my throat knows when to trust someone, long before I've made up my own mind about it. It was you who first observed that, I remember. Little Sharrar, do the grayheads tell you that *your* name means Wisdom? If they don't, they should.)

"I cannot bear to watch her," I confessed.

"Afraid she'll set someone's hair on fire?" He winked. "Can't really blame you. But she won't, you know."

"Not that. Only. . ." For a moment, my attention wandered back to the bride. Red flame. Red gown. Wheels of fire in the night. Her eyes. I looked away. "Only it would strike me blind if I gazed at her too long."

What he read in my face, I could not say (although I know you're wishing I'd just make something up), but he turned to follow her movements as she danced.

"Mmn," he grunted. "Can't say I see it, myself. She's just Hyrryai. Always has been. Once, several years back, my mother suggested I court her. I said I'd rather mesh with a giant squid. Hyrryai's all bone and sinew, you know. Never had any boobies to speak of. Anyway, even before Kuista died, she was too serious. Grew up with those Blodestone boys–learned to fight before she could talk. I wouldn't want a wife who could kill me with her pinkie, would you?"

My eyebrows went past my hairline. In fact, I have not located them since. I think they are hiding behind my ears. My new acquaintance grinned to see me at such a loss, but he grasped my forearm and gave it a hearty shake.

"What am I doing, keeping you from your grub? Eat up, man! You're that feral firemaid's husband now. I'd say you'll need all your strength for tonight."

And that, Nugget, is where I shall leave you. It is morning. As you see, I survived.

Your fond brother,

Shursta Blodestone

He was reading a book in the window seat of his room when Shursta heard the clamor in the courtyard. Wagon wheels, four barking dogs, several of the younger Blodestones who had been playing hoopball, an auntie trying to hush everyone down.

"Good morning, Chaos," a voice announced just beyond his line of sight. "My name is Sharrar Sarth. I've come to meet my mesh-kin."

Shursta slammed his book closed and ran for the door. He did not know if he was delighted or alarmed. Would they jostle her? Would they take her cane away and tease her? Would she whack them over the knuckles and earn the disapprobation of the elders? *Why had she come?*

The letter, of course. The letter. He had regretted it the moment he sent it. It had been too long, too full of things he should have kept to himself. He ought to have expected her. Would he have stayed at home, receiving a thing like that from her? Never. Now that she was here, he ought to send her away.

Sharrar stood amongst a seethe of Blodestones, chatting amiably with them. She leaned on her cane more crookedly than usual, the expression behind her smile starting to pinch.

No wonder. She'd come nearly twenty miles on the back of a rickety produce wagon. If she weren't bruised spine to sternum he'd be surprised.

When Shursta broke through the ranks, Sharrar's smile wobbled and she stumbled into his arms.

"I think you need a nap, Nugget," he suggested.

"You're not mad?"

"I am very happy to see you." He kissed the top of her head. "Always."

"You won't send me away on the next milknut run?"

"I might if you insist on walking up those stairs." He looked at his mesh-brothers. His mouth tightened. He'd be drowned twice and hung out to dry before asking them for help.

Hyrryai appeared at his side, meeting his eyes in brief consultation. He nodded. She slung one of Sharrar's arms about her shoulders while Shursta took the other.

"Oh, hey," said Sharrar, turning her head to study the newcomer. "You must be the Gleaming One."

"And you," said Hyrryai, "must be my sister."

"I've always wanted a sister," Sharrar said meditatively. "But my mother–may she sleep forever with the sea people–said, so help her, two children were *enough* for one woman, and that was two more than strictly necessary. She was a schoolteacher," Sharrar explained. "Awfully smart. But I don't think she understood things like sisters. She had so many herself."

For a moment, Shursta thought Hyrryai's eyes had flooded. But then she smiled, a warmer expression on her face than any Shursta had yet seen. "Perhaps you won't think so highly of them once I start borrowing your clothes without asking."

"Damisel," Sharrar pronounced, "my rags are your rags. Help yourself."

There was a feast four days later for the youngest of Hyrryai's brothers.

"Dumwei," Sharrar reminded Shursta. "I don't know why you can't keep them all straight."

"I do not have your elasticity of mind," he retorted. "I haven't had to memorize all three hundred epics for the entertainment of the Hall of Ages."

"It's all about mnemonic tricks. Let's see. In order of age, there's Lochlin the Lunkhead, Arishoz the Unenlightened, Menami Meatbrain–then Hyrryai, of course, fourth in the birth order, but we all know what *her* name means, don't we, Shursta?–Orssi the Obscene, Plankin Porkhole and Dumwei the Dimwitted. How could you mix them up?"

By this time Shursta was laughing too hard to answer. When Hyrryai joined them, he flung himself back onto the couch cushions and put a pillow over his face. Now and again, a hiccup emerged from the depths.

"I've never seen him laugh before," Hyrryai observed. "What is the joke?"

"Oh," Sharrar said blithely, "I was just mentioning how much I like your brothers. Tell me, who is coming to the feast tonight?"

Hyrryai perched at the edge of the couch. "Everybody."

"Is Laric Spectrox coming?"

"Yes. Why? Do you know him?"

"Shursta mentioned him in a letter."

Shursta removed his pillow long enough to glare, but Sharrar ignored him.

"I was curious to meet him. Also, I was wondering. . . What is the protocol to join the Sing at the end of the feast? One of my trades is storyteller–as my brother has just reminded me–and I have recently memorized a brave tale that dearest Dumwei will adore. It is all about, oh, heroic sacrifice, bloody deeds and great feats, despair, rescue, celebration. That sort of thing."

Observing the mischief dancing in Sharrar's eyes, a ready spark sprang to Hyrryai's. "I shall arrange a place of honor for you in the Sing. This is most kind of you."

Groaning, Shursta swam up from the cushions again. "Don't trust her! She is up to suh–*hic*–uhmething. She will tell some wild tale about, about–farts and–and burps and–billygoats that will–*hic*–will shame your grandmother!"

"My grandmother has no shame." Hyrryai stood up from the edge of the couch. She never relaxed around any piece of furniture. She had to be up and pacing. Shursta, following her with his eyes, wondered how, and if, she ever slept. "Sharrar is welcome to tell whatever tale she deems fit. Do not be offended if I leave early. Oron Onyssix attends the feast tonight, and I mean to shadow him home."

At that, even Sharrar looked startled. "Why?"

Hyrryai grinned. It was not a look her enemies would wish to meet by moonlight.

"Of late the rumors are running that his appetite for hedonism has begun to extend to girls too young to be mesh-fit. I go tonight to confirm or invalidate these."

"Oh," said Sharrar. "You're hunting."

"I am hunting."

Shursta bit his lip. He did not say, "Be careful." He did not say, "I will not sleep until you return." He did not say, "If the rumors are true, then bring him to justice. Let the Astrion Council sort him out, trial and judgement. Even if he proves a monster, he may not be *your* monster, and don't you see, Hyrryai, whatever happens tonight, it will not be the end? That grief like yours does not end in something so simple as a knife in the dark?"

As if she heard, Hyrryai turned her grin on him. All the teeth around her throat grinned too.

"It *is* a nice necklace," Sharrar observed. "I told Shursta it was a poem."

The edges of Hyrryai's grin softened. "Your brother has the heart of a poet. And you the voice of one. We Blodestones are wealthy in our new kin." She turned to go, paused, then added over her shoulder, "Husband, if you drink a bowl of water upside-down, your hiccups may go away."

When she was gone, Sharrar nudged him. "Oohee, brother mine. I like her."

"Ayup, Nugs," he sighed. "Me too."

It was with trepidation that Shursta introduced his sister to Laric Spectrox that night at the feast. He need not have worried. Hearing his name, Sharrar laughed with delight and raised her brown eyes to his.

"Why, hey there! Domo Spectrox! You're not nearly as tall as Shursta made you out to be."

Laric straightened his shoulders. "Am I not?"

"Nope. The way he writes it, I thought to mistake you for a milknut tree. Shursta, you said skinny. It's probably all muscle, right? Wiry, right? Like me?" Sharrar flexed her free arm for him. Laric shivered a wink at Shursta and gravely admired her bicep. "Anyway, you're not too proud to bend down, are you?"

"I'm not!"

"Good! I have a secret I must tell you."

When Laric brought his face to her level, she seized him by both big ears and planted an enormous kiss on his mouth. Menami and Orssi Blodestone, who stood nearby, started whooping. Dumwei sidled close.

"Don't I get one? It's my birthday, you know."

Sharrar gave him a sleepy-eyed look that made Shursta want to hide under the table. "Just you wait till after dinner, Dumwei my darling. I have a special surprise for you." She shooed him along and bent all her attention back to Laric.

"You," she said.

He pointed to his chest a bit nervously. "Me?"

"You, Laric Spectrox. You are going to be my friend for the rest of my life. I decided that ages ago, so I'm very glad we finally got to meet. No arguments."

Laric's shining black face broke into a radiance of dimple creases and crooked white teeth. "Do you see me arguing? I'm not arguing."

"I'm Sharrar, by the way. Sit beside me tonight and let me whisper into your ear."

When Laric glanced at Shursta, Shursta shrugged. "She's going to try and talk you into doing something you won't want to do. I don't know what. Just keep saying no and refilling her plate."

"Does that really work?"

Shursta gave him a pained glance and did not answer.

Hyrryai came late to the feast and took a silent seat beside Shursta. He filled a plate and shoved it at her, as if she had been Sharrar, but when she only picked at it, he shrugged and went back to listening to Laric and Orssi arguing.

Orssi said, "The Nine Islands drowned and the Nine Cities with them. There are no other islands. There is no other land. We are alone on this world, and we must do our part to repeople it."

"No, no, see–" Laric gestured with the remnants of a lobster claw, "that lacks imagination. That lacks gumption. What do we know for sure? We know that something terrible happened in our great-great grandparents' day. What was it really? How can we know? We weren't born then. All we have are stories, stories the grayheads tell us in the Hall of Ages. I value these stories, but I will not build my life on them, as a house upon sand. We call ourselves the Glennemgarra, the Unchosen. Unchosen by what? By death? By the wave? By the magic of the gods that protected the Nine Holy Cities even as they drowned, so that they live still, at the bottom of the sea? Let there be a hundred cities beneath the waves. What do we care? We can't go there."

Laric glanced around at the few people who still listened to him.

"Do you know where we *can* go, though? Everywhere else. Anywhere. There is no law binding us to Droon–or to Sif—" he nodded at Sharrar, whose face was rapt with attention, "or anywhere on this wretched oasis. We know the wind. We know the stars. We have our boats and our nets and our water casks. There is no reason not to set out in search of something better."

"Well, cousin," said Orssi. "No one could accuse you of lacking imagination."

"Yes, Spectrox," cried Arishoz, "and how *is* your big boat project coming along?"

Laric's round eyes narrowed. "It would go more quickly if I had more hands to help me."

The Blodestone brothers laughed, though not ill-naturedly. "Find a wife, cousin," Lochlin advised him. "Breed her well. People the world with tiny Spectroxes–as if the world needed more Spectroxes, eh? Convince *them* to build your boat. What else are children for?"

Laric threw up his hands. He was smiling too, but all the creases in his forehead bespoke a sadness. "Don't you see? When my boat is finished I will sail away from words like that and thoughts like yours. As if women were only good for wives, and children were only made for labor."

Hyrryai raised her glass to him. Shursta reached over to fill it from the pitcher and watched as she drank deeply.

"I will help you, Laric Specrox!" Sharrar declared, banging her fists on the table. "I am good with my hands. I never went to sea with the men of Sif, but I can swim like a seal– and I'd trade my good leg for an adventure. Tell me all about your big boat."

He turned to her and smiled, rue twining with gratitude and defiance. "It is the biggest boat ever built. Or it will be."

"And what will you name her?"

"*The Grimgramal*. After the wave that changed the world."

Sharrar nodded, as if this were the most natural thing. Then she swung her legs off the bench, took up her cane, and pushed herself to her feet. Leaning against the table for support, she used her cane to pound the floor. When this did not noticeably diminish the noise in the hall, she set her forefinger and pinkie to her lips and whistled. Everyone, from the crone's table where the elders were wine-deep in gossip and politics, to the children's table where little cakes were being served, hushed.

Sharrar smiled at them. Shursta held his breath. But she merely invoked the Sing, bracing against a bench for support, then raising both fists above her head to indicate the audience should respond to her call.

"Grimgramal the Endless was the wave that changed the world."

Obediently, the hall repeated, "*Grimgramal the Endless was the wave that changed the world.*"

Sharrar began the litany that preceded all stories. Shursta relaxed again, smiling to himself to see Hyrryai absently chewing a piece of flatbread as she listened. His sister's tales, unlike Grimgramal, were not endless; they were mainly intended to please grayheads, who fell asleep after fifteen minutes or so. Sharrar's habit had been to practice her stories on her brother when he came in from a day out at sea and was so tired he could barely keep his eyes open. When he asked why she could not wait until morning when he could pay proper attention, she had replied that his exhaustion in the evening best simulated her average audience member in the Hall of Ages.

But Shursta had never yet fallen asleep while Sharrar told a story.

"*The first city was Hanah and it fell beneath the sea
The second city was Lahatiel, and it fell beneath the sea*

The third city was Ekesh, and it fell beneath the sea
The fourth city was Var, and it fell beneath the sea
The fifth city was Thungol, and it fell beneath the sea
The sixth city was Yassam, and it fell beneath the sea
The seventh city was Saheer, and it fell beneath the sea
The eighth city was Gelph, and it fell beneath the sea
The ninth city was Niniam, and it fell beneath the sea. . ."

Sharrar ended the litany with a sweep of her hands, like a wave washing everything away. "But one city," she said, "did not fall beneath the sea." Again, her fists lifted. "That city was Droon!"

"That city was Droon!" the room agreed.

"That city was Droon, capital of the Last Isle. Now, on this island, there are many villages, though none that match the great city Droon. In one of these villages–in Sif, my own village–was born the hero of this tale. A young man, like the young men gathered here tonight. Like Dumwei whom we celebrate."

She did not need to coax a response this time. Cups and bowls and pitchers clashed.

"Dumwei whom we celebrate!"

"If our hero stood before you in this hall, humble as a Man of Sif might be before the Men of Droon, you would not say to your neighbor, your brother, your cousin, 'That young man is a hero.' But a hero he was born, a hero he became, a hero he'll remain, and I will tell you how, here and now."

Sharrar took her cane, moving it through the air like a paddle through water.

"The fisherfolk of Sif catch many kinds of fish. Octopus and squid, shrimp and crab. But the largest catch and tastiest, the feast to end all feasts, the catch that feeds a village–this is the bone shark."

"The bone shark."

"It is the most cunning, the most frightening, the most beautiful of all the sharks. A long shark, a white shark, with a towering dorsal fin and a great jaw glistening with terrible teeth. This is the shark which concerns our hero. This is the shark that brought him fame."

"This is the shark that brought him fame."

By this time, Sharrar barely needed to twitch a finger to elicit a response. The audience leaned in. All except Shursta, whose shoulders hunched, and Hyrryai, who drew her legs up onto the bench, to wrap her arms around her knees.

"To catch a shark you must first feed it. You must bloody the waters. You must send a slick of chum as sacrifice. For five days you must do this, until the sharks come tame to your boat. Then noose and net, you must grab it. Noose and net, you must drag it to the shore where it will die upon the sand. This is how you catch a shark."

"This is how you catch a shark."

"One day, our hero was at sea. Many other men were with him, for the fishermen of Sif do not hunt alone. A man–let us call him Ghoul, for his sense of humor was necrotic–had brought along his young son for the first time. Now, Ghoul, he did not like our hero.

Ghoul was a proud man. A strong man. A handsome man too, if you like that sort of man. He thought Sif had room for only one hero and that was Ghoul."

"*Ghoul!*"

"Ghoul said to his son, 'Son, why do we waste all this good chum to bait the bone shark? In the next boat over sits a lonesome feast. An unmeshed man whom no one will miss. Let us rock his boat a little, eh? Let us rock his boat and watch him fall in.'

"Father and son took turns rocking our hero's boat. Soon the other men of Sif joined in. Not all men are good men. Not all good men are good all the time. Not even in Droon. The waters grew choppy. The wind grew restless. The bone shark grew tired of waiting for his chum."

"*The bone shark grew tired of waiting–*"

"—Who can say what happened then? A wave too vigorous? The blow of a careless elbow as Ghoul bent to rock our hero's boat? A nudge from the muzzle of the bone shark? An act of the gods from the depths below? Who can know? But our hero saw the child. He saw Ghoul's young son fall into the sea. Like Gelph and Saheer, he fell into the sea. Like Ekesh and Var and Niniam he fell into the sea. Like Hanah and Lahatiel, Thungol and Yassam. Like the Nine Islands and all Nine Cities, the child fell."

"*The child fell.*"

"The bone shark moved as only sharks can move, lightning through the water, opening its maw for the sacrifice. But then our hero was there. There in the sea. Between shark and child. Between death and the child. Our hero was there, treading water. There with his noose and his net. He had jumped from his boat. Jumped–where no man of Sif could push him, however hard they rocked his boat. Jumped to save this child. And he tangled the shark in his net. He lassoed the shark with his noose and lashed himself to that dreadful dorsal fin! Ghoul had just enough time to haul his son back into his boat. The shark began to thrash."

"*The shark began to thrash.*"

"The shark began to swim."

"*The shark began to swim.*"

"Our hero clung fast. Our hero held firm. Our hero herded that shark as some men herd horses. He brought that shark to land. He brought that shark onto the sand, where the shark could not breathe, and so it died. Thus our hero slew the bone shark. Thus our hero fed his village. Thus our hero rescued the child. He rescued the child."

"*He rescued the child.*"

It was barely a whisper. Not an eye in that hall was dry.

"And that is the end of my tale."

Sharrar thumped her cane to the floor again. This time, the noise echoed in a resounding silence. But without giving even the most precipitous a chance to stir, much less erupt into the applause that itched in every sweaty palm present, Sharrar spun on her heel and glared at the table where the Blodestone brothers sat.

"It was Shursta Sarth slew the bone shark," she told them, coldly and deliberately. "Your sister wears its teeth around her neck. You are not worthy to call him brother. You are not worthy to sit at that table with him."

With that, she spat at their feet and stumped out of the room.

Shursta followed close behind, stumbling through bodies. Not daring to look up from his feet. Once free of the hall, he took a different corridor than the one Sharrar had stormed through. Had he caught her up, what would he have done to her? Thanked her? Scolded her? Shaken her? Thrown her out a window? He did not know.

However difficult or humiliating negotiating his new mesh-kin had been, Sharrar the Wise had probably just made it worse.

And yet . . .

And yet, how well she had done it. The Blodestones, greatest of the eight kinlines gathered together in one hall–and Sharrar had had them slavering. They would have eaten out of her hand. And what had she done with that hand? Slapped their faces. All six brothers of his new wife.

Shursta wanted his room. A blanket over his head. He wanted darkness.

When his door clicked open several hours later, Shursta jerked fully awake. Even in his half doze, he had expected some kind of retributive challenge from the Blodestone brothers. He wondered if they would try goading him to fight, now that they knew the truth about him. Well–Sharrar's version of the truth.

The mattress dipped near his ribs. He held his breath and did not speak. And when Hyrryai's voice came to him in the darkness, his heartrate skidded and began to hammer in his chest.

"Are you awake, Shursta?"

"Yes."

"Good." A disconsolate exhalation. He eased himself up to a sitting position and propped himself against the carven headboard.

"Did your hunting go amiss, Hyrryai?"

It was the first time he'd had the courage to speak her name aloud.

The sound she made was both hiss and plosive, more resigned than angry. "Oron Onyssix was arrested tonight by the soldiers of the Astrion Council. He will be brought to trial. I don't know–the crones, I think, got wind of my intentions regarding him. I track rumors; they, it seems, track me. In this case, they made sure to act before I did." She paused. "In this case, it might have been for the best. I was mistaken."

"Is he not guilty? With what, then, is he being charged?"

"The unsanctioned mentoring of threshold youths. That's what they're calling it."

She shifted. The mattress dipped again. Beneath the sheets, Shursta brought his hand to his heart and pressed it there, willing it to hush. Hush, Hyrryai is speaking.

"What does that mean?"

"It means Onyssix is not the man I'm hunting for!"

"How do you know?" he asked softly.

"Because . . ."

Shursta sensed, in that lack of light, Hyrryai making a gesture that cut the darkness into neat halves.

"Well, for one: the youths he prefers are *not*, after all, girls. A few young men came forward to bear witness. All were on the brink of mesh-readiness. Exploring themselves, each other. Coming of age. Usually the Astrion Council will assign such youths an older mentor to usher them into adulthood. One who will make sure the young people know that their duty as adult citizens of the Glennemgarra is to mesh and make children–no matter whom they may favor for pleasure or succor or lifelong companionship. That the privilege of preference is to be earned *after* meshing. There are rites. There is," her voice lilted mockingly, "paperwork. Onyssix sidestepped all of this. He will be fined. Watched a little more closely. Nothing else–there is no evidence of abuse. The young men did not speak of him with malice or fear. To them, he was just an older man with experience they wanted. I suppose it was a thrill to sneak around without the crones' consent. There you have it. Oron Onyssix is a reckless pleasure-seeker who thinks he's above the law. But hardly a murderer."

"I am sorry," Shursta murmured. "I wish it might have ended tonight."

From the way the mattress moved, he knew she had turned to look at him. Her hand was braced against the blankets. He could feel her wrist against his thigh.

"I wished it too." Hyrryai's voice was harsh. "All week I have anticipated... Some conclusion. The closing of this wound. I prepared myself. I was ready. I wanted to look my sister's killer in the eye and watch him confess. At banquet tonight, I wished it most–when Sharrar told her tale ..."

"The Epic of Shursta Sharkbait? You should not believe all you hear. Especially if Sharrar's talking."

"I've heard tell of it before," she retorted. "Certainly, when the story reached the Astrion Council, it was bare of the devices Sharrar used to hold our attention. But it has not changed in its particulars. It is, in fact, one measure by which the Astrion Council assessed your reputed stupidity. Intelligent men do not go diving in shark-infested waters."

The broken knife in his throat was laughter. Shursta choked on it. "No, they don't. I told you that day we met–I am everything they say."

"You did not tell me *that* story. Strange," Hyrryai observed, "when you mentioned they called you Sharkbait, you left out the reason why."

Shursta pulled the blankets up around his chin. "You didn't mention it either. Maybe it's not worth mentioning."

"It is why I chose you."

All at once, he could not breathe. Hyrryai had leaned over him. One fist was planted on either side of his body, pinning the blankets down. Her forehead touched his. Her breath was on his mouth, sharp and fresh, as though she had been chewing some bitter herb as she stalked Onyssix through the darkness.

"Not because they said you were stupid, or ugly, or poor. How many men in Droon are the same? No, I chose you because they said you were good to your sister. And because you rescued the child."

"I rescued the child," Shursta repeated in a voice he could barely recognize.

Of course, he wanted to say. Of course, Hyrryai, that would move you. That would catch you like a bone hook where you bleed.

"Had you not agreed to come to Droon, I would have attended the muster to win you at games, Shursta Sarth."

He would have shaken his head, but could do nothing of his own volition to break her contact with him. "The moment we met, you sent me away. You said–you said you were mistaken . . ."

"I was afraid."

"Of *me*?" Shursta was shivering. Not with cold or fear but something more terrifying. Something perilously close to joy. "Hyrryai, surely you know by now–surely you can see–I am the last man anyone would fear. Believe Sharrar's story if you like, but. . . But consider it an aberration. It does not define me. Did I look like a man who wrestled sharks when your brothers converged on me? When the crones questioned me? When I could not even speak my vows aloud at our meshing? That is who I am. That's all I am."

"I know what you are."

Hyrryai sat back as abruptly as she had leaned in. Stood up from the bed. Walked to the door. "When my hunt is done, we shall return to this discussion. I shall not speak of it again until then. But. . . Shursta, I did not want you to pass another night believing yourself to be a man whom. . . whom no wife could love."

The latch lifted. The door clicked shut. She was gone.

The Blodestones took their breakfast in the courtyard under a stand of milknut trees. When Shursta stepped outside, he saw Laric, Sharrar and Hyrryai all lounging on the benches, elbows sprawled on the wooden table, heads bent together. They were laughing about something–even Hyrryai–and Shursta stopped dead in the center of the courtyard, wondering if they spoke of him. Sharrar saw him first and grinned.

"Shursta, you must hear this!"

He stepped closer. Hyrryai glanced at him. The tips of her fingers brushed the place beside her. Taking a deep breath, he came forward and sat. She slid him a plate of peeled oranges.

"Your sister," said Laric Spectrox, with his broad beaming grin, "is amazing."

"My sister," Shursta answered, "is a minx. What did you do, Nugget?"

"Nugget?" Laric repeated.

"Shursta!" Sharrar leaned over and snatched his plate away. "Just for that you don't get breakfast."

"Nugget?" Laric asked her delightedly. Sharrar took his plate as well. Hyrryai handed Shursta a roll.

"Friends," she admonished them. "We must not have dissension in the ranks. Not now that we've declared open war on my brothers."

Shursta looked at them all, alarmed. "You declared. . . *What did you do?*"

Sharrar clapped her hands and crowed, "We sewed them into their bedsheets!"

"You . . ."

"We did!" Laric assured him, rocking with laughter in his seat. "Dumwei, claiming his right as birthday boy, goaded his brothers into a drinking game. By midnight, all six of them were sprawled out and snoring like harvest hogs. So late last night . . ."

"This morning," Sharrar put in.

"This morning, Sharrar and Hyrryai and I . . ."

"*Hyrryai*?" Shursta looked at his mesh-mate. She would not lift her eyes to his, but the corners of her lips twitched as she tore her roll into bird-bite pieces.

". . . Snuck into their chambers and sewed them in!"

Shursta hid his face in his hands. "Oh, by all the Drowned Cities in all the seas . . ."

Sharrar limped around the table to fling her arms about him. "Don't worry. No one will blame you. I made sure they'd know it was my idea."

He groaned again. "I'm afraid to ask."

"She signed their faces!" Laric threaded long fingers through his springy black hair. "I've not played pranks like this since I was a toddlekin. Or," he amended, "since my first-year wife left me for a man with more goats than brains."

Sharrar slid down beside him. "Laric, my friend—just *wait* till you hear my plans for the hoopball field!"

"Oh, the weeping gods. . ." Shursta covered his face again.

A knee nudged his knee. Hyrryai's flesh was warm beneath her linen trousers. He glanced at her between his fingers and she smiled.

"Courage, husband," she told him. "The best defense is offense. You never had brothers before, or you would know this. My brothers have been getting too sure of themselves. Three meshed already, their seeds gone for harvest, and they think they rule the world. Three of them recently come of age–brash, bold, considered prize studs of the market. Their heads are inflated like bladder balls."

Sharrar brandished her eating blade. "All it takes is a pinprick, my sweet ones!"

"Hush," Laric hissed. "Here come Plankin and Orssi."

The brothers had grim mouths, tousled hair, and murder in their bloodshot eyes. They had not bothered looking at themselves in the mirror that morning, for Sharrar's signature stood out bright and blue across their foreheads. Once they charged the breakfast table, however, they seemed uncertain upon whom they should fix their wrath. Sharrar had resumed her seat and was eating an innocent breakfast off three different plates. Laric kept trying to steal one of them back. Hyrryai's attention was wholly on the roll she decimated. Orssi glared at Shursta.

"Was it you, Sharkbait?" he demanded.

Shursta could still feel Hyrryai's knee pressed hard to his. His face flushed. His throat opened. He grinned at them both.

"Me, Shortsheets?" he asked. "Why, no. Of course not. I have minions to do that sort of thing for me."

He launched his breakfast roll into the air. It plonked Plankin right between the eyes. Unexpectedly, Plankin threw back his head, roaring out a laugh.

"Oh, hey," he said. "Breakfast! Thanks, brother."

Orssi, looking sly, made a martial leap and snatched the roll from Plankin's fingers. Yodeling victory, he took off running. With an indignant yelp, Plankin pelted after him. Hyrryai rolled her eyes. She reached across the table, took back the plate of oranges from Sharrar and popped a piece into Shursta's mouth before he could say another word. Her fingers brushed his lips, sticky with juice.

. . .

It did not surprise Shursta when, not one week later, Laric begged to have a word with him. "Privately," he said, "away from all these Blodestones. Come on, I'll take you to my favorite tavern. Very disreputable. No one of any note or name goes there. We won't be plagued."

Shursta agreed readily. He had not explored much of Droon beyond the family's holdings. Large as they were, they were starting to close in on him. Hyrryai's mother Dymorri had recently asked him whether a position as overseer of mines or of fields would better suit his taste. He had answered honestly that he knew nothing about either– and did the Blodestones have a fishing boat he might take out from time to time, to supply food for the family?

"Blodestones do not work the sea," she had replied, looking faintly amused.

Dymorri had high cheekbones, smooth rosy-bronze skin, and thick black eyebrows. Her hair was nearly white but for the single streak of black that started just off center of her hairline, and swept to the tip of a spiraling braid. Shursta would have been afraid of her, except that her eyes held the same sorrow permeating her daughter. He wondered if Kuista, the youngest Blodestone, had taken after her. Hyrryai had more the look of her grandmother, being taller and rangier, with a broader nose and wider mouth, black eyes instead of brown.

"Fishing's all I know," he'd told her.

"Hyrryai will teach you," she had said. "Think about it. There is no hurry. You have not been meshed a month."

True to his word, Laric propelled him around Droon, pointing out landmarks and places of interest. Shops, temples, old bits of wall, parks, famous houses, the seat of the Astrion Council. It was shaped like an eight-sided star, built of sparkling white quartz. Three hundred steps led up to the entrance, each step mosaiced in rainbow spirals of shell.

"Those shells came from the other Nine Islands," Laric told him. "When there were nine other islands."

"And you think there might be more?"

Laric cocked his ear for the hint of derision that usually flavored such questions. "I think," he answered slowly, "that there is more to this world than islands."

"Even if there isn't," Shursta sighed, "I wouldn't mind leaving this one. Even for a little while. Even if it meant nothing but stars and sea and a wooden boat forever."

"Exactly!" Laric clapped him on the back. "Ah, here we are. The Thirsty Seagull."

Laric Spectrox had not lied about the tavern. It was so old it had hunkered into the ground. The air was rank with fermentation and tobacco smoke. All the beams were blackened, all the tables scored with the graffiti of raffish nobodies whose names would never be sung, whose deeds would never be known, yet who had carved proof of their existence into the wood, as if to say, "Here, at least, I shall be recognized." Shursta fingered a stained, indelicate knife mark, feeling like his heart would break.

Taking a deep, appreciative breath, Laric pronounced, "Like coming home. Sit, sit. Let me buy you a drink. Beer?"

"All right," Shursta agreed, and sat, and waited. When Laric brought back the drinks, he sipped, and watched, and waited. The bulge in Laric's narrow throat bobbled. There was a sheen of sweat upon his brow. Shursta lowered his eyes, thinking Laric might find his task easier if he were not being watched. It seemed to help.

"Your sister," Laric began, "is . . ."

Shursta took a longer drink.

"Wonderful."

"Yes," Shursta agreed. He chanced to glance up. Laric was looking anywhere but at him, gesturing with his long hands.

"How is it that she wasn't snatched up by some clever fellow as soon as she came of age?"

"Well," Shursta pointed out, "she only recently did."

"I know, but. . . But in villages like Sif–small villages, I mean, well, even in Droon–surely some sparky critter had an eye on her these many years. Someone who grew up with her. Someone who thought, 'Soon as that Sarth girl casts her lure, I'll make damn sure I'm the fish for that hook! Take bait and line and pole and girl and dash for the far horizon . . .'"

Shursta cleared his throat. "Hard to dash with a game leg."

Laric plunked down from the high altitude of his visions. "Pardon?"

"Hard to run off with a girl who can't walk without a cane." Shursta studied Laric, who in turn tried to read the careful deadpan of his face. "And then, what if her children are born crooked? You'd be polluting your line. Surely the Spectroxes are taunted enough without introducing little lame Sharrar Sarth into the mix. Aren't you afraid what your family will say?"

"*Damisel* Sharrar Sarth," Laric corrected him stiffly, emphasizing the honorific. He tried to govern his voice. "And. . . And any Spectrox who does not want to claim wit and brilliance and derring-do and that glorious bosom for kin can eat my . . ."

Shursta clinked his mug to Laric's. "Relax. Sharrar has already told me she is going to elope with you on your big wooden boat. Two days after she met you. She said she'd been prepared to befriend you, but had not thought to be brought low by your, how did she put it, incredible height, provocative fingers and. . . adorable teeth." He coughed. "She went on about your teeth at some length. Forgive me if I don't repeat all of it. I'm sure she's composed a poem about them by now. If you find a proposal drummed up in couplets and shoved under your door tonight, you'll have had time to prepare your soul."

The look on Laric's face was beyond the price of gemmajas. He reached his long arms across the table and pumped Shursta's hand with both of his, and Shursta could not help laughing.

"Now, my friend," he said. "Let *me* buy *you* a drink."

It was at the bar Shursta noticed the bleak man in the corner. He looked as if he'd been sitting there so long that dust had settled over him, that lichen had grown over him, that spiders had woven cobwebs over his weary face. The difference between his despair and Laric's elation struck Shursta with the force of a blow, and he asked, when he returned to Laric's side, who the man might be.

"Ah." Laric shook his head. "That's Myrar Yaspir, poor bastard."

"Poor bastard?" Shursta raised his eyebrows, inviting more. It was this same dark curiosity, he recognized, that had made him press Hyrryai for details about Kuista's death the first day they met. He was unused to considering himself a gossip. But then, he thought, he'd had no friends to gossip with in Sif.

"Well." Laric knocked back a mouthful. His gaze wandered up and to the right. Sharrar once told Shursta that you could always tell when someone was reaching for a memory, for they always looked up and to the right. He'd seen the expression on her face often as she memorized a story.

"All right. I guess it began when he meshed with Adularia Yaspir three years ago. Second mesh-rite for both. No children on either side. He courted her for nearly a year. You could see by his face on their meshing day that there was a man who had pursued the dream of a lifetime. That for him, this was not about the Yaspir name or industry or holdings, but about a great burning love that would have consumed him had he not won it for his own. Adularia—well. I think she wanted children. She liked him enough. You could see the pink in her cheeks, the glow in her eyes on her meshing day. And you thought—if any couple's in it past the one year mesh-mark, this is that couple. It's usually that way for second meshings. You know."

Shursta nodded.

"So the first year passes. No children. The second year passes. No children. Myrar starts coming here more often. Drinking hard. Talk around Droon was that Adularia wanted to leave him. He was arrested once for brawling. A second time, on more serious charges, for theft."

"Really?" Shursta watched from the corner of his eye, the man who sat so still flies landed on him.

"Not just any theft. . . Gems from the Blodestone mines."

Shursta loosed a low whistle. "Diamonds?"

"Not even!" Laric leaned in. "Semi-precious stones, uncut, unpolished. Not even cleaned yet. Just a handful of green chalcedonies, like the one you're wearing."

The breath left Shursta's body. He touched the stone hanging from his ear. He remembered suddenly how Kuista Blodestone's gemmaja had come up missing on her person, how that one small detail had so disturbed him that he had admonished his sister to hide her own upon her person, as if the red-speckled stone were some amulet of death. He opened his mouth. His throat clicked a few times before it started working.

"Why. . . why would he take such a thing?"

Shrugging, Laric said, "Don't know. They made him return them all, of course. He spent some time in the stocks. Had to beg his wife to take him back. Promised her the moon, I heard. Stopped drinking. But she said that if she was not pregnant by winter, she'd leave him, and that was that."

"What happened?"

"A few months later, she was pregnant. There was great rejoicing." Laric finished his drink. "Of course, none of us were paying much attention to the Yaspirs at that time, because we were all still grieving for Kuista."

"Kuista. Kuista Blodestone?"

Laric looked at Shursta, perturbed, as if to ask, *Who else but Kuista Blodestone?*

"Yes. We burned her pyre not a month before Adularia announced her pregnancy. Hyrryai was still bedridden. She didn't leave the darkness of her room for six months."

"And the child?" Shursta's mouth tasted like dried out fish scales.

"Stillborn. Delivered dead at nine months." Laric sighed. "Adularia has gone back to live with her sister. Sometimes Myrar shows up for work at the chandlery, sometimes not. Owner's his kin, so he's not been fired yet. But I think that the blood is thinning to water on one end, if you know what I mean."

"Yes," said Shursta, who was no longer listening. "I... Laric, please... Please excuse me."

Shursta had no memory of leaving the Thirsty Seagull, or of walking clear across Droon and leaving the city by the sea road gates. He saw nothing, heard nothing, the thoughts boiling in his head like a cauldron full of viscera. He felt sick. Gray. Late afternoon, evening, and the early hours of night he passed in that lonely cove where Kuista died. Where he had met Hyrryai. Long past the hour most people had retired, he trudged wearily back to the Blodestone house. Sharrar awaited him in the courtyard, sitting atop the breakfast table, bundled warmly in a shawl.

"You're back!"

When his sister made as if to go to him, Shursta noticed she was stiff from sitting. He waved her down, joined her on the tabletop. She clasped his cold hand, squeezing.

"Shursta, it's too dark to see your face. Thunder struck my chest when Laric told me how you left him. Are you all right? What died in you today?"

"Kuista Blodestone," he whispered.

Sharrar was silent. She was, he realized, waiting for him to explain. But he could not.

"Sharrar," he said wildly, "Wise Sharrar, if stones could speak, what would they say?"

"Nothing quickly," she quipped, her voice strained. Shursta knew her ears were pricked to any clue he might let fall. Almost, he saw a glow about her skull as her riddle-raveling brain stoked itself to triple intensity. However he tried, he could not force his tongue to speak in anything more clear than questions.

"What does a stone possess other than... its stoneness? If not for wealth... or rarity... or beauty–why would someone covet... a hunk of rock?"

"Oh!" Sharrar's laughter was too giddy, almost fevered, with relief. She knew this answer. "For its magic, of course!"

"Magic."

It was not a common word. Not taboo–like incest or infanticide or cannibalism–but not common. Magic had drowned, it was said, along with the Nine Cities.

"Ayup." Sharrar talked quickly, her hand clamped to his, as if words could staunch whatever she thought to be his running wound. "See, in the olden days before the wave that changed the world, there was magic everywhere. Magic fish. Magic birds. Magic rivers. Magic... magicians. Certain gems, saith the grayheads, were also magic. A rich household would name itself for a powerful gem, so as to endow its kinline with the gem's essence. So, for instance, of the lost lines, there is Adamassis, whose gem was diamond, said to call the lightning. A stormy household, as you can imagine—quite impetuous—weather workers. The Anabarrs had amber, the gem of health, the gem that holds the sun, said to wake even the dead. Dozens more like this. Much of the lore was lost to us when the Nine Islands drowned. Of the remaining kinlines, let me think... The Sarths have sard—like the red carnelian—that can reverse the effects of poison. Onyssix wears onyx, to ward off demons. The jasper of the Yaspirs averts the eyes of an enemy..."

"And the Blodestones?" Shursta withdrew his hand from her stranglehold only to grip the soft flesh of her upper arm. "The Blodestones wear green chalcedony... Why? What is this stone?"

"Fertility," Sharrar gasped. Shursta did not know if she were frightened or in pain. "The green chalcedony—the bloodstone—will bring life to a barren womb. If a man crushes it to powder and drinks it, he will stand to his lover for all hours of the night. He will flood her with the seed of springtime. Shursta... Why are you asking me this, Shursta? Shursta, please..."

He had already sprinted from the courtyard. Faintly and far behind him, he heard the cry, "Let me come with you!"

He did not stop.

The Thirsty Seagull was seedier by night than by day. Gadabouts and muckrakes, sailors, soldiers, fisherfolk, washing women, street sweepers, lamplighters and red lamplighters of all varieties patronized the tavern. There were no tables free, so Shursta made his way to the last barstool.

Shursta did not have to pretend to stumble or slur. His head ached and he saw only through a distortion, as if peering through a sheet of water. But words poured freely from his mouth. None of them true, or mostly not true. Lies like Sharrar could tell. Dark lies, coming from depths within him he had never yet till this night sounded.

"*Women!*" he announced in a bleared roar. "Pluck you, pluck you right up from your comfy home. Job you like. Job you know. People you know. Pluck you up and say, it's meshing time. Little mesh-mesh. Come to bed, dear. No, you stink of fish, Shursta. Wash your hands, Shursta. Oh, your breath is like a dead squid, Shursta. Don't do it open-mouthed, Shursta. Shursta, you snore, go sleep in the next room. I mean, who are these people? These *Blodestones*? Who do they think they are? In Sif—in Sif at least the women know how to use their hands. I mean, they *know* how to use their hands, you know? And all this talk, talk, talk... All this whining and complaining... All this saying I'm not good enough. What does she expect, a miracle? How can a man function, how can he *function* in these circumstances? How can he rise to the occasion, eh? Eh?"

Shursta nudged the nearest patron, who gave him a curled lip and turned her back on him. Sneering at her shoulder blades, Shursta muttered, "You're probably a Blodestone, eh? *All women are kin.* Think that's what a man's about, eh? Think that's all he is? A damned baby maker? Soon's you have your precious daughters, your bouncing boys, you forget all about us. Man's no good to you till he gets you pissful of those shrieking, wailing, mewling, shitting little shit machines? Eh? Well, what if he can't? What if he cannot–is he not still a man? *Is he not still a man?*"

By now the barkeep of the Thirsty Seagull was scowling black daggers at him. Someone shoved Shursta from behind. He spun around with fists balled up. Nobody was there.

"Eh," he spat. "Probably a Blodestone."

When he turned back to the bar, a hand slid a drink over to him. Shursta drank before looking to see who had placed it there.

Myrar Yaspir stared at him with avid eyes.

"Don't know you," Shursta mumbled. "Thanks for the nog. Raise my cup. Up. To you. Oh. . . It's empty." He slammed it down. "Barkeep, top her up. Spill her over. Fill her full. Come on, man. Don't be a Blodestone."

Amber liquid splashed over the glass's rim.

"You're the new Blodestone man," Myrar Yaspir whispered. "You're Damisel Hyrryai's new husband."

Shursta snarled. "Won't be her husband once my year's up. She'll be glad to see the back of me. Wretch. Horror. Harpy. Who needs her? Who wants her?" He began to blubber behind shaking hands. "Oh, but by all the gods below! How she gleams. How she catches the light. How will I live without her?"

A coin clinked down. Bottle touched tumbler. Myrar's whisper was like a naked palm brushing the sandpaper side of a shark.

"Are you having trouble, Blodestone man? Trouble in the meshing bed?"

"Ayup, trouble," Shursta agreed, not raising his snot-streaked face. "Trouble like an empty sausage casing. Trouble like . . ."

"Yes, trouble," Myrar cut him off. "Yet you sit here. You sit here drunk and stupid–you. You of all men. You, whose right as husband gives you access to that household. Don't you see, you stupid Blodestone man?" His hand shot out to grab Shursta's ear. The cartilage gave a twinge of protest, but Shursta set his teeth. When Myrar's hand came back, he cradled Shursta's gemmaja in his palm.

"Do you know what this is?"

Shursta burped. "Ayup. Green rock. Wife gave me. Wanna see my coral?" He fished for the cord beneath his shirt. "True Sarths wear carnelian, she says. Carnelian's the stone for Sarths. You ask me, coral's just as good. Hoity-toity rich folk."

"Not rock. This–is–not–*rock*," Myrar hissed. His fingers clenched and unclenched around the green chalcedony. By the dim light of the wall sconces, Shursta could barely make out the red speckles in the stone, like tiny drops of blood.

"This is your *child.* This is the love of your wife. This is life. *Life,* Blodestone man. Do you understand?" Myrar Yaspir scooted his stool closer. His breath was cold, like the inside of a tomb. "I was you once. Low. A cur who knew it was beaten. Beaten by life. By work. By women. By those haughty, high-nosed Blodestone bastards who own more than half this island and mean to marry into the other half, until there is nothing left for the rest of us. But last thing before he died, my grandad sat me down. Said he knew I was unhappy. Knew my... my Adularia wept at night for want of a child. He had a thing to tell me. A thing about stones."

Dull-eyed, Shursta blinked back at him.

"Stones," he repeated.

"Yes. Stones. Magic stones. So." Myrar Yaspir set the green chalcedony tenderly, even jealously, into Shursta's palm. "Take your little rock home with you, Blodestone man. Put it in a mortar–not a wooden one. A fine one, of marble. Take the best pestle to it. Grind it down. Grind it to powder. Drink it in a glass of wine–the Blodestone's finest. They have fine wine in that house. Drink it. Go to your wife. Don't listen to her voice. Her voice doesn't matter. When she sees how you come to her, her thighs will sing. Her legs will open to you. Make her eat her words. Pound her words back into her. Get her with that child. Who knows?" Myrar Yaspir sank back down, his eyes losing that feral light. "Who knows. It may gain you another year. What more can a man ask, whose wife no longer loves him? Just one more year. It's worth it."

All down his gullet, the amber drink burned. In another minute, Shursta knew, he would lose it again, vomiting all over himself. He swallowed hard. Then he bent his head to the man beside him, who had become bleak and still and silent once more, and asked, very softly:

"Was it worth the life of Kuista Blodestone? Myrar Yaspir, was it worth the death of a child?"

If cold rock could turn its head, if rock could turn the fissures of its eyes upon a living man, this rock was Myrar Yaspir.

"What did you say?"

"My wife is hunting for you."

Myrar Yaspir became flesh. Flinched. Began to shudder. Shursta did not loose him from his gaze.

"I give you three days, Domo Yaspir. Turn yourself in to the Astrion Council. Confess to the murder of Kuista Blodestone. If you do not speak by the third day, I will tell my wife what I know. And she will find you. Though you flee from coast to bay and back again, she will find you. And she will eat your heart by moonlight."

Glass shattered. A stool toppled. Myrar Yaspir fled the Thirsty Seagull, fast as his legs could carry him.

Shursta closed his eyes.

The next three days were the happiest days of Shursta's life, and he drank them in. It was as if he, alone of all men, had been given to know the exact hour of his death. He filled the hours between himself and death with sunlight.

For the first day, Sharrar watched him as the sister of a dying man watches her brother. But his smiles and his teasing–"Leave off, Nugget, or I'll teach Laric where you're ticklish!"–and the deep brilliance of peace in his eyes must have eased her, for on the second day, her spirits soared, and she was back to playing tricks on her mesh-brothers, and kissing Laric Spectrox around every corner and under every tree, and reciting stories and singing songs to the children of the house.

Hyrryai, who still prowled Droon every night, spent her days close to home. She invited Shursta to walk with her, along paths she knew blindfolded. He asked her to teach him about spinning fire and she said, "Let's start with juggling maybe," and taught him patterns with handfuls of fallen fruit.

Suppers with the Blodestones were loud and raucous. Every night turned into a competition. Some Shursta won (ring tossing out in the courtyard) and some he lost (matching drinks with Lochlin, now known to all–thanks to Sharrar–as Lunkhead), but he laughed more than he ever had in his life, and when he laughed, he felt Hyrryai watching him, and knew she smiled.

On evening of the third day, he evaded his brothers' invitation to play hoopball. Sharrar immediately volunteered–so long as she and Laric could count as one player. She would piggyback upon his shoulders, and he would be her legs. Plankin, Orssi and Dumwei were still vehemently arguing against this when Shursta approached his mesh-mate and set a purple hyacinth into her hands.

"Will you walk with me, wife?"

Her rich, rare skin flushed with the heat of roses. She took the hand he offered.

"I will, husband."

They strolled out into the scented night, oblivious to the hoots and calls of their kin. Their sandals made soft noises on the pavement. For many minutes, neither spoke. Hyrryai tucked the hyacinth into her hair.

An aimless by and by had passed when they came to a small park. Just a patch of grass, a bench, a fountain. As they had when they met, they sat on the ground with their backs to the bench. Hyrryai, for once, slumped silkily, neglecting to jolt upright every few minutes. When Shursta sank down to rest his head in her lap, her hand went to his hair. She stroked it from his face, traced designs on his forehead. He did not care that he forgot to breathe. He might never breathe again and die a happy man.

The moon was high, waxing gibbous. To Shursta's eyes, Hyrryai seemed chased in silver. He reached to catch the fingers tangled in his hair. He kissed her fingertips. Sat up to face her. Her smile was silver when she looked at him.

"The name of your sister's murderer is Myrar Yaspir," he said in a low voice. "I met him in a tavern at the edge of Droon. He had three days' grace to confess his crime to the Astrion Council. Let them have him, I thought, they who made him. But when I spoke to your grandmother before dinner, she said no one had yet come forward. I believe he decided to run. I am sorry."

The pulse in her throat beat an inaudible but profound tattoo through the night air.

To an unconcerned eye, nothing of Hyrryai would have seemed changed. Still she was silver in the moonlight. Still the purple flower glimmered against her wing-black hair. Only her breath was transformed. Inhalation and exhalation exactly matched. Perfect and total control. The pale light playing on her mouth did not curve gently upward. Her eyes stared straight ahead, unblinking sinkholes. The gleam in them was not of moonlight.

"You have known this for three days."

Shursta did not respond.

"You talked to him. You warned him."

Again, he said nothing. She answered anyway.

"He cannot run far enough."

"Hyrryai."

"*You–do–not–speak–to–me.*"

"Hyrryai–"

"No!"

Her hand flashed out, much as Myrar Yaspir's had. She took nothing from him but flesh. Fingernails raked his face. Shursta did not, at first, suffer any sting. What he did feel, way down at the bottom of his chest, was a deep snap as she broke the strand of pearl and teeth and stone she wore around her throat. Pieces of moonlight scattered. Fleet and silver as they, Hyrryai Blodestone bounded into the radiant darkness.

One by one–by glint, by ridge, by razor edge–Shursta picked up pieces from the tufted grass. What he could salvage, he placed in the pouch he had prepared. His rucksack he retrieved from the hollow of a tree where he had hidden it the night before. The night was young, but the road to Sif was long.

Despite having begged her in his goodbye letter to go on and live her life in joy, with Laric Spectrox and his dream of a distant horizon, far from a brother who could only bring her shame and sorrow, Sharrar came home to Sif. And when she did, she did not come alone.

She brought her new husband. She brought a ragged band of orphans, grayheads, widows, widowers. Joining her too were past-primers like Adularia Yaspir, face lined and eyes haunted. Even Oron Onyssix had joined them, itching for spaces ungoverned by crones, a place where he might breathe freely.

Sharrar also brought a boat.

It was a very large boat. Or rather, the frame of it. It was the biggest boat skeleton Shursta had ever seen. They wheeled it on slats all the way along the searoad from the outskirts of Droon where Laric had been building it. Shursta, who had thought he might never do so again, laughed.

"What is this, Nugget? Who are all these people?"

But he thought he knew.

"These," she told him, "are all our new kin. And this–" with a grand gesture to the unfinished monstrosity listing on its makeshift wagon, "is Grimgramal–the ship that sails the world!"

Shursta scrutinized it and said at last, "It doesn't look like much, your ship that sails the world."

Sharrar stuck her tongue out at him. "We have to *finish* it first, brother mine!"

"Ah."

"Everyone's helping. You'll help too."

Shursta stared at all the people milling about his property, pitching tents, lining up for the outhouse, exploring the dock, testing the sturdiness of his small fishing boat. "Will I?" he asked. "How?"

Laric came over to clap him on the shoulder. "However you can, my mesh-brother. Mend nets. Hem sails. Boil tar. Old man Alexo Alban is carving us a masthead. He says it's a gift from all the Halls of Ages on the Last Isle to Sharrar." Taking his mesh-mate's hand, he indicated the dispersed crowd. "She's the one who called them. She's been speaking the name Grimgramal to anyone who'll stand still to listen. And you know Sharrar–when she talks, no one can help but listen. Some sympathizers–a very few–like Alexo Alban, started demanding passage in exchange for labor. Though," his left shoulder lifted in a gesture eloquent of resignation, "most of the grayheads say they'll safe stay on dry land to see us off. Someone, they claim, must be left behind to tell the tale. And see?"

Laric dipped into his pocket, spilling out a palmful of frozen rainbows. Shursta reached to catch a falling star before it buried itself in the sand. A large, almost bluish, diamond winked between his fingers. Hastily, he returned it.

"Over the last few weeks, the grayheads have been coming to Sharrar. Some from far villages. Even a few crones of the Astrion Council–including Dymmori Blodestone. Each gave her a gem, and told her the lore behind it. Whatever is known, whatever has been surmised. Alexo Alban will embed them in the masthead like a crown. Nine Cities magic to protect us on our journey."

Shursta whistled through his teeth. "We're really going then?"

"Oh, yes," Sharrar said softly. "All of us. Before summer's end."

It was not to Rath Sea that Shursta looked then, but to the empty road that led away from Sif.

"*All* of us," Sharrar repeated. "You'll see."

Dumwei Blodestone arrived one afternoon, drenched from a late summer storm, beady-eyed with irritation and chilled to the bone.

"Is Sif the last village of the world? What a stupid place. At the end of the stupidest road. Mudholes the size of small islands. Swallow a horse, much less a man. Sharkbait, why do you let your roof leak? How can you expect to cross an ocean in a wooden boat when you can't even be bothered to fix a leaky roof? We'll all be drowned by the end of the week."

"We?" Sharrar asked brightly, slamming a bowl of chowder in front of him. "Are you planning on going somewhere, Dimwit?"

"Of course!" He glanced at her, astonished, and brandished a spoon in her face. "You don't really think I'm going to let you mutants have all the fun, do you? Orssi wanted to come too, but now he's got a girl. Mesh-mad, the pair of 'em."

His gaze flickered to the corner where Oron Onyssix sat carving fishhooks from antler and bone. Onyssix raised his high-arched eyebrows. Dumwei looked away.

With a great laugh, Laric broke a fresh loaf of bread in two and handed the larger portion to Dumwei.

"Poor Orssi. You'll just have to have enough adventure for the two of you."

Dumwei's chest expanded. "I intend to, Laric Spectrox!"

"Laric Sarth," he corrected.

"Oh, yes, that's right. Forgot. *Maybe* because you didn't *invite* me to your *meshing*."

"Sorry," the couple said in unison, sounding anything but.

"And speaking of impossible mesh-mates. . ." Dumwei turned to Shursta, who knelt on the floor, feeding the firepit. "My sister wants to see you, Shursta."

For a moment, none of the dozen or so people crammed in the room breathed. Dumwei did not notice. Or if he noticed, he did not care.

"Mumsa won't talk about her, you know. Well, she talks, but only to say things like, if her last living daughter wants to run off like a wild dog and file her teeth and declare herself *windwyddiam*, that's Hyrryai's decision. Maybe no one will care then, she says, when she declares herself a mother with six sons and no daughters. And then she cries. And granmumsa and Auntie Elbanni and Auntie Ralorra all cluck their tongues and huddle close, and it's all hugs and tears and clacking, and a man can't hear himself think."

Shursta, who had not risen from his knees, comprehended little of this. If he'd held a flaming brand just then instead of ordinary wood, he might not have heeded it.

Sharrar asked, carefully, "Have you seen Hyrryai then, Dumwei?"

"Oh, ayup, all the time. She ran off to live in a little sea cave, in the. . . *That* cove." Dumwei seemed to swallow the wrong way, though he had not started eating. Quickly, he ducked his head, inspecting his chowder as if for contaminates. When he raised his face again, his eyes were overbright. "You know. . . You know, Kuista was just two years younger than I. Hyrryai was like her second mumsa, maybe, but I was her best friend. Anyway. I hope Hyrryai does eat that killer's heart!"

In the corner of the room, Adularia Yaspir turned her face to the wall and closed her eyes.

Dumwei shrugged. "I hope she eats it and spits it out again for chum. A heart like Myrar Yaspir's wouldn't make anyone much of meal. As she's cast herself out of the kinline, Hyrryai has no roof or bed or board of her own. And you can only eat so much fish. So I bring her food. It's not like they don't know back home. Granmumsa slips me other things, too, that Hyrryai might need. Last time I saw her. . . Yesterday? Day before?" He nodded at Shursta. "She asked for you."

Shursta sprang to his feet. "I'll go right now."

But Sharrar and Laric both grabbed fistfuls of Shursta's shirt and forced him down again.

"You'll wait till after the storm," said Laric.

"And you'll eat first," Sharrar put in.

"And perhaps," suggested Oron Onyssix from the corner, "you might wash your face. Dress in a clean change of clothes. Shave. What are they teaching young husbands these days?"

Dumwei snorted. "Think you can write that manual, Onyssix?"

"In my sleep," he replied, with the ghost of his reckless grin. Dumwei flushed past his ears, but he took his bowl of chowder and went to sit nearer him.

Obedient to his sister's narrowed eyes, Shursta went through the motions of eating. But as soon as her back was turned, he slipped out the front door.

It was full dark when Shursta finally squelched into the sea cave. He stood there a moment, dripping, startled at the glowing suddenness of shelter after three relentlessly rainy hours on the sea road. There was a hurricane lamp at the back of the cave, tucked into a small natural stone alcove. Its glass chimney was sooty, its wick on the spluttering end of low. What Shursta wanted most was to collapse. But a swift glance around the flickering hollow made it clear that amongst the neatly stacked storage crates, bedroll, the tiny folding camp table, the clay oven with its chimney near the cave mouth, the stockpile of weapons leaning in one corner, Hyrryai was not there.

He closed his eyes briefly. Wiping a wet sleeve over his wet face, Shursta contemplated stripping everything, wrapping himself in one of her blankets and waiting for her while he dried out. She hadn't meant to be gone long, he reasoned; she left the lamp burning. And there was a plate of food, half-eaten. Something had disturbed her. A strange sound, cutting through the wind and rain and surf. Or perhaps a face. Someone who, like he had done, glimpsed the light from her cave and sought shelter of a fellow wayfarer.

Already trembling from the cold, now Shursta's shivers grew violent, as if a hole had been bored into the bottom of his skull and was slowly filling his spine with ice water. Who might be ranging abroad on such a night? The sick or deranged, the elderly or the very young. The desperate, like himself. The outcasts, like Hyrrai. And the outlaws: lean, hungry, hunted. But why should they choose *this* cove, of all the crannies and caverns of the Last Isle? Why this so particular haunted place, on such a howling night? Other than Hyrryai herself, Shursta could think of just one who'd have cause to come here. Who would be drawn here, inexorably, by ghosts or guilt or gloating.

His stomach turned to stone, his knees to mud. He put his hand on the damp wall to steady himself.

And what would Hyrryai have done, glancing up from her sad little supper to meet the shadowed, harrowed eyes of her sister's killer?

She would not have thought to grab her weapons. Or even her coat. Look, there it was, a well-oiled sealskin, draped over the camp stool. Her fork was on the floor there by the bedroll, but her dinner knife was missing.

Shursta bolted from the cave, into the rain.

The wind tore strips from the shroud of the sky. Moonlight splintered through, fanged like an anglerfish and as cold. Shurta slipped and slid around the first wall of boulders and began to clamber back up the stone steps to the sea road. He clutched at clumps of marram grass, which slicked through his fingers like seaweed. Wet sand and crumbled rock shifted beneath his feet. Gasping and drenched as he was, he clung to his claw-holds, knowing that if he fell he'd have to do it all over again. He'd almost attained the headland, had slapped first his left hand onto the blessedly flat surface, was following it by his right, meaning to beach himself from the cliff face onto the road in one great heave and lie there awhile, catching his breath, when a hand grasped his and hauled him up the rest of the way.

"Domo Blodestone!" gasped Myrar Yaspir. "You must help me. Your wife is hunting me."

The first time Shursta had seen Yaspir, he had looked like a man turned to stone and forgotten. The second time, his eyes had been livid as enraged wounds. Now he seemed scoured, nervous and alive, wet as Shursta. He wore an enormous rucksack and carried a walking stick which Shursta eyed speculatively. It had a smooth blunt end, well polished from age and handling.

"Is that how you killed Kuista Blodestone?" he blurted.

Myrar Yaspir followed his gaze. "This?" he asked, blankly. "No, it was a stone. I threw it into the sea, after." He grasped Shursta's collar and hefted. Myrar Yaspir was a ropy, long-limbed man whose bones seemed to poke right through his skin, but rather than attenuated, he seemed vigorously condensed, and his strength was enormous, almost electrical. Hauled to his feet, Shursta felt as though a piece of mortal-shaped lightning had smote down upon the Last Isle just to manhandle him. "Come," he commanded Shursta. "We must keep moving. She is circling us like a bone shark, closer, ever closer. Come, Domo Blodestone," he said again, blinking back rain from his burning eyes. "You must help me."

Shursta disengaged himself, though he felt little shocks go through him when his wrists knocked Myrar Yaspir's fists aside. "I already helped you, child-killer. I gave you three days to turn yourself into the Astrion Council. I am done with you."

Myrar Yaspir glanced at him, then shook his head. "You are not listening to me," he said with exasperated patience. "Your wife is hunting me. I will be safe nowhere on this island. Not here and not in Droon cowering in some straw cage built by those doddering bitches of the council." He bent his head close to Shursta's and whispered, "No, you must take me to Sif where you live. Word is you are sailing from this cursed place on a boat the size of a city. I will work for my passage. I work hard. I have worked all my life." He opened his hands as if to show the callouses there; as if, even empty, they had always been enough.

Shursta felt his voice go gentle, and could not prevent it, although he knew Myrar Yaspir would think him weakening.

"The Grimgrimal is the size, maybe, of a large house, and we who will sail on it are family. You, Domo Yaspir, are no one's family."

"*My wife is on that boat!*" Myrar flashed, his fist grasping the sodden cloth at Shursta's throat. His expression flickered from whetted volatility to bleak cobweb-clung despair, and after that, it seemed, he could express nothing because he no longer had a face. His was merely a sand-blasted and sun-bleached skull, dripping dark rain. The skull whispered, "My Adularia."

Shursta was afraid. He had only been so afraid once in his entire life, and that was last year, out on the open ocean, in that breathless half second before he jumped in after Gulak's young son, realizing even as he leapt that he would rather by far spool out the remainder of his days taunted and disliked and respected by none than dive into that particular death, where the boy floundered and the shark danced.

Now the words came with no stutter or click. "You have no wife."

The skull opened its mouth and screamed. It shrieked, raw and wordless, right into Shursta's face. Its fists closed again on the collar of Shursta's coat, twisted in a chokehold and jerked, lifting him off his feet as though he had been a small child. Shursta's legs dangled and his vision blackened and he struck out with his fists, but it was like pummeling a waterspout. Myrar was still screaming, but the sound soon floated off to a far away keening. Shursta, weightless between sky and sea, began to believe that Myrar had always been screaming, since the first time Shursta had beheld him sitting in the tavern, or maybe even before. Maybe he had been screaming since killing Kuista, the child he could not give his wife, and who, though a child, had all the esteem, joy of status, wealth and hope for the future that Myrar Yaspir, a man in his prime and a citizen of proud Droon, lacked.

Is it any wonder he screamed? Shursta thought. This was followed by another thought, further away: *I am dying.*

The moment he could breathe again was the moment his breath was knocked out of him. Myrar had released his chokehold on Shursta, but Shursta, barely conscious, had no time to find his feet before the ground leapt up to grapple him. He tried to groan, but all sound was sucked from the pit of his stomach into the sky. Rain splattered on his face. The wind ripped over everything except into his lungs.

By and by, he remembered how to breathe, and soon could do so without volunteering the effort. His mouth tasted coppery. His tongue was sore. Something had been bitten that probably should not have been. Shursta's hands closed over stones, trying to find one jagged enough to fend off further advances from a screaming skull-faced murderer. Where was his mesh-gift, the black knife Hyrryai had given him? Back in Sif, of course, in a box with his gemmaja, and the pressed petals of purple hyacinth that had fallen from her hair that night she left him. All his fingers found now were pebbles and blades of grass, and he could not seem to properly grip any of them. Shursta sat up.

Sometime between his falling and landing the awful screaming had stopped. There was only sobbing now: convulsive, curt, wretched, interrupted by bitter gasps for breath and short, sawtoothed cries of rage. Muffled, moist thumps punctuated each cry. Shursta had barely registered that it could not be Myrar Yaspir who wept–his tears had turned to dust long ago–when the thumps and sobs stopped. For a few minutes it was just rain and wind. Shursta blinked his eyes back into focus and took in the moon-battered, rain-silvered scene before him. His heart crashed in his chest like a fog-bell.

Hyrryai Blodestone crouched over the crumpled body of Myrar Yaspir. She grasped a large stone in her dominant hand. Myrar's bloody hair was tangled in her other. Her dinner knife was clamped between her teeth. As he watched, she let the head fall–another pulpy thump–tossed the dripping stone to one side and spat her knife into her hand. Her movements ragged and impatient, she sliced Myrar's shirt down the middle and laid her hand against his chest. She seemed startled by what she felt there–the last echoes of a heartbeat or the fact there was none, Shursta did not know.

"It's not worth," he said through chattering teeth, "the effort it would take to chew."

Hyrryai glanced at him, her face a shocky blank, eyes and nose and mouth streaming. She looked away again, then spat out a mouthful of excess saliva. The next second, she had keeled over and was vomiting over the side of a cliff. Shursta hurried to her side, tearing a strip from his sleeve as he did so, to gather her hair from her face and tie it back.

His pockets were full of useless things. A coil of fishing line, a smooth white pebble, a pencil stub–ah! Bless Sharrar and her clever hands. A handkerchief. He pulled it out and wiped Hyrryai's face, taking care at the corners of her mouth.

Her lips were bloodied, as though she had already eaten Myrar Yaspir's heart. He realized this was because she had been careless of her teeth, newly filed into the needle points of the *windwyddiam*. Even a nervous gnawing of the lip might pierce the tender flesh there.

Blotting cautiously, he asked, "Did that hurt?"

The face Hyrryai lifted to Shursta was no longer hard and blank but so wide open that he feared for her, that whatever spirits of the night were prowling might seek to use her as a door. He moved his body more firmly between hers and Myrar Yaspir's. He wondered if this look of woeful wonder would ever be wiped from her eyes.

"Nothing hurts," she mumbled, turning away again. "I feel nothing."

"Then why are you crying?"

She shrugged, picking at the grass near her feet. Her agitated fingers brushed again a dark and jagged stone. It was as if she had accidently touched a rotten corpse. She jerked against Shursta, who flailed out his foot to kick the stone over the cliff's edge. He wished he could kick Myrar Yaspir over and gone as well.

"Hyrryai–"

"D-Dumwei f-found you?" she asked at the same time.

"As you see."

"I c-called you to w-witness."

"Yes."

"I was going to make you, make you w-watch while I–" Hyrryai shook her head, baring her teeth as if to still their chattering. More slowly, she said, "It was going to be your punishment. Instead I came upon him as he was, as he was k-killing you."

And though his soul was sick, Shursta laughed. "Two at one blow, eh, Hyrryai?"

"Never," she growled at him, and took his face between her hands. "Never, never, *never*, Shursta Sarth, do you hear me? No one touches you. I will murder anyone who tries. I will eat their eyes, I will . . ."

He turned his face to kiss her blood-slicked hands. First one, then the other.

"Shh," he said. "Shh, Hyrryai. You saved my life. You saved me. It's over. It's over."

She slumped suddenly, pressing her face against his neck. Wrenched back, gasping. A small cut on her face bled a single thread of red. When next she spoke, her voice was wry.

"Your neck grew fangs, Shursta Sarth."

"Yes. Well. So."

Hyrryai fingered the strand of tooth and stone and pearl at his throat. Shursta held his breath as her black eyes flickered up to meet his, holding them for a luminous moment.

"Thief," she breathed. "That's mine."

"Sorry." Shursta ducked his head, unclasped the necklace, and wound it down into her palm. Her fist snapped shut over it. "Destroy it again for all of me, Hyrryai."

Hyrryai leaned in to lay her forehead against his. Even with his eyes shut, Shursta felt her smile move against his mouth, very deliberately, very carefully.

"Never," she repeated. "I'd sooner destroy Droon."

They left Myrar Yaspir's body where it lie, for the plovers and the pipers and the gulls. From the sea cave they gathered what of Hyrryai's belongings she wanted with her when she sailed with the Grimgrimal into the unknown sky, and they knelt and kissed the place where Kuista Blodestone had fallen. These last things done, in silent exhaustion Shursta and Hyrryai climbed back up to the sea road.

Setting their faces for Sif, they turned their backs on Droon.

Discussion Questions and Writing Activities

1. What did the inversion of gender norms surrounding marriage do in this story? How did this story dissect or disrupt the arranged marriage trope?

2. Why does the postapocalyptic setting of this world matter to the story? How would it be different without it?

3. Analyze point of view. How does the protagonist's worldview and voice infuse the narrative?

4. How does Cooney build the world of the story without explaining it overtly?

5. What internal and external pressures drive the characters in this story? How do these pressures impact the actions and reactions of the characters?

6. What do Cooney's characters want and fear? How do you know?

7. Write a fantasy story in a world where the sea levels rose long ago, and now people live in islands that used to be mountains. How would the constraints of this situation impact the culture of the world, and the beliefs and values of the characters?

8. Write a fantasy short story, à la Cooney's, where a romance is part of the story, but not the entire story.

Emrys Donaldson's   from *The Fairy Tale Review* (Charcoal Issue)

Biography (from their official website and their faculty profile)

Donaldson's work has recently appeared in *Electric Literature*, *TriQuarterly*, *Passages North*, *Redivider*, and *The Rupture*, among other venues. They hold a BA summa cum laude from Cornell University and an MFA from the University of Alabama. Originally from Vermont, they are now an Assistant Professor of English at Jacksonville State University. Their main areas of research concern speculative ecologies, science fiction, and cli-fi.

Literary Introduction

Donaldson's short story "The Albatrosses" is an original fairy tale. Rather than retelling an existing fairy tale, Donaldson takes recognizable fairy tale patterns, such as the fuzzy boundary between humans and animals, transformations, and utopian wish fulfillment, in order to tell a story of trans identity and community. It is told in the flat language of the oral fairy-tale tradition, where the story is simply related, with no explanation, the dream logic irrefutable. Donaldson works in the long and honorable tradition of using fairy tale motifs (retellings or originals) to give voice to that which is often unvoiced. Literary ancestors in this tradition include Angela Carter's "The Snow Child," and many others.

The Albatrosses

We warned the boys about the cliff, the one out there in the island cove. It loomed over the beach, with scraggly trees and grass alive in its crevices. Behind the island, the water darkened until it blurred with the horizon. Every time a boy swam out, an uncle floating on an inner tube would try to shoo them back to shore, but they never listened. Up they climbed.

If the leap from the top of the cliff didn't kill the boys, plummeting like stones, they turned into albatrosses or sometimes they turned into girls. Assigned *boy* by hospitals, they desired most to turn into *girl*. Without knowledge of the clinic on the mainland, they thought jumping was the only way. Don't ask us what made the few of them girls. Feathers iridesce, but so does young skin coming out of saltwater.

One day, three boys swam out to the island. Droplets glistened in the uncle's chest hair as he shook his finger at them, but again they ignored him. Finding footholds in the rock, the boys climbed, wet trunks sticking to their soft legs. It was hard going.

At the top of the island, a single twisted tree grew from a crag. The boys, beautiful boys, stood in a line. On the cusp of puberty, their limbs had begun to lengthen, stones growing at the bases of their throats. Two tied their hair back in topknots, one came forward with a fistful of grass. As they drew straws, sawn edges of grass blades tickled their cupped palms.

The first one to jump fell through the air half-formed, with bird wings and human legs. Half-changes happened sometimes, but they were rare. The boy sank below the surface of the water, and one of the people on shore began to scream. But then, just as drowning seemed likely, a form broke the surface of the water. Mid-transformation, head elongating into a beaked skull, wet wings dragging on the sand, the changeling walked to shore, receding from view beyond the first line of trees.

The second one to jump closed his eyes and dove. He was not so lucky.

The last boy took a running start, then pulled his legs up to his chest and held them as he went down. He seemed to hover in the air, just beyond the edge of the ledge, before he disappeared downward.

Spread wings skimmed water, but the albatross was determined. In the throes of changing selfhood, it returned to the ledge. Its eyes were beady black, its feathers blue and green, the sound of its beak snapping like teeth coming together after a big yawn. We used to say that if an albatross tried to jump again, it would fall so hard and so fast into the water that its beak would fill up with sand. We used to think that failure doomed a second transformation.

Spreading its webbed toes and folding in its wings, the albatross hopped off the cliff. It made only a small plonk when it hit the water. Kelp parted and reformed. Something bobbed up, out of the waves, and she was human.

The girl brushed water out of her eyes. She giggled, and the sound echoed in the cove. Floating on her back, she hit the water with her hands and feet, pummeling it into waves that splashed high up the side of the cliff, that tickled the toes of people sunning on the mainland shore. She was happy.

When the girl walked out from the sea, iridescent and new, the women in the beachside resort sat her down and fed her fish. She stood dripping wet on the tiles as one by one they chided her for taking such a risk when there was another way. They told her had they known, they would have helped her—held her hand on the way to the clinic, gone from verandah to verandah to ask for spare funds. These women took her in.

Sometimes, we go to the restaurant and see the girl there, tapping away at her keyboard, drinking a soda. We lay on the beach until it gets dark. At night, if we stay up and listen, we can hear the women's outboard motor, their soft laughter, and the lapping of the waves.

Discussion Questions and Writing Activities

1. What is the impact of using the matter-of-fact flat tone of a traditional oral folktale? How would this narrative be different if told from the point of view of one of the boys jumping off the cliffs?

2. Donaldson's short story is flash fiction. How does the brevity of the story influence the way it is read? Would a longer story in this same style be as effective? Why, or why not?

3. What opportunities does the fairy tale genre afford this story? What can a writer do in a fairy tale that they can't in a straightforward realistic story?

4. Analyze the prose in Donaldson's story. It has the simple language of an oral tale, but its imagery is incredibly precise. What patterns can you find in how Donaldson uses their prose to weave the tone and imagery in this story?

5. How is an original fairy tale different from a retelling? What constraints and opportunities are afforded the writer of an original fairy tale?

6. Write your own original fairy tale, using some the ingredients, or grammar, as Marina Warner would say, of fairy tales to create something new that still feels like a fairy tale.

7. Try writing a flash fairy tale in a similar flat oral prose, and then rewriting it from the point of view of one of the characters within. What changes? How do the different stylistic and point of view choices give your story different strengths?

Theodora Goss "England Under the White Witch" from *Clarkesworld 73*.

Biography (from her website)

Theodora Goss was born in Hungary and spent her childhood in various European countries before her family moved to the United States, where she completed her PhD. She has a BA in English Literature from the University of Virginia, a JD from Harvard Law School, and an MA and PhD in English Literature from Boston University. She is also a graduate of the Odyssey and Clarion writing workshops. She is the World Fantasy, Locus, and Mythopoeic Award-winning author of the short story and poetry collections *In the Forest of Forgetting* (2006), *Songs for Ophelia* (2014), and *Snow White Learns Witchcraft* (2019), as well as the novella *The Thorn and the Blossom* (2012), debut novel *The Strange Case of the Alchemist's Daughter* (2017), and sequels *European Travel for the Monstrous Gentlewoman* (2018) and *The Sinister Mystery of the Mesmerizing* Girl (2019). She has been a finalist for the Nebula, Crawford, and Shirley Jackson Awards, as well as on the Tiptree Award Honor List. Her work has been translated into fifteen languages. She teaches literature and writing at Boston University.

Literary Introduction

"England Under the White Witch" is an alternate-history apocalyptic fantasy story. Goss's prose is lyrical and draws upon the tradition of the literary fantasy story, among the traditions of the genres already named above. This story takes a Second-World-War-era England, but adds another party to the war, a White Witch. The story investigates issues of oppressive regimes, surveillance states, and what happens when people are brainwashed into informing on their neighbors. It has environmental overtones, since the omnipresent winter brought by the White Witch causes environmental and social devastation. Goss alludes to the White Witch of Narnia, as well as real-life oppressive states. Goss is also a fairy tale and folklore scholar; fairy tale imagery infuses the story. Novels that could be seen as literary ancestors to this story include *Lud-In-The-Mist* by Hope Mirlees and *Bend Sinister* by Vladimir Nabokov.

England Under the White Witch

It is always winter now.

When she came, I was only a child—in ankle socks, my hair tied back with a silk ribbon. My mother was a seamstress working for the House of Alexandre. She spent the days on her knees, saying Yes, madame has lost weight, what has madame been doing? When madame had been doing nothing of the sort. My father was a photograph of a man I had never seen in a naval uniform. A medal was pinned to the velvet frame.

My mother used to take me to Kensington Gardens, where I looked for fairies under the lilac bushes or in the tulip cups.

In school, we studied the kings and queens of England, its principal imports and exports, and home economics. Even so young, we knew that we were living in the waning days of our empire. That after the war, which had taken my father and toppled parts of London, the sun was finally setting. We were a diminished version of ourselves.

At home, my mother told me fairy tales about Red Riding Hood (never talk to wolves), Sleeping Beauty (your prince will come), Cinderella (choose the right shoes). We had tea with bread and potted meat, and on my birthday there was cake made with butter and sugar that our landlady, Mrs. Stokes, had bought as a present with her ration card.

Harold doesn't hold with this new Empress, as she calls herself, Mrs. Stokes would tell my mother. Coming out of the north, saying she will restore us to greatness. She's established herself in Edinburgh, and they do say she will march on London. He says the King got us through the war, and that's good enough for us. And who believes a woman's promises anyway?

But what I say is, England has always done best under a queen. Remember Elizabeth and Victoria. Here we are, half the young men dead in the war, no one for the young women to marry so they work as typists instead of having homes of their own. And trouble every day in India, it seems. Why not give an Empress a try?

One day Monsieur Alexandre told my mother that Lady Whorlesham had called her impertinent and therefore she had to go. That night, she sat for a long time at the kitchen table in our bedsit, with her face in her hands. When I asked her the date of the signing of the Magna Carta, she hastily wiped her eyes with a handkerchief and said, As though I could remember such a thing! Then she said, Can you take care of yourself for a moment, Ann of my heart? I need to go talk to Mrs. Stokes.

The next day, when I ran home from school for dinner, she was there, talking to Mrs. Stokes and wearing a new dress, white tricotine with silver braid trim. She looked like a princess from a fairy tale.

It's easy as pie, she was saying. I found the office just where you said it was, and they signed me right up. At first I'm going to help with recruitment, but the girl I talked to said she thought I should be in the rifle corps. They have women doing all sorts of things, there. I start training in two days.

You're braver than I am, said Mrs. Stokes. Aren't you afraid of being arrested?

If they do arrest me, will you take care of Ann? she asked. I know it's dangerous, but they're paying twice what I was making at the shop, and I have to do something. This world we're living in is no good, you and I both know that. Nothing's been right since the war. Just read this pamphlet they gave me. It makes sense, it does. I'm doing important work, now. Not stitching some Lady Whortlesham into her dress. I'm with the Empress.

In the end, the Empress took London more easily than anyone could have imagined. She had already taken Manchester, Birmingham, Oxford. We had heard how effective her magic could be against the remnants of our Home Forces. First, she sent clouds that covered the sky, from horizon to horizon. It snowed for days, until the city was shrouded in white. And then the sun came out just long enough to melt the top layer of snow, which froze during the night. The trees were encased in ice. They sparkled as though made of glass, and when they moved I heard a tinkling sound.

Then, she sent wolves. Out of the mist they came, white and gray, with teeth as sharp as knives. They spoke in low, guttural voices, telling the Royal Guards to surrender or have their throats ripped out. Most of the guards stayed loyal. In the end, there was blood on the snow in front of Buckingham Palace. Wolves gnawed the partly-frozen bodies.

Third and finally came her personal army, the shop girls and nursemaids and typists who had been recruited, my mother among them. They looked magnificent in their white and silver, which made them difficult to see against the snow. They had endured toast and tea for supper, daily indignity, the unwanted attention of employers. Their faces were implacable. They shot with deadly accuracy and watched men die with the same polite attention as they had shown demonstrating a new shade of lipstick.

Buckingham Palace fell within a day. On the wireless, we heard that the King and his family had fled to France, all but one of his sisters, who it turned out was a sympathizer. By the time the professional military could mobilize its troops, scattered throughout our empire, England was already hers to command.

I stood by Mrs. Stokes, watching the barge of the Empress as it was rowed down the Thames. She stood on the barge, surrounded by wolves, with her white arms bare, black hair down to her feet, waving at her subjects.

No good will come of this, you mark my words, said Mr. Stokes.

Hush! Isn't she lovely? said Mrs. Stokes.

You have seen her face in every schoolroom, every shop. Perhaps in your dreams. It is as familiar to you as your own. But I will never forget that first glimpse of her loveliness. She looked toward us, and I believed that she had seen me, had waved particularly to me.

The next day, our home economics teacher said, From now on, we are not going to learn about cooking and sewing. Instead, we are going to learn magic. There was already a picture of our beloved Empress over her desk, where the picture of the King used to be.

At first, there were resistance movements. There were some who fought for warmth, for light. Who said that as long as she reigned, spring would never come again. We would never see violets scattered among the grass, never hear a river run. Never watch young lovers hold each other on the embankment, kiss each other not caring who was watching. There was the Wordsworth Society, which tried to effect change politically. And there were more radical groups: the Children of Albion, the Primrose Brigade.

But we soon learned that our Empress was as ruthless as she was beautiful. Those who opposed her were torn apart by wolves, or by her girl soldiers, who could tear men apart with their bare hands and were more frightening than any wolves. Sympathizers were rounded up and imprisoned, encased in ice. Or worse, they were left free but all the joy was taken from them, so that they remained in a prison of their own perpetual despair.

Her spies were everywhere. Even the trees could not be trusted. The hollies were the most dangerous, the most liable to inform. But resistance groups would not meet under pines, firs, or hemlocks. In many households, the cats were on her side. Whispers of disloyalty would bring swift retribution.

And many said, such traitors deserved punishment. That winter was good for England, that we needed cold, needed toughening. We had grown soft after the war, allowed our dominions to rebel against us, allowed the world to change. But she would set things right. And so the resistance movements were put down, and our soldiers marched into countries under a white flag that did not mean surrender. Those who had tried to be free of us were confronted with winter, and sorceresses, and wolves. Their chiefs and rajahs and presidents came to London, bringing jewels and costly fabrics to lay before her feet, and pledged their loyalty.

Our empire spread, as indeed it must. A winter country must import its food, and as winter spreads, the empire must expand to supply the lands under snow, their waters locked in ice. That is the terrible, inescapable logic of empire.

I was a Snowflake, in a white kerchief with silver stars. Then, I was an Ice Maiden. The other girls in school nodded to me as I walked by. If they did not wear the white uniform, I asked them why they had not joined up yet, and if they said their parents would not let them, I told them it was their responsibility to be persuasive. I won a scholarship to university, where I was inducted into the Sisterhood of the Wolf.

My den mother encouraged me to go into the sciences. Scientists will be useful to the Empress in the coming war, she said. Science and magic together are more powerful, are greater weapons, than they are apart. And there is a war coming, Ann. We hear more and more from our spies in Germany. A power is rising in that part of the world, a power that seeks to oppose the reign of the Empress. Surely not, I said. Who would oppose her? A power that believes in fire, she said. A fire that will burn away the snow, that will scorch the earth. That does not care about what we have already achieved—the security, the equality, the peace we will achieve when her empire spreads over the earth.

When I graduated, the Empress herself handed me a diploma and the badge of our order. My mother, who had been promoted to major-general, was so proud! All of us in the Sisterhood had been brought to Buckingham Palace, in sleighs drawn by reindeer with silver bells on their antlers. We waited in a long room whose walls were painted to look like a winter forest, nibbling on almond biscuits and eating blancmange from silver cups with small bone spoons. At last, we were summoned into her presence.

You have seen our beloved Empress from far away, from below while she stands on a balcony, or from a sidewalk as she is drawn through the city streets in her sleigh. But I have met her, I have kissed her hand. It was white and cold, with the blue veins visible. Her grip was strong—stronger than any man's, as she was taller than any man. Her face was so pale that I could only look at it for a moment without pain. Her black hair trailed on the floor.

You have done well, she said to me, and I could hear her voice in my head as well as with my ears. To hear that voice again, I would consent to being torn apart by wolves.

You have never seen, you will never see, anything as magnificent as our Empress.

Where did she come from? Some say she came from the stars, that she is an alien life-form. Some say that she is an ancient goddess reborn. Some say she is an ordinary woman, and that such women have always lived in the north: witches who command the snows.

The question is whispered, in secret places where there are no hemlocks, no cats: does human blood flow in her veins? Can our Empress die?

I met Jack in the basic physical training program required for all recruits to the war effort. My mother had used her influence to have me chosen for the Imperial Guard, the Empress's personal girl army, which could be deployed throughout the empire. After basic training, I was going to advanced training in the north, and then wherever the war effort needed me. He was a poet, assigned to the Ministry of Morale. He had been conscripted after university—this was in the early days of general conscription. He was expected to write poetry in praise of the Empress, and England, and those who served the empire. But first, we all had to pass basic training.

We stayed in unheated cabins, bathed in cold water, all to make us stronger, to bring the cold inside us. Each morning, we marched through the woods. The long marches, hauling weapons and equipment through the snow, were not difficult for me. I had been training since my university days, waking at dawn to run through the snow or swim in the icy rivers with the Sisterhood. But he was not as strong as I was. He would stumble over roots or boulders beneath the snow, and try to catch himself with chilled, chapped hands—the woolen gloves we had been issued were inadequate protection against the cold. I would help him up, holding him by the elbow, and sometimes I would carry part of his equipment, transferring it into my pack surreptitiously so the Sergeant did not see me.

Why are you so kind to me, Ann? he asked me once. Someone has to be, I said, smiling.

The other girls laughed at him, but I thought his large, dark eyes were beautiful. When he looked at me, I did not feel the cold. One day, I sat next to him at dinner. He told me about Yorkshire, where he was born—about the high hills, the sheep huddled together, their breaths hanging on the air.

Perhaps I should have been more like my father, he said. It was my headmaster at school who first read my poems and told me to apply for a scholarship. There I was, a farmer's son, studying with the children of ministers and generals, who talked about going to the palace the way I talked about going to the store. I kept to myself, too proud or ashamed to approach them, to presume they might be my friends. But my tutor sent my poems to the university literary magazine, and they were published. Then, I was invited to join the literary society. I thought it was an honor—until we all received letters from the war office. So here I am, losing my toes to frostbite so I can write odes for the dead in Africa—or for the war they say is coming.

We all believed that war was coming. The newspapers were already talking about a fire rising in the east, burning all before it.

It's a great honor to write for the Empress, I said.

Yes, of course it is, he said after a moment. He looked at me intently with those dark eyes. Of course, he said again, before finishing the thin broth with dumplings that we were told was Irish stew.

We spent more and more time together, huddled in the communal showers when we could, telling each other about our childhoods, the foods we liked, the books we had read. We wondered about the future. He hoped that after his compulsory service, he could work as a schoolteacher, publish his poems. I did not know where I would be assigned—Australia? South America? There was always unrest in some part of the empire.

One day, the Sergeant said to me, Ann, I'm not going to tell you what to do. I'm just going to warn you—there's something not right about Jack Kirby. I don't know what it is, but Thule—who was her wolf—can't stand him. I don't think a general's daughter should show too much interest in that boy. You don't want anyone questioning your loyalty, do you?

Her words made me angry. He was going into the Ministry—wasn't that good enough? That night, we met in the showers. I don't want to talk, I said. I kissed him—slid my hands under his jacket, sweater, undershirt. His body was bony, but I thought it had its own particular grace. He told me that I was beautiful, breathing it into my neck as we made love, awkwardly, removing as few layers of clothing as possible. You're beautiful, Ann—I hear it in my mind and remember the warmth of his breath in that cold place. There had been others, not many, but he may as well have been my first. He is the one I remember.

During our week of leave, he asked me to come home with him, to Yorkshire. His father met us at the train station. He was a large, quiet man who talked mostly of sheep. Look at these pelts, he told me. Feel the weight of them. Didn't use to get wool like this, in Yorkshire. It's the perpetual winter as does it. Grows twice as thick and twice as long. But he grumbled about the feed from the communal granaries—not as nourishing as the grass that used to grow on the hillsides, never seen such sickly lambs. And the wolves—not allowed to shoot them anymore. Those who complained were brought before a committee.

We had suppers of Yorkshire pudding and gravy, and walked out over the fields holding hands. I asked Jack about his mother. She had died in the influenza epidemic, which he had barely survived. That was before the coming of the Empress. I could see, from the photograph of her on the bureau, that he had inherited her delicacy, her dark eyes and thick, dark hair. Late at night, when his father was asleep, he would sneak into the guest room and we would make love under the covers, as quietly as possible, muffling our laughter, whispering to one another.

The day before we were to return from leave, his father told him that a ewe was giving birth in the snow. She had become trapped in a gully, and could not be lifted out in her condition. There was no chance of bringing her into the barn, so he and his father, one of the two farm hands, and the veterinarian went out, grumbling about the cold.

I wandered through the house, then sat in his room for a while, looking through the books he had read as a child. Books from before the Empress came, and from after—Prince Frost and the Giants, the Wolf Scout series, the Treasury of English Poems we had all studied in school. I can't tell you why I chose to look though the battered old desk he had used as a schoolboy. It was wrong, a base impulse. But I loved him, and on this last day before we went back to the camp, I wanted to feel close to him. I wanted to know his secrets, whatever they were—even if they included love letters from another girl. I tortured myself for a moment with that thought, knowing how unlikely it was that I would find anything but old schoolbooks and pens. And then I pulled open the drawer.

In the desk was a notebook, and in the notebook were his poems—in his handwriting, with dates at the tops of the pages indicating when they had been written. The latest of them was dated just before camp. They spoke of sunlight and warmth and green fields. Next to the notebook was a worn copy of one of the forbidden books: *The Complete Poetical Works of Wordsworth*. I opened to the page marked with a ribbon and read,

I wandered lonely as a cloud
That floats on high o'er vales and hills,
When all at once I saw a crowd,
A host, of golden daffodils . . .

I slammed the book shut. My hands were shaking. I remembered what the Sergeant had said: You don't want anyone questioning your loyalty, do you?

By the time Jack, his father, and the other men had returned, I was composed enough to seem almost normal. That night, he came to my room. We made love as though nothing had happened, but all the time I could hear it in my head: *I wandered lonely as a cloud—a host of golden daffodils.* I remembered daffodils. I could almost see them, bright yellow against the blue sky.

The next morning, as Jack and his father were loading our bags into the sleigh that would take us to the train station, I told them I had forgotten something. I ran back into the house, up the stairs and into Jack's room, then quickly slid the notebook and book into my backpack.

When we arrived back at camp, I went to the Sergeant and denounced Jack Kirby as a traitor.

I told myself that I was doing the right thing. He would be sent for reeducation. He would become a productive citizen, not a malcontent longing for what could never be. Perhaps someday he would even thank me.

He was sent to a reeducation camp in the north of Scotland. I graduated from basic training, went on to advanced training for the Imperial Guard, and was eventually given my wolf companion, Ulla. Together, we were sent to France, where the war had already started. We were among the first to enter Poland. We were in the squadron that summoned ice to cover the Black Sea so our soldiers could march into Turkey. My den mother had been right: science and magic together created powerful weapons. It took five years, but the fire in the east was defeated, and our empire stretched into the Russian plains, into the deserts of Arabia.

When I returned to England, I asked for Jack's file. It told me that he had died in the camp, shortly after arriving. The causes of death were listed as cold and heartbreak.

During the Empress's reign, England has changed for the better, some say. There is always food in the shops, although it has lost its flavor. Once, carrots were not pale, like potatoes. Cabbages were green. They were not grown in great glass houses. The eggs had bright yellow centers, and all meat did not taste like mutton. Once, there were apple trees in England, and apples, peaches, plums were not imported from the distant reaches of our empire, where winter has not yet permanently settled. There was a sweetness in the world that you have never tasted. There was love and joy, and pain sharp as knives, rather than this blankness.

Our art, our stories, our poems have changed, become ghosts of their former selves. Mothers tell their daughters about Little White Hood and her wolf companion. About Corporal Cinder, who joined the liberation army and informed on her wicked sisters.

Our soldiers move on from conquest to conquest, riding white bears, white camels. Parts of the world that had never seen snow have seen it now. I myself have sent snow drifts to cover the sands of the Sahara, so we could deploy our sleighs. I have seen the Great Pyramid covered in ice, and crocodiles lying lethargic on ice-floes in the Nile.

Our empire stretches from sea to sea to sea. Eventually, even the republics that now fight against us will come under our dominion. And then perhaps the only part of the world that has not bowed down to our Empress, the wild seas themselves, will be covered in ice. What will happen to us then, when there are no more lands to send provisions to the empire? I do not know. Our Empress has promised us a perfect world, but the only perfection is death.

You have heard stories of primroses and daffodils, and you do not believe them. You have heard that there were once green fields, and rivers that ran between their banks, and a warm sun overhead. You have never seen them, and you believe they are merely tales. I am here to tell you that they are true, that in my childhood these existed. And cups of tea that were truly hot, and Christmas trees with candles on their branches, and church bells. Girls wore ribbons in their hair rather than badges on their lapels. Boys played King Arthur or Robin Hood rather than Wolf Scout.

I'm here to tell you that the fairy tales are true.

And that, sitting in this secret place, looking at each other in fear, wondering who among you is an informant, you must decide whether to believe in the fairy tales, whether to fight for an idea. Ideas are the most powerful things—beauty, freedom, love. But they are harder to fight for than things like food, or safety, or power. You can't eat freedom, you can't wield love over another.

You are so young, with your solemn faces, your thin bodies, nourished on pale cabbage and soggy beef and slabs of flavorless pudding! I do not know if you have the strength. But that, my children, you will have to find out for yourselves.

Your leaders, who have asked me here tonight, believe that winter can end, if you have the courage to end it. They are naive, as revolutionaries always are. Looking at your faces, I wonder. You have listened so intently to an old soldier, a woman who has seen much, felt much, endured. I have no strength left to fight, either for or against the Empress. Everyone I have ever loved—my mother, Mrs. Stokes, Jack Kirby, Ulla—is dead. I have just enough strength to tell you what the world was once, and could be again: imperfect, unequal, and in many ways unjust. But there was warmth and light to counteract the cold, the darkness.

What do I believe? Entropy is the law of the universe. All things run down, all things eventually end. Perhaps, after all, she is not an alien, not a witch, but a universal principal.

Perhaps all you can do is hold back the cold, the darkness, for a while. Is a temporary summer worth your lives? But if you do not fight, you will never feel the warmth of the sun on your cheeks, or smell lilacs, or bite into a peach picked directly from the tree. You will never hold each other on the embankment, watching the waters of the Thames run below. The old stories will be forgotten. Our empire will spread over the world, and it will be winter, everywhere, forever.

Discussion Questions and Writing Activities

1. What is the effect of using historical fantasy to talk about real-life historical and contemporary traumas, like surveillance, and militarization of societies? What is gained in this story through combining the real and the unreal?

2. Why use the White Witch as the villain and authoritarian leader in this story? What impact does the intertextuality of the name make on the story's meaning?

3. Analyze the way the environment and the characters are impacted by the White Witch as the story progresses. Do you see any connections between what happens to the natural world, and to the characters?

4. How does this story control the flow of time in order to cover a long period? How does point of view assist in this process?

5. Is there a historical period or event you are super-nerdy about? If so, imagine inserting another actor into that event or period, one that is in some way magical or fantastical, that would destabilize the power structures at play. What might happen as a result? Write a story from the resulting imaginative exercise.

6. Imagine Goss's story told from another point of view, such as that of the Witch herself. How would the point of view shift change this story?

7. Try writing a short fantasy story that takes place in the aftermath of a war. What happens when you set a story after what is often the climatic event of many epic fantasy and historical narratives?

Rachael K. Jones "The Night Bazaar for Women Becoming Reptiles" from *Beneath Ceaseless Skies*

Biography (from her website)

Rachael K. Jones grew up in various cities across Europe and North America, picked up (and mostly forgot) six languages, and acquired several degrees in the arts and sciences. Now she writes speculative fiction in Portland, Oregon. Her debut novella was *Every River Runs to Salt* (2018). Contrary to the rumors, she is probably not a secret android. Rachael is a World Fantasy Award nominee and Tiptree Award honoree. Her fiction has appeared in dozens of venues worldwide, including *Lightspeed*, *Beneath Ceaseless Skies*, *Strange Horizons*, and *PodCastle*. Follow her on Twitter @RachaelKJones.

Literary Introduction

Jones's short story "The Night Bazaar for Women Becoming Reptiles" is a secondary-world fantasy. Its prose is lyrical and characterized by concrete imagery and an intimate psychological portrait of the point of view character, Hester. This story takes part in the time-honored tradition of fantasy fiction that disrupts gender norms by creating a world in which relational arrangements, sexuality, and gendered expectations are different from the real world. Its character-driven approach and focus on gender recall works as recent as *When the Tiger Came Down the Mountain* by Nghi Vo and *A Taste of Honey* by Kai Ashante Wilson, and earlier works like *Swordspoint* by Ellen Kushner.

The Night Bazaar for Women Becoming Reptiles

In the desert, all the footprints lead into Oasis, and none lead out again. They come for water, and once they find it, no one returns to the endless sand. The city is a prison with bars of thirst and heat.

Outside the gates the reptiles roam: asps and cobras, great lazing skinks, tortoises who lie down to doze in the heat. Where they go as they pad and swish and claw their way through the sand, no one knows, save the women who look over the walls and feel the deep itching pressure in their bones, the weight of skin in need of sloughing.

Though Hester has sold asp eggs at the night bazaar for five years, she has never become a reptile herself, no matter what she tries.

She takes eggs wherever she finds them. She has eaten those of skinks and geckos. She has tasted sun-warmed iguana eggs. She has traced water-snake paths through Oasis and dug for their nests. She has braved the king cobra's sway and dart, and devoured its offspring too. Once, she found an alligator egg, and poked a hole in the top and sucked out the insides. But no matter what she tries, Hester has never broken free and escaped the city like the other women do.

She even tried the asp eggs once, the ones that were her livelihood. It was the day after Marick the mango seller asked to take her as his sunside lover. Hester left home and dug asp eggs from the clay by the river. The sun spilled long red tongues across the sand, over the footprints always entering the city, never leaving, and Hester's skin itched all over, and her flesh grew hot and heavy, and she longed for cool sand sliding against her bare belly.

One, two, three eggs into her mouth, one sharp bite, and the clear, viscous glair ran down her throat. The shells were tougher than she expected. They tasted tart, like spoiled goat's milk. She waited for the change, but the sun crawled higher and nothing happened.

She has never told anyone about the day with the asp eggs. Not her mother the batik dyer, who spatters linen in hot running wax and crafts her famous purple cloth. Not Marick her sunside lover, who sells indigo cactus flowers and mango slices on a wooden tray. Not Shayna the butcher, her moonside lover, whose honey-gold verses roll from her tongue, smooth and rounded as sand-polished pebbles. Hester hasn't told them, because they are why she longs to leave.

The night bazaar meets on a different street each week. Each morning before, at sunrise, Hester finds three blue chalk symbols sketched on the doorjamb behind the perfumed jasmine bush. Sometimes she sees a falcon, a crane beneath a full moon, and a viper climbing a triple-columned temple portico. This means *We assemble where the Street of Upholsterers intersects the Street of Priests, when the Crane rises.* Or it might be a hand holding an eye, a wavy river, and a kneeling woman, which would mean *Meet where Oasis runs to mud, and beware the police.* Hester memorizes the message and wipes off the chalk with her sleeve.

They meet in secret, because the night bazaar was outlawed when the emperor stepped down from her throne and became a snapping turtle. No one knew if she chose to change, or if a traitor had slipped her the eggs unawares. These days, vendors caught selling such goods moonside are made to drink poison sunside. Even possessing the eggs earns a speedy execution. But in Oasis, women at their wits' end have always eaten the eggs, and fled.

Hester packs the asp eggs in damp red clay and binds them, in sets of three. Any more would be a waste, and any less, insufficient to cause the change. At the meeting point, booths have already popped up in the dark. Hester drapes her bamboo frame in purple and gold batik, fringed with the shiny onyx hair of some young customer who bought eggs long ago.

She lays out packets in three reed baskets and lights a lamp that burns tallow made from women's fat. At moonrise, Hester's chin lifts, and over vendors hawking their wares, she sings:

Eggs of the asp
collected riverside
in the new moon dark
Come, buy, and eat!

Opal-white eggs
cool as desert's night

against your belly
Come, buy, and eat!

The customers arrive, ghosts cut from darkness by moonlight's blade. They are no two alike. They are old and young. They are blind and deaf and whole of body. They have hats and sandals, sunburns and calluses. They come singing and weeping and completely silent. The vendors sing to them all, a cacophony and a tapestry. Hester's bones buzz from the dissonance, her skin as a quivering lizard bolting from rock to rock.

On slow nights, Hester bargains for rare eggs, which she devours on the spot. They never work. *A waste of good coin*, the merchants say, clucking their tongues, but they take payment anyway. *Traders should not eat their wares.* Most vendors prosper from the illegal trade, but Hester barely makes ends meet because she spends so much on eggs. Shayna, her moonside lover, often teases her about her bad business sense.

Marick never asks what she does moonside. By this, Hester has come to fear him. He does not ask because he already knows.

Hester has to wait for sundown to pack for the next bazaar, since Marick won't leave for work before then. People often compliment her attentive sunside lover—how he won't leave her side until sunset requires it. When they are alone, he keeps his distance. He has not once touched her, not as a lover does. Perhaps he mistakes her distance for demure shyness, the way she lies still in bed, how she curls into herself during the midday nap.

Ever since they met, Hester has a recurring dream where her body is a golden pot with an amethyst lid and she an asp inside it. In the dream, Marick plays the oboe, charming her out with music. She slithers to him, and he grabs her and devours her.

When she wakes, she feels hollow and hungry inside. Her mouth tastes sour, like the eggs that will not change her.

Truthfully, her shoulders relax when Marick leaves for moonside life, and she can go to the night bazaar. Hester wonders if Marick's moonside lover is any different from her. Perhaps he loves Marick better. Perhaps he likes mangoes. Perhaps Marick touches him. Perhaps he is less afraid than she is.

Hester's first customer that night wears a priest's robe tied all wrong, knotted at the shoulder like they do on the Street of Blacksmiths to keep their sleeves from the hot anvil. People often pretend to be another thing when they come to the night bazaar. The woman's fingers stroke a linen packet, thumb caressing the round bulges.

After payment, the woman unwraps the eggs and eats them. The moon glints on her teeth. Hester cannot hear the eggs burst above the din, but her insides quiver anyway.

The woman falls into a heap before Hester's booth. Her flesh splits open and she slithers out from her own breastbone, her shining black length cutting crescents in the sand. The newborn asp slithers through the gutter, making westward toward the desert.

Hester drags the blacksmith's sloughed-off body behind her booth for later processing. There will be more before the night's end.

They seem so sure when they approach the booth, like they know it will work for them. They often stop to browse the other wares, but their eyes slide until their fingers find the asp eggs. They do not waver. Assurance steadies their voices. She used to ask them why, back when she first started selling. *Why the bazaar? Why tonight? Why this shape?*

"Because this body has grown too tight around me."

"Because breathing weighs me down, and I am exhausted."

"Because each night, I dream of walking into the desert and not returning."

"Because each morning, I watch the merchants pass into the gates, and I want to scream, 'Stay away!'"

At the night bazaar, they shed their skin and leave as asps and tortoises and crocodiles. They pass the gates unimpeded. They go out into the desert and erase the footprints leading inward.

The night Hester met Marick, the bazaar assembled where the Street of Cobblers bisected the Street of Zither Players. Someone must have betrayed them. Perhaps a sharp-eyed officer traced the steady stream of determined lizards and serpents and tortoises scampering through the gutters and under the gates and out into the darkness. A cry cut through the selling-songs: *Run! Run!*

It had happened before. It was why the booths collapsed so easily. Hester grabbed her basket and yanked the batik down. The crowd surged toward the Street of Cobblers, pressed from the rear by police with battering sticks. The cloth sheet tangled in the bamboo bars, and Hester wrestled with it.

"Hester?" It was a young policeman, stick in hand. "The batik dyer's daughter. I would know you anywhere." She knew him too: Marick the mango seller. Now moonside, his crooked teeth became a cobra's fangs. "Wait. I need to speak with you."

His boot pinned the batik sheet to the cobblestone. Hester yanked harder, heart thudding against her ribs. *Poison,* she thought. *Bloated bodies at the wall.* The sheet ripped, and she fled into the crowd.

The next day, Marick arrived at her mother's shop with six ripe mangoes wrapped in a tattered batik scrap, and a proposition.

To mark her as his sunside lover, he gave Hester a gold earring shaped like a pot set with an amethyst for a lid. It was heavy for its size.

Marick never mentioned that night at the bazaar. What happened moonside wasn't discussed sunside. She could not tell if the coercion was deliberate or accidental on his part.

It all amounted to the same for Hester. Marick's love was a prison. His smile tightened when she glanced out the window to check the sun's position. *Test me, and you shall learn my nature,* said that tightness. His gaze followed her everywhere. She always checked the doorjamb for the chalk signs before sunrise and erased them. Propriety forced him to stay away until dawn touched the rooftop.

When they were alone together, she mirrored his smile, and the woman who gathered asp eggs curled in on herself, deep down where no one could ever find her sunside. She dreamed and dreamed of being consumed, of escape.

Near moonset, as the crowd thins to a trickle and the reptiles depart, a hand rests on Hester's shoulder. "Never trust a woman who gathers asp eggs, for she may become one," Shayna whispers, breath warm and licorice-scented.

"They don't work for me, I'm afraid." Hester turns so Shayna's kiss falls on her cheek.

"You cannot become what you already are," she jokes. Shayna stops trying to steal kisses and counts the shedded bodies. Eight women lie bisected and cold: a good night. Shayna's blades flick and twist, opening seams, probing apart joints. The hair goes to the weavers, the bones to the lemon tree growers and to the scribes, and the meat goes to the vulture breeders and the candlemakers.

The two women work quickly, distributing the haul to runners who buy for the sunside merchants. If any time remains, they slip off to Shayna's bower on the Street of Butchers for a few hours in the dark together before sunrise. Their infant son, too young for a name yet, sleeps in a basket nearby. He has hair like damp sand. "He gets it from his father," Shayna explains when Hester pets his soft head. Shayna talks about her sunside lover more than anyone Hester has ever met. It was especially tiresome during her pregnancy last year.

Hester rolls over in the hammock in the dark. "Shayna, have you ever wished to leave Oasis?"

Shayna turns, and the hammock sways. "I prefer not dying of thirst and exposure, thank you. I like my life here. I have my family, and business. Why?"

"Sometimes I wonder where the reptiles go. They say there is an ocean out there, beyond the desert."

Shayna yawns wide. "You spend too much time at the night bazaar. You should start a proper family. When are you going to give me a moonside baby of my own?"

"You sound like my mother." With Marick and Shayna in her life, it is what everyone expects. Children thrive best with two mothers and a father. Hester only has one mother, though. Perhaps that is why she cannot become a reptile.

"You haven't answered my question," Shayna points out, stirring, and the baby wakes and cries.

Hester climbs from the hammock and rocks him until he calms. Outside, the dark sky is gray and heavy. Softly it starts to rain. Too late, she realizes her mistake. "Oh, damnation! It's morning, Shayna." She dresses and sprints out the door, through the rain, toward the Street of Dyers.

An oil lamp sits lit on the stoop when Hester gets home, and the door is ajar. Marick, home from his moonside life, curls in bed with his back toward the door. Hester listens to his breathing for ten heartbeats, slow and regular like wind in the olive tree branches. When she is sure he is asleep, she stows her basket of asp eggs beneath the bed and lies down beside him. Marick always smells like incense and cinnamon at dawn, the way Hester smells faintly of butcher's blood. In this way, they bring their moonside lovers home with them. At sunrise, the scents make a family.

She dreams of Shayna and Marick and the unknown men who love them. Of her mother, alone by sunside, and Hester a child only half-mothered, now half-mother again to the nameless baby with the damp sand hair. If only she had hatched from an egg. Reptiles needed no mothers or father. They birthed themselves and named themselves and no one kept them from the desert.

She is dreaming of the desert when she wakes in the evening, the day's heat slipping away. Marick isn't in bed, nor is he in the kitchen cutting up mangoes. It is only then she realizes: in her hurry to return from Shayna's home, she forgot to erase the chalk from the doorjamb. Marick's muddy footprints squat below that spot, the jasmine branches forced back, but he is already gone.

So is her bundle of asp eggs.

The moment Hester notices, she ransacks their home, searching for the missing eggs. She strips the bed and shakes out the linen sheets. She dumps the reed baskets piled by the door. She plunges both hands elbow deep into the refuse heap outside the window. Worms ooze around her knuckles.

Never in all this time has she left evidence of the night bazaar. Never so much as a glance toward the doorjamb and its tiny chalk symbols. Her bones quiver inside the bag of her skin. The sky is streaked angry red, and moonrise bears down with vicious weight. Marick could return at any time with the other policemen, with the poison.

Her fingers dig into her palms so hard they draw blood. It is against every rule for him to police her by day: against law, against custom, against decency. But poison makes no such distinctions, and if he found the eggs, she would have no defense. She could beg Shayna to hide her, but how would she explain it without exposing her sunside life?

Hester wraps her head in batik and hurries to the western wall, where the reptiles emerge in a thin, long line across the sands. Above them, bodies swing to and fro over the gates, dry and mummified by weather and time. It was always a major affair when they hung out a new one. Marick took Hester to watch once. He held her hand, and neither smiled.

If she could be that kind of creature. If she could cross the desert. If she could break free of the spidersilk bonds Oasis imposed, the thin invisible obligations tying woman to man to woman to child, a web which caught and snared.

Hester finds herself at home again, standing before the darkened door. Behind the jasmine bush, she finds the chalk symbols: a pot, an oboe, and an egg.

We gather in the alley on the Street of Midwives where the Emperor was born.

She considers going into the house, lying down in the dark, and waiting for Marick, but her feet are already drawing her back toward the night bazaar.

Hester's money buys her half a dozen crocodile eggs, two cobra eggs, and a large speckled monitor lizard egg still warm to the touch. She swallows them down and will not let her stomach vomit them up, no matter how much her guts twist. Her head buzzes like when she drinks too much palm wine. Her hands tingle as if the poison courses inside her veins already. She hurries from booth to booth, begging for more eggs, but her colleagues only cluck their tongues and offer her rose petal tea, or silken shawls, or cool hands to the forehead.

"I am not sick," Hester insists. "I need to buy more eggs." But they will not sell them to her.

At last she hunches behind her booth, shivering in the chill, waiting, hoping yet for transformation. She has no asp eggs to sell, so the customers pass her by, until at last one does not.

Despite his broad-brimmed veiled hat, Hester recognizes Marick, when he sets the missing eggs on the booth's counter. He smells like incense and cinnamon. "Do not try to run now. Not this time."

Fear twists her gut hard, and all the raw eggs roil in her stomach. She gags and vomits into the sand behind the booth. The slimy white glair pools with her bile, studded with chunks of undigested shell. Her last hope of transformation, absorbed into the sand. The desert will take even this before it will take her. As her hope dribbles away, so does the fear. Hester laughs a short, sharp hyena bark.

"Everyone pretends to be something different at the night bazaar, Marick. What are you supposed to be?"

He hesitates, then twitches the veil up. Rose-colored moonlight bathes his face, a rare lunar eclipse. He looks small and fragile as a pressed flower, not at all like the man she has feared for five years.

He leans forward, voice low and secret. "I need to know how the eggs work. Is there a spell?"

Hester snorts. "You want our secrets before you betray me. You think you can ask, and I will tell you, as if this is not my bazaar and you are not a customer. As though the price is not my life."

Marick shakes his head hard. "No, no, you've got it all wrong, Hester. Have the police found the night bazaar since we became lovers? Do you think that is a coincidence? Whatever I am, I am no traitor."

It has the ring of truth to it, though she does not want to trust him. "What do you want from me? You take me for a lover and do not touch me. You follow me here and do not arrest me. You say you've been protecting me. What do you want?"

He casts his eyes toward the gutter, which is littered with tiny reptile prints. When he speaks, his voice is not a mango-seller's cries or a policeman's growl but trembling and weak, a flute cracked and leaking air. "I am done, trying to live in this body. It doesn't fit. Not with dayside lovers, or nightside lovers. Touches do not reach me. I wear my own flesh like a cloak, and I am alone inside. It isn't mine. Maybe I was supposed to be a reptile? A woman? Half a mother to complete some child? I do not know. I only know that if I don't shed this body, I will suffocate in it. Do you understand?"

He sounds just as sure as every woman who has come before. "You just eat them, Marick. There is no spell. The eggs don't work for men, though."

He shrugs, and the corner of his mouth lifts. "I will try, anyway. I don't know any other way." Marick unwraps the eggs and rubs off the clay. He cracks them one by one, sucks out their insides, chews and swallows the shells. Around his ankles, women skitter and slither westward on scaled claw and belly.

Hester waits for his disappointment, but instead he collapses before her booth. An asp springs from his breastbone, a fine golden-eyed creature damp from heart's-blood, and it joins the reptile exodus in the gutter. As she watches him go, a hollow place inside her rips open, as though the last of her hope has also left her and slithered into the desert.

Mechanically she drags his unwanted body behind the booth. It has been many years since this chore unsettled her, since a customer's discarded eyes fixed upon her face, but

Marick was her dayside lover, the only one she had. For the first time since she joined the bazaar, a body becomes a corpse.

When Shayna sees Marick, she steadies her head between her hands. "Oh, Hester, what have you done? The law might turn a blind eye to the night bazaar as long as we're discreet, but it won't ignore a dead policeman."

"He isn't dead. He became an asp, Shayna!"

The two women slump together behind the booth while Hester confesses everything. "What did he do? Why did it work for him?"

Shayna jerks her chin toward the sky. "Eclipses are strange. Moonside and sunside join hands and pass. Perhaps the desert calls to its own."

Hester curls up tight and tries not to retch. No eggs for her, because she is already empty inside. She does not say, *Why won't it work for me?*

Shayna holds her at arm's length. "You think I don't know. You think I don't pay attention." She undoes Marick's earring, holds the matching golden pot to Hester's ear. "Tell me, lover, what makes you so afraid? Afraid enough to piss away your profit on all those eggs? Scared enough to leave me too?"

"You are so happy here," Hester manages through hitching breath.

Shayna's eyebrows pinch together like when she is considering the best way to slice open a ribcage. "Maybe the eggs do not work for you because you do not need them. You're practically an asp already. You spend enough time among their nests."

Somehow, the thought comforts her. "And you, Shayna? What are you?"

Shayna's smile is all teeth. "I am a butcher, of course."

They drag Marick's shell into an alley. In the night bazaar's bustle, no one notices. Hester grabs the booth's batik fabric and drapes it over the ground. Shayna is a good butcher, well-practiced and quick, skilled at separating muscle from skin and meat from bone. The waxed batik absorbs the blood in brown-bordered swirls.

Shayna cuts, and Hester sorts the pieces. Hester lays Marick's heart in the pile for the vulture breeders. It is soft and round like a ripe mango on a plate, plum-red as an amethyst, tattered where the asp ripped through the flesh.

As the heart drips onto the batik, Hester sees maybe there is another path to freedom, one she never considered before Marick transformed. How she could leave behind the mass of bodies—the heralds, the upholsterers, the weavers, the potmakers, the herbalists, the papyrus-rollers, the inksetters—all the close, warm mammalian musks, the raised voices, the songs and tambourines. How she could slip beneath the gates, slither into the desert, the sand burning her belly into hard scales; her tongue flickering, testing the air. Some irresistible pull inside knows exactly where lies the ocean she has never seen, beating on a far shore. Her flesh feels heavy and cumbersome, and she thinks she could shake it loose, leave it behind to mummify in the heat and sand.

If this other path will work for her.

Hester saves Marick's heart carefully, wrapped tight in stained batik until the blood no longer soaks through. They sell the meat and bones to the vendors, but the skin they burn at Shayna's bower on the Street of Butchers. Its wetness makes the fire smoke and sputter.

"I can hide you for tonight, but you'll have to leave tomorrow," Shayna says as they wash up at home. "We can slow down their investigation, but they will find you. There were witnesses. Someone will talk eventually."

"Yes, of course. I understand." Hester inhales Shayna's familiar licorice smell, and longing prickles down her back. If this path works for her, there will be no more sunside or moonside, no lovers to fear and tend to and worry over. There will be no night bazaar, because in the desert, everyone is a reptile. Asps are asps by day or night.

Hester waits until Shayna sleeps before she draws her last gift in chalk on the doorjamb: two stones, a dead woman's eye, and an asp. *Find me at the wall where criminals are made to drink poison, and come alone.* Then she kisses her sleeping lover and their moonside baby, and she leaves.

At this hour, the night bazaar must be packing up. A few snakes and lizards skitter through the gutters. Hester follows them to the gouge in the sand where they have dug a hole beneath the wall. They slither and wriggle and just slip through. Overhead, ropes creak as the mummified corpses swing.

Before she can lose her courage, Hester unwraps Marick's heart, sliced into strips like a mango, her final hope on a wooden tray.

Hearts are eggs, she realized when Shayna slit open Marick's body and piled his organs on the stained batik. Hester wonders what will hatch from hers.

Hester eats it, piece by piece. If this fails, the police will find her. Her body will swing overhead with the rest, always within sight of the desert but never able to go there.

The heart slides into her belly, easier than glair, and settles in the empty space which once held fear. The quivering in her bones becomes a violent shudder. A change is coming, churning her like a sandstorm. She slips and twists inside her own flesh, full to the brim, a straining wineskin, a sated leech, an egg about to burst.

It does not hurt much, the hatching, the shedding. No worse than picking off a scab. When it is over, she slides free onto her segmented belly, the sand warm, the wind drying her damp newborn back. Her tongue tests the air, and tastes water far to the west, beyond the husk of her old body, through the gouge beneath the wall.

Over the wall the bodies swing and creak on their ropes, but they are only shells, and the poison rests between her teeth now, a gift for those she chooses to kiss. Oasis shrinks toy-like under her unblinking reptilian gaze. It is a nest, a golden pot with an amethyst lid, trapping asps until the music plays, but it cannot hold her anymore. All over the city, people pitch and turn inside themselves, sliding against the smooth walls of their prison, but only a few buck against the shell and break it.

But the desert is a city too, vaster than Oasis, and the reptiles are its people. Hester tastes them on the wind. Blood and incense, jasmine and mango, they call to her, all the ones who went before, the peasants and merchants, the old women and the young, the Emperor and Marick all, now fully themselves, unchanging day or night. Their prints erase the footsteps trailing into Oasis. Their bodies are arrows which point to the sea. They are waiting for her. It is almost time to go.

Hester waits beside her cooling body until sunrise breaks upon the city. Oasis turns over in its old familiar rhythm. Moonside lovers kiss and part. Footsteps hurry from house to house, and chalk symbols are found and read and quickly erased. And then, for the first time sunside, Hester sees her: Shayna the moonside butcher, come to unseam her body.

Hester knows Shayna will sell the parts piece by piece, a last providence for her Oasis family. A family can live for a month on the price a human body would fetch. Her hair will go to the weavers, her bones to feed the lemon tree groves, her fat to fuel the lamps, everything given back to the city that bore her.

Except her heart.

Shayna saves it in the same scrap of bloodstained batik that once held Marick's. Hester hopes it will be enough.

But now, the part of her that cannot be bought or sold slips beneath the wall, tastes the distant water, and goes to find it.

Discussion Questions and Writing Activities

1. In fantasy fiction that questions contemporary social norms via positing different ones, the fantastical aspects of the story can be interpreted simultaneously literally and metaphorically. The women in this story, like Hester, are literally becoming serpents, while at the same time, transformation can also be read as a metaphor for aspects of human experience. How does the transformation into a reptile in this story work both literally and metaphorically? What are some of the potential metaphorical readings? Why is it important for the story to work literally as well as metaphorically?

2. What is the origin of Hester's desperation to escape her body? How do you know? How does her desperation drive the plot of the story?

3. How do you interpret the ending of this story? What can this ending teach us about creating endings that are both surprising and fitting?

4. Analyze the way the story is predicated upon Hester's point of view. How does her perspective influence the words used, the sensory experiences given, and what information is released at what time?

5. Write a story that uses the transformation of a human into a nonhuman animal as a central plot point. Avoid transformations that are well known (such as werewolves). What avenues for storytelling open up for you? Is this transformation sought after? Feared? Or something else?

6. How would this story be different if it wasn't a secondary-world fantasy, but set in a fantastical version of a real time or place? What does a writer gain by creating an entirely new world?

7. Pick a fantasy story you've already written, or a fantasy world you've designed, and write a short, focused story set in that world, covering the experiences of

one particular character, dealing with something deeply personal. Use a close third point of view like the one in Jones's story. Afterwards, analyze how writing a fantasy story this way impacts plot, characterization, and release of information. How is it different or similar to how you've written this story, or a story set in this world before?

Ursula K. Le Guin "The Ones Who Walk Away from Omelas"

Biography (from her website)

Ursula Kroeber Le Guin (1929–2018) was a celebrated author whose body of work includes twenty-three novels, twelve volumes of short stories, eleven volumes of poetry, thirteen children's books, five essay collections, and four works of translation. Le Guin's major titles have been translated into forty-two languages and have remained in print, often for over half a century. Her fantasy novel *A Wizard of Earthsea,* the first in a related group of six books, has sold millions of copies worldwide. The breadth and imagination of her work earned her six Nebula Awards, seven Hugo Awards, and SFWA's Grand Master, along with the PEN/Malamud and many other awards. In 2014 she was awarded the National Book Foundation Medal for Distinguished Contribution to American Letters, and in 2016 joined the short list of authors to be published in their lifetimes by the Library of America. Ursula Kroeber was born in 1929 and grew up in Berkeley, California. Her parents were anthropologist Alfred Kroeber and writer Theodora Kroeber, author of *Ishi.* She attended Radcliffe College and did graduate work at Columbia University. She married historian Charles A. Le Guin, in Paris in 1953; they lived in Portland, Oregon, beginning in 1958, and had three children and four grandchildren. Le Guin died peacefully in her home in January 2018. Few American writers have done work of such high quality in so many forms.

Literary Introduction

"The Ones Who Walk Away from Omelas" was originally published in 1973, as Le Guin was first coming into fame. In many respects, it is typical of her work, in its preoccupations with ethics, its refusal to give easy answers to the moral and ethical questions it poses, its lyrical prose, and attention to detail. It is sometimes viewed as fantasy and sometimes as science fiction. Reading it, one can't know from the text itself if Omelas is a secondary-world fantasy universe, or a story on another planet. This represents another aspect of Le Guin's writing. She has written work that is definitively fantasy (all of the Earthsea books and stories) as well as work that is more firmly science fiction (such as *The Dispossessed,* and *The Lathe of Heaven*), but is more interested in culture than technology. The worlds of her stories ask, "What if a society existed with x as a given?" and extrapolate from there. She dissected everything from socioeconomic structures, to gender, sexuality, and the human relationship to the environment. She often wrote from the point of view of scientists, including social scientists, like anthropologists. "The Ones Who Walk Away from Omelas" is widely assigned not only in literature and creative writing classes, but in ethics and political science courses. In some respects, she is inimitable, from the sheer depth and breadth of her body of work. However, writers with a similar degree of interests in ethics (as well as her fine attention to human nature, and the personhood of all life, including nonhuman life), who deserve acclaim include Octavia Butler (one of our most important science fiction writers, the first science fiction writer to win a MacArthur, and one of the first women of color to gain renown in the science fiction community), N. K. Jemisin, Matt Bell, David Mitchell, Jeff VanderMeer, Peter S. Beagle, and Guy Gavriel Kay.

The Ones Who Walk Away from Omelas

With a clamor of bells that set the swallows soaring, the Festival of Summer came to the city Omelas, bright-towered by the sea. The ringing of the boats in harbor sparkled with flags. In the streets between houses with red roofs and painted walls, between old moss-grown gardens and under avenues of trees, past great parks and public buildings, processions moved. Some were decorous: old people in long stiff robes of mauve and gray, grave master workmen, quiet, merry women carrying their babies and chatting as they walked. In other streets the music beat faster, a shimmering of gong and tambourine, and the people went dancing, the procession was a dance. Children dodged in and out, their high calls rising like the swallows' crossing flights over the music and the singing. All the processions wound towards the north side of the city, where on the great water-meadow called the Green Fields boys and girls, naked in the bright air, with mud-stained feet and ankles and long, lithe arms, exercised their restive horses before the race. The horses wore no gear at all but a halter without bit. Their manes were braided with streamers of silver, gold, and green. They flared their nostrils and pranced and boasted to one another; they were vastly excited, the horse being the only animal who has adopted our ceremonies as his own. Far off to the north and west the mountains stood up half encircling Omelas on her bay. The air of morning was so clear that the snow still crowning the Eighteen Peaks burned with white-gold fire across the miles of sunlit air, under the dark blue of the sky. There was just enough wind to make the banners that marked the racecourse snap and flutter now and then. In the silence of the broad green meadows one could hear the music winding throughout the city streets, farther and nearer and ever approaching, a cheerful faint sweetness of the air from time to time trembled and gathered together and broke out into the great joyous clanging of the bells.

Joyous! How is one to tell about joy? How describe the citizens of Omelas?

They were not simple folk, you see, though they were happy. But we do not say the words of cheer much anymore. All smiles have become archaic. Given a description such as this one tends to make certain assumptions. Given a description such as this one tends to look next for the King, mounted on a splendid stallion and surrounded by his noble knights, or perhaps in a golden litter borne by great-muscled slaves. But there was no king. They did not use swords, or keep slaves. They were not barbarians, I do not know the rules and laws of their society, but I suspect that they were singularly few. As they did without monarchy and slavery, so they also got on without the stock exchange, the advertisement, the secret police, and the bomb. Yet I repeat that these were not simple folk, not dulcet shepherds, noble savages, bland utopians. There were not less complex than us. The trouble is that we have a bad habit, encouraged by pedants and sophisticates, of considering happiness as something rather stupid. Only pain is intellectual, only evil interesting. This is the treason of the artist: a refusal to admit the banality of evil and the terrible boredom of pain. If you can't lick 'em, join 'em. If it hurts, repeat it. But to praise despair is to condemn delight, to embrace violence is to lose hold of everything else. We have almost lost hold; we can no longer describe happy man, nor make any celebration of joy. How can I tell you about the people of Omelas? They were not naive and happy children–though their children were, in fact, happy. They were mature, intelligent, passionate adults whose lives were not wretched. O miracle! But I wish I could describe it better. I wish I could convince you. Omelas sounds in my words like a city in a fairy tale, long ago and far away, once upon a time. Perhaps it would be best if you imagined it as your own fancy bids, assuming it will rise to the occasion, for certainly I cannot suit you all. For instance, how about technology? I think that there would be no cars or helicopters in and above the streets; this follows from the fact that the people of Omelas are happy people. Happiness is based on a just discrimination of what is necessary, what is neither necessary nor destructive, and what is destructive. In the middle category, however–that of the unnecessary but undestructive, that of comfort, luxury, exuberance, etc.–they could perfectly well have central heating, subway trains, washing machines, and all kinds of marvelous devices not yet invented here, floating light-sources, fuelless power, a cure for the common cold. Or they could have none of that: it doesn't matter. As you like it. I incline to think that people from towns up and down the coast have been coming to Omelas during the last days before the Festival on very fast little trains and double-decked trams, and that the train station of Omelas is actually the handsomest building in town, though plainer than the magnificent Farmers' Market. But even granted trains, I fear that Omelas so far strikes some of you as goody-goody. Smiles, bells, parades, horses, bleh. If so, please add an orgy. If an orgy would help, don't hesitate. Let us not, however, have temples from which issue beautiful nude priests and priestesses already half in ecstasy and ready to copulate with any man or woman, lover or stranger, who desires union with the deep godhead of the blood, although that was my first idea. But really it would be better not to have any temples in Omelas–at least, not manned temples. Religion yes, clergy no. Surely the beautiful nudes can just wander about, offering themselves like divine souffles to the hunger of the needy and the rapture of the flesh. Let them join the processions. Let tambourines be struck above the copulations, and the gory of desire be proclaimed upon the gongs, and (a not unimportant point) let the offspring of these delightful rituals be beloved and looked after by all. One thing I know there is none of in Omelas is guilt. But what else should there be? I thought at first there were no drugs, but that is puritanical. For those who like it, the faint insistent sweetness of *drooz* may perfume the ways of the city, *drooz* which first brings a great lightness and brilliance to the mind and limbs, and then after some hours a dreamy languor, and wonderful visions at last of the very arcane and inmost secrets of the Universe, as well as exciting the pleasure of sex beyond all belief; and it is not habit-forming. For more modest tastes I think there ought to be beer. What else, what else belongs in the joyous city? The sense of victory, surely, the celebration of courage. But as we did without clergy, let us do without soldiers. The joy built upon successful slaughter is not the right kind of joy; it will not do; it is fearful and it is trivial. A boundless and generous contentment, a magnanimous triumph felt not against some outer enemy but in communion with the finest and fairest in the souls of all men everywhere and the splendor of the world's summer: This is what swells the hearts of the people of Omelas, and the victory they celebrate is that of life. I don't think many of them need to take *drooz*.

Most of the processions have reached the Green Fields by now. A marvelous smell of cooking goes forth from the red and blue tents of the provisioners. The faces of small children are amiably sticky; in the benign gray beard of a man a couple of crumbs of rich pastry are entangled. The youths and girls have mounted their horses and are beginning to group around the starting line of the course. An old woman, small, fat, and laughing, is passing out flowers from a basket, and tall young men wear her flowers in their shining hair. A child of nine or ten sits at the edge of the crowd alone, playing on a wooden flute. People pause to listen, and they smile, but they do not speak to him, for he never ceases playing and never sees them, his dark eyes wholly rapt in the sweet, thin magic of the tune.

He finishes, and slowly lowers his hands holding the wooden flute.

As if that little private silence were the signal, all at once a trumpet sounds from the pavilion near the starting line: imperious, melancholy, piercing. The horses rear on their slender legs, and some of them neigh in answer. Sober-faced, the young riders stroke the horses' necks and soothe them, whispering. "Quiet, quiet, there my beauty, my hope. . ." They begin to form in rank along the starting line. The crowds along the racecourse are like a field of grass and flowers in the wind.

The Festival of Summer has begun. Do you believe? Do you accept the festival, the city, the joy? No? Then let me describe one more thing.

In a basement under one of the beautiful public buildings of Omelas, or perhaps in the cellar of one of its spacious private homes, there is a room. It has one locked door, and no window. A little light seeps in dustily between cracks in the boards, secondhand from a cobwebbed window somewhere across the cellar. In one corner of the little room a couple of mops, with stiff, clotted, foul-smelling heads, stand near a rusty bucket. The floor is dirt, a little damp to the touch, as cellar dirt usually is. The room is about three paces long and two wide: a mere broom closet or disused tool room. In the room, a child is sitting. It could be a boy or a girl. It looks about six, but actually is nearly ten. It is feeble-minded. Perhaps it was born defective, or perhaps it has become imbecile through fear, malnutrition, and neglect. It picks its nose and occasionally fumbles vaguely with its toes or genitals, as it sits hunched in the corner farthest from the bucket and the two mops. It is afraid of the mops. It finds them horrible. It shuts its eyes, but it knows the mops are still standing there; and the door is locked; and nobody will come. The door is always locked; and nobody ever comes, except that sometimes–the child has no understanding of time or interval–sometimes the door rattles terribly and opens, and a person, or several people, are there. One of them may come in and kick the child to make it stand up. The others never come close, but peer in at it with frightened, disgusted eyes. The food bowl and the water jug are hastily filled, the door is locked; the eyes disappear. The people at the door never say anything, but the child, who has not always lived in the tool room, and can remember sunlight and its mother's voice, sometimes speaks. "I will be good," it says. "Please let me out. I will be good!" They never answer. The child used to scream for help at night, and cry a good deal, but now it only makes a kind of whining, "eh-haa, eh-haa," and it speaks less and less often. It is so thin there are no calves to its legs; its belly protrudes; it lives on a half-bowl of corn meal and grease a day. It is naked. Its buttocks and thighs are a mass of festered sores, as it sits in its own excrement continually.

They all know it is there, all the people of Omelas. Some of them have come to see it, others are content merely to know it is there. They all know that it has to be there. Some of them understand why, and some do not, but they all understand that their happiness, the beauty of their city, the tenderness of their friendships, the health of their children, the wisdom of their scholars, the skill of their makers, even the abundance of their harvest and the kindly weathers of their skies, depend wholly on this child's abominable misery.

This is usually explained to children when they are between eight and twelve, whenever they seem capable of understanding; and most of those who come to see the child are young people, though often enough an adult comes, or comes back, to see the child. No matter how well the matter has been explained to them, these young spectators are always shocked and sickened at the sight. They feel disgust, which they had thought themselves superior to. They feel anger, outrage, impotence, despite all the explanations. They would like to do something for the child. But there is nothing they can do. If the child were brought up into the sunlight out of that vile place, if it were cleaned and fed and comforted, that would be a good thing, indeed; but if it were done, in that day and hour all the prosperity and beauty and delight of Omelas would wither and be destroyed. Those are the terms. To exchange all the goodness and grace of every life in Omelas for that single, small improvement: to throw away the happiness of thousands for the chance of happiness of one: that would be to let guilt within the walls indeed.

The terms are strict and absolute; there may not even be a kind word spoken to the child. Often the young people go home in tears, or in a tearless rage, when they have seen the child and faced this terrible paradox. They may brood over it for weeks or years. But as time goes on they begin to realize that even if the child could be released, it would not get much good of its freedom: a little vague pleasure of warmth and food, no real doubt, but little more. It is too degraded and imbecile to know any real joy. It has been afraid too long ever to be free of fear. Its habits are too uncouth for it to respond to humane treatment. Indeed, after so long it would probably be wretched without walls about it to protect it, and darkness for its eyes, and its own excrement to sit in. Their tears at the bitter injustice dry when they begin to perceive the terrible justice of reality, and to accept it. Yet it is their tears and anger, the trying of their generosity and the acceptance of their helplessness, which are perhaps the true source of the splendor of their lives. Theirs is no vapid, irresponsible happiness. They know that they, like the child, are not free. They know compassion. It is the existence of the child, and their knowledge of its existence, that makes possible the nobility of their architecture, the poignancy of their music, the profundity of their science. It is because of the child that they are so gentle with children. They know that if the wretched one were not there sniveling in the dark, the other one, the flute-player, could make no joyful music as the young riders line up in their beauty for the race in the sunlight of the first morning of summer.

Now do you believe them? Are they not more credible? But there is one more thing to tell, and this is quite incredible.

At times one of the adolescent girls or boys who go see the child does not go home to weep or rage, does not, in fact, go home at all. Sometimes also a man or a woman much older falls silent for a day or two, then leaves home. These people go out into the street, and walk down the street alone. They keep walking, and walk straight out of the city of Omelas, through the beautiful gates. They keep walking across the farmlands of Omelas. Each one goes alone, youth or girl, man or woman. Night falls; the traveler must pass down village streets, between the houses with yellow-lit windows, and on out into the darkness of the fields. Each alone, they go west or north, towards the mountains. They go on. They leave Omelas, they walk ahead into the darkness, and they do not come back. The place they go towards is a place even less imaginable to most of us than the city of happiness. I cannot describe it at all. It is possible that it does not exist. But they seem to know where they are going, the ones who walk away from Omelas.

Discussion Questions and Writing Activities

1. This description of a society is from the voice of a very nongeneric narrator, though they are unnamed. They directly address their audience, and call attention to the audience's potential belief/disbelief. What is the effect of this kind of narrator? Why is it important for the sake of the story to not simply tell the story objectively from a generic narrator's point of view?

2. What is the ethical conundrum at the center of the story? For help on this, do an internet search of utilitarianism and Kantian ethics. How does Le Guin implicate the reader? How does the society you live within have its own child in the basement? Who is exploited for the prosperity of others?

3. How does Le Guin get the reader to wrestle with ethical questions without lecturing, or directly telling the reader how to think?

4. This story is barely over a thousand words, almost flash fiction. How does length play into the success of this story? Explain your answer.

5. Are readers meant to agree with any of the choices made by the people of Omelas, those who stay, or those who walk away? Or are they meant to find problems with all parties in the story? How do you know? N. K. Jemisin wrote a story in dialogue with this one called, "The Ones Who Stay and Fight." Some people argue that those who walk away are meant to be lauded. Others argue that Le Guin implicates both those who walk away, and those who stay, and do nothing. What do you think, and why?

6. Write your own addition or answer to Omelas. What is the experience of writing in dialogue with another story like?

7. Try to write a story that is a short description of a society, with an opinionated narrator, who breaks the fourth wall and addresses the reader. What do you discover in the process? What opportunities and/or difficulties does this type of narrator create for you as a storyteller?

8. Write a fantasy story with an ethical conundrum at its heart, where there are no easy answers for the protagonist.

Ken Liu "Good Hunting" from *Strange Horizons*.

Biography (from press kit on his website)

Ken Liu (http://kenliu.name) is an American author of speculative fiction. A winner of the Nebula, Hugo, and World Fantasy Awards, he wrote the *Dandelion Dynasty*, a silkpunk epic fantasy series (starting with *The Grace of Kings*), as well as short story collections *The Paper Menagerie and Other Stories* and *The Hidden Girl and Other Stories*. He also authored the Star Wars novel *The Legends of Luke Skywalker*. Prior to becoming a full-time writer, Liu worked as a software engineer, corporate lawyer, and litigation consultant. Liu frequently speaks at conferences and universities on a variety of topics, including futurism, cryptocurrency, history of technology, bookmaking, narrative futures, and the mathematics of origami. Liu is also the translator for Liu Cixin's *The Three-Body Problem*, Hao Jingfang's "Folding Beijing" and *Vagabonds*, Chen Qiufan's *Waste Tide*, as well as the editor of *Invisible Planets* and *Broken Stars*, anthologies of contemporary Chinese science fiction. Liu lives with his family near Boston, Massachusetts.

Literary Introduction

"Good Hunting" is a silkpunk story, a term and genre that Liu coined, which refers to an aesthetic where technologies from East Asia's classical antiquity are elaborated upon and brought into a fantastical and futuristic setting. When "punk" is added to a genre description (such as cyberpunk, steampunk, silkpunk, or solarpunk), it denotes an orientation that is anti-authoritarian, and prone toward questioning established hierarchies. In the case of silkpunk, that orientation is a deliberate pushback against the centering of Western narratives, cultures, and technologies in fantasy and science fiction. Most of the "punk" genres like silkpunk and steampunk are hybrid genres, existing somewhere between fantasy and science fiction. This story employs both traditional East Asian folklore through the kitsune tale, and advanced technology. Kitsune are trickster fox spirits common in Shinto and Buddhist lore. Liu engages in the tradition of the folktale, as well as wrestles with issues of colonialism, gender, and modernity. Writers whose work engages with related themes include Sequoia Nagamatsu, Nghi Vo, Julie Kagawa, Angela Mi Young Hur, Charles Yu, and Aliette de Boddard, among many others. Liu's prose is characterized by its attention to detail and psychological acuity.

Good Hunting

Night. Half-moon. An occasional hoot from an owl.

The merchant and his wife and all the servants had been sent away. The large house was eerily quiet.

Father and I crouched behind the scholar's rock in the courtyard. Through the rock's many holes I could see the bedroom window of the merchant's son.

"Oh Hsaio-jung, my sweet Hsaio-jung . . ."

The young man's feverish groans were pitiful. Half-delirious, he was tied to his bed for his own good, but Father had left a window open so that his plaintive cries could be carried by the breeze far over the rice paddies.

"Do you think she really will come?" I whispered. Today was my thirteenth birthday, and this was my first hunt.

"She will," Father said. "A *hulijing* cannot resist the cries of the man she has bewitched."

"Like how the Butterfly Lovers cannot resist each other?" I thought back to the folk opera troupe that had come through our village last fall.

"Not quite," Father said. But he seemed to have trouble explaining why. "Just know that it's not the same."

I nodded, not sure I understood. But I remembered how the merchant and his wife had come to Father to ask for his help.

"How shameful!" the merchant had muttered. "He's not even nineteen. How could he have read so many sages' books and still fall under the spell of such a creature?"

"There's no shame in being entranced by the beauty and wiles of a hulijing," *Father had said. "Even the great scholar Wong Lai once spent three nights in the company of one, and he took first place at the Imperial Examinations. Your son just needs a little help."*

"You must save him," the merchant's wife had said, bowing like a chicken pecking at rice. "If this gets out, the matchmakers won't touch him at all."

A *hulijing* was a demon who stole hearts. I shuddered, worried if I would have the courage to face one.

Father put a warm hand on my shoulder, and I felt calmer. In his hand was Swallow Tail, a sword that had first been forged by our ancestor, General Lau Yip, thirteen generations ago. The sword was charged with hundreds of Daoist blessings and had drunk the blood of countless demons.

A passing cloud obscured the moon for a moment, throwing everything into darkness.

When the moon emerged again, I almost cried out.

There, in the courtyard, was the most beautiful lady I had ever seen.

She had on a flowing white silk dress with billowing sleeves and a wide, silvery belt. Her face was pale as snow, and her hair dark as coal, draping past her waist. I thought she looked like the paintings of great beauties from the Tang Dynasty the opera troupe had hung around their stage.

She turned slowly to survey everything around her, her eyes glistening in the moonlight like two shimmering pools.

I was surprised to see how sad she looked. Suddenly, I felt sorry for her and wanted more than anything else to make her smile.

The light touch of my father's hand against the back of my neck jolted me out of my mesmerized state. He had warned me about the power of the *hulijing*. My face hot and my heart hammering, I averted my eyes from the demon's face and focused on her stance.

The merchant's servants had been patrolling the courtyard every night this week with dogs to keep her away from her victim. But now the courtyard was empty. She stood still, hesitating, suspecting a trap.

"Hsiao-jung! Have you come for me?" The son's feverish voice grew louder.

The lady turned and walked—no, glided, so smooth were her movements—towards the bedroom door.

Father jumped out from behind the rock and rushed at her with Swallow Tail.

She dodged out of the way as though she had eyes on the back of her head. Unable to stop, my father thrust the sword into the thick wooden door with a dull thunk. He pulled but could not free the weapon immediately.

The lady glanced at him, turned, and headed for the courtyard gate.

"Don't just stand there, Liang!" Father called. "She's getting away!"

I ran at her, dragging my clay pot filled with dog piss. It was my job to splash her with it so that she could not transform into her fox form and escape.

She turned to me and smiled. "You're a very brave boy." A scent, like jasmine blooming in spring rain, surrounded me. Her voice was like sweet, cold lotus paste, and I wanted to hear her talk forever. The clay pot dangled from my hand, forgotten.

"Now!" Father shouted. He had pulled the sword free.

I bit my lip in frustration. *How could I become a demon hunter if I was so easily enticed?* I lifted off the cover and emptied the clay pot at her retreating figure, but the insane thought that I shouldn't dirty her white dress caused my hands to shake, and my aim was wide. Only a small amount of dog piss got onto her.

But it was enough. She howled, and the sound, like a dog's but so much wilder, caused the hairs on the back of my neck to stand up. She turned and snarled, showing two rows of sharp, white teeth, and I stumbled back.

I had doused her while she was in the midst of her transformation. Her face was thus frozen halfway between a woman's and a fox's, with a hairless snout and raised, triangular ears that twitched angrily. Her hands had turned into paws, tipped with sharp claws that she swiped at me.

She could no longer speak, but her eyes conveyed her venomous thoughts without trouble.

Father rushed by me, his sword raised for a killing blow. The *hulijing* turned around and slammed into the courtyard gate, smashing it open, and disappeared through the broken door.

Father chased after her without even a glance back at me. Ashamed, I followed.

The *hulijing* was swift of foot, and her silvery tail seemed to leave a glittering trail across the fields. But her incompletely transformed body maintained a human's posture, incapable of running as fast as she could have on four legs.

Father and I saw her dodging into the abandoned temple about a *li* outside the village.

"Go around the temple," Father said, trying to catch his breath. "I will go through the front door. If she tries to flee through the back door, you know what to do."

The back of the temple was overgrown with weeds and the wall half-collapsed. As I came around, I saw a white flash darting through the rubble.

Determined to redeem myself in my father's eyes, I swallowed my fear and ran after it without hesitation. After a few quick turns, I had the thing cornered in one of the monks' cells.

I was about to pour the remaining dog piss on it when I realized that the animal was much smaller than the *hulijing* we had been chasing. It was a small white fox, about the size of a puppy.

I set the clay pot on the ground and lunged.

The fox squirmed under me. It was surprisingly strong for such a small animal. I struggled to hold it down. As we fought, the fur between my fingers seemed to become as slippery as skin, and the body elongated, expanded, grew. I had to use my whole body to wrestle it to the ground.

Suddenly, I realized that my hands and arms were wrapped around the nude body of a young girl about my age.

I cried out and jumped back. The girl stood up slowly, picked up a silk robe from behind a pile of straw, put it on, and gazed at me haughtily.

A growl came from the main hall some distance away, followed by the sound of a heavy sword crashing into a table. Then another growl, and the sound of my father's curses.

The girl and I stared at each other. She was even prettier than the opera singer that I couldn't stop thinking about last year.

"Why are you after us?" she asked. "We did nothing to you."

"Your mother bewitched the merchant's son," I said. "We have to save him."

"*Bewitched*? *He's* the one who wouldn't leave *her* alone."

I was taken aback. "What are you talking about?"

"One night about a month ago, the merchant's son stumbled upon my mother, caught in a chicken farmer's trap. She had to transform into her human form to escape, and as soon as he saw her, he became infatuated.

"She liked her freedom and didn't want anything to do with him. But once a man has set his heart on a *hulijing*, she cannot help hearing him no matter how far apart they are. All that moaning and crying he did drove her to distraction, and she had to go see him every night just to keep him quiet."

This was not what I learned from Father.

"She lures innocent scholars and draws on their life essence to feed her evil magic! Look how sick the merchant's son is!"

"He's sick because that useless doctor gave him poison that was supposed to make him forget about my mother. My mother is the one who's kept him alive with her nightly visits. And stop using the word *lure*. A man can fall in love with a *hulijing* just like he can with any human woman."

I didn't know what to say, so I said the first thing that came to mind. "I just know it's not the same."

She smirked. "Not the same? I saw how you looked at me before I put on my robe."

I blushed. "Brazen demon!" I picked up the clay pot. She remained where she was, a mocking smile on her face. Eventually, I put the pot back down.

The fight in the main hall grew noisier, and suddenly, there was a loud crash, followed by a triumphant shout from Father and a long, piercing scream from the woman.

There was no smirk on the girl's face now, only rage turning slowly to shock. Her eyes had lost their lively luster; they looked dead.

Another grunt from Father. The scream ended abruptly.

"Liang! Liang! It's over. Where are you?"

Tears rolled down the girl's face.

"Search the temple," my Father's voice continued. "She may have pups here. We have to kill them too."

The girl tensed.

"Liang, have you found anything?" The voice was coming closer.

"Nothing," I said, locking eyes with her. "I didn't find anything."

She turned around and silently ran out of the cell. A moment later, I saw a small white fox jump over the broken back wall and disappear into the night.

It was *Qingming*, the Festival of the Dead. Father and I went to sweep Mother's grave and to bring her food and drink to comfort her in the afterlife.

"I'd like to stay here for a while," I said. Father nodded and left for home.

I whispered an apology to my mother, packed up the chicken we had brought for her, and walked the three *li* to the other side of the hill, to the abandoned temple.

I found Yan kneeling in the main hall, near the place where my father had killed her mother five years ago. She now wore her hair up in a bun, in the style of a young woman who had had her *jijili*, the ceremony that meant she was no longer a girl. We'd been meeting every *Qingming*, every *Chongyang*, every *Yulan*, every New Year's, occasions when families were supposed to be together.

"I brought you this," I said, and handed her the steamed chicken.

"Thank you." And she carefully tore off a leg and bit into it daintily. Yan had explained to me that the *hulijing* chose to live near human villages because they liked to have human things in their lives: conversation, beautiful clothes, poetry and stories, and, occasionally, the love of a worthy, kind man.

But the *hulijing* remained hunters who felt most free in their fox form. After what happened to her mother, Yan stayed away from chicken coops, but she still missed their taste.

"How's hunting?" I asked.

"Not so great," she said. "There are few Hundred-Year Salamanders and Six-Toed Rabbits. I can't ever seem to get enough to eat." She bit off another piece of chicken, chewed, and swallowed. "I'm having trouble transforming too."

"It's hard for you to keep this shape?"

"No." She put the rest of the chicken on the ground and whispered a prayer to her mother.

"I mean it's getting harder for me to return to my true form," she continued, "to hunt. Some nights I can't do it at all. How's hunting for you?"

"Not so great either. There don't seem to be as many snake spirits or angry ghosts as a few years ago. Even hauntings by suicides with unfinished business are down. And we haven't had a proper jumping corpse in months. Father is worried about money."

We also hadn't had to deal with a *hulijing* in years. Maybe Yan had warned them all away. Truth be told, I was relieved. I didn't relish the prospect of having to tell my father that he was wrong about something. He was already very irritable, anxious that he was losing the respect of the villagers now that his knowledge and skill didn't seem to be needed as much.

"Ever think that maybe the jumping corpses are also misunderstood?" she asked. "Like me and my mother?"

She laughed as she saw my face. "Just kidding!"

It was strange, what Yan and I shared. She wasn't exactly a friend. More like someone who you couldn't help being drawn to because you shared the knowledge of how the world didn't work the way you had been told.

She looked at the chicken bits she had left for her mother. "I think magic is being drained out of this land."

I had suspected that something was wrong, but didn't want to voice my suspicion out loud, which would make it real.

"What do you think is causing it?"

Instead of answering, Yan perked up her ears and listened intently. Then she got up, grabbed my hand, and pulled until we were behind the buddha in the main hall.

"Wha—"

She held up her finger against my lips. So close to her, I finally noticed her scent. It was like her mother's, floral and sweet, but also bright, like blankets dried in the sun. I felt my face grow warm.

A moment later, I heard a group of men making their way into the temple. Slowly, I inched my head out from behind the buddha so I could see.

It was a hot day, and the men were seeking some shade from the noon sun. Two men set down a cane sedan chair, and the passenger who stepped off was a foreigner, with curly yellow hair and pale skin. Other men in the group carried tripods, levels, bronze tubes, and open trunks full of strange equipment.

"Most Honored Mister Thompson." A man dressed like a mandarin came up to the foreigner. The way he kept on bowing and smiling and bouncing his head up and down reminded me of a kicked dog begging for favors. "Please have a rest and drink some cold tea. It is hard for the men to be working on the day when they're supposed to visit the graves of their families, and they need to take a little time to pray lest they anger the gods and spirits. But I promise we'll work hard afterwards and finish the survey on time."

"The trouble with you Chinese is your endless superstition," the foreigner said. He had a strange accent, but I could understand him just fine. "Remember, the Hong Kong–Tientsin Railroad is a priority for Great Britain. If I don't get as far as Botou Village by sunset, I'll be docking all of your wages."

I had heard rumors that the Manchu Emperor had lost a war and been forced to give up all kinds of concessions, one of which involved paying to help the foreigners build a road of iron. But it had all seemed so fantastical that I didn't pay much attention.

The mandarin nodded enthusiastically. "Most Honored Mister Thompson is right in every way. But might I trouble your gracious ear with a suggestion?"

The weary Englishman waved impatiently.

"Some of the local villagers are worried about the proposed path of the railroad. You see, they think the tracks that have already been laid are blocking off veins of *qi* in the earth. It's bad *feng shui*."

"What are you talking about?"

"It is kind of like how a man breathes," the mandarin said, huffing a few times to make sure the Englishman understood. "The land has channels along rivers, hills, ancient roads that carry the energy of *qi*. It's what gives the villages prosperity and maintains the rare animals and local spirits and household gods. Could you consider shifting the line of the tracks a little, to follow the *feng shui* masters' suggestions?"

Thompson rolled his eyes. "That is the most ridiculous thing I've yet heard. You want me to deviate from the most efficient path for our railroad because you think your idols would be angry?"

The mandarin looked pained. "Well, in the places where the tracks have already been laid, many bad things are happening: people losing money, animals dying, household gods not responding to prayers. The Buddhist and Daoist monks all agree that it's the railroad."

Thompson strode over to the buddha and looked at it appraisingly. I ducked back behind the statue and squeezed Yan's hand. We held our breaths, hoping that we wouldn't be discovered.

"Does this one still have any power?" Thompson asked.

"The temple hasn't been able to maintain a contingent of monks for many years," the mandarin said. "But this buddha is still well respected. I hear villagers say that prayers to him are often answered."

Then I heard a loud crash and a collective gasp from the men in the main hall.

"I've just broken the hands off of this god of yours with my cane," Thompson said. "As you can see, I have not been struck by lightning or suffered any other calamity. Indeed, now we know that it is only an idol made of mud stuffed with straw and covered in cheap paint. This is why you people lost the war to Britain. You worship statues of mud when you should be thinking about building roads from iron and weapons from steel."

There was no more talk about changing the path of the railroad.

After the men were gone, Yan and I stepped out from behind the statue. We gazed at the broken hands of the buddha for a while.

"The world's changing," Yan said. "Hong Kong, iron roads, foreigners with wires that carry speech and machines that belch smoke. More and more, storytellers in the teahouses speak of these wonders. I think that's why the old magic is leaving. A more powerful kind of magic has come."

She kept her voice unemotional and cool, like a placid pool of water in autumn, but her words rang true. I thought about my father's attempts to keep up a cheerful mien as fewer and fewer customers came to us. I wondered if the time I spent learning the chants and the sword dance moves were wasted.

"What will you do?" I asked, thinking about her, alone in the hills and unable to find the food that sustained her magic.

"There's only one thing I *can* do." Her voice broke for a second and became defiant, like a pebble tossed into the pool.

But then she looked at me, and her composure returned.

"The only thing *we* can do. Learn to survive."

The railroad soon became a familiar part of the landscape: the black locomotive huffing through the green rice paddies, puffing steam and pulling a long train behind it, like a dragon coming down from the distant, hazy, blue mountains. For a while, it was a wondrous sight, with children marveling at it, running alongside the tracks to keep up.

But the soot from the locomotive chimneys killed the rice in the fields closest to the tracks, and two children playing on the tracks, too frightened to move, were killed one afternoon. After that, the train ceased to fascinate.

People stopped coming to Father and me to ask for our services. They either went to the Christian missionary or the new teacher who said he'd studied in San Francisco. Young men in the village began to leave for Hong Kong or Canton, moved by rumors of bright lights and well-paying work. Fields lay fallow. The village itself seemed to consist only of the too-old and too-young, and their mood one of resignation. Men from distant provinces came to inquire about buying land for cheap.

Father spent his days sitting in the front room, Swallow Tail over his knee, staring out the door from dawn to dusk, as though he himself had turned into a statue.

Every day, as I returned home from the fields, I would see the glint of hope in Father's eyes briefly flare up.

"Did anyone speak of needing our help?" he would ask.

"No," I would say, trying to keep my tone light. "But I'm sure there will be a jumping corpse soon. It's been too long."

I would not look at my father as I spoke because I did not want to look as hope faded from his eyes.

Then, one day, I found Father hanging from the heavy beam in his bedroom. As I let his body down, my heart numb, I thought that he was not unlike those he had hunted all his life: they were all sustained by an old magic that had left and would not return, and they did not know how to survive without it.

Swallow Tail felt dull and heavy in my hand. I had always thought I would be a demon hunter, but how could I when there were no more demons, no more spirits? All the Daoist blessings in the sword could not save my father's sinking heart. And if I stuck around, perhaps my heart would grow heavy and yearn to be still too.

I hadn't seen Yan since that day six years ago, when we hid from the railroad surveyors at the temple. But her words came back to me now.

Learn to survive.

I packed a bag and bought a train ticket to Hong Kong.

The Sikh guard checked my papers and waved me through the security gate.

I paused to let my gaze follow the tracks going up the steep side of the mountain. It seemed less like a railroad track than a ladder straight up to heaven. This was the funicular railway, the tram line to the top of Victoria Peak, where the masters of Hong Kong lived and the Chinese were forbidden to stay.

But the Chinese were good enough to shovel coal into the boilers and grease the gears.

Steam rose around me as I ducked into the engine room. After five years, I knew the rhythmic rumbling of the pistons and the staccato grinding of the gears as well as I knew my own breath and heartbeat. There was a kind of music to their orderly cacophony that moved me, like the clashing of cymbals and gongs at the start of a folk opera. I checked the pressure, applied sealant on the gaskets, tightened the flanges, replaced the worn-down gears in the backup cable assembly. I lost myself in the work, which was hard and satisfying.

By the end of my shift, it was dark. I stepped outside the engine room and saw a full moon in the sky as another tram filled with passengers was pulled up the side of the mountain, powered by my engine.

"Don't let the Chinese ghosts get you," a woman with bright blond hair said in the tram, and her companions laughed.

It was the night of *Yulan*, I realized, the Ghost Festival. *I should get something for my father, maybe pick up some paper money at Mongkok.*

"How can you be done for the day when we still want you?" a man's voice came to me.

"Girls like you shouldn't tease," another man said, and laughed.

I looked in the direction of the voices and saw a Chinese woman standing in the shadows just outside the tram station. Her tight western-style cheongsam and the garish makeup told me her profession. Two Englishmen blocked her path. One tried to put his arms around her, and she backed out of the way.

"Please. I'm very tired," she said in English. "Maybe next time."

"Now, don't be stupid," the first man said, his voice hardening. "This isn't a discussion. Come along now and do what you're supposed to."

I walked up to them. "Hey."

The men turned around and looked at me.

"What seems to be the problem?"

"None of your business."

"Well, I think it *is* my business," I said, "seeing as how you're talking to my sister."

I doubt either of them believed me. But five years of wrangling heavy machinery had given me a muscular frame, and they took a look at my face and hands, grimy with engine grease, and probably decided that it wasn't worth it to get into a public tussle with a lowly Chinese engineer.

The two men stepped away to get in line for the Peak Tram, muttering curses.

"Thank you," she said.

"It's been a long time," I said, looking at her. I swallowed the *you look good*. She didn't. She looked tired and thin and brittle. And the pungent perfume she wore assaulted my nose.

But I did not think of her harshly. Judging was the luxury of those who did not need to survive.

"It's the night of the Ghost Festival," she said. "I didn't want to work any more. I wanted to think about my mother."

"Why don't we go get some offerings together?" I asked.

We took the ferry over to Kowloon, and the breeze over the water revived her a bit. She wet a towel with the hot water from the teapot on the ferry and wiped off her makeup. I caught a faint trace of her natural scent, fresh and lovely as always.

"You look good," I said, and meant it.

On the streets of Kowloon, we bought pastries and fruits and cold dumplings and a steamed chicken and incense and paper money, and caught up on each other's lives.

"How's hunting?" I asked. We both laughed.

"I miss being a fox," she said. She nibbled on a chicken wing absent-mindedly. "One day, shortly after that last time we talked, I felt the last bit of magic leave me. I could no longer transform."

"I'm sorry," I said, unable to offer anything else.

"My mother taught me to like human things: food, clothes, folk opera, old stories. But she was never dependent on them. When she wanted, she could always turn into her true form and hunt. But now, in this form, what can I do? I don't have claws. I don't have sharp teeth. I can't even run very fast. All I have is my beauty, the same thing that your father and you killed my mother for. So now I live by the very thing that you once falsely accused my mother of doing: I *lure* men for money."

"My father is dead, too."

Hearing this seemed to drain some of the bitterness out of her. "What happened?"

"He felt the magic leave us, much as you. He couldn't bear it."

"I'm sorry." And I knew that she didn't know what else to say either.

"You told me once that the only thing we can do is to survive. I have to thank you for that. It probably saved my life."

"Then we're even," she said, smiling. "But let us not speak of ourselves anymore. Tonight is reserved for the ghosts."

We went down to the harbor and placed our food next to the water, inviting all the ghosts we had loved to come and dine. Then we lit the incense and burned the paper money in a bucket.

She watched bits of burnt paper being carried into the sky by the heat from the flames. They disappeared among the stars. "Do you think the gates to the underworld still open for the ghosts tonight, now that there is no magic left?"

I hesitated. When I was young I had been trained to hear the scratching of a ghost's fingers against a paper window, to distinguish the voice of a spirit from the wind. But now I was used to enduring the thunderous pounding of pistons and the deafening hiss of high-pressured steam rushing through valves. I could no longer claim to be attuned to that vanished world of my childhood.

"I don't know," I said. "I suppose it's the same with ghosts as with people. Some will figure out how to survive in a world diminished by iron roads and steam whistles, some will not."

"But will any of them thrive?" she asked.

She could still surprise me.

"I mean," she continued, "are you happy? Are you happy to keep an engine running all day, yourself like another cog? What do you dream of?"

I couldn't remember any dreams. I had let myself become entranced by the movement of gears and levers, to let my mind grow to fit the gaps between the ceaseless clanging of metal on metal. It was a way to not have to think about my father, about a land that had lost so much.

"I dream of hunting in this jungle of metal and asphalt," she said. "I dream of my true form leaping from beam to ledge to terrace to roof, until I am at the top of this island, until I can growl in the faces of all the men who believe they can own me."

As I watched, her eyes, brightly lit for a moment, dimmed.

"In this new age of steam and electricity, in this great metropolis, except for those who live on the Peak, is anyone still in their true form?" she asked.

We sat together by the harbor and burned paper money all night, waiting for a sign that the ghosts were still with us.

Life in Hong Kong could be a strange experience: from day to day, things never seemed to change much. But if you compared things over a few years, it was almost like you lived in a different world.

By my thirtieth birthday, new designs for steam engines required less coal and delivered more power. They grew smaller and smaller. The streets filled with automatic rickshaws and horseless carriages, and most people who could afford them had machines that kept the air cool in houses and the food cold in boxes in the kitchen—all powered by steam.

I went into stores and endured the ire of the clerks as I studied the components of new display models. I devoured every book on the principle and operation of the steam engine I could find. I tried to apply those principles to improve the machines I was in charge of: trying out new firing cycles, testing new kinds of lubricants for the pistons, adjusting the gear ratios. I found a measure of satisfaction in the way I came to understand the magic of the machines.

One morning, as I repaired a broken governor—a delicate bit of work—two pairs of polished shoes stopped on the platform above me.

I looked up. Two men looked down at me.

"This is the one," said my shift supervisor.

The other man, dressed in a crisp suit, looked skeptical. "Are you the man who came up with the idea of using a larger flywheel for the old engine?"

I nodded. I took pride in the way I could squeeze more power out of my machines than dreamed of by their designers.

"You did not steal the idea from an Englishman?" his tone was severe.

I blinked. A moment of confusion was followed by a rush of anger. "No," I said, trying to keep my voice calm. I ducked back under the machine to continue my work.

"He is clever," my shift supervisor said, "for a Chinaman. He can be taught."

"I suppose we might as well try," said the other man. "It will certainly be cheaper than hiring a real engineer from England."

Mr. Alexander Findlay Smith, owner of the Peak Tram and an avid engineer himself, had seen an opportunity. He foresaw that the path of technological progress would lead inevitably to the use of steam power to operate automata: mechanical arms and legs that would eventually replace the Chinese coolies and servants.

I was selected to serve Mr. Findlay Smith in his new venture.

I learned to repair clockwork, to design intricate systems of gears and devise ingenious uses for levers. I studied how to plate metal with chrome and how to shape brass into smooth curves. I invented ways to connect the world of hardened and ruggedized clockwork to the world of miniaturized and regulated piston and clean steam. Once the automata were finished, we connected them to the latest analytic engines shipped from Britain and fed them with tape punched with dense holes in Babbage-Lovelace code.

It had taken a decade of hard work. But now mechanical arms served drinks in the bars along Central and machine hands fashioned shoes and clothes in factories in the New Territories. In the mansions up on the Peak, I heard—though I'd never seen—that automatic sweepers and mops I designed roamed the halls discreetly, bumping into walls gently as they cleaned the floors like mechanical elves puffing out bits of white steam. The expats could finally live their lives in this tropical paradise free of reminders of the presence of the Chinese.

I was thirty-five when she showed up at my door again, like a memory from long ago.

I pulled her into my tiny flat, looked around to be sure no one was following her, and closed the door.

"How's hunting?" I asked. It was a bad attempt at a joke, and she laughed weakly.

Photographs of her had been in all the papers. It was the biggest scandal in the colony: not so much because the Governor's son was keeping a Chinese mistress—it was expected that he would—but because the mistress had managed to steal a large sum of money from him and then disappear. Everyone tittered while the police turned the city upside down, looking for her.

"I can hide you for tonight," I said. Then I waited, the unspoken second half of my sentence hanging between us.

She sat down in the only chair in the room, the dim light bulb casting dark shadows on her face. She looked gaunt and exhausted. "Ah, now you're judging me."

"I have a good job I want to keep," I said. "Mr. Findlay Smith trusts me."

She bent down and began to pull up her dress.

"Don't," I said, and turned my face away. I could not bear to watch her try to ply her trade with me.

"Look," she said. There was no seduction in her voice. "Liang, look at me."

I turned and gasped.

Her legs, what I could see of them, were made of shiny chrome. I bent down to look closer: the cylindrical joints at the knees were lathed with precision, the pneumatic actuators along the thighs moved in complete silence, the feet were exquisitely molded and shaped, the surfaces smooth and flowing. These were the most beautiful mechanical legs I had ever seen.

"He had me drugged," she said. "When I woke up, my legs were gone and replaced by these. The pain was excruciating. He explained to me that he had a secret: he liked machines more than flesh, couldn't get hard with a regular woman."

I had heard of such men. In a city filled with chrome and brass and clanging and hissing, desires became confused.

I focused on the way light moved along the gleaming curves of her calves so that I didn't have to look into her face.

"I had a choice: let him keep on changing me to suit him, or he could remove the legs and throw me out on the street. Who would believe a legless Chinese whore? I wanted to survive. So I swallowed the pain and let him continue."

She stood up and removed the rest of her dress and her evening gloves. I took in her chrome torso, slatted around the waist to allow articulation and movement; her sinuous arms, constructed from curved plates sliding over each other like obscene armor; her hands, shaped from delicate metal mesh, with dark steel fingers tipped with jewels where the fingernails would be.

"He spared no expense. Every piece of me is built with the best craftsmanship and attached to my body by the best surgeons—there are many who want to experiment, despite the law, with how the body could be animated by electricity, nerves replaced by wires. They always spoke only to him, as if I was already only a machine.

"Then, one night, he hurt me and I struck back in desperation. He fell like he was made of straw. I realized, suddenly, how much strength I had in my metal arms. I had let him do all this to me, to replace me part by part, mourning my loss all the while without understanding what I had gained. A terrible thing had been done to me, but I could also be *terrible*.

"I choked him until he fainted, and then I took all the money I could find and left.

"So I come to you, Liang. Will you help me?"

I stepped up and embraced her. "We'll find some way to reverse this. There must be doctors—"

"No," she interrupted me. "That's not what I want."

It took us almost a whole year to complete the task. Yan's money helped, but some things money couldn't buy, especially skill and knowledge.

My flat became a workshop. We spent every evening and all of Sundays working: shaping metal, polishing gears, reattaching wires.

Her face was the hardest. It was still flesh.

I poured over books of anatomy and took casts of her face with plaster of Paris. I broke my cheekbones and cut my face so that I could stagger into surgeons' offices and learn from them how to repair these injuries. I bought expensive jeweled masks and took them apart, learning the delicate art of shaping metal to take on the shape of a face.

Finally, it was time.

Through the window, the moon threw a pale white parallelogram on the floor. Yan stood in the middle of it, moving her head about, trying out her new face.

Hundreds of miniature pneumatic actuators were hidden under the smooth chrome skin, each of which could be controlled independently, allowing her to adopt any expression. But her eyes were still the same, and they shone in the moonlight with excitement.

"Are you ready?" I asked.

She nodded.

I handed her a bowl, filled with the purest anthracite coal, ground into a fine powder. It smelled of burnt wood, of the heart of the earth. She poured it into her mouth and swallowed. I could hear the fire in the miniature boiler in her torso grow hotter as the pressure of the steam built up. I took a step back.

She lifted her head to the moon and howled: it was a howl made by steam passing through brass piping, and yet it reminded me of that wild howl long ago, when I first heard the call of a *hulijing*.

Then she crouched to the floor. Gears grinding, pistons pumping, curved metal plates sliding over each other—the noises grew louder as she began to transform.

She had drawn the first glimmers of her idea with ink on paper. Then she had refined it, through hundreds of iterations until she was satisfied. I could see traces of her mother in it, but also something harder, something new.

Working from her idea, I had designed the delicate folds in the chrome skin and the intricate joints in the metal skeleton. I had put together every hinge, assembled every gear, soldered every wire, welded every seam, oiled every actuator. I had taken her apart and put her back together.

Yet, it was a marvel to see everything working. In front of my eyes, she folded and unfolded like a silvery origami construction, until finally, a chrome fox as beautiful and deadly as the oldest legends stood before me.

She padded around the flat, testing out her sleek new form, trying out her stealthy new movements. Her limbs gleamed in the moonlight, and her tail, made of delicate silver wires as fine as lace, left a trail of light in the dim flat.

She turned and walked—no, glided—towards me, a glorious hunter, an ancient vision coming alive. I took a deep breath and smelled fire and smoke, engine oil and polished metal, the scent of power.

"Thank you," she said, and leaned in as I put my arms around her true form. The steam engine inside her had warmed her cold metal body, and it felt warm and alive.

"Can you feel it?" she asked.

I shivered. I knew what she meant. The old magic was back but changed: not fur and flesh, but metal and fire.

"I will find others like me," she said, "and bring them to you. Together, we will set them free."

Once, I was a demon hunter. Now, I am one of them.

I opened the door, Swallow Tail in my hand. It was only an old and heavy sword, rusty, but still perfectly capable of striking down anyone who might be lying in wait.

No one was.

Yan leapt out like a bolt of lightning. Stealthily, gracefully, she darted into the streets of Hong Kong, free, feral, a *hulijing* built for this new age.

. . . once a man has set his heart on a hulijing, *she cannot help hearing him no matter how far apart they are . . .*

"Good hunting," I whispered.

She howled in the distance, and I watched a puff of steam rise into the air as she disappeared.

I imagined her running along the tracks of the funicular railway, a tireless engine racing up, and up, towards the top of Victoria Peak, towards a future as full of magic as the past.

Discussion Questions and Writing Activities

1. Liu's story follows his protagonist from childhood into adulthood. How does Liu move the reader through time, and choose which moments in the protagonist's life to show?

2. Describe the effect of blending the mythic and the technological in this story. How is technology and myth regarded in this narrative? Is one more positive or negative than the other? Or are they complementary?

3. How does Liu relate gender and colonialism in this story? How are these two areas of exploitation interrelated in the text?

4. Analyze Liu's cultural critiques. How do you as a reader get a sense of the points he wants to make, without any overlecturing ever occurring? Why is it important for anti-colonial fantasy and science fiction to exist?

5. What drives the protagonist of this story? How do you know?

6. Imagine if this story were told from the point of view not of the current protagonist, but through the eyes of his kitsune friend? What would change? How would her point of view change the prose, the plot, and the tone? Explain your answer.

7. Write a story that combines a character or being from myth and folklore with a futuristic form of technology. What techniques can you glean from Liu's story to help make that fusion feel natural and inevitable?

8. Write a story from the point of view of a character in a marginalized position in the society of your story. Think carefully about the ways in which marginalization would impact the character's point of view, their dreams, and dreads, as well as constrain their choices. What do you learn from thinking about the impacts of power on individual characters?

China Miéville "The Condition of New Death" from *Three Moments of an Explosion*

Biography (from his publisher's webpage and other online sources)

China Miéville is the author of numerous books, including *This Census-Taker, Three Moments of an Explosion, Railsea, Embassytown, Kraken, The City & The City*, and *Perdido Street Station*. He lives and works in London. He describes his work as weird fiction aligned with the loose association of speculative fiction writers referred to as the New Weird. Miéville has won awards for his fiction, including the Arthur C. Clarke Award (three times), British Fantasy Award, BSFA Award, Hugo Award, Locus Award, and World Fantasy Award. He holds degrees from several universities, including a PhD in international relations from the London School of Economics. He is interested in Marxist theory and is active in politics in London.

Literary Introduction

Miéville is one of the writers credited with bringing weird fiction into prominence in the fantasy and science fiction community. He positions himself as working in a tradition of the fantastic that does not derive from Tolkien. He has listed his influences from Mervyn Peake to Michael Moorcock and is included in the groups of writers who were influenced by H. P. Lovecraft but who abhor his politics and beliefs and so write works that are influenced by the Lovecraft mythos but also deliberately take down and tackle Lovecraft's worldview. His work engages with many social issues, particularly the ways in which economic systems exploit the lives and bodies of people. He does so through elements of body horror, such as a criminal justice system that punishes people by grafting machines onto their bodies, turning them into literal instruments of labor. He doesn't use traditional fantasy cultures or beings—he makes up his own. Even when he uses something slightly familiar (like a vampire), he radically changes the mythos and puts that changed magical being in a setting completely unfamiliar. "The Condition of New Death" works, like much weird fiction, to create a feeling of alienation and strangeness, and refuses rational explanations. Other writers of weird fiction include Jeff VanderMeer, K. J. Bishop, Paul Di Filippo, M. John Harrison, Jeffrey Ford, Storm Constantine, Alastair Reynolds, Justina Robson, Steph Swainston, Mary Gentle, Michael Cisco, and others. Weird fiction generally doesn't fit tidily into genre categories.

The Condition of New Death

The first reported case of New Death occurred on 23 August 2017, in Georgetown, Guyana. At approximately 2:45 p.m., Jake Morris, a fifty-three-year-old librarian, entered his living room and found his wife, pharmacist Marie-Therese Morris, fifty-one, motionless and supine on the floor. "I opened the door onto the soles of her feet," he has said.

Mr. Morris testifies that he checked his wife's pulse and found her cold. His claim to have *gone to her side* to do so has been the source of much controversy in neothanatology, this action of course being impossible in the case of the New Dead. Mainstream opinion is that this is the inaccurate memory of a distraught man. A substantial minority insist that there are no grounds to assume such error, and that Ms. Morris must therefore be assumed to have been Old Dead at this point, and that her status changed seconds after discovery.

Mr. Morris went to the telephone in the northeastern corner of the room and summoned an ambulance. When he turned back to his wife's body, New Death had unmistakably taken hold.

"I turn around," he has said, "and her feet are right in front of me again. Pointing directly at me. Again."

During his call, Ms. Morris's corpse appeared to have silently rotated on a horizontal axis approximately 160 degrees, around a point somewhere close to her waist.

With great alarm, Mr. Morris began to walk around the body, but he stopped when, in his words, "those feet wouldn't stop pointing at me." Ms. Morris's body appeared to him to be swiveling like a needle on a compass, her feet always facing him.

He remained frozen, his wife's feet a few inches from his own shoes. He was unwilling to move and thereby provoke that smooth and perfectly silent motion. That was how the paramedics found him, by his dead wife.

At one point in the highly confused moments that followed, a medic demanded that Mr. Morris be careful not to tread on his wife's hair. Which was, however, from Mr. Morris's perspective, on the other side of her body from him.

Thus the specificity of New Death began to emerge.

After the Morris case was that of the Bucharest aneurysm, then the Toronto crosswalk, then the Hong Kong twins. New Death spread at accelerating rates. News coverage, which had started as sporadic, amused, and skeptical, grew rapidly more serious. Two weeks after Mrs. Morris New Died, the sinking of the overloaded ferry *Carnivale* sailing between the Eritrean coast and the Italian port of Lampedusa gave the world its first harrowing scene of *mass* New Death.

Now, with the last verified Old Death having occurred six years ago, and the upgrading of all human death seemingly complete, we are inured enough to the scenes of countless New Dead left by drone strike, terrorist attack, landslide, and pandemic that it can be hard to recall the shock occasioned by that first spectacle.

The shots of almost a hundred drowned migrants, dead despite their life belts, their bodies oddly stiff, their legs not slanting, their feet not sinking but visible at the surface of the water, are still iconic. It might be thought that, occurring on water, the apparent rotations of the New Dead would not appear quite so unnatural (old-natural, to use the now-preferred term) as the same phenomenon on land. This, however, was not the case.

The quickly leaked footage showed the instant and exact swivels by which every drowned migrant's feet always precisely faced every camera. These remained in perfect synchrony. All feet always faced all cameras no matter what abrupt and contingent motions the boats or helicopters made, or where they were when they made them. These movements were obviously not the results of currents, winds, or hidden engines.

The feeds from the headcams of rescue divers were even more shocking. In it, the drowned dead without floatation devices all sink slowly, and every one of the bodies, at every level, is stiffly oriented perfectly horizontally, with its feet pointing toward every rising, panicking diver. This of course is the case even in the footage shot simultaneously from quite different directions, in which the same corpses can be identified.

In the weeks that followed, more and more scenes of the smooth, precisely flat and silent rotation of the dead were released, the bodies horizontal on slopes of varying inclines, in a Baghdad plaza or on a Mexican hillside or the site of a Danish school shooting. It was, however, the *Carnivale* disaster that inaugurated the era of New Death.

There is variation among New cadavers. Arms and legs may be splayed to various degrees, though the range is attenuated relative to that possible in Old Death. The bodies of victims of dismemberment or explosive force do not reconstitute, though their components, even if scattered, lie according to the condition of New Death—they are, in other words, New Dead in pieces.

Stated most simply, New Death is the condition whereby human corpses now lie always on a horizontal vector—no matter the angle of the surface or the substance below them—and now orient so that their feet are facing all observers, all the time.

Two facts about this epochal thanatological shift were quickly established:

i)   New Death is *subjective*.

All observers in the presence of New Dead, in person or via imaging technology, will perceive that body or those bodies as oriented with feet toward them. This remains the case when those observers are directly opposite each other. *Perception* and *observation* is constitutive of New Death.

ii)   New Death is *objective*.

Physical interventions have verified that these subjective impressions are *not illusory*. The New Dead have mass. They can be interacted with. The basic positional predicates of New Death, however, cannot be overcome. As the notorious Bannif-Murchau experiment showed, multiple observers of a New Dead, all perceiving the body's feet to be toward them, all instructed to take hold of the cadaver at the same instant, all coming from different directions, *will all grasp the feet at the same time*. This sometimes shocking and occasionally dangerous vectoral/locational slippage would of course have been impossible in the pre-ND era. It is not just biology, but physics, that have changed.

New Death has had no impact on death rates or causes. Nor has the agential status of the dead vis-à-vis the living changed—they remain as quiet as their Old Dead precursors. New Death is a phenomenon not of *dying*, nor of *death*, but of the *quiddity of deadness*.

Philosophies of its causes, effects, and meanings (if any) are, of course, in their infancy. But they have, very recently, taken an exciting turn.

At the 2024 Mumbai Conference "The New Dead and Their Critics." PJ Mukhopadhyay, a graduate student of digital design, gave a paper on "New Death as a Game." In the course of her presentation she pointed out, almost in passing, that a *locus classicus* of a foot-to-viewpoint orientation of the dead was the earliest generation of First-Person Shooters.

In such games, no matter where "you" stood, your defeated enemies would lie with their feet toward you, shifting as you shifted. This would be the case until, finally, after a programmed time, their bodies winked out of play.

With this insight, we have entered a new era of New Death studies. In the words of the most recent issue of the *Cambridge Journal of Philosophy*, "no one is yet clear on why Mukhopadhyay's observation is important. That it is important—that it changes everything—no doubt remains."

Understanding remains evasive, but culture is pragmatic and quick. Those for whom showing the soles of feet has been an insult adapt no less than do those who delight in insulting them. A plethora of ceremonies are emerging around the interment and veneration of New Dead. Theologies of all traditions are, mostly, smoothly accommodating them, with new interpretations of old texts and ways. The New Dead are already completely banalised representationally in movies, television dramas, and other commodities—including, of course, video games. The point is not that rotating sugar skeletons with windup handles are sold by Mexican vendors: the point is that they sell in similar numbers to any other *Día de los Muertos* items.

This insouciance is admirable. But it is also somehow inadequate. We have tweaked our various bells and smells, but we still die as we always died, and live as we did before we died.

We are not ready. What would being ready constitute? What might the endgame of New Death be?

This is not a manifesto. It is not even a prequel to such. We don't know what to call for, to live up to the potentiality of New Death. This is a call for a manifesto to be written. An exhortation for an exhortation, a plea to have it demanded of us to live as we must and New Die well.

We must proceed according to a presumption that we might have something up to which to live, that there might be a telos to all our upgraded dead, that we might eventually *succeed* in something, that we might unlock achievements, if we die correctly. And, conversely, that if we do not, we will continue to fail.

What the stakes of that success and that failure might be, none of us yet know.

We will all learn.

Discussion Questions and Writing Activities

1. Based upon your understanding of weird fiction, how is "The Condition of New Death" weird fiction?

2. Characterize the imagery used in this story, describe it. How does the imagery in this story influence the tone and mood of the piece?

3. How does the form of the story, made up of artifacts, a report, some interviews, a few scenes, and some unclassifiable musings by the author of the report/narrator, create meaning, and add to the feeling of alienation/discomfort?

4. What is your sense of who the narrator is, and what drives them? How can the inconclusive ending begin to give the reader clues as to the narrator and their motivations?

5. How does Miéville use details to give a sense of verisimilitude to the story? In other words, how do Miéville's details make New Death feel real within the bounds of the story?

6. Try to write a story in the form of a report. Then analyze the experience. What was challenging about writing such a story? How did you craft a narrative within a form that is not itself inherently narrative?

7. Write a weird fiction story with the goal of making some kind of point. How can you use the sense of the strange, the uncanny, the inexplicable to lead your readers to a particular conclusion?

8. Check out "Reading the Weird" on tor.com. Read a few of the columns and add a book or two from the column to your reading list. Which ones did you pick, and why?

Fantasy Fiction

Yxta Maya Murray "La Llorona" from The North American Review Vol. 281

Biography (taken from her faculty webpage at Loyola Marymount School of Law, Wikipedia, and her author page on Amazon; she doesn't have a writer webpage)

Yxta Maya Murray is a novelist, art critic, playwright, and law professor. She holds a JD from Stanford. The author of nine fiction books, her most recent story collection, *The World Doesn't Work That Way, but It Could* (2020), was named a 2020 Best Book by BuzzFeed News. The winner of a Whiting Award and an Art Writer's Grant, she has been named a fellow at the Huntington Library in Pasadena, California. Her play *Advice and Consent* was also made into a short film in collaboration with Kathleen Kim. Her legal scholarship focuses on Community Constitutionalism, Criminal Law, Property Law, Gender Justice, and Law and Literature. She also writes about the relationship between law and visual, conceptual, and performance art. She has curated an art show looking at the intersection of legal practice and art.

Literary Introduction

Murray's fiction ranges across genres and forms, her novels engaging with everything from the New World adventure narrative, folkloric narrative, academic mystery, and noir. Most of her work uses these forms and genres to examine issues of gender, sexuality, and colonialism. She often employs Latin American folklore and history to examine the aforementioned issues, while simultaneously telling crackling good adventure stories infused with the supernatural via folklore. "La Llorona" is a dark feminist folkloric fantasy, retelling the Mexican folktale of the weeping woman, a vengeful ghost mourning her children who drowned. It is a story often associated with the colonial era in Mexico and the exploitative and violent dynamic between conquistadors and indigenous women. Many versions of the story focus on making the titular character horrific or reducing her to her motherhood. Murray's version gives her a voice, and humanizes her, very much engaging in the long tradition of feminist retellings, but with an emphasis on the ways in which racism, colonialism, and gendered oppression work together.

La Llorona

I could have cooked them up and eaten them with some fine dark wine, a few dry crackers. Like a mad Greek goddess, searching out the bones, searching her sons' blank eyes for a last song then gulping them down like that, ferociously.

Instead I fed them to the water. There is a deep, silty river by my house, it is purple black at night with strains of shaded blue like royal velvet beneath the surface. The fish live here, quietly, staring up at the light during the day with their small electric eyes, gulping in the watery air with their fishy mouths opening and shutting, their gills fluttering in the current. You can skim your hand through the force of the water, then plunge it in and feel the hard rushing push as it runs back toward the sea.

A man never knew how angry a woman could be until the very last moment, the last second when he glanced up at her and saw nothing but red, hot volcanoes. How could he love another, with his smooth skin and hard legs, his hands as strong as river rocks, and as soft? A husband is forever, he belongs to you, as do his children. They cannot leave no matter how hard they try, it will turn them into beasts, it will make you into a monster.

I have green gills now, I breathe the water as the fish do, as my children did, living down here at the bottom of the river, caressing myself and remembering.

I was once like you are. I spoke quietly, my head turned down and my mouth bending up slightly into a small smile, satisfied. I cooked warm, spicy meals with meat and rice and beans in them, milk on the table and spirits for my husband after. Putting the children to bed with stories of an Aztec king, a Mayan princess living among jaguars and wild horses, fighting in their bloody wars. My sons would sleep like trees.

What is a woman? A woman is waiting. Waiting for the day to begin and then the lights to dim at night. A woman is praying to God. To think of the things that will happen to you, that you will let others do to you, it is madness. There is a limit to those things, but it stretches on and on, like a desert, like you are dying of thirst in the sandy ocean, seeing nothing all around but a thin, grey line at the horizon.

I have black eyes, big like a deer's. And a nose so sharp it can sniff out a beetle. My hands would have turned into claws if anyone threatened my family, I would have died for them, spread out my body like a blanket, opened to any knife, just to keep them safe, to keep them mine forever. And then the lies came, and I had to protect myself. I had to do the hardest things, and sing and cry and let the heavens know that I was doing them.

My husband began turning away from me in bed. Cold sheets of air between us, between our bodies. A woman may not ask, not ever, she must keep to herself, patient until the time when the man reaches over, when he decides that it is time for love. So I did not ask. I said nothing, only lying there surrounded by the whispering air, my skin lonely, my eyes open all through the night, seeing the black walls, listening to the rats gather their food in the dark corners of our home.

And so I was the dying person in the desert, stretching myself out over the horizon, a vast sheet of skin and blood and bone, of endless hope, of patience. I would wait forever until this time passed, until he would want me again.

Once a woman like me waited until there was no more time. Then she gathered herself like the brown bear, collected all her strength and made a gold ball gown, with fine filigree and a headdress, with jewels on the sleeves and bodice, gold lace, gold petticoat, gold slip, air-spun and weightless. She sat in her small sewing room and bent over the sheets of fine, burning gold, so careful not to tear it with her thin fingers, pulling the needle in and out, the thread only a gold breath, invisible, like the thoughts in her mind.

It was her finest craft. And it was so beautiful on her husband's lover, who had the same shade of hair, the same jewel-tone lips like fine rubies. The girl smiled when she saw her wedding present and offered her body to its fiery cloth, letting it burn her into ash. There were colors then, more than in any art, there was the color of vengeance, blood red and bone-white, and the stinking pull of pale skin folding over.

But I would take my creation home. I would become it. Because it is in the blood, in the soil from where we grow our food, in the black, southern dirt, with our darker skin. The women are only their families, and their husbands and sons feel every drop of them.

He would not have me, he said. He would not have me anymore, and he hid his washed hands in his pockets. I looked over at our home with its thick wooden walls, the stone floors, my small garden with the flowers and the herb plants for making teas, the quiet and beauty of the rooms, each holding us like a mother.

I will wait, I told him.

He was gone many nights, and then there was more than a cool sheet of air around me in bed, it was a tornado, and I was sinking. My children still laughed and played out by my garden, squeezing the flowers with their hands, wanting more food, as they grew and widened, expanded into broader, demanding men. I saw how they would only become bigger, how they would grow dark shadows above their lips, their voices getting harder and thicker, their footfalls heavy.

I would pray to God.

The sky will not forgive stones, if you toss one up in the air it will be thrown back to you, harder and faster than before. God is like that, He is like the sky with your stones. He is like an echo, only giving back the same, spare thing, without a sign.

I burnt sage and candles and sprinkled the house with my holy water, purifying myself with it, praying from my books with a low whisper. We have many devices for calling on God. There are the plants to tuck into pillows and to burn in small clay pots, there is starvation, turning from food and water until the day gets clearer, until everything has a crisp, silver outline. You may kill small animals, breathing in the mist from their hot bodies in the morning, leaning over them after your knife has done its work. God may speak with you then, if you are lucky.

But He saw what was in me, what was rightly mine, and He turned away from the sight with the same cool force as all my nights alone in my swallowing bed.

My sons lengthened, their legs stretching out like watered weeds.

I became a mongoose. Secret and moving at night. My skin leathered and my eyes narrowed from sifting through the darkness to see the sleeping world. I burrowed through the dirt faster than a running horse, with my ugly humped back and my spiky dirt-covered fur.

There are deceptions for the quiet ones to see, the small silent animals traveling at midnight. I wandered through my neighbors' homes, splintering their wood floors with my digging claws. I saw how other men take their lovers in different houses, the noise of their sex filling the late sky, sweeter than the simple duty of home. I saw the married women who lay like stone in their sleeping beds. These women were not like me any more.

My husband would return some days, giving me his old smile. He would tell me lies with a slick voice. That he had fallen asleep at a bar, drinking with his friends, playing cards, discussing the new regime. He wanted me to see him there in my mind, on an old wood stool with a cognac, smoking cigars with the other good men. To believe.

But I had hardscrabbled my small, spindly animal body over the floorboards of his new woman's house. With my raw fangs I had nibbled on her linen sheets while they slept, listening to the pace of their breathing, and had seen their breath twining up in the cold night in a pale, lingering fog. His lover is the color of parchment, pale against him.

He would tell me these things, how he had lost track of time with his friends, and I would stare into his flat, familiar face.

He has the look of our lost people, the old bloodlines, with his flint-sharp nose and widening cheeks, his skin a weathering bronze. We are twins, I used to say, my face mirroring his with the color of an ancient pot buried under the sand. I would smile with my teeth shining out. We are the same.

But now I am dark skinned like the mongoose, like the brown bear, and not like him any longer. I am not like any woman or man, only godless, and I was digging tunnels in the dirt and preying on grasshoppers, small mice. Practicing.

And as with the other woman who sewed night and day to make a beautiful burning gown, there came a day when I saw that all the time in the world would run out. It bled out of me, flowing and rushing out of my body like this river, the night and the day, the dark and the light became the same, and there was only a flat, dank grey to the world. The wind ceased. I could not hear it anymore, nor the birds, any laughter or music, and I wondered if I would die, quieter than dust.

Children are their mothers. They can only belong to the women. We kiss their faces and feed them, we know the fresh scents of their heads, their questions. When they will cry. Children belong to mothers, because they are of the same body. They do not become separated from us until a certain age, until they lose that gleam, the shining of their simple, pure faces. When they become like the other people all around.

My sons were still only mine, they were unformed yet and simple minded. And they were the only path to my wandering husband, who was reaching past me faster and farther. I could barely see him then, only the top of his head down the road, and I knew it would be over soon, that I would fold into the earth with no more sound.

Women are weak like glass. Life will offer them only few gifts, a drawer full of trinkets. The memories of our children, of our husband and our home, the scent of a clean room, a fine meal. They will be offered for a handful of years, and then they are gone.

And so I brought my sons to the edge of the river bank, stroked their beautiful heads, their ink black hair and sturdy frames, and whispered into their ears of my love for them. They reached for me with their small hands, curved like beach shells. I saw that my own hands against their gleaming heads were starving, the meat shrunk away, only a few sticks and a layer of bark, and I remembered my husband with his clove skin, his lover's white face.

My sons did my bidding then, and swam under the river with the strength of a shark, their faces becoming its same grey color. They asked no questions, only smiling up at me until the very end, the sounds of the water rushing and their raised cheeks, letting me fold them into the murk, into the cold water like the sky in the dark night. My arms were like iron, my teeth set in a stone line while I plunged them in, and I shrieked to the sky with all the sound of the wind and the roaring ocean, all the music of rain. I thought I might grow blind, with the black water in my eyes, my hair wet ropes like eels, and the thick feel of silt on my face as I tried to swim too.

At the riverbed there are the copper coins that the children throw in for luck, and the small sucking bottom fish and tangled feathery plants. The men and the women refuse to come near, they whisper about what I did. How my husband fell ill with the news of me, of our sons, how he cried and screamed just as a woman would, a woman with a heart in her. He would kill himself, he said, and I held my breath at this news, waiting and watching at this small shore. Then he came and took our sons away from me, he dredged up their hard bodies, their little heads with their open eyes and mouths, their few baby teeth showing. He showed no fear as he did this, but I let him feel my presence, the ice of it, as I draped my shadowy body over his and laughed into his ear.

But men live. They live without the blood running through them to keep them alive, somehow they stay on the earth to walk and work and eat and sleep just like before, only now their eyes are round and blank like eggs. My victory was small, taking life from the living, but he could not smile again with the memory of us.

There was that day when all the time poured out of me like the ocean, and now time feeds in and out of me the same as the wind, winding its way down my spine, through my fingers, it wraps its thick cloak about my body. I sit by this river and sing out loud, so that my boys might hear me, so that my husband will stop what he is doing and look up, a dazzled look on his face.

Women are weak but now I am the strong one, here in the river with the sucking fish. The townsfolk say that I hated men, that I would kill all men and boys with a cutting smile, my hands like scythes. The women cluck their tongues when they hear my singing, calling me bruja, llorona. They tell their own sons to behave, to not wander, warning them that I will kill them with my knife and tear them with my big teeth. I am the rumor now, the thing that they will whisper about, and I torture them with my songs, my voice a low violin, a grand piano, a symphony full of men in tuxedos, their heads bent over their instruments, their eyes closed.

The dirt on the riverbank is green and dust brown, it is wet with the river water, a thick muck where I sleep. I will sing the people my songs, and I appear to them, dressed in green plants and old skirts, my hair these wild wet ropes around my breasts, wrapping my hips, coiling my legs like snakes. I see my old friends' frightened white egg eyes, their open mouths, and I love to hear them speak my name out loud in the living world. But there are the times when I will remember and cry, seeing the grey faces of my two sons like stone, their teeth like pebbles just showing out of their open mouths, as they were with me.

It shadows my joy, a dark bog, when I remember the time before I was a mongoose, when I could not yet become a jaguar, a muskrat, a beetle. Before I could make myself heard as the thunder is and have the whole sky tumble down like weeds. I felt different then, I could let my hands linger on my husband's back, I could kiss him below his hair, my children would rush to me, like the water does. Those pictures are my ghosts now, haunting me as I will haunt all of you.

I would have a war here. If I could summon men I would bring them here with their pistols and their drums, and they would fight before me and die only for my amusement, waving their silly flags and their trumpets. I know the world works like that. But here at the marshy river my voice only carries into a few small homes, my legend travels a short distance, and the small brown fish and the spiders, the plants and the flies around me are my only family now.

They say I hate all the men and the small boys, that I drowned my sons here and will walk along this bank until the sun dies, singing and crying like a hard wind. If I could have done it again, I would have been a cannibal, eating them all like lunch. If my husband had given me a daughter I would have forced her in me like that, even harder than I tucked my sons under the lapping water. I would want to breathe in the air with her same nose, her same lungs, to see the clouds with the eyes I imagine she would have had. I would want to take them all in, my husband, my sons, my daughter, one by one until they were gone.

Discussion Questions and Writing Activities

1. Do an internet search on the La Llorona folktale. How is Murray in dialogue with traditional folklore? What are the effects of her changes?

2. This short story is in first person, and thus entirely situated in the perspective of the titular character. How does the choice of first person impact the story? How would you characterize the tone and voice of our narrator? How do you know?

3. How does this story use storytelling techniques from both horror and folkloric retellings? Examine it for useful techniques, and then find a folktale to retell with an edge of dark fantasy or horror and try it yourself.

4. How does Murray humanize the narrator, and in doing so, make social critiques without being didactic?

Rebecca Roanhorse "Harvest" from *New Suns*

Biography (from her website)

Rebecca Roanhorse is a *New York Times* bestselling and Nebula, Hugo, and Locus Award-winning speculative fiction writer and the recipient of the 2018 Astounding (Campbell) Award for Best New Writer. Rebecca has published multiple award-winning short stories and five novels, including two in *The Sixth World* series, *Star Wars: Resistance Reborn*, *Race to the Sun* for the Rick Riordan imprint, and her latest novel, the epic fantasy *Black Sun*. She has also written for Marvel Comics and for television, and had projects optioned by Amazon Studios, Netflix, and Paramount TV. She lives in northern New Mexico with her husband, daughter, and pup. She drinks a lot of black coffee. Find more at https://rebeccaroanhorse.com/ and on Twitter at @RoanhorseBex. She has written fantasy, science fiction, and comics. She holds a JD from the New Mexico School of Law.

Literary Introduction

Rebecca Roanhorse splashed onto the science fiction and fantasy writing scene with her award-winning short story "Welcome to Your Authentic Indian Experience" (published by *Apex Magazine*). Her work has continued to be distinguished by many of the traits visible in that story. Character-driven writing, that is simultaneously action- packed, focused on pushing fantasy and science fiction away from Tolkien knock-offs, centering indigenous characters, pushing back against colonialism and erasure. Her novels have ranged from tie-in work with *Star Wars* and Rick Riordan Presents, to her own original *Sixth World* series (a postapocalyptic urban fantasy series set among Southwest native peoples) and her *Between Earth and Sky* series (an epic fantasy novel inspired by various pre-Columbian American cultures). Her fantasy work, with its anti-colonialist orientation and tight pacing, has aesthetic ancestors in the early work of Samuel Delaney, and Octavia Butler. Other contemporary speculative writers who center indigenous characters and themes, working in fantasy, horror, and science fiction, include Stephen Graham Jones, Darcie Little Badger, Cherie Dimaline, and Louise Erdrich. Erdrich is a particularly important comparison in this case, since Roanhorse's story "Harvest" uses the deer woman motif of Native American folklore, arguably putting it into conversation with Erdrich's novel, *The Antelope Wife*.

Harvest

Never fall in love with a deer woman. Deer women are wild and without reason. Their lips are soft as evensong, their skin dark as the mysteries of a moonless forest. A deer woman will make you do terrible things for a chance to dip your fingers inside her, to have her taste linger on your tongue. You will weep before it is over, the cries of one who has no relatives. But you will do whatever she asks.

"Tansi, Tansi," my lover whispers my name. "Is it time to harvest the hearts?"

The horror of her question is always fresh, always a shock. I suppose in the daylight hours when she is not here, I am able to tell myself that it never happened. That her words are other than what I know them to be. As long as I don't look at what we keep in the old cooler on the fire escape, as long as I ignore her bloody breath.

The hand she rests against my cheek is still damp and smells faintly of rot. The air clots my nose with a coppery sweetness that has become familiar. Her eyes meet mine, vast and luminous. They say that if you gaze into someone's eyes, you can see their soul, but my lover has no soul. Her eyes are mirrors, showing me only myself, and I turn away from what I see. I reach for her instead, my hands compelled by something primal. If desire were a thing made physical, it would be the curve of my lover's neck, the slope of her shoulders. It would taste like the salt of her skin. It would sound like the susurrus of her breath. So, of course I say what I always say, every time she asks me to kill for her:

"Yes."

"We only need a few more hearts now," she says. "Two? Three? I've lost count. Are you counting?"

"Three." Last week when she asked, it was five. The fifth we harvested on a Monday night in the empty parking lot of a deserted travel stop off I-95, a blonde-haired clerk whose steps were heavy with minimum wage and payday loan debt. Fourth was a grey-eyed mother of two, the backbone of her family. She fought hard, a strong heart, a worthy sacrifice, something to break the best of her people.

"They were monsters," my lover says to me. "And it does no good to have mercy on a monster. They will not have mercy on you." She tucks herself against my ribs and rests her head on my shoulder. The silver moonlight through the open window snags in her hair, the light of distant stars caresses her skin. She tilts her face up for a kiss. I lean in, eager, but she moves away, laughing. She rolls to her feet, drags at my hand. "Let's go!"

I go, stumbling out of bed, barefoot across peeling and cold plastic tiles, ignoring the residue of filth that sticks to my soles. I pull on my jeans, an old stained hoodie. Grab the black leather roll of chef knives from the console by the door. Hesitate at the feel of the leather in my hands, the blades of sharp steel unrevealed. And for a moment, I remember. A life before. Before I met my lover.

"It only has one knife right now," my fiancé Jeffery explains as I open the brightly wrapped box. It's a warm day in early September, the heat of summer still idling over upstate New York. He has obviously taken care in the wrapping of this gift, and my usually deft fingers fumble awkwardly with the green ribbon. When I finally crack open the box, I grin. The chef roll is the one I've always wanted, aged leather, smooth and supple with enough compartments to hold a whole catalogue of knives. Butcher and chop and paring.

"I could only afford one knife right now," he repeats, watching my face for disappointment. "But maybe after school, when you come back home. And we get married. . ." He pauses, waits for my reaction. When I offer him nothing but silence, he goes on. "I know one is not enough, but it's a start, right?"

"One knife is a start," I agree. I don't mention the other thing. "Thank you."

We sit a little longer in this impossible place. A bench on a sprawling leafy campus like something out of a movie about bright college years, a wonderland of green sloping hills on the banks of the Hudson. It is more water, and more things that need water to grow, than I have ever seen in my entire life.

"When will you come home?" he asks.

Home. A tiny reservation town that I outgrew the day I won a local cooking contest, then a statewide competition, and then it was a Food Network culinary cook-off show for teen chefs. The red-haired celebrity chef who hosted it took an interest in my talent. Then an interest in other things. Enough that when I demanded more of his time, he found me a scholarship to a culinary school on the other side of the country, far away from his wife and child.

I unfold the leather bag. Draw the solitary butcher knife from its sheath and run my hands across the silver shine of the blade. I press the tip of the knife into the pad of my thumb until blood rises to the surface. I suck the redness from my skin, eyes closed.

"I thought you weren't doing that anymore," Jeffery says, alarm in his voice and eyes on the bloody thumb in my mouth.

"I'm not."

"I mean, it's okay if you are. I just think maybe you should see someone about it? Especially up here. I bet they have great doctors in a place like this." Jefferey babbles on some more about the superior health care available in the Mid-Hudson Valley, but I've already stopped listening. When he finally tapers off I give him a smile.

"I'm not trying to change you," he insists. "I already told you that."

The smile stays firmly in place. "Let me walk you to your car," I say. "It's a long drive back to New Mexico."

Never fall in love with a deer woman. Deer women are cunning and can see the past and the future all at once. Their eyes are deep and still as well water, their legs as long and slender as the high aspens. A deer woman will make you do terrible things for a chance to stroke the back of her knees, to hear her whisper your name. She will promise you home.

We did not meet in a chance encounter in a moonlit wood, in the way of fairytales. I did not chase her fleeing shadow through a dappled grove of ancient trees to the banks of an enchanted pool. I was not lured away, as is the way of hunters who have, on a solstice eve, somehow become the prey themselves.

I met my lover in a bar on a weekend trip to Manhattan, an impetuous late train from my upstate culinary school down to the city, a solo escape from a mind-numbing week spent on gastronomy etiquette. Spirit dulled by the proper way to sit at a table, the hand to use for the seafood fork, the ordering of stemware. I am lost in this white man's world, drowning in a sea of their buttery sauces and unfamiliar histories, wishing for something known, something to remind me of home. I overhear a boy in class mention a food truck somewhere on the Lower East Side that serves oven bread and prune pastelitos. It feels like a sign.

New York City is big, noisy, a foreign place. But I am not afraid of it. It beckons, asking me to let go, to become someone else. I wander, looking fruitlessly for that truck, until I hear a deep drum beat, a high wailing through the open door of a corner bar.

She is there, wearing white. A dress that leaves her brown shoulders bare, a skirt that gambols lovingly around her long legs to brush the floor. Another Native woman. In New York City? What are the chances?

She dances the kind of dance that draws stares. The dance that reminds you of the whirl of the starry heavens, of places that exist far away from concrete canyons. She is graceful and undisciplined all at once, an invitation to question one's life choices.

When she stops, she falls into the high-backed chair next to me at the bar, laughing and flushed. She ignores the others, men and women, who crowd around her offering to buy her a drink. She looks at me.

And I make the mistake of looking back.

We drink St. Germain. Her, neat, in a shot glass, because she says it's like a shot of summer straight to the vein. I take mine with gin and ice and lemon, and agree. We drink, and then we dance, until the night moves on without us until the bartender calls last call. And laughing, dizzy, reckless, we share a nectar-tinged kiss. I should have known then, but in the way of new lust, all I could know was the slip of her hips and the flirt of her long fingers. The flavor of white flowers staining her lips.

Now I understand, in the way of those doomed, that I was being seduced. But like all fools whose desires leave them dashed upon rocks or lost in a faerie's lair, knowledge comes too late for salvation.

I never find that food truck that tasted like home.

The first time she convinces me to kill for her, it is a hot June evening. The sun has already set, but the oppressive humidity refuses to allow the day to cool, so we idle, naked, in my bed, eating ice chips and huddling in front of the fan. The first year of school is done; instead of going back to New Mexico and Jeffery, I'm working an internship at a prestigious midtown restaurant. Long hours of backbreaking work for almost nothing. I sleep days and spend my nights in the fury of the kitchen or, on my rare nights off, in her arms. I am in love. I am naïve.

"Why do you only visit me at night?" I ask her. I trace the delicate lines of her back with a finger, brush her hair away from her face. I keep my voice light, teasing. "Maybe we should try to do something during the day."

She rolls over on her side. "Like what?"

"Go to Central Park. Catch a movie."

She groans and flops on her back.

"It's just a thought."

She waves a hand weakly in the air, clearing away my "just a thought." "Tell me about your people, Tansi."

"What do you mean?" We haven't spoken of our families, either of us. A strange thing for two Natives to do, but it seemed an understood condition of her attention. Until now.

"Your people back home in New Mexico," she repeats. "Your family."

"We don't talk. They wouldn't approve. If they knew about us—"

"My family is gone," she says, her face focused on the ceiling. She pulls a hair from her head, stretches it out above her. "They were murdered. A long time ago. But sometimes, it feels like only yesterday."

"I-I'm sorry," I stutter out, shocked at her confession.

She drops the strand of hair and rolls to face me, her dark eyes intent. "Tell me. What would you do if people murdered your family?"

"What do you mean?"

"What would you do? Justice? Revenge?"

"Justice, I guess." I'm still reeling, trying to find my way through the sudden thorns of this conversation. "Revenge sounds scary," I add airily, a poor attempt to laugh off her black mood.

"Whatever you call it, you would make it right, wouldn't you? If it was in your power, you would make it right?"

A trickle of fear now. Deep down I know that this is not a question lightly asked. That what I say now, it is an oath.

I should run. I should not answer. But I am frozen in the bright headlights.

"Yes."

Her nod is grim, satisfied. "Where are those knives, Tansi?"

"What?"

"The ones you always carry. Your chef knives."

"Here. Well, over there. By the door."

"Tansi," she says my name like an invocation. "I want you to do something for me."

I don't say anything, breath stuck in my throat.

"I want you to help me make it right."

My hands up to the elbow are covered in blood. My heart is thumping wildly in my chest, but perhaps not as wildly or desperately as it should be for what I have done. Shouldn't I be vomiting? Crying? Shouldn't I feel more than a desire for her blessing?

She smiles and my spirit soars, giddy. She leans forward to catch the drip of blood in her small hands, brings it to her mouth and drinks. Her eyes are bright, dancing flames of wildfire. Her long hair catches the light.

"Did you know the Aztecs could remove a beating heart in less than two minutes? But that took a team. Two men to hold the body still and prone, at just the right angle. Two men to hold the legs."

"I didn't. Know, I mean."

"But you and I, we only need each other." She laughs and twirls, her long white skirt flaring around her, blood soaking the hem. She licks her fingers clean.

"What do we do now?" I ask. At least my voice has the sense to shake, to sound too high with fear. "Will the police come? Will I go to jail?"

"We leave the body here in the forest," she says. "You'd be surprised what deer will eat."

"And this?" I hold up the heart, still warm and pulsing in my hand. Just another piece of meat. Not so different from preparing *coeur de boeuf*. At least, that's what I tell myself.

"We'll collect them, Tansi. For my family. For. . .justice."

I look at the dead white woman at my feet.

"Are you sure this is justice?"

She puts a finger to my lips, then her lips to mine. "I certainly feel better. Don't you?"

After that I don't see my lover for days. I start to forget the screams, the smell, the horror. I go to the movies alone. I wander through Central Park. At night, I am thrown back into the insanity of the kitchen, taught to master fire and sharp steel and the incessant demands of perfectionists. After two weeks without her, I can almost believe it never happened. When the chef invites us all out for after-work drinks, I go. But I am lonely in the company of my co-workers, a foreigner unable to follow their words, their jokes all spoken in a language unfamiliar. I make excuses to leave early.

She is waiting for me when I get home. She steps out of her white dress and parts her legs. Runs trembling hands over her breasts. "Please don't leave me, Tansi," she whispers, tears wetting her cheeks. "Please don't leave me."

I miss work the next day. And then the next. A terse voicemail from the restaurant manager, and terser message from the chef de cuisine. I delete them both. Finally, a concerned email from school about my internship status. I don't answer.

We don't leave my bed for a week.

"You're ruined, Tansi," she says, laughing. "Now all you have is me."

Her face dips down between my legs and I shudder. She is enough. She is my work. She is my home.

After, she asks. "Is it time to harvest the hearts?"

We're in a parking lot of a Quikmart. We have stopped to wash the blood from my hands, to clean my knives in the anonymous restrooms. The cooler in the back of the car is heavy and sated.

"Are we done?" I ask.

She nods. Somewhere in the distance, the sound of a police car streaks down the parkway. The summer has become one for the record books. The internet is splashed with the sensational story. Thirteen women missing between the City and upstate New York. All matching a description.

The streetlights flicker, casting shadows across her heart-shaped face. She sighs and runs a hand across my hair, tucks a strand behind my ear. I shudder down to the marrow of my bones. Even now, after all she has made me do for her, I want her.

"Let's go home now," I beg.

"And where is that, Tansi?"

"Wherever. Just. . .somewhere. We don't have to do this anymore, right?"

She leaves her hand but turns her head away from me, eyes toward the dark night, the myriad trails that vivisect the forest beyond the parking lot. The call of the wind through the thick trees that line the parkway.

"Home," she says, her voice breaking with sorrow. "I want my home back, too."

Our last night together, while we're still in my little Brooklyn walkup and whatever comes next is still a sunrise and sunset away, she pulls something from her bag. A notebook, its velvet cover the deep green of secrets.

"I've been keeping a list," she says. "Of my family that were murdered."

She thrusts it towards me. The pages are full of tiny practiced handwriting. Name after name. Wessagusset. Pamunky. Massapequa. Pound Ridge. Susquehannock. Great Swamp. Occoneechee. I flip the page, and then another. Another. Skull Valley. Sand Creek. Wounded Knee.

The roar in my head is grief, wide and vast enough to drown whole new worlds. I know it is not mine, but hers. The book tumbles from my shaking hand. "I'm so sorry . . ."

"I felt them all when they died," she whispers, a hand to her heart, her eyes lined with tears. "Every one."

Her dark eyes find mine and she whispers the truth.

"Revenge."

I lug the full cooler across the National Mall, past the band playing the Star-Spangled, the screaming children with their Rainbow Rocket pops, the picnics and laughter and shouting masses waiting for sunset and the promised fireworks.

"What if this doesn't work?" I ask, nerves making my voice rattle. "What if doesn't bring your home back? What if it doesn't quiet the dead?"

I watch her ponder my question and for a moment, the night holds its breath. On its exhale she laughs, as free and enchanting as a rushing mountain stream.

"But, Tansi, what if it does?"

I place the last heart on the grass. Turn to where she lies sprawled in the middle of the circle. Some curious tourists are already starting to come closer, to see what ancient conjuration I am working with blood and muscle and grief on this most American of holidays. It is only a matter of time now.

I stretch out beside her. Gather her close to me, breathe in her scent for the last time.

"Are you sad?" she asks.

"No," I whisper, and it's true, but not. "Only that I will miss you," I say, picking words so inadequate they rise to the level of a lie. "Do I have to go?"

She draws a finger across my mouth and I taste the salt of my own tears.

I close my eyes and the children are gone, their melting popsicles only memories discarded on the lawn. The fireworks, reduced to suggestions of smoky trails in a blackening sky. The curious tourists, the monuments, the city. All vanished.

Time, rolled back to silence.

"Are they all gone?" I ask.

"Keep your eyes closed and they are gone."

"And your family?"

"They cannot come back, but their children are still here."

"Then we're home?"

When she doesn't answer, I open my eyes.

I am alone on the lawn. The crowd rushes back in, the noise, the children, the tourists, the smoke, the screams of horror, the sound of sirens.

Love a deer woman. Deer women are wild and without reason. A deer woman will make you do terrible things for a chance to raise up nations, to lie down with a dream. You will weep before it is over, the tears of the blessed, the cries of one who has found lost relatives. And if they ever let you out of your cell, tell them that you will do it again.

Discussion Questions and Writing Activities

1. Roanhorse's story blends traits of a revenge thriller, horror, and folkloric fantasy together. What is the impact of blending these genres together? How do these various threads help create the story that you have just read?

2. Deer women, who appear in many indigenous storytelling traditions, are often pursued by men, and exploited, the deer-self kept from them, or in some way putting them in danger. How does "Harvest" both engage with that tradition, and change it? What is the effect of that change? What point do you think Roanhorse is attempting to make?

3. This story takes place at least partially in an urban setting. What does the urban setting, and the decentering of the heterosexual experience so common to deer women stories, do for the narrative?

4. What is at stake for the protagonist? How are her stakes and the stakes of her lover connected? Are their goals and motivations in any way in conflict?

5. Write a fantasy story that reverses traditional and normative power structures for the characters, as Roanhorse does here. Pick a different folk tradition, a different story type, and try to pull it off. What do you learn from the experience?

6. Read up on deer women. Afterwards, reread the story. How does your additional knowledge add to your reading of the tale?

7. Write a fantasy story where your protagonist, much like the protagonist of "Harvest," has conflicting desires. The push and pull between their conflicting longings should drive their actions in some way. What happens when you give a character this kind of tangled motivation?

Sofia Samatar "Meet Me in Iram" from *Lightspeed Magazine*

Biography (from her website and interviews she's given)

Sofia Samatar is the author of the novels *A Stranger in Olondria* and *The Winged Histories*, the short story collection *Tender*, and *Monster Portraits,* a collaboration with her brother, the artist Del Samatar. Her work has won several awards, including the World Fantasy Award. She holds a PhD in Arabic Literature from the University of Wisconsin Madison. She has lived and taught English abroad, in countries including Egypt and Sudan. She speaks multiple languages: English, Arabic, and some Swahili. She now teaches African literature, Arabic literature, and speculative fiction at James Madison University.

Literary Introduction

Sofia Samatar's work is noted for its poetic language and interest in looking at the literature of diaspora, and the creation of fantasy worlds with global inspiration, often centering characters of color. Her writing frequently looks at language and storytelling itself through the lens of the fantastic. In interviews she has discussed how her experiences living abroad and her family life (her father was the Somali scholar and writer Said Sheikh Samatar, and her mother was a Swiss-German Mennonite from North Dakota) has influenced her scholarly and artistic interests. Many of her characters are at home in multiple places, or living in exile, especially in her debut novel, *A Strange in Olondira*, and its standalone follow up, *The Winged Histories*. "Meet Me in Iram" is a hallucinatory description of a lost city. The speaker longs to find their family there, but with the loss of a place, so, too, comes the loss of sensory experiences, and of community. Iram is a fabled desert city, lost to time and sand, mentioned in both the Qur'an and *A Thousand and One Nights*. The city simultaneously exists and doesn't exist. The narrator desperately wants to get back there. She has cited Mervyn Peake, Ursula K. Le Guin, and the Brontë sisters as literary inspiration. She shares with Le Guin a tendency toward scholar thinker characters, and fantasy stories that are epic in scope, without glorifying armed conflict. Writers who share her interest in language, in fantasy that hybridizes different cultural influences, and speculative storytelling oriented toward ethical questions include Brenda Peynado, Isabel Yap, Sequoia Nagamatsu, Ursula K. Le Guin, Vandana Singh, Carmen Maria Machado, and Gene Wolfe.

Meet Me in Iram

We are familiar with gold, says Hume, and also with mountains; therefore, we are able to imagine a golden mountain. This idea may serve as an origin myth for Iram, the unconstructed city.

The city has several problems. (1) It is lacking in domestic objects. (2) It is lacking in atmospheres that produce nostalgia. In cities without the correct combination of—for example—hills, streetlights, and coffee, it is difficult to get laid. A playbill in a gutter, bleeding color, the image of a famous actress blurring slowly into pulp: This would be perfect. The word *playbill* is perfect. There are many ways to achieve the desired conditions. Iram has none.

No continuity without desire. There is no desire in Iram; the time of Iram is *not yet.*

oh do you remember when we were courting
when my head lay upon your breast
you could make me believe by the falling of your arm
that the sun rose in the west

—American folksong

The reversal of time expressed in these lines is impossible in Iram. In Iram, there is nothing to reverse. Every time I go there, I see my uncle on the same bridge, and he raises his hand to greet me in the same way. He always tells me not to say *every time*, but I can't help it, it's a habit. He wishes I had come to visit him in Jeddah. I couldn't go, I tell him. It would have meant an expensive trip. I would have had to wear an abaya. I couldn't do it.

My uncle is not at all angry. Well, he says. He pats my shoulder. Well. He's wearing the most magnificent orange suit. Like my father, who is waiting for us at the restaurant, my uncle has style. The men in my family are all very beautiful.

When I say that Iram is lacking in domestic objects, I mean that we haven't gathered enough. I try to bring something with me every time. Last time it was a collection of my father's audiotapes, crammed into a pair of black plastic bags. The tapes are dusty with cigarette ash and poetry. It is only possible to listen to them in the worst light. A white, ugly, institutional light that, despite its harshness, is too weak to travel more than a couple of feet.

Fortunately the tapes create the sort of light they need.

At the restaurant, my father has already ordered. As always, he's gotten the huge appetizer plate, more than a hundred appetizers arranged around a bowl of blue flame. I kiss his cheek. He waves, expansive: Sit down! It's important to order the biggest thing. The entire restaurant must smell my father's cologne. In Iram, this makes me happy. This is the good life. I don't know what the blue flame is made of, but it keeps everybody warm.

You can stop there.

My mother says: Your father had beautiful skin. This was before he began to suffer from psoriasis. Now he goes out in a hat and gloves, even on the hottest days. My father has become allergic to sunlight. How is that possible, my mother asks. He's a Somali, he grew up in the sun! My father puts on his hat and goes out to his car. His beautiful skin, my mother says sadly. The car starts up: a throbbing sound that remains, for me, after all these years, synonymous with fear.

The car pulls into the driveway. The children hear its long, low note. They hear the door slam. The children run upstairs and hide inside their rooms. They're giggling because it's beautiful and exciting to be a child. They're smart; like bugs, they can squeeze into any kind of space. The children make bug-nests for themselves out of torn-up letters and photos. They squirm around in the nests and eat a lot of paper. The children are going to turn out fine, but they'll be the kind of people who do not have many things they can take to Iram.

In a city where one could find—for example—dogs, graffiti, and palm trees, it would be possible to fall in love.

Have you not considered how your Lord dealt with Aad, with Iram—who had lofty pillars, the likes of whom had never been created in the lands? And with Thamud, who carved out the rocks in the valley? And with Pharaoh, owner of the stakes? All of whom oppressed within the lands, and increased therein the corruption. So your Lord poured upon them a scourge of punishment.

—Qur'an 89: 6–13

The Wikipedia article on Iram warns: This article *needs attention from an expert in Archaeology.* The specific problem is: *The article is a confusing mix of myth, supposition, popular sources and very little science, scholarship, or sense; the result is a meaningless overview of the subject, accompanied by random facts and inexplicable leaps of logic.*

According to the article, Iram is also known as *the City of the tent poles.* It is *a lost city* or perhaps *a tribe.*

The passage from the Qur'an quoted here appears in the article. A note at the end reads: *translated by error.*

I walk to the restaurant with my uncle. There's nothing, no atmosphere. It's like anywhere. Iram, the windless city, is buried underground. I wish there were more of a glow so that I could see my uncle's suit. Once, I remember, I told a friend I was disgusted by the idea of a Daddy-Daughter Dance. So heterosexist, I said. I mean—ugh! My friend said she had gone to a dance like that with her father when she was a little girl. Magic, she said. If there were a glow, I could take my uncle's arm. She felt so special. It was the happiest night of her life.

Translated by error.

In Iram, my uncle understands me perfectly. I realize we've been speaking in Somali. We sing the song about the Prophet Issa's birth, the one about the darkest night. The very darkest night.

It almost doesn't matter that I'm carrying these awkward plastic bags.

In the window of the restaurant, there's a small blue light. My father waits for us inside. It's the way I told you before. Happy, happy. I'm the only woman there.

There are hardly any women in Iram. This is a problem, because without women, nothing happens. Nothing goes on without them. You will have realized at once that there's a connection between these missing women and the missing domestic objects. In Iram, there are windows but no curtains. I'm not saying women have to create these objects, I'm saying they do. Sometimes, after dark, I catch sight of a woman just disappearing around a corner. I recognize her from her photograph.

According to the ninth edition of the *Encyclopedia Britannica*, Iram is a lost city *which yet, after the annihilation of its tenants, remains entire, so Arabs say, invisible to ordinary eyes, but occasionally, and at rare intervals, revealed to some heaven-favoured traveler.*

I write on a scrap of paper: *Q-tips. Deodorant. Small hand lotion.*

I have a terrible longing to visit Iram again. I'm full of plans. I want to take a beaded wooden spoon with me next time—I think it's somewhere in my parents' house. The Somali pillow, too, and the little stool we used to call the African Stool. I'm sure that, when I reach Iram, I will know its true name. Perhaps that sounds romantic, but I believe things have true names. I believe everything has a name that I don't know.

In the restaurant, my father and uncle laugh together. My father grips my uncle's shoulder, chuckling naturally and with pleasure. It's not the explosive, uncontrollable laugh that seized him in our house the night some Somali guests came for dinner. My father had invited them. Everything was going well, and then something happened—I believe my brother made a face at one of his kids—and my father started laughing and couldn't stop. I remember we all laughed, too; we kept telling each other how terribly funny it was. Our guests smiled politely. You have to understand that at this time it was very rare for my father to eat with us, even rarer for him to invite guests to the house. The production of a normal family required immense effort. We were all keyed up to the highest pitch of excitement. My father's laughter seemed to go on forever, past bearing. At one point I felt pinned inside it. I couldn't move. Later I would experience that kind of laughter myself, when I was working in South Sudan during the war.

When you're outside, you can picture exactly what you want it to be like, but once you get in, all you can do is follow along.

You can help me. You can tell me if these feelings are universal. What is normal? I've felt for a long time that *normal* is something suspect, that embedded in the idea of the normal is something dangerous, an erasure of everything *abnormal*, a death or a series of deaths. But isn't it actually normal to want to be normal? I would like to build an entire philosophy out of Iram, the absent city. This philosophy would serve all the children of immigrants, many of the immigrants, and many others who found themselves at a loss. Eventually people would come to say: *This philosophy is available to all. Anybody can go to Iram.* All sorts of people, many of whom looked nothing at all like me, would disembark in the unconstructed streets. They'd bring their own bags, their photographs, their desire. Early in the morning, you'd find teenagers putting up playbills on the walls. Their sense of satisfaction would be so strong, it would color the air. For the first time, Iram would have a color of its own. But of course that can't happen until we import more objects, until we have succeeded in creating the conditions for nostalgia. For this reason, I fear that my feelings are not universal. Surely love cannot exist outside of time. It depends upon small objects.

The fact is, when my uncle died, he and my father were barely on speaking terms. My mother told me that my father disliked my uncle's gifts, specifically the gifts my uncle gave to my mother and me: gold jewelry, dresses heavy with beads. My mother, who is often sad, and not without reason, was sad because of this split between my uncle and my father. She and I wore our glittering beaded dresses to a New Year's Eve party. Everyone said we looked beautiful, exotic.

My father didn't go to the party. My father went somewhere else. I don't know where. Perhaps he was helping to draft the Somali constitution. When he disappears, I always imagine him doing heroic work. Once someone asked if I thought he worked for the CIA. I said I don't know.

We never eat anything after the appetizers. We're drinking tea from my uncle's thermos. My father and I use cups and my uncle uses the lid. In the radiance of the cobalt flame in the center of the table, of my uncle's marigold suit, I am dreaming of things to bring to Iram. I wish I could bring a bathroom door from the library at the University of Wisconsin–Madison, but how would I take it off, how could I get it out of the building? I'm picturing myself in the snow and ice, sliding down State Street with the big gray door clasped somehow under my arm. Impossible. And anyway, I don't know if that object would work. I don't think it's sacred in the way that a piece of cloth worn by a relative is sacred. Something that holds perfume. The door of a public bathroom stall—it's so anonymous, it doesn't even hold the imprint of my shoe. The imprint of my shoe where I kicked the metal door in a rage. A Somali student had told me his name was Waria. I knew it wasn't a name. He was making fun of me. It couldn't be a name, because it was just a sort of word. It was just something you said, not you but my father, on the phone. A sort of preface, like *Hey* or maybe *Hey you*. I realized I didn't know what it meant. Something melted in my face. Excuse me, I said. I went to the bathroom.

I question this idea of the *heaven-favoured traveler*. What kind of favor is it to arrive at an empty city? A city that goes on, lifeless, *after the annihilation of its tenants*? I'm just standing here on the corner with my bags.

To have no one to blame but yourself is to have no one. It's the worst fate.

a lost city or perhaps *a tribe*

I want to fall down in Iram. I've never tripped or fallen there. It's the sort of thing you can't organize; it has to come up and catch you unawares. I want to be caught and thrown to the ground in Iram, to scrape my knee. Look, there's blood. That's me. If that happened, I feel certain a new kind of light would arrive. I'd look down at my blood on the pavement, and my blood would show me the edge of a flight of steps. That's really what it's called. A flight.

If it gets too painful, you can stop.

When my uncle died, he left six children. Two sets of triplets. Three boys and three girls. I don't know them, because my father is on bad terms with my uncle's widow—in fact, he is estranged from her whole family. My uncle and his wife had their children through IVF treatment. When I was a child myself—long before my uncle's children were born—I remember being told that my uncle was unable to have children, because of what had been done to him in Somalia, in prison.

You can stop.

The woman is smiling in the photograph. I'm on her lap. I'm three or four years old. I asked my mother who she was, but my mother didn't know; she couldn't remember; she said, You'll have to ask your dad. I was getting ready to move somewhere—perhaps

Cairo, perhaps Wisconsin. My father had not been home for several days. I put the photograph away with the others. I was afraid to ask, afraid to find out that this lovely woman, my relative, was dead. Now I consider this an act of cowardice. I remember the picture. The smile. It seems to me that one corner of the photograph was cut off. Was someone else there? This woman was happy; she loved me. She smiled so fully, with such golden warmth, as she disappeared around the corner in Iram. Next time, I think, I'll rush to catch her, I'll shout, perhaps I'll fall down in the empty street. But of course there's no *next time*, only *not yet*. At one point I thought I was writing this to force myself to ask my father about the photograph. But I must have lost it, because it's gone. I can't ask now.

i wish i was a little swallow
that i had wings and i could fly
My uncle was shot and killed in his bed. Addis Ababa, 2010.
I'm just standing here on the corner, holding my plastic bags.
Very little science, scholarship, or sense.

I'm just trying to hold them both. Let's all laugh together. Sweet blue light. Let's pour a little more tea. Let's order more appetizers. Dad, let's stay here, let's not go. I remember when I was a kid, on long car trips, I'd imagine a giant saw was attached to my side of the car. The saw could cut through anything. It sliced fences, it sliced trees. The fences gave a swift groan and exposed the hollow insides of their poles. The trees went *snick* and fell over with juicy ease, the tops of the stumps left gleaming moist and pale, like a wound before the blood comes. I was leveling the whole country from my seat in the back of the car. I don't know why it gave me so much pleasure. The world was coming down to size. I know it sounds like the opposite of what I'm trying to do in Iram, but the feeling is the same.

The chapter of the Qur'an that mentions the city of Iram is called *al-Fajr*. Dawn.

Because we are familiar with gold and we are familiar with mountains. Because we are familiar with pillows and spoons. Because we are familiar, we can imagine. Is that true? Look, here I am, at my desk on the highest roof of the city. I sit up here at night so that you can find me if you come. I am listening to my father's cassettes. You will have noticed that there is sound in Iram, and this is why I come back, I think, to these blank and shrouded streets. I am trying to imagine sound as an object. As soon as I press *play* the light comes on, that white ceramic glare, and cigarette ashes lift away from the tape recorder and disappear in the air of Iram, where it is always night. Light pins me to my seat. When my father was in the basement listening to poetry, we knew we mustn't disturb him. The door was edged with grainy fluorescent light, the stairs coated with black rubber. It was a terrible, terrible place. And poetry came up as it comes to me now. I know the words for *pearl* and *water*. I am singing of the moon, of a great-limbed tree. Amber necklaces come to me and thorns and rain and a fiery horse and a lonely dhow adrift on a trackless sea. In Iram, I know the names. I sit repeating them, enraptured, frozen in an ecstasy of bad light. No continuity without desire. Look for me if you come. You'll know me by the falling of my arm.

Discussion Questions and Writing Activities

1. "Meet Me in Iram" is both a meditation on loss and loneliness, a description of a lost city, and semi-autobiographical since aspects of the narrator's experience line up directly with Samatar's. What does this blend of the fantastic, the personal, and real add to the story? Why cast one's experience into a fictional fantastic light?

2. There's a long history in the fantasy and science fiction community of writing about lost cities, from Atlantis to Roanoke, to entirely made-up cities, which in the 19th century were often placed in Africa, as though the continent was a blank slate where one could write anything. How does focusing a lost-city story on a place that is so deeply grounded in the Islamic Arabic tradition engage with the fantasy community's history of lost-city stories. How does it push back, revise, or expand that tradition?

3. How does Samatar structure the arc of the narrative within the hallucinatory structure? What are the main threads of the narrative? What is gained by creating the hallucinatory quality that this story exudes?

4. This is in some respects a story about memory, and family. How does Samatar turn memory into not just content, but form?

5. Think of a few bits of your real life, like where you went to school, your family's background, and then weave it in with the fantastic, creating a highly fictionalized reflection of yourself. Does this reveal anything to you about your identity? What do you think it adds to the story for someone who doesn't know anything about you?

6. Try to write a story that is both hallucinatory, but very clear at the same time. Each piece alone should be clear and easy to visualize, yet each piece together should make the story feel like a bit of a fever dream. Afterwards, reflect on the challenges of writing a story that is dreamlike, yet readable.

7. Pick your favorite image from "Meet Me in Iram" to analyze. How is the image used to add emotional heft to the story? Does imagery in this story function like imagery in prose, or does it have a lot in common with poetry?

Vandana Singh "A Handful of Rice" from Steampunk Revolution

Biography (information taken from her website and other articles about her; she doesn't have a third-person biography on her webpage)

Vandana Singh is an Indian writer and physicist. She was born and raised in New Delhi, fluent in both English and Hindi; she has spoken and written in both since she was a child. She writes speculative fiction, encompassing both fantasy and science fiction. She holds a PhD in Particle Physics and teaches at a state university not far from Boston. She has spoken often about how growing up in India with parents who both hold graduate degrees in English Literature infuses her writing and life. She has said that she's forgotten more epics in two languages than most people will ever know. Her academic work and her creative writing have shifted to looking at environmental issues, grappling with climate change, and its implications for social and environmental justice. Her short stories have won her many accolades, including inclusion in year's best anthologies, as well as work with Arizona State University's Center for Science and the Imagination. She has written two short story collections, *Ambiguity Machines* and *The Woman Who Thought She Was a Planet*, as well as a children's book.

Literary Introduction

"A Handful of Rice" is very different from much of Singh's work, insofar as it is primarily fantastical, rather than science fiction (most of her work blends the two, or is straight science fiction), while at the same time it is typical, in the beauty of the prose, and the fusion of many literary influences, from steampunk to the Indian epic. The story is also representative of her work in that her short stories, like this one, often contain the scope of an epic fantasy novel into the length of a short story, through grounding the epic events in the personal. While the protagonist of this story is setting out to kill a ruler that he views as despotic, the story itself isn't focused on large-scale conflict, but on the deeply emotional and personal consequences of current events on the protagonist. It also wrestles with deeply philosophical questions, such as: Can one good outcome justify other evils? Can the ends justify the means? Her focus on the personal and the political intersecting connect Singh's work with Ursula K. Le Guin (I know, she's everywhere!), Sofia Samatar, Silvia Moreno-Garcia, Abbey Mei Otis, and Ken Liu. Her environmental justice work connects her to Le Guin, VanderMeer, and Catherine Valente.

A Handful of Rice

At last Vishnumitra saw the king.

The city was alive with beasts, mechanical and organic; there were elephants in the procession, stately and benign, draped with silk and brocade, bearing silk howdahs on their backs; then the metal men, marching in formation, sun glinting off their armor; the king's black horse, riderless and unsaddled, hooves ringing, leading the king's glory, the tallest howdah on the tallest elephant. Crowds leaned out of balconies, lined the roads, throwing rose petals into the parade. Horseless carriages of the latest fashion, just out from the king's own factories, led the procession, but it would not do for the king to sit in one of those. There were few things, said the traitor to Vishnumitra, as royal as elephants.

To Vishnumitra the elephants looked out of place. He was an outsider from a village in the far reaches of the kingdom, and the bright, ringing clamor of the streets, the heavy scent of roses and sweat, were all too much for him. His opinion was of no account, so he said nothing. But he thought with some nostalgia about the home he had left behind these many, weary months, although the picture that came into his mind was one from his boyhood. Kind-eyed elephants bathing on the shore of the Ganga with the village boys, the water a grey sheet under a cloudy sky. Ahead were the steps of the ghat going down to the water and on the steps his mother and sisters, saris billowing red and orange. It was early morning; it was going to rain. On the rise along the shore the shisham trees spoke sibilantly in the breeze, their leaves a tender green. He saw his mother bend down and release the little earthen diya in the water, in its garland-boat of woven leaves and marigolds. Her hands cupped the small flame to make certain it did not go out in the wind, but the currents pulled the diya away from her, and she straightened and looked at the little boat—fire on water—sail off mid-stream. Fire on water, a prayer released into the world.

He shook his head to clear it of old memories and immediately the noise and pomp of the procession assaulted his senses again. Annoyed with himself for dwelling so much on the past lately, he tried to turn his attention to the task at hand: to get a good look at that elusive, all-powerful monarch, the great man who ruled Hindustan, the man who, it was said, would live for ever. Harbinger of Peace and Prosperity, they called him, this mysterious man who would not let anybody draw his portrait or take his picture. He was not quite mortal, it was said. He had held off She Shah's kingdom in the North-West, the Portuguese colony in the East, and the British territories to the South, and only magic of some kind could have accomplished that, said the sycophants and admirers of the king.

Vishnumitra did not believe in magic; instead he believed in rigorous observation and systematic study. The glimpse was the first step: after that he didn't know whether he was going to do it, or how he was going to do it. He was not an assassin, he had told the traitor.

The traitor nodded as though to imply that all the assassins said that anyway, and Vishnumitra had felt soiled by the man's polite disbelief. Somehow these days of waiting and plotting in the great nation's capital had been the hardest period since he had left home two years ago. Perhaps it was no wonder that he was tired; that his resolve was shaken by that deep, inexpressible desire to go home. Looking at the King's portrait on the coinage of the country, the abstract, fluid lines suggesting a face beautiful in repose, he had thought about his mother making kheer in the kitchen. A portrait of the king, made illegally and paid for in blood, showed the lean, aristocratic face, the eyes large, clear, cold. "This is not very accurate, but maybe it is good enough?" the traitor had said. Vishnumitra had a sudden clear vision of the schoolroom in his village, the foot-thick mud walls, the golden thatch overhead, the view of the distant river. It took him some time to frown and say that he really needed to be able to recognize the king clearly before he could be certain he had killed the right man. It was known that the king had proxies who sometimes spoke for him on lesser public occasions. At least once, such a proxy had been killed. No, Vishnumitra needed to see the king face-to-face.

"How can I be certain," he asked the traitor, "that the man in the procession is indeed the king!"

"For the anniversary of his coronation? Only the real king rides the royal elephant, my friend."

The broad way was divided in the middle by a long water channel that had been sprinkled with rose petals. Along each side of the road was a five-foot-high divan, a raised platform bristling with tall, plumed soldiers. The noise was tremendous, with shouts and the baying of horns.

And Vishnumitra saw the king.

The room he was in was level with the howdah in which the king rode. The building was too far from the street for clear viewing with the naked eye; they had already been searched for weapons by guards. So Vishnumitra put the telescope in position and squinted through it, waiting for the attendant inside the howdah to do his job.

The attendant, in the pay of the traitor, did his job. He had an embroidered palm-leaf punkha in his hand and while fanning the king he let it catch in one of the king's long braids. The king wore his ceremonial turban above his coiffure; the crown shifted, the black braids parted. The king turned instinctively toward the punkha, his hand already up to adjust the braid, his mouth an O of surprise and irritation, and in that moment Vishnumitra saw him.

The procession continued. Vishnumitra lowered the telescope, stood staring out through the latticed window, his mind a maelstrom.

No wonder he had been thinking so much about his youth.

The king—surely there could be no mistaking it—the king was no other than Upamanyu, the young man he had befriended in his boyhood, the wanderer who had made a home with them for four unforgettable years, closer than a brother. But no, it could not be. In the interim Vishnumitra had aged; despite his practice of the forbidden sciences, he had a few gray hairs. He looked younger than his fifty-seven years, but the king looked twenty-five.

Upamanyu... the face burned into his mind, thirty-eight years ago, never forgotten, Remembered always, with yearning.

If the king was, indeed, Upamangu, that could only mean one thing.

"Well?" said the traitor, "Can you... will you do it?"

Vishnumitra took a deep breath. He controlled the needless dissipation of his body's prana with an effort, a skill learned over years, and felt his mind and body getting back to equilibrium. He now understood that his wanderings in search of the hidden sciences and their practitioners, his investigations into the murder of the girl Shankara, whose name he still could not say without pain, were all intended to bring him to this place at this point. He was the only man in the four kingdoms who knew who the king was.

"This is where our association ends," Vishnumitra said to the traitor. "You have been paid. If I do it, I will do it alone."

That night. Vishnumitra went walking through the long, lamp-lit streets of Dilli.

The city rose over the banks of the Yamuna like a poet's dream. Here was the delicate arch of a doorway, the doors carved with scenes from a fairy tale; there was a temple spire, beside the dark crown of mango tree. The dome of a mosque, silver in the twilight, and above it the fort itself, red sandstone, turrets, and tessellations. Closer at hand: a man selling roasted shakarkand under a tree by the road side: the smell of coal and sweetness and spices, the flare of the fire. Voices from within a walled garden where somebody was watering rosebushes. He could smell wet earth and the inescapable fragrance of roses. The horseless carriages still startled him as they went by, leaving behind a wet smell, coal and steam, and the image of a face or faces at a window. Here and there were patrols of the king, guards in red and brown, with green turbans, riding horses. And the ornate carriages filled with nobility, pulled by the great, white, humped oxen that stood six feet high at the shoulder. One time he saw a patrol accompanying those curious artifacts, the metal men (borrowed for the parade), back to the factories where they worked. The metal men walked stiffly; with each step the joints clanged faintly, metal on metal, and there was a sigh of steam. Vishnumitra could not get used to their swiveling heads, their eyeless gaze.

He walked swiftly, like a man with a purpose, so as not to draw attention to himself. But his back was against the wall. There really was no place to go anymore. This place, this moment, was where the last two decades had brought him. He could give himself the illusion of being free, the stranger in the city who must be on his way soon, but he was chained by his promise to the dead. He had to kill the king.

But Upamanyu . . .

If even that is his real name, Vishnumitra thought, with bitter humor. The king called himself Akbar Khan. Every child in the kingdom knew how he had come to occupy the throne of the Mughals; in towns all over, people still enacted the story. The British forces fighting their way all the way to Dilli from the South, burning and looting, setting the bazaar on fire. The valiant Mughal army, with the king, Mirza Mughal, in the lead. All the king's sons fall in battle that black day, until there is only Mirza Mughal chasing a knot of enemy soldiers into an alleyway and out in the open by the river. He is known for his swordsmanship; he dispatches three of them quickly, a few of the others flee, but there is one left. Mirza Mughal leaps from his great black horse, fighting hard, blood on his sword, his armor broken across the chest. Last of the Mughals, he is holding back a pale, yellow-haired youth with a bayonet. There's the Yamuna before him, and in the black water he can see his city burning. At the last minute, when Mirza Mughal is so tired he almost wants to die, there comes a madman leaping into the fray, challenging the British soldier, wielding a sword but in a style Mirza Mughal has never seen. Then a strange thing happens: the bayonet falls from the British soldier's hand as if of its own accord; the boy seems surprised, horrified, and the madman's sword makes short work of him. The stranger bows, introduces himself to his king. His name is Akbar Khan. The king and his subject return to the fray, fighting side by side until a stray bullet hits the king. In the last scene of the tragedy, Mirza Mughal is dying in Akbar Khan's arms while Dilli burns. The river is burning too: boats succumb first to fire, then water. In the presence of what is left of his army, Mirza Mughal tells Akbar Khan: my sons are dead. I give you my kingdom. Drive out the enemy and rule!

Over the body of the dead king, Akbar Khan rouses the soldiers and the common people of the city with a speech that is still recited today in the dramas. Men leap over courtyard walls, where they have been cowering, and throng the streets; mothers lock the children in their homes and take up kitchen knives and burning brands, and leap into the fray. It is as though a tsunami has suddenly hit the invaders.

In the narrow alleyways, the once-gracious city squares, in courtyards and on the riverbank the British are cut to bits. The invading armies flee.

In the dark and smoke, the smell of blood and burning flesh, the wails of the bereaved, Akbar Khan stands still for a moment, outlined in the archway of a garden that has become a charnel house. Watchers see him limned in the light from the fires behind him, his bloody, smoking sword by his side.

Then, in a moment immortalized by innumerable dramas, Mirza Mughal's great black horse comes up to Akbar Khan. He has lost his saddle, and there is a gash on his side, but the great beast simply bows his head, stands and waits. Akbar Khan pauses for a moment, strokes the horse's head, and with a lithe movement that no theater performer can quite emulate, leaps upon the horse. The horse bears the new king to the fort.

Vishnumitra had to concede that it was quite a story: how the nobody, Akbar Khan, ascended the throne of Dilli. But holding on to that throne for so many years was an even greater achievement. What Akbar Khan did, the stories went, was to first consolidate that nexus of power, the harem. Mirza Mughal's harem was fairly modest, with two chief queens, seventy-five lesser wives and about five hundred concubines, along with hundreds of female administrators, a corps of eunuchs and female guards. This was where the king had lived, where the affairs of state were decided, and where he opened reports from his spies. It was said that Akbar Khan won over the queen mother first. The dead princes were given elaborate funerals and the queens shown the utmost respect. So when the intrigues and assassination attempts began, Akbar Khan was not without friends. His pleasing mien and obvious wizardry with the sword were rivaled only by his political acumen. When Mirza Mughal's relatives challenged him he played one faction against the other until most of his rivals were eliminated. As for the rest, he invited them to challenge him in a duel unto death.

Those were the early years. The challenges were issued mostly by nobles outraged that a man without a lineage, let alone a proper Persian lineage, could sit upon the throne of Hindustan with such insouciant ease. Such challenges were the talk of the citizenry, because Akbar Khan received and accepted them in the public durbar. Sometimes the challenger wanted a game of chess; sometimes it was a duel by arms, but always it was the throne at stake, and always, failure meant death. The challenge itself was held in a private room off the durbar, with only the king and the challenger present. And always, the challenger would be found dead the next morning, in the trash heap outside the city walls. There was no evidence of poison or other underhand means, only a bruising about the skin, and a neat sword-cut to the throat. The victim didn't bleed much, it was said. There were rumors of magic and other skullduggery, but the king, while contradicting these, did not work too hard to suppress the imaginations of the credulous. Always, he generously compensated the families of the victims.

After his first two years in office, Akbar Khan stopped accepting challenges. The occasional madman would still issue a challenge but Akbar Khan showed great compassion in turning such fools away.

Enough blood had been shed. His kingdom was established.

Having silenced his critics. Akbar Khan had set his skill and charisma to work on the rest of the country, bringing to it a relatively stable economy and a robust peace. He befriended Sher Shah of the North-West Kingdom and played the Portuguese and the British against each other while making neighborly noises to both. It was rumored that he gave covert support to the revolutionaries in the South so the British had their hands full. This was the king who embraced the modern science of Europe's industrial revolution, and in doing so revived the metallurgical genius of the ancient Indians by searching for and bringing to his capital all indigenous talent: he brought over some of Europe's finest engineers to work with them. The manufactories of Dilli rolled out horseless carriages of gleaming steel that moved on the new-paved roads like boats on still water. They were becoming popular in Britain; the manufactories were having a difficult time keeping up with the frenzied demands from abroad.

At the same time, Akbar Khan had been careful not to create a culture of demand in his own land. Very few Indians owned their own cars; for long-distance travel there were the railways, laid across the land like lines on a palm. Vishnumitra had, during his wanderings, acquired a reluctant fascination for this mode of transport; there was something about the sway and rhythm of these sleek, serpentine monsters that brought to his heart an inexplicable joy. It was also easy to think while traveling like this, and he had spent some of his most contemplative moments in the last two years on a train, watching the countryside flash by.

It was said that while the South-West reeled under the despotism of the Portuguese king, and the South itself knew mass poverty and economic collapse for the first time under the rule of the British general, Hindustan was free. And prosperous. Glory be to the king, Akbar Khan the First. So what if he used magic and was rumored to be unconventional, even heretical? So what if he defied the kazis and brought back the syncretic, hybrid Hindu-Muslim culture of his namesake, Akbar the Great? So what if he kept his hair in long braids, had private quarters outside the harem atop a small tower, where only he and invited guests could go?

So what if his eccentricities included banning the ancient science of healing?

Vishnumitra had, from afar, supported the rise of Akbar Khan until then. For him Akbar Khan had been a person of legend in distant Dilli, a man of whom absurdly tall tales were told, who had somehow been able to consolidate the kingdom and keep its enemies at bay. Then the news came, slowly at first, trickling into the outer reaches of the kingdom from wanderers and tradespeople, and finally from local officials: the practice of the ancient arts was banned. Some of the herbal lore was all right to practice, but the rest of it, referred to by the king as quackery, was no longer allowed. Significant parts of the ancient medical system of Ayurveda, particularly those concerned with the prana vidya, as well as the various methods of acupuncture brought by Chinese scholars, were now forbidden. A system of national medical care had been set up by the king, employing a mishmash of traditions, from the European to the Yunnani, and the textbooks had been standardized and rewritten. So while a practitioner of Ayurveda would have studied the works of, say, Charaka, or Patanjali, now only "relevant" extracts were read, the implication being that the rest was not worth learning. The king claimed he wanted to modernize the country. Yet he did nothing to stop other kinds of quackery; charlatan astrologers could wander the land at will, but a traditional healer could find himself thrown in jail. Yoga as exercise was all right, but healing through the control and manipulation of prana was quackery, and its practice punishable by imprisonment. Vishnumitra had been angry and bewildered, but there was nothing to be done. He had to keep his true vocation a secret and lie about his age.

But now, walking through the city like a man possessed, Vishnumitra thought he knew why the king had banned the ancient sciences of healing, while reserving them for himself under the guise of magic.

Still, it made no sense that a man who was sixty-two years old should look twenty-five, even with the practice of the prana vidya. They gave good health, not immortality. Something was very wrong.

He thought of the girl Shankara, whom he himself had trained in the forbidden sciences. For his first year of wandering she and a handful of others had been his dear companions. She had cut off he hair and disguised herself as a man so as to be able to travel with less trouble. With their help Vishnumitra had established over much of Hindustan a secret network of the practitioners of prana vidya, all of whom had once operated alone, and in fear. The fear was still there but with it now there was comradeship, the exchange and enhancement of knowledge. No longer did one healer or scholar of such arts fear that the knowledge would die with him or her.

And the best of them had been Shankara.

She had gone to Dilli against his advice, to challenge the king.

Since the months after a friend discovered her body on the refuse pile outside the city, Vishnumitra had wondered how it had happened.

Why had the king, who no longer accepted challenges, accepted one from Shankara? And how had someone of Shankara's skill been outmaneuvered?

Oh, those months of grief and rage . . .

Vishnumitra paused by a shop selling sugarcane juice. He had a cupful so he could sit down for a moment, away from the crowd around the stall. There was a cracked marble platform around the roots of a pipal tree; he sat himself down on it. Behind him, under the tree's great canopy, was the mausoleum of a minor Sufi poet. He could smell incense and flowers.

Upamanyu . . .

He could not let himself feel what he had once felt, but even now, thinking of the name was enough to quicken his pulse. Once dearest friend, dearer than a brother! How lonely the years had been without him. He could never have imagined that he, Vishnumitra, who would once have defended Upamanyu with his life, would one day be plotting his death. He took a deep, shaky breath. A great wave of resistance to the notion rose in him, and along with it a desire to see Upamanyu again, and to leave this matter of revenge and murder to someone else. After all, there was all of Hindustan at stake. What would happen to its freedom and prosperity when Upamanyu was gone? He had thought through it all before, before he knew who the king was, and settled on the idea that what is right is right, and if a right act leads to great evil, then that evil must be thought of as independent of the act that preceded it, and fought on its own terms. But here, in the great city, with its show of might, power and glory, and the terrible news streaming in from the South as though to say: this is what will happen to Hindustan if you kill the king, it was difficult enough to justify this reasoning. And now that he knew who the king was, could he lift a hand against him?

And yet, and yet . . .

Shankara.

And the rest of the practitioners, who now worked in fear and secrecy, and the ones who had been found and killed. He had to do what he had set out to do.

He thought: after this I will go back home to my village, to what is left of my father's ashram by the Ganga. He did not tell himself that the very air, there, would remind him of Upamanyu. That after this Upamanyu's name might well be written on the paths they had once walked in the forests, together, or on the mud walls of the now-abandoned ashram.

The ashram was the place of his earliest memory. The walls were nearly a foot thick, made from a mixture of mud and straw; in the sun they glowed as though they were made of gold. Some of the walls were carved with images such as a god on a chariot or a hero atop an ele-phant. To the small boy he had been, the walls of the ashram told stories without saying a word. Inside, under the thatch roof, it was always cool in summer and warm in winter; even now he remembered leaning his head against the textured surface, feeling safe, feeling he was home.

The first time he saw Upamanyu . . . Nearly forty years ago. The face, in its youthful, unchanged beauty, had burned in his memory for all these years.

He remembered. How could he not? It was the first time that the world had come to his doorstep, after all, in the form of a young man, wanderer and eternal traveler. On his clothes was the dust of Baluchistan, Mysore, and Assam. He had stories to tell about the fall of Travancore in the South, the winds of the Western Desert, the arid cliffs of the North-West where Sher Shah had his citadel.

That morning Vishnumitra had been reading a copy of the Charika Samhita on the verandah, practicing his Sanskrit while trying to learn something about healing. He was fifteen, a tall, quiet boy grown golden in the sun like the walls, and had acquired some of their contemplative silence. He wanted to be a healer, to use the knowledge of the ancients to heal the sick. His world had been whole, complete, until Upamanyu walked into it.

The children had been singing multiplication tables out in the courtyard, swaying with the music of it, making Vishnumitra feel pleasantly sleepy, so that he couldn't go beyond stanza one of the first verse of the Charaka Sambita (that great medical treatise being written in poetry, as was once the norm). The other children were bringing in mustard leaves from the garden they had been tending, the leaves scenting the air with their delicate pungency. And there was the stranger at the gate, as though the air had conjured him up: a tall long-limbed fellow in the outlandish loose pants and long shirt of the North-West, with a mane of unruly black hair. He stood there unhurried and smiling, hefting his cloth bag on his shoulder, rubbing the stubble on his chin with his other hand.

Vishnumitra rose to greet the stranger but his father had already waved the children to silence. His father loved wanderers and outcasts, having been one himself for so long. In a few minutes the stranger was seated on a low wooden seat under the pipal tree. Water was brought for his hands and feet, and to drink. That was what he had stopped for: water, and five minutes of rest before wandering on to the town twelve miles away. Later Upamanyu would tell Vishnumitra: I stopped for five minutes and stayed five years—I, who have never stayed in a place longer than a month!

All these years later Vishnumitra wondered why Upamanyu had stayed so long. He had always thought it was because of the love that had arisen between them, the love of brother for brother and friend for friend; but now he was not so sure. Perhaps all that had been an illusion. His mentor and dear friend, who had taught him sword-fighting and filled his ears with the knowledge of a world far greater than the little ashram, may have had other reasons to linger. Who knew if even Upamanyu were his real name?

Every morning Vishnumitra would recite verses from the Charaka Sambita for his father. Upamanyu would be leaning against the wall, his mane of hair tied casually into a knot, his eyes bright with curiosity.

Maitreya would explain each concept.

"Prana is the life force. Some people call it breath but it is that which comes before breath. In every healthy living being prana flows unimpeded through its designated channels. Sickness is when there is a blockage or abnormality in the prana flow, and then the healer must restore its pathways in order to restore health. . ."

"But is prana not the same as blood?" This from Upamanyu.

"No, indeed. Prana cannot be seen, heard, or felt, except by the one trained in the ancient art of healing. Such a practitioner can tell the state of the prana flow when he feels the patient's pulse, for the quality of the flow is reflected in the characteristics of the pulse. But the true sage can induce in himself a state of direct prana perception, in which the flow of prana appears manifest to the inner eye as the flow of the Ganga is manifest to the outer."

"Can you do this, Guruji? Will you teach me?"

Maitreya laughed.

"It is not so easily done. It takes the discipline of years. You will have to set down your traveling staff, my son, and study like Vishnumitra here. I myself have only touched the edge of that perceptive state. This knowledge is very arcane; I have found one version of it in a Tibetan text that I found by chance. But here too the greater truth is hinted at and concealed in a morass of lesser truths. This is the language of the twilight, as they say. It takes a lifetime to interpret these hints and intimations."

"Teach me, then, Guruji! For you I lay down my staff. You will find your pupil unused to instruction and too full of questions and impatience, but he will be grateful to be schooled . . ."

What Vishnumitra realized was that his father was in fact pleased. Later he wondered if Upamanyu had reminded his father of his own youth. Upamanyu's habit of asking questions as though he were issuing a challenge in a duel instigated in Maitreya delight instead of anger, and in fact Vishnumitra spent the next few days hating their guest, thinking himself less loved, a boring, overly obedient, dull sluggard of a student. But it all changed when Uparnanya asked Vishnumitra if he would help him achieve a better hand—his writing was atrocious, After that they went for walks in the forest, swam in the river, and engaged the village youth in games like kho and stick-fighting, Upamanyu revealed himself to be skilled with stick and sword, prideful and quick to temper, but just as easily recovering his good nature. In the forest one day Upamanyu brushed his hand across a chamel bush. Its white, scented flowers were like stars.

"Do you think plants have prana too, Vishnu?"

Vishnumitra thought, with a little surge of triumph: so you don't know everything, my friend!

Aloud he said:

"They do. My father has not yet taught you about cosmic prana. The prana that is in us flows into us and out again, and into and out of other things also. I don't quite understand it myself. But once, during meditation, he achieved the deepest state of prana perception—just for a few seconds—and he told me later it was like rivers of light falling out of the sky, flowing in and out of everything Like the delta of a river, small streams coming together and then flowing apart . . ."

"That's what I want to see," Upsmanyu said enthusiastically. Ahead of them the Ganga lay silver in the semi-darkness. They sat on the bank in companionable silence.

So long ago, it had been. It amazed Vishnumitra to think that the ashram had so long withstood the depredation of time and prejudice. His father had been a maverick, a madman. An outcast who had given up the Brahmin's sacred thread to marry a Muslim woman and not even insist on her conversion, let alone the various purification rituals! It was said that while she performed Hindu rituals such as the chhat fast, she also kept to her daily Islamic prayers! So Maitreya had lost caste and status, been turned out with his wife to roam the world. In his late youth he had finally found this place by the great, slow river, where among the trees a new kind of ashram had been founded. Eklavya, where any child could come to learn, irrespective of caste or creed or religion. The Brahmins kept their sons at home but in time the other castes sent their children, afraid to miss out on such an education. Apart from learning the duties of a householder, they would learn mathematics, music, astronomy, Ayurveda, yoga, tending a garden, cooking, sword-fighting and wrestling. Maitreya found teachers from the ranks of swordsmen and wandering dervishes, Sufi healers and itinerant craftsmen. So in time the children of petty tradesmen, Hindu or Muslim, sat with those of cow-herds, rich landowners, and the occasional defiant Brahmin and sang their multiplication tables, or learned to cook and eat together and thus destroy both caste and religion. But what they created, Maitreya would say, was more important: a hybrid culture, a *din-i-illahi* made real, imbued with the best of both traditions. Friendship, community, a temple of knowledge.

And it was that. In the kitchen Vishnumitra's mother, Tasleem, took the clay pot of rice off the earthen stove and carried it out to the courtyard, swept clean by the children. There was a daal and some vegetables, and berries the children had picked in the forest. Everyone was sitting cross-legged on the ground, in a row, waiting to be served. The platters were made of dried, woven leaves, and soon each held a mound of rice, the famous red-tinged rice of that region. Many years after he had left home, Vishnumitra remembered the aroma of that rice: rich, earthy, with a touch of walnut. Whenever he met a trader from those parts he was sure to buy enough red rice to last him some time.

And in the night-time, sleeping in the open under the stars, with the crickets singing in the undergrowth, and from the forest the low, sweet call of a koel. His father would tell the small ones stories of pirs, or gods, or kings.

"And so Krishna became the king of Dwarka, but his friend of childhood, Sudama, remained poor even as a grown man. He lived in a hut with his wife and children, and they were hungry many times. One day he decided he would go to Dwarka to see his old friend. All he had that he could bring as a gift was a bag of rice, just the kind you ate today. So he walked all the way to Dwarka ..."

It was an old, comforting story: the friend, Sudama, in his rags, with his lowly gift, being laughed at by the courtiers until the king saw him and came to him and embraced him, and expressed inordinate delight at the gift of rice. And Sudama spent a few days with Krishna, and when he returned home he found that his fortunes had changed. Where his rude hut had been, there stood a mansion, and his wife and children were well-fed and well-clothed.

"So, children, wherever you go when you are grown, may you remember your days together and be friends to each other as Krishna and Sudama were ..."

Somewhere a queen-of-the-night bush was in bloom; its heavy scent was wafted by the breeze from the river. In the quiet after the story, Vishnumitra stole a glance at his friend, who was stretched out in the next pallet. He wanted to touch Upamanyu's hand, to make real his feeling that they were and always would be as Krishna and Sudama had been to each other, but shyness held him back. Upamanyu's fine, clever face was soft with moonlight, and listening.

And after all, Upamanyu had been the first to leave. He wanted to go to Tibet, he said, to look for the lost books on prana lore.

But even before that Vishnumitra had sensed a restlessness in him, a preoccupation. He had known, but not admitted to himself until years later, that what called to Upamanyu was not just old palm-leaf manuscripts on prana lore but the long journey, the new sights along the way, and new adventures. He was tired of staying in one place. It was time to move on.

He had gone away one day with promises to be back in a year or two. There were disturbances from the South: the British invaders were marching north. Nothing was certain.

Maitreya knew he wouldn't be back, and he kept his disappointment and sorrow to himself. Vishnumitra's heart broke. The world became empty to him, and every familiar place reminded him of Upamanyu's absence. Only a few years later his father died in a skirmish during the confusion of the first British incursion north. Vishnumitra ran the ashram as best he could until his mother died. Some years after that the news came that the new king had banned the practice of the ancient arts. Vishnumitra could have kept the ashram going with all the remaining disciplines, but its existence was already a thorn in the side of the new provincial governor, who frowned upon such sacrilegious intermingling of caste and religion. Vishnumitra had no heart left for trouble. When the ashram closed he found that the wanderlust had come to him after all.

He set off into the world, not knowing what it held in store for him. He hid his true occupation, calling himself a scribe or a scholar, practicing his healing arts when they were truly needed. He found that if he stayed in a place more than a few days after a healing, others would come to him in the dark of night, begging for help to save a life or work a miracle. Sometimes he could do something; at other times he found himself on the run like a criminal.

But what he valued most was the discovery of those already versed in the arts; although few were superior to him, it was a delight to be able to discuss the finer points of prana control and manipulation, and the techniques to restore harmony for different conditions.

When he met such people he taught them what he knew and learned from them as well. He found that his travels could help connect one practitioner with another, across cities and villages. And as he wandered, he picked up companions who wanted to be trained in the art. Mostly young people who became his family.

Now they were all scattered, doing the same work he had set out to do. Except for Shankara, who was dead.

After all, it was the bag of rice that did it.

The clerk in the royal court had shaken his old head as he watched Vishnumitra sign the document of challenge. He had reluctantly agreed to submit the bag of rice that Vishnumitra handed him with the scroll. "He will not see you." he had said, darkly. "He turns away all. . . nearly all who challenge him."

But the summons came two days later. The king would receive Vishnumitra—not in the Diwan-i-Khas but in his private room atop the tower. In the hour of twilight.

In the late afternoon Vishnumitra hired a boatman to take him to the opposite bank of the Yamuna. He chose a small pipal tree on the bank and sat down in the lotus position. Slowly he steadied his wildly beating heart. In the golden light the fort was a vision in red sandstone and marble.

Breathing slowly, Vishnumitra calmed his body, balancing out the prana flow in the two main channels on either side of his spine. He felt the slow shock of kundalini energy flowing up the sushumna channel toward the crown of his head, a wave of exhilaration, of limitless strength flooding him. He let his consciousness flow and become one with the prana, softening the flow in the seventy-two thousand distributories of the subtle body. In this deep, receptive state he opened his inner eye. With years of discipline he had come close to mastering what his father had taught him: the perception of the mahaprana, the cosmic channels of the life force. He saw the mahaprana as a faint skein of unearthly light, limning every living thing: tree or grazing cow or the waiting boatman. Raining down from the vastness of the sky were the greater channels, joining and connecting one life to another, from the smallest beetle now crawling along his arm to the King himself, awaiting him at the palace. When Vishnumitra had first glimpsed this cosmic marvel, two years after Upamanyu's own initiation, he had asked his father the same question Upamanyu had: From whence did the mahaprana flow? What was the source of it, beyond the sky? His father did not know.

Slowly Vishnumitra drew himself out of the meditation. He brushed the beetle from his arm with infinite tenderness and watched it scuttle away over the rock on which he was sitting. He waved to the silent boatman. It was time to go.

Between the fort walls are wonders: gracious gardens abloom with flowers, fountains that sing as water soars up into the air, a metal woman dancing in the center of a stone circle. Officials in small groups leave lighted rooms and confer in the scented gloom, as lamps flicker on, creating moving shadows. Vishnumitra is deep in the centered peacefulness that any glimpse of the mahaprana affords him—he has accepted what he must do, with all its moral ambiguity. Dharma is dharma, and if it is his fate to commit murder of one dearer to him than a brother, he will meet it like a scholar and a man.

To his surprise the king meets him at the base of the tower. His face is luminous in the light of the lamps, he makes an impatient gesture and his guards leave his side, watching from several paces away, out of earshot. Vishnumitra hesitates, but the king is holding out his arms.

The braids are held back, the face open, young as when Vishnumitra last saw him, filled with humor and intelligence, and at this moment—yes, this is so—the king's eyes are moist with tears.

"Dear brother! Vishnumitra!"

Vishnumitra cannot but accept the embrace, feeling tears pricking his own eyelids while simultaneously his mind warns him not to deviate from his purpose.

"Upamanyu!"

"Hush! Only to you, my friend!"

They stand apart, looking at each other. Vishnumitra feels his purpose like a burden whose weight he can hardly bear. Under other circumstances this would be a joyous reunion. He breathes deep

"You know why I am here."

"We will talk of that in a few moments. As a condemned man surely I have a right to ask for one last wish: a walk with my brother in the gardens? Come now, do not deny me!"

The old, affectionate, mocking tone. Vishnumitra's composures shaken; he finds himself being led through the magical garden, with one wonder after another being pointed out. His heart is a traitor—this is what he has yearned for since Upamanyu left: this reunion, where he is Sudama to Upamanyu's Krishna, treated like an honored guest. Now the king's guards fling open the great doors of a large, circular building surrounded by ashoka trees. Within are bright lights, the hiss of steam and the noise of metal upon metal. Mechanical men are working in clusters, monitoring pulleys and wheels, fitting together beautifully wrought pieces of metal with exquisite precision.

Vishnumitra, his mouth agape in wonder, understands nothing, recognizes nothing. What are they building? This is no manufactory of horseless carriages.

"This is my personal laboratory," the king says with pride. "For these many years I have become interested in the forces of nature apart from . . . from the life force itself. I have read the ancient Yunnanis Aristut, and Sukrat, and our own atomist schools. I have perused the barbarian vilayati scholar Niyuton. You have seen for yourself what wonders their discoveries have brought to us! Yet what I seek is to understand how these different imperatives, these forces, are related. Observe, my friend!"

He hands Vishnumitra a wooden tray upon which silver wires have been arranged in a rectangular array. Within this lattice are small canisters of metal. The king asks Vishnumitra to place his finger in such a way as to bridge a gap between the wires. Vishnumitra does so and feels the faintest shock, a jolt not unlike the sting one feels touching a metal gate before a thunderstorm. Not unlike the first experience of kundalini energy for a beginner. He jerks his finger away, raises startled eyes to Upamanyu.

"Ah. I see you are wondering if I have captured a storm in a few pieces of wire! Or is it a jolt of prana? So similar, yet the two forces are different—this one arises from inanimate matter, and the other from life itself! A mystery, is it not?"

They emerge from the chamber; the doors clang behind them, and a sweet silence descends. In the lamp-lit dark the king is leading him to the tower. Courtiers and guards watch curiously from afar.

The stairs spiral upwards and at the top there is a door, and a room furnished relatively simply—a small Persian rug over the marble foot, a low divan, a few chairs. A table with neat stacks of paperwork.

Shelves filled with books—forbidden books! The Charaka Sambita, the works of the great physician Sushruta, Patanjali's Yoga Sutra, works on the tantric mysteries, tomes in Tibetan, Pali, and Sanskrit, and in languages he does not know. Vishnumitra stares at the books and then at Upamanyu, who is smiling indulgently, as an older brother might.

"You've seen what I've wrought in this kingdom, dear brother. And yet through all these years I have been alone. A decade ago I sent my spies to find you, but all they found was the ashram, abandoned, and you flown. And now you stand before me, bent upon revenge. And yet when we embraced there were tears in your eyes in answer to my own. Dear friend! Let us forget about this challenge! I have needed you for a long time, and you are here at last."

Vishnumitra feels his purpose weakening. The promise he has made to his art, to his dead, feels now like a burden whose weight he can hardly bear. Bitterness and sorrow rise in his throat like bile. He wants to say: Why didn't you come back and keep your promise? Why did you abandon me? Why did you betray us all, betray the prana vidya itself?

Vishnumitra draws himself up, remembers his dharma. He brings deliberately to memory the imprisonments and murders that have befallen his dear companions, the practitioners of the art. He remains standing, ignoring Upamanyu's invitation to sit down.

"I need answers, Upamanyu, not pretty speeches. Tell me, why did you ban the prana vidya? Why have your spies pursued and killed the practitioners these many years?"

"Come, my friend, can I afford to have every fool in the empire learn and use what is the most arcane of arts? Why do you think I look so young, although I am older than you in years? Ah, I can see from your face that you know, or suspect. I am the best practitioner of the art in the empire, and it is that which has kept me young. It is that which allows me to defend myself from my enemies. Do you blame me for making sure that nobody else can be an adept in the art?"

"I am also an adept," Vishnumitra says softly. "And I might look twenty years younger, but I have aged, Upamanyu. What you are doing is against cosmic order. The prana vidya is not to be misused to confer immortality."

"Cosmic order will survive, my friend! Do you not recall the old stories about the sages who lived for thousands of years? Here I thought you'd congratulate me upon my great discovery! I have wandered far, from mountain to desert, read countless ancient tomes, studied under the most learned of teachers to teach myself what nobody else would, or could. The manipulation of the mahaprana itself."

Looking at him, Vishnumitra is struck by how young Upamanyu is, not only in appearance but in mind. It is as though the companion of his boyhood is back, with his lively intelligence, his curiosity, his unending propensity for play. The playful look is in those bright eyes.

"I wish to choose my weapon."

"What if I refuse your challenge?"

"You will not refuse, Upamanyu."

An unreadable expression in Upamanyu's eyes. The shoulders drop, and when he speaks it is the same light tone, but resigned. Regretful.

"Choose, then."

"I choose combat by prana vidya."

Vishnumitra has done this before, used manipulation of prana to kill. When someone is dying in great pain, it is a mercy to let the individual prana flow cease, to draw life out gently, as one draws the last of thread from a spindle. He has never used this skill to murder. But his way is clear.

Upamanyu is shaking his head as though Vishnumitra has just proposed something quite absurd, but he comes up to Vishnumitra, and their hands meet. Fingertip to fingertip, then clasping lightly, as though they might be about to draw each other into an embrace.

Vishnumitra can sense the prana flow in the other's body—thick and strong. He senses the other finding his own prana flow as a bird on the wing might sense the landscape below. The duel begins.

Vishnumitra attempts to still the flow, to draw life and breath and consciousness from Upamanyu, and in the beginning Upamanyu simply resists. He is smiling a little, but Vishnumitra hardly notices. He is intent upon the task, looking for weaknesses in the chakras, turbulence in the nadis. The thing is to take Upamanyu by surprise, to strike without warning, as he scans his friend's subtle body with that gentle inner gaze. Then he's hit.

It feels as though the world has suddenly grown dark. Controlling his breath, Vishnumitra finds his balance; the light returns. He fights back. They are going back and forth, sending great waves of weakness, invisible sword-cuts that might stop the heart or constrict a blood vessel. Every few minutes Vishnumitra is aware of that gaze, so light, contemplative even. He is aware that deep within him there is a great resistance to kill the man he loves. Surely there is another way! In his pain and love he cries out:

"In the name of the art, which you betrayed, in the names of those whom you had imprisoned and killed, for Shankara, who was innocent in her fierceness and courage, I beg you, Upamanyu, to repent by choosing death! Do not make me kill you!"

Upamanyu's face is intent, sweat has broken out over his brow.

"*Nobody* can kill me . . ."

And Vishnumitra sees with his inner eye what Upamanyu has done, how he can kill an adept in the art, how he must have killed Shankara. The columns of mahaprana that rain down from the sky are joining and coalescing, coming down at him, filling every part of his being with the life force, a fullness that his body cannot take. For a moment Upamanyu is Indra himself, wielding the thunderbolt. Vishnumitra knows for a split second the beauty of the cosmic prana, the vastness of the mystery that they have barely begun to comprehend, and he knows that he has done wrong, just as Upamanyu has, to use the prana vidya for murder. As he accepts his death, welcomes it as a man guided by dharma must, he senses the capillaries on his skin bursting. A pain in his chest, his lungs, and he is losing consciousness, falling to the floor. Then blessed darkness and he knows nothing at all.

When Vishnumitra came to, the first thing he noticed was the smell.

It was a rotten odor, sickly sweet, like spoiled fruit. He hurt all over, Gradually, through the pain, he realized he was alive. He was lying on a great pile of refuse, above which he could see the silhouette of the fort wall, a dark wave against the starlit sky. He tried to sit up and groaned as the pain hit him anew. Lying back in the filth, he tasted his defeat, and the struggles that still lay ahead, and the bitterness of knowing that he, greatest of the practitioners of the art (or so he'd thought), defender of the prana vidya, had ultimately betrayed it and failed all the ones he loved. He shuddered in the cold air

Why had Upamanyu left him alive?

He should be dead!

He must have lain there for many hours before he noticed the horse. There was a faint radiance in the eastern sky, although the darkness was still profound. Against that sky stood the king's stallion, black, strong, unmistakable. There was no rider.

Vishnumitra dragged his broken body off the pile of trash and crawled to where the stallion stood. The horse bent its great head, snorting softly, blowing twin puffs of breath from the enormous nostrils. Vishnumitra saw the pale shape of a rolled scroll hanging from the saddle and reached for it. He lay gasping on the hard ground, waiting for the light. The horse waited too.

Dear brother, [Upamanyu wrote]

I regret the pain I have caused you, but perhaps it is better this way.

As I said I have awaited your coming these many years. Kingship has been very interesting but I grow weary of it. You recall that your father's explanation of the mahaprana when I was just a boy launched me on a journey of discovery. My kingdom was but a stop on the way to greater adventures, one that enabled me to consolidate my knowledge and distracted me pleasantly with interesting dilemmas. I have as yet no answer to the question I once posed your father: From whence does the cosmic prana arise? What is the origin of the life force beyond this earth? Some invoke gods but I seek no such convenient answers. My dabbling with the knowledge of the mechanical forces convinces me that one will lead me to the other. The Chinese have been experimenting with propulsion power for eons, and in my own small laboratory I have found enough evidence that a carefully designed craft might bear the weight of a man to the endless skies. There I will fly as the Vidyadharas are said to do, and seek the adventures that have constantly beckoned my soul.

Meanwhile, I leave you my horse (with great regret as he, strengthened by my knowledge of prana vidya, has been my dear companion these many years). And I leave you my kingdom. I have talked all night with my chief queen, the peerless Jabanara, who has known for some time that I have a brother in spirit. She is to be trusted, as is Noori, her slave and my best spy, who is an expert archer and fighter. My minister, Sukbwant Singh, will guide you as well. Your name, my friend, is Ambar Khan, and you are born of a Muslim father and a Hindu mother (this small reversal of the truth I deemed necessary in order to explain away any Hindu traits that you, the next Mughal king, might display). Do not fear that such a thing would betray you, for I have attempted to re-create as much as possible the vibrant hybrid culture that I so enjoyed in your father's ashram. I have prepared the ground, you see, for the past few years, in the hope that you might come, although what it took to draw you out was the girl Shankara's death. It might comfort you to know that she fought bravely to the end, and that spared her pain at the passing. So I bid you, dear brother, to save and keep what I have built—the most prosperous kingdom in the hemisphere, if not the world. This morning at dawn one of my proxies will appear at the jharokha as usual, for the people of the city must see their king daily. I will be well on my way by then, on the north road out of Dilli, once more a traveler on a quest, unhampered by the burdens of the settled life. My heart will be as light as my pack, which contains little besides a device or two of my invention, a few books—and a handful of rice from the one place that felt like home to me.

Now you must take my horse to the inn an hour's journey from the gate, and rest and recover a while. Just before sunset I bid you ride into the city from the Eastern gate on my horse. The smallest child in the city knows that the new king will, like Akbar Khan, take the kingdom without a single weapon, riding in on this very horse, the noble Vikram. I have signed documents stating that none of my offspring will inherit the throne, which is perhaps the main reason they have not killed each other. Apparently the latter is a tradition among the Mughals.

If you do not wish to be king, simply let my horse return to the city. Sukhwant Singh will know what to do. But I am confident that you, who have always been led by your dharma, will not betray the people who await you.

Through all my life I have resisted giving my heart to another. It would only be a distraction from my quest, which is to comprehend the mysteries that surround me, and thus to comprehend myself. I have never even told anyone the name I was born with—I have worn names as another man might wear clothes. Yet you, Vishnumitra, took my heart from me without my knowledge or permission. I knew this as I stood over your body. My anger—unused to defiance all these years, and honed by the sutras of the ancient, rageful sage Durvasa, who lived five thousand years—flared up as we dueled. In that moment I would have given up my careful plans to install you in my place (a wise ruler always has other options prepared)—I would have killed you, my friend, but when I held the hand that had brought me the rice from his mother's kitchen, I could not do it. So have I learned that my knowledge of myself is far from complete, and this humbles me.

I do not know if you will forgive me. I will not insult you or those dear to you I killed by asking it of you. But consider this: you have a vast network of practitioners of the prana vidya spread all over the country. This great instrument I have forged as much as you have, by pruning the incompetent or the rash. Use it as you will, for in the days ahead there will be much turmoil. Sher Shah in the North-West shows signs of impatience, there are rumors the Portuguese king is mad, and as the British lose their hold over the South, their envious gaze turns northwards.

So, dear brother, farewell! I go north to China now, to the next adventure. Only the sky—Ambar!—is my limit! May you and yours find peace.

Your brother in spirit,

Upamanyu

Vishnumitra read this missive three times. The horse whinnied softly, and at last he put the scroll away in his shirt and staggered shakily to his feet. He leaned against the horse's side and wept for all he had lost, and for all the losses still to come. He thought of the curve of the great river of his home, and the steps of the ghat leading down to the grey water, and the kind-eyed elephants sporting by the shore. He saw in memory the bright saris of his mother and sisters, and the golden walls of the ashram. Then, with great difficulty, he hoisted himself upon the horse, and lay for a moment against his neck, panting. He wiped his tears with his tattered sleeve and turned the horse away from the city toward the inn, to await the sunset of all he had known. Above him the last stars went out in the vast bowl of the sky.

Discussion Questions and Writing Activities

1. Structurally, "A Handful of Rice" begins with the present of the story, with the protagonist planning an assassination, the revelation that he knows the monarch, and then from there it braids the past and the present. Why begin this way, rather than go chronologically through the story? How is the past infused with more tension and stakes because we know from the beginning what he must do?

2. What is the difference between using memory in a story, and using flashback? Why does the difference matter?

3. What is the effect of combining steampunk, a genre often associated with Victoriana, with a postcolonial anti-colonialist story? Why do you think Singh made this choice?

4. Where a writer begins and ends a short story matters a great deal. How does Singh's choice of beginning and end help her write an epic story in a short space? How might it have been different if this story were being told in another length, say a novella or a novel?

5. This is an epic made personal. How does the personal nature of the conflict in this story make a national and internationally significant event feel more emotionally impactful?

6. Imagine an epic fantasy story, either one that you've thought of before or tried to write and write it as a short story by beginning just before the climax. Distill it down to one very personal conflict. What do you notice about this process? What can it teach you about boiling a story down to the essentials?

7. This is alternate-history epic steampunk fantasy. Try to write your own alternate-history epic steampunk fantasy story. Afterwards, think about what opportunities and constraints result from combining so many genres.

8. Imagine Singh's story from a different point of view. How does point of view change what story is told?

Jessie Ulmer "Red" from *Corvid Queen*

Biography (from the Sword & Kettle Press website)

Jessie Ulmer is a queer writer and editor, an identical twin, and a swan by birth. She holds a degree from Western Washington University. She uses aspects of speculative fiction to explore themes of ability, physical and mental illness, gender, sexuality, and the intersections of identity within her work. She loves ghosts, impossible forests, the carnivorous sea, and believes in magic. She delights in editing for Sword & Kettle Press and her work has been featured in *Gordon Square Review*, *Gingerbread House*, *Syntax & Salt*, *Corvid Queen*, *3Elements Review*, *Yellow Chair Review*, *Sweet Tree Review*, *Dose of Dread*, *Rune Bear*, *Pins & Needles: A Journal of Contemporary Fairy Tales*, *Translunar Travelers Lounge*, and Washington's *Best Emerging Poets* Anthology. In 2020 her work was nominated for a Best of the Net Award.

Literary Introduction

"Red" participates in a long literary tradition of feminist fairy tale retellings, from the recent work of Amber Sparks to Angela Carter, all the way back to the root of fairy tales, which is oral tradition, stories usually told by women to other women. As flash fiction, its emphasis is not only on the story, but on the language itself. Flash fiction and prose poetry are in many respects cousins, if not close to the same thing. In this piece Ulmer takes the story of Little Red Riding Hood and disrupts it, emphasizing its bloody beating heart, as well as its liberatory potential. This piece alludes to Angela Carter's work, "The Company of Wolves" (which was made into a deeply weird movie).

Red

Whether it was her name or her color it's hard to say. Red. Red hair, red clothes, red shoes, they clash horribly. Red. Scarlet. Ruby. Rose. Crimson. Her mother's baby book had one section only. She was doomed from the start. Red. She'd seen it once, two flimsy pages, ripped out and bound together. By who? Who knows? Does it matter? Her poor mother, never knowing. Her poor grandmother, knowing too much. Her woodsman father, never coming home.

Red. Red shoes. Red lips. Red teeth. Too far.

Red. There's nothing little about her. Nothing diminutive. Red. Leader of children. Befriender of wolves. It's true. You never ran. Just asked for a name and where he was going. Red. You grew with the forest. You knew what to fear. Red. In a word where god can curse your feet, your family, your dear, sweet brother, wolves are so small in comparison. Red. There was no path you could follow. Red. Your mother knew. She cursed you twice. Don't stray, she said. Too late.

Red. Grandmother. Namesake. Leader of wolves. Baker of bread. She called for you. Spoke of communion. Consume body. Consume blood. Details are important. There are reasons widows move to wolf-infested woods, build a house, call it home. Your baby teeth boil on the hearth. You've been trouble from the start. Silent baby. You never cried. What dark eyes you had, my dear. Your mother, she feared you. Your father, he left you. Your grandmother, she taught you to run. Red. There is a wolf at the door. Won't you let your cousin in?

Discussion Questions and Writing Activities

1. How does the language and imagery in this piece influence the tone of the story? Explain your answer.

2. This story depends upon the reader having some knowledge of the traditional story of Little Red Riding Hood. How does Ulmer disrupt categories from the original, including Red herself, the grandmother, and wolves?

3. Who is the speaker of this story? How do you know?

4. Look up the Angela Carter story, "The Company of Wolves." Read it. Then come back to Ulmer's story. How is "Red" in dialogue with Carter's story? What do these two pieces have to say to each other? What can this tell you about the intertextual and/or metafictional quality of fairy tale retellings?

5. Try to write a Little Red Riding Hood retelling yourself that in some way comments on or responds to Ulmer's story.

6. Write a flash fairy tale retelling of any story but mimic the fragments and image-driven language choices of Ulmer. Then, try rewriting it in a different prose style. What do you notice about how your own story changes based upon form and prose style?

7. Write a poem about a fairy tale character. Then break it out of lines and into a paragraph. Or try the reverse. Write a piece of micro flash fiction, one hundred words or less, and then break it into lines. What happens as you transform a flash piece from poetry to prose, or vice versa?

Genevieve Valentine "From the Catalogue of the Pavilion of the Uncanny and Marvelous, Scheduled for Premiere at the Great Exhibition (Before the Fire)" from *Queen Victoria's Book of Spells*

Biography *(taken from her website, with additions from various interviews)*

Genevieve Valentine is an American science fiction and fantasy author. She is the author of *Mechanique: A Tale of the Circus Tresaulti* (2012 Crawford Award), *The Girls at the Kingfisher Club*, *Persona*, and *Icon*. She has written Catwoman for DC Comics, and Xena: Warrior Princess for Dynamite. Her short stories have appeared in over a dozen Best of the Year anthologies, including *Best American Science Fiction and Fantasy*. Her cultural criticism has appeared at *NPR.org*, *The AV Club*, *LA Review of Books*, *Vice*, *Vox*, and the *New York Times*, among others. She blogs about the entertainment industry, fashion, and writes nonfiction about literary and cultural history, especially British literature, and the great 19th-century gothic novels (*Frankenstein*, *Dracula*, etc.).

Literary Introduction

Valentine's work has changed over time. Her earliest work, including her award-winning debut novel *Mechanique*, and many of her short stories, were primarily historical fantasy, usually gas-lamp, frequently with a steampunk twist. *The Girls at the Kingfisher Club* is set during the 1920s and fuses the twelve-dancing-princess fairy tale with a jazz club, and a side of the gothic. Her later novels, particularly *Persona* and *Icon*, are science fiction, but share with her earlier work a preoccupation for fusing multiple types of stories together, playing with form, and a subversive gothic heart. From feminism to environmental justice, Valentine's work forces readers to ask uncomfortable questions, while pulling them in with gorgeous language and compelling narrative. Her literary ancestors are the likes of Mary Shelley's *Frankenstein*, Sheridan Le Fanu's *Carmilla*, and many others. Like the Victorians, Valentine is concerned with social issues, and will combine forms and genres as much as she likes. They did it because genres hadn't solidified yet. Valentine does it because she can and does it well. Contemporary books in a similar vein include *Smoke* by Dan Vyleta, *Little Big* by John Crowley, and *Vampires in the Lemon Grove* by Karen Russell. More broadly, her aesthetic vibes with that of Theodora Goss, Kelly Link, Elizabeth Hand, Cherie Priest, and Helen Oyeyemi.

From the Catalogue of the Pavilion of the Uncanny and Marvelous, Scheduled for Premiere at the Great Exhibition (Before the Fire)

It may be called a bazaar or a fair, but it is such a bazaar or fair as Eastern genii might have created. It seems as if only magic could have gathered this mass of wealth from all the ends of the earth—as if none but supernatural hands could have arranged it thus, with such a blaze and contrast of colours and marvellous power of effect.

—from Charlotte Brontë's letters, 1851

London's Great Exhibition more than lived up to its name, providing nearly 100,000 exhibits' worth of spectacle, at a price the public could afford, from an Empire that had by then reached heretofore unimaginable levels of expansion and technological advancement.

It also stands as a confluence of two of the era's strangest bedfellows: its passion for intellectualism, and its unquenchable thirst for spectacle. It was an era that idolized the gentleman scientist even as it queued for the grotesque and the fraudulent.

Perhaps the most obvious marriage of these two attitudes was in the visibility of non-Western cultures (most under the banner of the voracious Empire) whose displays of "exotic" offerings provided the trappings of science with the thrill of the fair.

By then, the Crown had more spoils than could be displayed at once, and many of the items offered to the Exhibition were never displayed. Many of these pieces exist today in the Victoria and Albert Museum (a watered-down replica of the colony-maker's might).

Among the Exhibition's many achievements (the most lasting of which were the ephemeral successes of public perception), it was a triumph of finance. The only true material losses to the Crown during the Exhibition were China's decision not to participate (solved by buying out an importer's inventory and leaving the public unaware of the slight), and the fire that consumed the Pavilion of the Uncanny and Marvellous.

Even with these losses, however, the Exhibition turned enough profit to finance construction of the Victoria and Albert Museum itself.

—Sarah Powers, "Opiate of the Masses: The Great Exhibition and Its Legacy in England," Journal of Victorian Studies, 1984

BY AUTHORITY OF THE ROYAL COMMISSION

OFFICIAL CATALOGUE

Of

THE PAVILION OF THE UNCANNY AND MARVELLOUS

Presented as a Special Attraction at the

GREAT EXHIBITION

Of the works of

INDUSTRY OF ALL NATIONS

1851

"[   ] *therefore as a stranger give it welcome.*

[   ] *are more things in heaven and earth, Horatio,*

[   ]*an are dreamt of in your philosophy."*

[   ] *ONDON:*

[   ] *Brothers, Printers*

—handwritten cover craft of the catalogue, Victoria and Albert Museum Archives (fire damage in brackets)

14 January 1851

Have hired two young ladies at the suggestion of the Commission—Mary Hammond, Rose Smith—to assist in compilation of the Catalg-s [*sic*]. Miss Smith shows promise—meticulous in her work—but Miss Hammond—can only recommend penmanship and punctuality. Still—in this city one must take such as can be found.

—from the diaries of Alfred York, Undersecretary to the Commission

The Biddenden Maids [Germany]—Pair of "Siam-ese" conjoined twins fastened from the shoulder through the torso by supernatural means. Several surgeries have been attempted, but none has yet severed them. Taken from a pagan mother and christened Eve and Mary, the Maids remain wards of the German state and appear in this exhibition with the greatest caution, as their heritage and the spell that binds them suggest the influence of witchcraft. As such, the Biddenden Maids should not be viewed by any ladies in a delicate state, or the very young.

The Scythian [Greece]—Authentic mermaid specimen, a scientific discovery of a most unusual kind. After many hoaxes and fabrications, the true mermaid is presented after due scrutiny of scientific minds. With the head and torso of an ill-favored woman and a lower half of slimy scales, this mermaid is thought to be a direct descendant of the line feared by the ancient Greeks. It is of vicious nature, and ruthless in its attempts to escape captivity; this hunting trophy is a gift from Greece to Her Majesty's exhibition. Though displayed in silhouette and intact to the general public, as a medical lesson the mermaid is bisected laterally to allow examination of its singular anatomy. Academic viewings may be arranged at the Exhibition Committee's offices.

Walter Goodall, a London artist, was hired by the commission to paint watercolours of Exhibition highlights. Designed to be "snapshots" of the event, they were actually painted before the opening, as some of the exhibits he depicts were unfinished—the howdah in the India Pavilion, for example was painted *sans* the taxidermy elephant on which it would be displayed.

Many of these watercolours were made available as lithographs in *Recollections of the Great Exhibition*; though not all survived, the extant watercolours give a fascinating glimpse into the Exhibition itself.

—introductory card from "Impressions of the Great Exhibition," Victoria and Albert Museum

March 27, 1851

My Dear Ed,

Since the Commission asked me to paint these watercolours, I have chanced to see some of the workings of such an endeavour, and how each thing is decided. Never again shall I make complaint about the processes of the Royal Academy—very unfortunate, as that was my favourite pastime.

In the offices there are a vast number of very busy persons cataloguing the contents for this Pavilion and that one, making sure each piece of rope is accounted for. You would not believe the quantities of rope that will be on display in Hyde Park this summer. Thankfully I am tasked with painting their more majestic offerings. The howdah made for Her Majesty is truly a wonder.

The Pavilion of the Uncanny and Marvellous, which I understand has half a dozen or so live elements that must be present, is to be painted last. There is a Miss Hammond assigned to assist me—I feel quite the professor—though she seems solemn as a nun whenever the Pavilion is mentioned. Suspect it must be grim stuff. Let us pray it is not a display of insects—my least favorite of God's creatures.

Give my love to Mother.

Your Very Affectionate Brother,

Walter

Some of the most telling developments of the Exhibition were those that changed *in situ* to reflect the difference between the initial grand design and the eventual compromise that formed the Exhibition itself. The most famous of these is the arched atrium in the centre of the Exhibition hall that is now considered to be an architectural focal point, but was in fact added as an afterthought to preserve the large trees around which the Exhibition itself was built. There were several such obstacles that had to be overcome for the Exhibition to be successfully staged.

The Pavilion of the Uncanny and Marvellous, which was to stand alongside the scientific displays in the British Wing, and can still be seen in Paxton's initial sketches, was not present when the doors were opened to the final exhibition, and would have provided an interesting barometer to the limits of public interest.

The Exhibition as a whole had several draws (such as the Austrian perfume fountain which guests could sample *gratis*) that gave attendees a sense of being treated to something unique. Conversely, this Pavilion would have charged an extra shilling admittance.

The Committee's archives record this price differential as an attempt to underwrite "the many expenditures and dangers undertaken to provide the Crown with the exhibits to be displayed," though one wonders if, surrounded by so many other marvels, there would have been much appeal to part with another shilling.

Whatever the attractions might have been, the plan was moot; the fire (mere weeks before the Exhibition was scheduled to open) erased the planned displays, and no attempt was made by the Exhibition's organisers to provide an official inventory of what had been lost.

Perhaps this is due to the fact that, prior to the Exhibition's opening, it came under widespread scrutiny, and was primed in public opinion to be a disastrous expenditure; in this atmosphere, an entire Pavilion going up in smoke would have been an opportunity no newspaperman could have resisted. (It is likely that those who saw it were paid for their silence, perhaps with a reminder how close the Exhibition was to the Queen's heart, and the duty of a good subject to keep his counsel.)

—from "Opiate of the Masses"

2 April 1851

Work on the Catalg-s [*sic*] shall take remainder of the spring. HRH the Prince has requested early inventory of the British wing—to examine number and kind of machinery on display. Suspect French display at fault. Miss Smith seems equal to the task—excellent notes from all quarters.

Miss Hammond taking dictation from the Secretary for the Uncanny and Marvellous as exhibits arrive and are classified—she seems soured of it all but her penmanship second to none. Will postpone presentation to HRH until satisfied—this is the Crown.

—from the diaries of Alfred York

Osiris [Egypt]—From the heart of this desert country comes a beautiful deaf-mute, given the name Osiris by his people, whose seizures were regarded by those of his own tribe to be communion with the ancient gods. English doctors have determined his seizures are of a medical nature, though Osiris provides an excellent opportunity to study the connection between nature and the supernatural that may have been eliminated forever from more advanced minds, and experimentation continues to determine if there is, indeed, some spiritual force at work. Osiris has been put under the care of a physician familiar with the very latest in electric current treatment, and his seizures are examined by spectrograph as they occur throughout his hours of display, each day of the week from eleven o'clock in the morning until four o'clock in the afternoon.

On the Bonny Sweet Hills of Kilkenny [Ireland]—A tableau of the Fey, taxidermied in the finest style. Exclusive to the Exhibition, the fairy folk have never before been seen outside the Isle that is their native land. Eight examples of this species have been carefully preserved as they were found down to the smallest detail, dressed in Classical costume, and set in a garden scene that recreates some of Ireland's most beautiful flora. This rare prey has been procured at great risk for the wonder and enjoyment of Her Majesty's subjects.

You will behold there A MONUMENT OF NATIONAL GREATNESS. Britain, viewed in her insular situation and her geographical dimensions, is amongst the least of all the nations of the earth. Her own immediate territories of England, Scotland, and Ireland, are, comparatively speaking, of very limited extent.

What are we in relation to France, Austria, Russia, or America? A mere speck in the bosom of the ocean deep; yet the sea is our strong rampart, our chosen element, and our undisputed empire; and great indeed is Britain, by the confession of every tongue.

—from "Sermons on the Great Exhibition," the Reverend

George Clayton, York St. Chapel, Walworth, 1851

10 April 1851

My Dear Ed,

The Committee would not be pleased to know I am writing this. I hope you shall handle this letter accordingly once you have read it.

I have seen some of the Pavilion of the Uncanny and Marvellous. It is troubling in a way I dare not say—if India has refrained from displaying living things at their exhibit, surely England might, but in even worse. There is grotesquery here that does no credit to the Crown.

When I told Miss Hammond, she seemed pleased in the way a gravekeeper is pleased, and said, "Would that others felt the same as you about what's happening here, sir," and I find myself agreeing. There really is no wonder she looks so sepulchral.

She has an odd face—I did not think her very pretty when I met her first, but now I am thinking I should like to sketch her. You might, too, if you liked women as much as you like birds.

Give my love to Mother.

Your Very Affectionate Brother,

Walter

The Martyr-Bird (Gallicolumba sanctus) [Italy]—This rare specimen, a species properly identified only in this year of Her Majesty's reign, was previously dismissed as Papist sentimentality, before it was examined this year by faculty at Oxford and determined to be an authentic phenomenon. The Martyr-Bird is immortal; no attempt to end its life has been successful, nor any mark remains save a single red wound on its chest, which beg when it is injured. Demonstration killings and resurrections are enacted on Saturdays at one o'clock in the afternoon.

Salome [Ottoman Empire]—A harem prisoner of the savage Sultan until her rescue by British troops, Salome is a descendant of the succubae of legend, and was scheduled to be put to death for her ruthless seduction of men. Her beauty is beyond imagining, but those who look upon her risk being the victims of a most powerful and relentless lust; while she was good only for the gallows according to Ottoman law, the Sultan himself still murdered six Englishmen during her liberation, helpless under her spell. Though robbed of much of her power outside the lands of her people, Salome is still presented veiled and shackled, and behind a guarded partition past which ladies and children shall expressly not be admitted, to preserve their moral character.

The Dressing Table [India]—This display is the original dressing table of Lady Penelope Howard, who, during her husband's time as an envoy of the Crown in India, became an expert in native remedies and poisons. Her demise is assumed to have been a casualty of her hidden and occult passions. Transported here and recreated *in situ*, the dressing table contains dozens of unusual vials, talismans, and other artefacts whose purposes are, in some cases, still unknown. Visitors should be most careful not to touch any part of this display.

18 April 1851

Mr York,

Yesterday, as I followed Mr Pentney through the final preparations for the Pavilion of the Uncanny and Marvellous displays, I noticed Eve and Mary—perhaps known to you as the Biddenden Maids—taking a glass vial from Lady Howard's dressing table as they were guided to their places beside the Martyr-Bird for the sketches that Mr Goodall is making.

When they saw me watching them, they gave me such looks as I shall never forget, but I only nodded as I would to a fellow on the street. I said nothing of it to Mr Pentney. For this I am not sorry.

I know from cataloguing its arrival that the vial they took smells of camphor: I suspected then what they intended. When I returned to the offices, I gathered the draft of the Pavilion's catalogue and all its other papers, and waited until darkness to leave the building with them in hand. I stole your satchel in which to carry them. I ask forgiveness.

When I arrived back at the Pavilion, as if by assignation, the sisters were there also. The Martyr-Bird sat in one of the old trees—even in the dark I could never mistake that bird for any other—and I believe I saw behind the partition that the woman who must have been Salome stood beside the man who has been named Osiris, and knew that whatever means the sisters had used to escape from their captivity, they had done the same to free their fellows.

Without looking at me, the sisters passed their hands over the camphor and murmured strange words. A violet flame sprung up, and they flung the vial inside, where it caught on all objects that had the supernatural in them, and left the rest untouched.

You are not a man of imagination, but if I could explain to you the terror of a scentless fire, the sight of all those things vanishing into smoke, disappearing into the night!

But I will go on. Osiris and Salome soon vanished into the park. The flames inside the Pavilion rose quickly, and I threw the papers into the fire, where they were at once consumed, and within moments it was as though the Pavilion itself had never existed. For this I am not sorry.

The sisters and I said nothing to one another, as I speak no German and they no English, but we watched the flames together until they seemed satisfied and departed, I know not where. The Martyr-Bird flew after them, and then the Park was as quiet as if nothing had occurred.

I came here to write this letter. I have before made my feelings about this Pavilion clear, so you will not be surprised I am sure that I would be so eager to rid England of this low display, but I do not want the sisters to be accused of taking anything that was not theirs. I alone burnt the Catalogue, this is my sworn confession.

I have no plans to take flight. I remain at my lodgings. You may send the police, if you choose. I know the Crown might find me guilty of a crime, though you and I shall know differently.

Please take this as my notice to resign from my post, and I wish you great success in the Exhibit.

With best wishes, and most sincerely,

Mary Hammond

18 April 1851

My Dear Ed,

Last night I got an unusual visit from Miss Hammond, who had some news about recent developments to the Pavilion. Despite her certainty that nothing shall be said about it in the papers, I still think it best I say nothing here. One never knows, these days.

Have disposed of some of my sketches for the Exhibition watercolours. Suggest you do the same with some of our correspondence—you know which.

When will you be in London next? You should meet Miss Hammond—a singular young lady.

Yours, etc.,

Walter

19 April 1851

An incident with fire has consumed the Pavilion of the Uncanny and Marvellous. No loss to the Exhibit or the Crown. Some setbacks in the Catalogue—work continues. Dismissed Miss Hammond.

—from the diaries of Alfred York

The effect the Great Exhibition had on Britain cannot be precisely quantified, but neither can it be overstated. Its attractions spurred an industrial and cultural rivalry with other nations that was unheard of until that time (and which, many of those involved admitted later, had been largely the point of the Exhibition all along).

However, the estimated six million visitors were in themselves a force to be reckoned with; they brought tourism (both from within the United Kingdom and without) to an all-time high, which in turn had far-reaching consequences for London's economy.

Savvy businesspeople took advantage of the crowds for tertiary displays of their own, hoping to siphon some of the wealth that was pouring into the Crystal Palace. While the Pavilion of the Uncanny and Marvellous was a casualty of circumstance in this respect, entrepreneurs outside the Commission's purview were still scrambling to make a good showing. A savvy few did.

In particular, John Gould's remarkable stuffed-hummingbird exhibit at the Zoological Gardens in Regent's Park attracted more than 75,000 visitors. The display included several rare breeds and brought the colourful birds squarely into the public's scope of interest; they would continue to have a strong presence in fashion and design for the next century.

—from "Opiate of the Masses"

Alexander, on the shore of the Indian Ocean, sighed that he had no more worlds to conquer, the triumvirate of the Crystal Palace appear to be very differently situated. Having overrun the globe, and gathered in spoils within a glass case, they do not fold their arms and sit down contented. They wish to be useful in turning to the best account the opportunities thus created.

—*Guardian* **newspaper, May 7, 1851**

That majestic palace of iron and glass! A while ago, its pillars were coarse rude particles, clotted together in some deep recess of the earth, and its transparent plates were sandy masses, without beauty or coherence. How a little fire and a little art have changed them! … Oh, 'tis indeed wonderful, how God gives man skill to make an inheritance of all things!

—from "The World's Great Assembly," *English Monthly Tract Society*, **London, J. F. Shaw, 1851**

About "From the Catalogue of the Pavilion of the Uncanny and Marvelous, Scheduled for Premiere at the Great Exhibition (Before the Fire)"

Though the Pavilion of the Uncanny and Marvellous is fictional, it's probably not through any lack of trying on the part of the Victorians.

The comparatively rapid development of the natural sciences and a boom in occult pastimes among the upper and middle classes led to the popularity of séances, ghost photography, and quasi-scientific sideshows, of which the Pavilion of the Uncanny and Marvellous would have been welcome. And for a setting, nothing was more natural than the Great Exhibition, which arose in tandem with the swelling of patriotic sentiment accompanying the reign of Queen Victoria, which was, at its best, a myopic view of globalization that put British sentiments before all, and at its worst, xenophobia.

The Great Exhibition (a notable precursor to both the modern museum and the modern shopping mall) was designed as a celebration of industry, but it was also a ready platform for displays of the "exotic," and a handy pat on the back for anyone who wanted to feel that the British Isles was at the apex of the cultural ladder. The public reaction to the Exhibition was enthusiastic (the extensive catalogue of its wonders was one of the bestselling books of 1851); for some, it was a nearly religious event that demonstrated how Providence had smiled on England.

The Pavilion of the Uncanny and Marvellous is an imaginary missing chapter from this fraught and fascinating event. Some of the narrative excerpts in this story are fictional; others are real historical documents from the most pivotal cultural event of Victoria's reign.

Discussion Questions and Writing Activities

1. This gaslamp fantasy is also an alternate-history fantasy, since it adds a new pavilion to the Great Exhibition, and then takes the form of entries from and about the catalog for that pavilion, as well as letters and other documents. How do the form, genre, and content work together?

2. Run an internet search on the Great Exhibition. Read about why it occurred, what it meant at the time, and why it is generally considered significant by literary scholars and historians. Then, reread the short story. How is your understanding expanded by knowing the history the story references? What changes if you read it informed after reading it uninformed?

3. This story critiques the colonialism and eurocentrism embedded in the Great Exhibition. Dissect the story with this critique in mind. Do you see any other arguments implicit in the text? What connections can you make between the social problems of the Victorian era, and contemporary culture?

4. Why write the story in this form, rather than in a more traditional narrative structure? Does it create a sense of discomfort or alienation? Or force you to read slower? Or?

5. Write a gaslamp fantasy of your own. If you like, do one set during the Great Exhibition as well, or pick some other setting or situation.

6. Write a fantasy story in the form of a catalog. How do you give meaning and narrative to a nonnarrative form?

7. Imagine another "marvelous" person/being from the titular pavilion in Valentine's story. Then write a story from the point of view of that being.

NOTES AND REFERENCES

Chapter 1

1. "Victorian England: Birthplace of Fantasy." *BIBLIOTHÈQUE NATIONALE DE FRANCE.* https://fantasy.bnf.fr/en/understand/victorian-england-birthplace-fantasy/

2. "Mexico." *Encyclopedia of Science Fiction.* https://sf-encyclopedia.com/entry/mexico

3. Alter, Alexander. "How Chinese Sci-Fi Conquered America." *New York Times Magazine.* December 3, 2019. https://www.nytimes.com/2019/12/03/magazine/ken-liu-three-body-problem-chinese-science-fiction.html

4. "A Brief History of Russian Science Fiction." *Clarkesworld.* https://clarkesworldmagazine.com/shvartsman_05_21/

5. "Fantasy in France: The Road Goes Ever On." *BIBLIOTHÈQUE NATIONALE DE FRANCE.* https://fantasy.bnf.fr/en/understand/fantasy-france-road-goes-ever/

6. Altick, Richard. *The English Common Reader: A Social History of the Mass Reading Public.* Ohio State University Press, 1998.

7. Anderson, Hepzibah. "The Shocking Tale of the Penny Dreadful." *BBC.* The shocking tale of the penny dreadful – BBC Culture

8. Altick, Richard. *Victorian People and Ideas.* Ohio State University Press, 1973.

9. Zipes, Jack. *The Irresistible Fairy Tale: The Cultural and Social History of a Genre.* Princeton University Press, 2012.

10. Des Cars, Laurence. *The Pre-Raphaelites: Romance and Realism.* Abrams, 2000.

11. Trumpener, Kate. *Bardic Nationalism: The Romantic Novel and the British Empire.* Princeton University Press, 1997.

12. Smith, Karen Patricia. *The Fabulous Realm: A Literary Historical Approach to British Fantasy 1780–1890.* Scarecrow Press, 1993.

13. Sessarego, Carrie. "Supernatural Brontes." *Clarkesworld.* https://clarkesworldmagazine.com/sessarego_05_19/

14. "Gothic Novel." *Encyclopedia Britannica.* Gothic novel Definition, Elements, Authors, Examples, Meaning, & Facts | Britannica

15. Feldman, Burton, and Robert D. Richardson. *The Rise of Modern Mythology, 1680–1860.* Indiana University Press, 2000.

16. Grenby, M. O. "Fantasy and Fairytale in Children's Literature." *British Library.* https://www.bl.uk/romantics-and-victorians/articles/fantasy-and-fairytale-in-childrens-literature

17. James, Henry. "The Art of Fiction." *Longman's Magazine* 4. 1884.

18. Ashley, Mike. "The Golden Age of Pulp Fiction." *The Pulp Magazines Project.* https://www.pulpmags.org/contexts/essays/golden-age-of-pulps.html

19. Larbalestier, Justine. *The Battle of the Sexes in Science Fiction.* Wesleyan University Press, 2002.

20. Roberts, Robin. *A New Species: Gender and Science in Science Fiction.* University of Illinois Press, 1993.

21. VanderMeer, Jeff, and Ann VanderMeer. *The Big Book of Classic Fantasy.* Vintage, 2019.

22. Bowers, Maggie Ann. *Magic(al) Realism: The New Critical Idiom.* Routledge, 2004.

23. Lusty, Natalya. "Explainer: Surrealism." *The Conversation.* Explainer: Surrealism (theconversation.com)

24. Hyles, Vernon. "Lord Dunsany: The Geography of the Gods." *More Real than Reality: The Fantastic in Irish Literature and the Arts.* Eds. Morse, Donald E., and Csilla Bertha. Greenwood Press, 1991.

25. Fimi, Dimitra. *Tolkien, Race, and Culture History: From Faeries to Hobbits.* Macmillan, 2008.

26. Duriez, Colin. *The C. S. Lewis Encyclopedia: The Complete Guide to His Life, Thought and Writings.* Crossway Books, 2000.

27. "Mervyn Peake." *Wikipedia.* https://en.wikipedia.org/wiki/Mervyn_Peake

28. "Dungeons and Dragons controversies." *Wikipedia.* https://en.wikipedia.org/wiki/Dungeons_%26_Dragons_controversies

29. "Samuel R. Delaney." *Wikipedia.* https://en.wikipedia.org/wiki/Samuel_R._Delany

30. "Marion Zimmer Bradley." *Wikipedia.* https://en.wikipedia.org/wiki/Marion_Zimmer_Bradley

31. Li, Hua. *Chinese Science Fiction During the Post Mao Thaw.* University of Toronto Press, 2021.

32. Anders, Charlie Jane. "How Harry Potter Changed Publishing." *Gizmodo.* https://gizmodo.com/how-harry-potter-changed-publishing-5821271

33. Buzacott-Spear, Eliza. "The Harry Potter Effect: How Seven Books Changed Children's Publishing." *ABC.* https://www.abc.net.au/news/2017-06-26/harry-potter-effect-how-seven-books-changed-childrens-publishing/8630254

34. Shawl, Nisi. *Writing the Other.* https://writingtheother.com/the-book/

35. Khatchadourian, Raffi. "N.K. Jemisin's Dream Worlds." *New Yorker.* https://www.newyorker.com/magazine/2020/01/27/nk-jemisins-dream-worlds

36. Wikipedia. "Sad Puppies." https://en.wikipedia.org/wiki/Sad_Puppies

37. The Hugo Awards. https://www.thehugoawards.org/hugo-history/

Chapter 2

1. See books like *The Chronicles of Narnia* by C. S. Lewis, or Seanan Mcguire's *Wayward Children* series.

2. While most epic fantasy has historically been secondary-world fantasy, there are exceptions, such as N. K. Jemisin's *The City We Became*, which is epic invasive weird fantasy, not a secondary world. Similarly, there are secondary-world fantasies that take place on an intimate scope.

3. Tolkien's *The Lord of the Rings*, Dunsany's *The King of Elfland's Daughter*, Morris's *The Well at World's End*.

4. Bond, Sarah E., and Joel Christensen. "The Man Behind the Myth: Why We Should Question the Hero's Journey." *LARB.* August 12, 2021. https://lareviewofbooks.org/article/the-man-behind-the-myth-should-we-question-the-heros-journey/

5.   Datlow, Ellen. "Introduction." *Queen Victoria's Book of Spells: An Anthology of Gaslamp Fantasy*. Eds. Ellen Datlow and Terri Windling. Tor, 2013.

6.   "Novel of Manners." *Encyclopedia Britannica*. https://www.britannica.com/art/novel-of-manners

7.   VanderMeer, Jeff. "Blowing off Steam." https://www.jeffVanderMeer.com/2007/11/28/blowing-off-steam/

8.   Liu, Ken. "What is Silkpunk?" https://kenliu.name/books/what-is-silkpunk/

9.   Shanoes, Veronica. "Historical Fantasy." *Cambridge Companion to Fantasy Literature*. https://www.cambridge.org/core/books/abs/cambridge-companion-to-fantasy-literature/historical-fantasy/B748D0CABEDE43390F5BF0CA1EE96359 Cambridge University Press, 2012.

10. Ashe, Laura. "Love and Chivalry in the Middle Ages." *British Library*. https://www.bl.uk/medieval-literature/articles/love-and-chivalry-in-the-middle-ages

11. Wikipedia. "Romantic Fantasy." https://en.wikipedia.org/wiki/Romantic_fantasy#:~:text=Romantic%20fantasy%20is%20a%20subgenre,of%20the%20chivalric%20romance%20genre

12. SF-Encyclopedia. "Gothic SF." https://sf-encyclopedia.com/entry/gothic_sf

13. CBC Radio. "How Writers are Turning H.P. Lovecraft's Racist Work on Its Head." *CBC.CA*. https://www.cbc.ca/radio/ideas/how-writers-are-turning-h-p-lovecraft-s-racist-work-on-its-head-1.5883881

14. Carroll, Tobias. "Weird Fiction: A Primer." *Literary Hub*. https://lithub.com/weird-fiction-a-primer/

15. Endicott Studios. "A Mythic Fiction Reading List." *A Journal of Mythic Arts*. https://endicottstudio.typepad.com/jomareadinglists/2007/10/a-mythic-fictio.html

16. Anderson, Graham. *Fairytale in the Ancient World*. Routledge, 2000.

17. Fimi, Dimitra. "Mad Elves and Elusive Beauty: Some Celtic Strands of Tolkien's Mythology." *Dimitra Fimi.com*. https://dimitrafimi.com/mad-elves-and-elusive-beauty-some-celtic-strands-of-tolkiens-mythology/

18. Munro, T. O. "4 Categories of Fantasy." *Fantasy Hive*. https://fantasy-hive.co.uk/2019/07/the-4-categories-of-fantasy-applying-some-ideas-from-rhetorics-of-fantasy-by-farah-mendlesohn/

19. *Witch Week* by Diane Wynn Jones and *The Wizard of Earthsea* by Ursula K. Le Guin.

20. "Urban Fantasy." *SFE*. https://sf-encyclopedia.com/fe/urban_fantasy.

21. Peynado, Brenda. "Is Fabulism the New Sincerity?" *Literary Hub*. https://lithub.com/is-fabulism-the-new-sincerity/

22. Allman, Emma. "What Is Magical Realism?" *Book Riot*. https://bookriot.com/what-is-magical-realism/

23. Wikipedia. "Science Fantasy." *Wikipedia*. https://en.wikipedia.org/wiki/Science_fantasy

Chapter 3

1.   For a lengthier discussion of this topic, see my scholarly essay in *Imaginative Teaching Through Creative Writing*, Bloomsbury Academic, 2021.

2. Alte, Alexandra. "For Kazuo Ishiguro 'The Buried Giant' Is a Departure." *New York Times*. February 15, 2015. https://www.nytimes.com/2015/02/20/books/for-kazuo-ishiguro-the-buried-giant-is-a-departure.html

3. Cain, Siam. "Writer's Indignation: Kazuo Ishiguro Rejects Claims of Genre Snobbery." *The Guardian*. March 8, 2019. https://www.theguardian.com/books/2015/mar/08/kazuo-ishiguro-rebuffs-genre-snobbery

4. Gussoff, Caren. "Lit Fic Mags for Spec Fic Writers 101: Five Things You Have to Know." *SFWA*. November 26, 2013. https://www.sfwa.org/2013/11/lit-fic-mags-spec-fic-writers-101-five-things-know/

5. Michel, Lincoln. "When Popular Fiction Isn't Popular: Genre, Literary, and the Myths of Popularity." *Electric Literature*. April 2, 2016. https://electricliterature.com/when-popular-fiction-isnt-popular-genre-literary-and-the-myths-of-popularity/

6. Strickland, Donna. "Taking Dictation: The Emergence of Writing Programs and the Cultural Contradictions of Composition Teaching." *College English* 63.4 (2001): 457–79.

7. Bennett, Eric. *Workshops of Empire: Stegner, Engle, and American Creative Writing During the Cold War*. University of Iowa Press, 2015. 32–3.

8. Bennett, 10–13.

9. Bennett, 46.

10. Bennett, 33.

11. Menand, Louis. "Pulp's Big Moment." *New Yorker*. January 5, 2015. https://www.newyorker.com/magazine/2015/01/05/pulps-big-moment

12. Roberts, Robin. *A New Species: Gender and Science in Science Fiction*. University of Illinois Press, 1993. 40–65.

13. Enns, Anthony. "The Poet of the Pulps: Ray Bradbury and the Struggle for Prestige in Postwar Science Fiction." *Distinctions that Matter: Popular Literature and Material Culture* 13.1 (2015). https://journals.openedition.org/belphegor/615

14. Saler, Michael. "'Clap if You Believe in Sherlock Holmes': Mass Culture and the Re-Enchantment of Modernity." *The Historical Journal* 46.3 (2003): 599–662.

15. Hughes, 544.

16. Flanders, Judith. "Discovering Literature, The Romantics and the Victorians: The Penny Dreadful." *The British Library*. May 15, 2014, https://www.bl.uk/romantics-and-victorians/articles/penny-dreadfuls

17. Knoepflmacher, U. C. "The Balancing of Child and Adult: An Approach to Victorian Fantasies for Children." *Nineteenth-Century Fiction* 37.3 (1983): 497–530.

18. Knoepflmacher, 498.

19. Hughes, 544.

20. James, Henry. "The Art of Fiction." *Longman's Magazine* (1884). Washington State University. May 16, 2019, https://public.wsu.edu/~campbelld/amlit/artfiction.html

21. Pastoor, Kate. "Magic in the Classroom: The Controversial *Harry Potter*." *Prized Writing: UC Davis*. ucdavis.edu. 2002, https://prizedwriting.ucdavis.edu/magic-classroom-controversial-harry-potter

22. Garcia, Mary Elizabeth. "*Harry Potter* course leaves students spell bound." *News Center: UC Santa Cruz*. June 5, 2018. https://news.ucsc.edu/2018/06/harry-potter-class.html

Chapter 4

1. The elements of fiction refers to an idea that permeates creative writing craft and pedagogy, where generally there are believed to be five major elements of fiction: 1) plot, 2) setting, 3) character, 4) theme, and 5) point of view. Some people include a sixth, style. These ideas can't be attributed to any one person, though some people believe the breakdown originates with E. M. Forster's *Aspects of the Novel*.

2. Quoted here and reprinted in its entirety with permission from Liu in our anthology. Liu, Ken. "Good Hunting." *The Paper Menagerie and Other Stories*. Saga Press, 2016.

3. Bagarino, Christine. "Where Does Japan's Name Come From?" *The Culture Trip*. https://thecultoretrip.com/asia/japan/articles/where-does-japans-name-come-from/

4. Jemisin, N. K. *The Broken Earth Trilogy*. Orbit, 2015.

5. Quoted and reprinted in our anthology with permission from C. S. E. Cooney. Original venue of publication: Cooney, C. S. E. "Martyr's Gem." *Bone Swans*. Mythic Delirium Books, 2015.

6. Gailor, Denis. "Early Modern English Contractions and Their Relevance to Present-Day English." *English Today* 27 (March 2011): 10–15.

7. Clarke, Susanna. *Jonathan Strange & Mr. Norrell*. Tor, 2006.

8. Kay, Guy Gavriel. *The Last Light of the Sun*. Ace, 2005.

9. *A Knight's Tale*. Directed by Brian Helgeland, performances by Heath Ledger, Mark Addy, and Rufus Sewell. Columbia Pictures, 2001.

10. Quoted and reprinted in our anthology with the permission of Emrys Donaldson. Donaldson, Emrys. "The Albatrosses." *The Fairy Tale Review: Charcoal Issue*, 2018.

11. Atwood, Margaret. *The Handmaid's Tale*. McClelland and Stewart, 1985.

12. Hobb, Robin. *Assassin's Apprentice*. Spectra, 1996.

13. Quoted and reprinted in our anthology with permission from Rebecca Roanhorse. Roanhorse, Rebecca. "Harvest." *New Suns: Original Speculative Fiction by People of Color*. Solaris, 2020.

14. Bernheimer, Kate. "Fairy Tale is Form, Form is Fairy Tale." *The Writer's Notebook*. Tin House Books, 2010.

15. Beal, Jane. "Tolkien, Eucatastrophe, and the Re-Creation of Medieval Legend." *Journal of Tolkien Research* 4.1 (2017).

16. Quoted and reprinted with permission from Ursula K. Le Guin's agent. Le Guin, Ursula K. "The Ones Who Walk Away from Omelas." *New Dimensions 3*. Ed. Robert Silverberg. Doubleday, 1973.

17. Salesses, Matthew. *Craft and the Real World*. Catapult Books, 2021.

18. Lewis, C. S. *The Lion the Witch and the Wardrobe*. HarperCollins, 1950.

19. Rothfuss, Patrick. *The Kingkiller Chronicles*. DAW.

20. Chakraborty, S. A. *The Daevabad Trilogy*. HarperVoyager.

21. Kay, Guy Gavriel. *A Brightness Long Ago*. Berkeley, 2020.

22. Beagle, Peter S. *Summerlong*. Tachyon Publications, 2017.

23. Vo, Nghi. *Empress of Salt and Fortune*. Tor.com, 2020.

24. Djèlí Clark, P. *The Haunting of Tram Car 015*. Tor.com, 2019.

25. Howard, Kat. *Roses and Rot*. Saga Press, 2017.

26. Brennan, Marie. *A Natural History of Dragons*. Tor Books, 2014.

27. Addison, Katherine. *The Goblin Emperor*. Tor Fantasy, 2015.

28. Reprinted in our anthology and quoted with permission of the author. Singh, Vandana. "A Handful of Rice." *Steampunk III: Steampunk Revolution*. Ed. Ann VanderMeer. Tachyon Publications, 2012.

Chapter 5

1. Fitzgerald, F. Scott. *The Great Gatsby*. Scribner, 1925.

2. Link, Kelly. "The Faery Handbag." *Magic for Beginners*. Random House, 2014.

3. Link, Kelly. "The Wrong Grave." *Pretty Monsters*. Speak, 2010.

4. Reprinted in our anthology and referenced with permission of the author. Valentine, Genevieve. "From the Catalogue of the Pavilion of the Uncanny and Marvelous, Scheduled for Premiere at the Great Exhibition (Before the Fire)." *Queen Victoria's Book of Spells*. Eds. Ellen Datlow and Terri Windling. Tor Books, 2013.

5. Patchett, *Ann. Bel Canto*. Harpers, 2005.

6. Moore, Lorrie. "How to be an Other Woman." *Self Help*. Vintage, 2007.

7. Quoted and reprinted our anthology with permission from the publisher. Miéville, China. "The Condition of New Death." *Three Moments of an Explosion*. Del Rey, 2016.

8. Jones, Rachael K. "Night Bazaar for Women Becoming Reptiles." *Beneath Ceaseless Skies* 207, July 2016.

9. Carter, Angela. *The Bloody Chamber and Other Stories*. Penguin Classics Reprint Edition, 2015.

10. Douglass, Sara. *The Wayfarer Redemption*. Tor Fantasy, 2001.

11. Lyons, Jenn. *The Ruin of Kings*. Tor Books, 2019.

12. Liu, Ken. *The Grace of Kings*. Saga Press, 2016.

13. Martin, George R. R. *A Game of Thrones*. Bantam Reprint Edition, 2002.

14. Hairston, Andrea. *Master of Poisons*. Tor.com, 2021.

15. Thackeray, William Makepeace. *Vanity Fair: A Novel Without a Hero*. 1848.

16. Moreno-Garcia, Silvia. *Mexican Gothic*. Del Rey, 2021.

17. Anders, Charlie Jane. *All the Birds in the Sky*. Tor Books, 2017.

18. Nghi, Vo. The Chosen and the Beautiful. Tor.com, 2022.

19. Priest, Cherie. *Maplecroft*. Ace, 2014.

20. Harrow, Alix E. *Ten Thousand Doors of January*. Redhook, 2020.

21. Jemisin, N. K. *The Hundred Thousand Kingdoms*. Orbit, 2010.

Chapter 6

1. Kardos, Michael. *The Art and Craft of Fiction*. Bedford/St. Martin's, 2016.

2. VanderMeer, Jeff. *The Wonderbook*. Abrams, 2013.

3. VanderMeer, Jeff. *The Wonderbook*. Abrams, 2013.

4. Miller, William. "The Matter of Screenplay Structure." *Journal of Film and Video* 36.3 (1984).

5. Quoted, referenced, and reprinted in the anthology with permission of Sophia Samatar. Samatar, Sophia. "Meet Me in Iram." *Lightspeed*, 2018.

6. Carter, Angela. *The Bloody Chamber and Other Stories*. Penguin Classics Reprint Edition, 2015.

7. Johnson, Kij. "The Apartment Dweller's Bestiary." *Clarkesworld*, 2015.

8. Blandiana, Ana. "The Phantom Church." *The Phantom Church and Other Stories from Romania*. Eds. and trans. Georgiana Farnoaga and Sharon King. University of Pittsburgh Press, 1997.

9. Okungbowa, Suyi Davies. "We Come as Gods." Tor.com, 2020.

10. Dodson, Zachary Thomas. *Bats of the Republic*. Doubleday, 2015.

11. Wilson, Kai Ashante. *A Taste of Honey*. Tor.com, 2016.

12. El-Mohtar, Amal, and Max Gladstone. *This is How You Lose the Time War*. Tor.com, 2019.

13. *The Princess Bride*. Directed by Rob Reiner, performances by Cary Elwes, Mandy Patinkin, and Robin Wright. Twentieth Century Fox, 1987.

14. Calvino, Italo. *If On Winter's Night a Traveler*. Harcourt Brace, 1982. Byatt, A. S. *Possession*. Vintage, 1991. Vonnegut, Kurt. *Slaughterhouse Five*. Delacorte, 1969. Fforde, Jasper. *The Eyre Affair*. Penguin Books, 2003.

15. Hergenrader, Trent. *Collaborative Worldbuilding for Writer's and Gamers*. Bloomsbury Academic, 2019.

16. LaValle, Victor. *The Changeling*. One World, 2018.

17. Roanhorse, Rebecca. *Black Sun*. Saga Press, 2021.

Chapter 7

1. Michel, Lincoln. "Against Worldbuilding." *Electric Literature*. April 6, 2017. https://electricliterature.com/against-worldbuilding/

2. Wendig, Chuck. "25 Things You Should Know About Worldbuilding." *TerribleMinds.com*. April 4, 2021. http://terribleminds.com/ramble/2013/09/17/25-things-you-should-know-about-worldbuilding/

3. Ng, Celeste. *Little Fires Everywhere*. Penguin, 2017.

4. Loughrey, Clarisse. "Charlotte Brontë 200th Anniversary: How the Brontës Created a Completely Secret Game of Thrones Style World." *The Independent*. April 21, 2016. https://www.independent.co.uk/arts-entertainment/books/news/charlotte-bronte-200th-anniversary-how-the-brontes-created-a-completely-secret-game-of-thronesstyle-world-a6994786.html

5. Polk, C.L. *Kingston Cycle*. Tor.com, 2019–21.

6. Nicholls, Stan. *Orcs*. Orbit, 2008.

7. Hergenrader, Trent. *Collaborative Worldbuilding for Writers and Gamers*. Bloomsbury Academic, 2019.

8. VanderMeer, Jeff. "Chapter 6: Worldbuilding." *The Wonderbook*. Abrams Image, 2013.

9. Referenced, quoted, and included in our anthology with permission of the author. Singh, Vandana. "A Handful of Rice." *Ambiguity Machines and Other Stories.* Small Beer Press, 2018.

10. Jones, Rachael, K. "Night Bazaar for Women Becoming Reptiles." *Beneath Ceaseless Skies* 203 (2016). http://www.beneath-ceaseless-skies.com/stories/the-night-bazaar-for-women-becoming-reptile

11. Referenced, quoted, and included in the anthology with permission of the author. Goss, Theodora. "England Under the White Witch." *Clarkesworld* 73 (2012). https://clarkesworldmagazine.com/goss_10_12/

12. Le Guin, Ursula K. *The Dispossessed: An Ambiguous Utopia.* Harper & Row, 1974.

13. Quoted and reprinted with permission from Ursula K. Le Guin's agent. Le Guin, Ursula K. "The Ones Who Walk Away from Omelas." *New Dimensions 3.* Ed. Robert Silverberg. Doubleday, 1973.

14. "Episode 12: The Wounded." *Star Trek: The Next Generation Season 4.* Directed by Chip Chalmers. Paramount Domestic Television, 28 January 1991.

15. Mariller, Juliet. *Sevenwaters Trilogy.* Pan Macmillan Australia, 1999–2001.

16. Showalter, Ross. "Writing Fantasy Lets me Show the Whole Truth of Disability." *Electric Literature,* October 1, 2021.

17. Schwab, V. E. *Shades of Magic.* Tor, 2015.

18. Kay, Guy Gavriel. *The Last Light of the Sun.* Ace, 2005.

19. Brennan, Marie. *A Natural History of Dragons.* Tor, 2014.

20. Rothfuss, Patrick. *The Name of the Wind.* Daw Books, 2008.

21. Muir, Tamsyn. *Gideon the Ninth.* Tor.com, 2019.

Chapter 8

1. Beagle, Peter. S. *The Last Unicorn.* Viking Press, 1968.

2. Hobb, Robin. *The Farseer Trilogy.* Spectra, 1998.

3. Hobb, Robin. *The Rainwilds Chronicles.* HarperVoyager, 2014.

4. Older, Daniel Jose. *Half Resurrection Blues.* Ace, 2015.

5. "W.B. Yeats." *Britannica.com.* https://www.britannica.com/biography/William-Butler-Yeats#ref205494

6. Roanhorse, Rebecca. "Harvest." *New Suns: Original Speculative Fiction by People of Color.* Ed. Nisi Shawl. Solaris, 2019.

7. Quoted, referenced, and reprinted in anthology with the permission of the author. Samatar, Sofia. "Meet Me in Iram." *Lightspeed* 102 (2018). https://www.lightspeedmagazine.com/fiction/meet-me-in-iram/

8. Kushner, Ellen. *Swordspoint.* Arbor House, 1987.

9. Chee, Alexander. "Research Your Life." *Center for Fiction.*

Chapter 9

1. Morris, William. *The Roots of the Mountains.* Reeves and Turner, 1889.

2. Carter, Angela. *The Bloody Chamber and Other Stories*. Penguin Classics Reprint Edition, 2015.

3. "I Want to Vote." *The Hugo Awards.org*. https://www.thehugoawards.org/i-want-to-vote/#:~:text=The%20Hugo%20Awards%20voting%20process,of%20the%20previous%20calendar%20year

4. "Sad Puppies." *Wikipedia*.

5. Fimi, Dimitra. *Tolkien, Race, and Cultural History: From Faeries to Hobbits*. Palgrave Macmillan, 2008.

6. Caplan, Walker. "On the Time J.R.R. Tolkien Refused to Work with Nazi Leaning Publishers." *Literary Hub*. January 5, 2022. https://lithub.com/on-the-time-j-r-r-tolkien-refused-to-work-with-nazi-leaning-publishers/

7. Tolkien, J. R. R. "On Fairy Stories." *Essays Presented to Charles Williams*. Eds. C. S. Lewis and Charlies Williams. Oxford University Press, 1947.

8. "Cultural Appropriation View Guide." "Cultural Appropriation vs Appreciation." *What I Hear When You Say* Episode 5, 15 March 2017, Franchesa Ramsey, Jamin Warren, and Alyasha Owerka-Moore. PBS. https://bento.cdn.pbs.org/hostedbento-prod/filer_public/whatihear/9-Cultural_Approp-Viewing_Guide.pdf

9. Shawl, Nisi, and Cynthia Ward. *Writing the Other: A Practical Approach*. Aqueduct Press, 2005.

10. Stitch Media. "Too White Bread for this Shit: Race and Racism in Laurell K Hamilton's Urban Fantasy Series." *Stich Media*. https://stitchmediamix.com/2018/08/07/too-white-bread-for-this-shit-race-and-racism-in-laurell-k-hamiltons-urban-fantasy-series/

11. Alter, Alexander. "She Pulled Her Debut Book When Critics Found it Racist, Now She Plans to Publish." *NYtimes.com*. https://www.nytimes.com/2019/04/29/books/amelie-wen-zhao-blood-heir.html

12. Shawl, Nisi. "Appropriate Cultural Appropriation." *Writing the Other.com*. August 20, 2016. https://writingtheother.com/appropriate-cultural-appropriation/

13. Schappell, Elissa, and Claudia Brodsky Lacour. "Toni Morrison: The Art of Fiction: No 134." *The Paris Review* 128 (1993). https://www.theparisreview.org/interviews/1888/the-art-of-fiction-no-134-toni-morrison

14. Sutton, Rebecca. "Toni Morrison: Write, Erase, Do it Over." *NEA.gov*. https://www.arts.gov/stories/magazine/2014/4/art-failure-importance-risk-and-experimentation/toni-morrison

15. Shawl, Nisi. "Appropriate Cultural Appropriation." *Writing the Other.com*. August 20, 2016. https://writingtheother.com/appropriate-cultural-appropriation/

16. Anders, Charlie Jane. "Never Say You Can't Survive. When is It Okay to Write About Someone Else's Culture or Experience?" *Tor.com*. October 6, 2020. https://www.tor.com/2020/10/06/never-say-you-cant-survive-when-is-it-okay-to-write-about-someone-elses-culture-or-experience/

17. Goto, Hiromi. "Wiscon 38 Guest of Honor Speech." *Hiromi Goto.com*. https://www.hiromigoto.com/wiscon38-guest-of-honour-speech/

18. Ng, Jeannette. "Cultural Appropriate for the Worried Writer: Some Practical Advice." *Medium*. October 29, 2018. https://medium.com/@nettlefish/cultural-appropriation-for-the-worried-writer-some-practical-advice-ac21710685e3 and "Cultural Appropriation: Some More practical Advice." *Medium*. September 17, 2020. https://medium.com/@nettlefish/cultural-appropriation-some-more-practical-advice-5da23a29349d

19. Ng, Jeannette. *Under the Pendulum Sun*. Angry Robot, 2017.

20. Le Guin, Ursula K. "Is Gender Necessary? Redux." *Dancing at the Edge of the World: Thoughts on Words, Women, and Places.* Grove Press, 1989.

21. Eberhardt, Jennifer. *Biased: Uncovering the Hidden Prejudice that Shapes What We See, Think, and Do.* Penguin Books, 2020.

22. Connor, Dylan Shane, and Michael Storper. "The Changing Geography of Social Mobility in the United States." *PNAS.* November 16, 2020. https://www.pnas.org/doi/10.1073/pnas.2010222117

23. Salvatore, R. A. *The Dark Elf Trilogy.* Wizards of the Coast, 1991.

24. Chakraborty. S. A. *The Daevabad Trilogy.* HarperVoyager, 2020.

25. Miéville, China. "The Condition of New Death." *Three Moments of an Explosion.* Del Rey, 2016.

26. Jemisin, N. K. *The Broken Earth trilogy.* Orbit, 2015.

27. Shawl, Nisi. *Everfair.* Tor Books, 2017.

28. Harrow, Alix E. *Ten Thousand Doors of January.* Redhook, 2020.

29. Lynch, Scott. *The Lies of Locke Lamora.* Del Rey, 2007.

Chapter 10

1. Encyclopedia Britannica. "The Baroque Period: Summary." https://www.britannica.com/summary/Baroque-art-andarchitecture#:~:text=Baroque%20period%2C%20(17th%E2%80%9318th,%2C%20decorative%20arts%2C%20and%20music

2. American Writer's Museum. "Minimalism vs. Maximalism." https://americanwritersmuseum.org/minimalism-vs-maximalism/

3. Ulmer, Jessie. "Red." *Corvid Queen.* https://corvidqueen.com/stories/red-jessie-ulmer Quoted and reproduced in our anthology with permission of the author.

4. Murakami, Haruki. *After the Quake.* Vintage, 2003.

5. Donoghue, Emma. "The Tale of the Shoe." *Kissing the Witch: Old Tales in New Skins.* HarperTeen, 1999.

6. Faber, Michel. *The Crimson Petal and the White.* Harvest, 2003.

7. Reprinted in our anthology and referenced with permission of the author. Valentine, Genevieve. "From the Catalogue of the Pavilion of the Uncanny and Marvelous, Scheduled for Premiere at the Great Exhibition (Before the Fire)." *Queen Victoria's Book of Spells.* Eds. Ellen Datlow and Terri Windling. Tor Books, 2013.

8. Clarke, Susanna. *Jonathan Strange & Mr. Norrell.* Tor, 2006.

9. Quoted, referenced, and reprinted in the anthology with permission of Sophia Samatar. Samatar, Sophia. "Meet Me in Iram." *Lightspeed,* 2018.

10. VanderMeer, Jeff. "Approaches to Style." *The Wonderbook.* Abrams Image, 2018.

11. Quoted and reprinted in our anthology with permission from Rebecca Roanhorse. Roanhorse, Rebecca. "Harvest." *New Suns: Original Speculative Fiction by People of Color.* Solaris, 2020.

12. Referenced, quoted, and included in the anthology with permission of the author. Goss, Theodora. "England Under the White Witch." *Clarkesworld* 73 (2012). https://clarkesworldmagazine.com/goss_10_12/

13. Carroll, Tobias. "Weird Fiction: A Primer." *Literary Hub*. July 21, 2015. https://lithub.com/weird-fiction-a-primer/

14. The Shirley Jackson Awards. https://www.shirleyjacksonawards.org/

15. The Bram Stoker Awards. https://www.thebramstokerawards.com/

16. Yolen, Jane. "Granny Rumple." *How to Fracture a Fairy Tale*. Tachyon Publications, 2018.

17. Beckett, Galen. *The Magicians and Mrs. Quent*. Spectra, 2009.

18. Polk, C. L. *The Midnight Bargain*. Erewhon, 2020.

19. Kushner, Ellen. *Swordspoint*. Arbor House, 1987.

20. *Shakespeare in Love*. Dir. John Madden. Miramax, 1998.

21. Kerouac, Jack. *On the Road*. Viking, 1957.

22. "On the Road." Wikipedia. https://en.wikipedia.org/wiki/On_the_Road

23. NaNoWriMo. https://nanowrimo.org/

24. Grunenwald, Jill. "8 Bestselling Books Written during Nanowrimo." *Overdrive*. https://company.overdrive.com/2019/11/01/8-bestselling-books-written-during-nanowrimo/

25. Robb, Alice. "'The Flow State': Where Creative Work Thrives." *BBC.com*. February 5, 2019. https://www.bbc.com/worklife/article/20190204-how-to-find-your-flow-state-to-be-peak-creative

26. King, Stephen. *On Writing: A Memoir of the Craft*. Scribner, 2010.

27. Moxley, Joseph M. "The Writing Process." *Writing Commons*. https://writingcommons.org/section/writing-process/

28. Percy, Benjamin. *Thrill Me: Essays on Fiction*. Graywolf Press, 2016.

29. Michel, Lincoln. "Plotter, Pantser, Scribbler, Scribe." *Countercraft*. December 14, 2021. https://countercraft.substack.com/p/plotter-pantser-scribbler-scribe?s=r

30. Mitchell, David. *Cloud Atlas*. Random House, 2004.

31. Jemisin, N. K. *The Fifth Season*. Orbit, 2015.

32. Harlequin Submission Manager. https://harlequin.submittable.com/submit

33. Briggs, Patricia. https://www.patriciabriggs.com/

34. VanderMeer, Jeff. "Chart of Revision." *The Wonderbook*. Abrams Image, 2018.

Chapter 11

1. "High Fantasy." *Encyclopedia of Fantasy*. https://sf-encyclopedia.com/fe/high_fantasy

2. "Epic Fantasy." *Encyclopedia of Fantasy*. https://sf-encyclopedia.com/fe/epic_fantasy

3. "Elric of Melnibon." *Wikipedia*. https://en.wikipedia.org/wiki/Elric_of_Melnibon%C3%A9

4. Cobb, Marat. "Morgan Le Fay: How Arthurian Legend Turned a Powerful Woman From a Healer to a Villian." *The Conversation*, 2019. https://theconversation.com/morgan-le-fay-how-arthurian-legend-turned-a-powerful-woman-from-healer-to-villain-109928

5. Tolkien, J. R. R. *The Two Towers*. George Allen Unwin, 1954.

6. "Epic." Poets.org: Glossary of Poetic Terms. https://poets.org/glossary/epic

7. "World Epics." Columbia. https://edblogs.columbia.edu/worldepics/

8. Ortez, Patrick. "Modern Epics: Fantasy Translation." *World Literature Today*. October 1, 2019. https://www.worldliteraturetoday.org/blog/lit-lists/modern-epics-fantasy-translation-t-patrick-ortez

9. Stubby the Rocket. "Our Favorite Science Fiction and Fantasy in Translation—Redux." *Tor. com*. November 10, 2014. https://www.tor.com/2014/11/10/favorite-science-fiction-a-fantasy-in-translation-redux/

10. Sapkowski, Andrzej. *The Witcher Saga*. Orbit, 2013.

11. Le Guin, Ursula K. *The Books of Earthsea: Completed Illustrated Edition*. Saga Press. 2018.

12. Jemisin, N. K. *The Hundred Thousand Kingdoms*. Orbit, 2010.

13. Marillier, Juliet. *Daughter of the Forest*. Tor Books, 2002.

14. Carey, Jacqueline. *Kushiel's Dart*. Tor Fantasy, 2001.

15. Bujold, Lois McMaster. *The Paladin of Souls*. Eos, 2003.

16. McKinley, Robin. *The Blue Sword*. Greenwillow Books, 1982.

17. Yang, Neon. *The Red Threads of Fortune*. Tor.com Publishing, 2017.

18. Roanhorse, Rebecca. *Black Sun*. Saga Press, 2020

19. James, Marlon. *Black Leopard Red Wolf*. Riverhead Books, 2020.

20. Lyons, Jenn. *The Ruin of Kings*. Tor Books, 2019.

21. Robin Hobb. http://www.robinhobb.com/works.htm

22. Rothfuss, Patrick. *The Name of the Wind*. DAW Books, 2008.

23. Guy Gavriel Kay. https://brightweavings.com/

24. Cook, Glen. *The Chronicles of the Black Company*. Tor, 2007.

25. Salesses, Matthew. *Craft in the Real World*. Catapult, 2021.

26. Reprinted in our anthology and quoted with permission of the author. Singh, Vandana. "A Handful of Rice." *Steampunk III: Steampunk Revolution*. Ed. Ann VanderMeer. Tachyon Publications, 2012.

Chapter 12

1. Whitehead, Colson. *The Underground Railroad*. Doubleday, 2016.

2. Walton, Jo. "What Is Historical Fantasy?" *Tor.com*. July 31, 2009. https://www.tor.com/2009/07/31/what-is-historical-fantasy-anyway/

3. Huber, Kayla. "How the Work of Marie Curie Restricted the Advancement of Future Female Scientists." *Wake Forest College News*. April 28, 2022. https://www.lakeforest.edu/news/how-the-work-of-marie-curie-restricted-the-advancement-of-future-female-scientists

4. Shawl, Nisi. *Everfair*. Tor Books, 2017.

5. Coates, Ta-Nehisi. *The Water Dancer*. One World, 2020.

6. Butler, Octavia. *Kindred*. Doubleday, 1979.

7. Hoffman, Alice. *The World That We Knew*. Scribner, 2020.

8. Kay, Guy Gavriel. *The Lions of Al-Rassan*. HarperVoyager, 2005.

9. Brennan, Marie. *A Natural History of Dragons*. Tor Books, 2014.

10. Djèlí Clark, P. *The Haunting of Tram Car 015*. Tor.com, 2019.

11. Goss, Theodora. *The Strange Case of the Alchemist's Daughter*. Saga Press, 2017.

12. Vo, Nghi. *The Chosen and the Beautiful*. Tor, 2021.

13. Horrocks, Caitlin. "On the Anxiety of Writing Historical Fiction: A User's Manual." *Literary Hub*. August 9, 2019. https://lithub.com/on-the-anxiety-of-writing-historical-fiction-a-users-manual/

14. *A Knight's Tale*. Dir. Brian Helgeland. Columbia, 2001.

15. Martin, Ben L. "From Negro to Black to African America: The Power of Names and Naming." *Political Science Quarterly* 106 (1991).

16. Wilkerson, Isabel. "'African-American' Favored by Many of America's Blacks." *New York Times Archives*. January 31, 1989. African-American' Favored By Many of America's Blacks – The New York Times (nytimes.com)

17. Mantel, Hilary. "Why I Became a Historical Novelist." *The Guardian*. June 3, 2017. https://www.theguardian.com/books/2017/jun/03/hilary-mantel-why-i-became-a-historical-novelist

18. *Peaky Blinders* Season 1. Dir, Otto Bathhurst. BBC Two, 2013.

19. Moreno-Garcia, Silvia. *Mexican Gothic*. Del Rey, 2021.

20. Gabaldon, Diana. *Outlander*. Dell, 1991.

21. Robertson, Blythe. "Why Does Women's Writing About Relationships Need to be 'Relatable'?" *Literary Hub*. January 10, 2019. https://lithub.com/why-does-womens-writing-about-relationships-need-to-be-relatable/

22. Mantel, Hilary. *Wolf Hall*. Picador, 2010.

23. Zhang, C. Pam. *How Much of These Hills Is Gold*. Riverhead, 2020.

24. Crowley, John. *Little, Big*. William Morrow, 2006.

Chapter 13

1. Emrys, Ruthanna, and Anne M. Pillsworth. "A (Re)Introduction to Reading the Weird." *Tor.com*. September 16. 2020. https://www.tor.com/2020/09/16/reintroduction-to-reading-the-weird/

2. Moreno-Garcia, Silvia. *Mexican Gothic*. Del Rey, 2021.

3. "The Sublime." Tate Museum. https://www.tate.org.uk/art/art-terms/s/sublime

4. "Dark Fantasy." *Historical Dictionary of Science Fiction*. https://sfdictionary.com/view/255/dark-fantasy

5. "Weird Tales." *The Pulp Magazines Project*. https://www.pulpmags.org/content/view/issues/weird-tales.html

6. Carroll, Tobias. "Weird Fiction: A Primer." *Literary Hub*. July 15, 2021. https://lithub.com/weird-fiction-a-primer/

7. VanderMeer, Jeff, and Ann VanderMeer. *The Weird*. Tor Books, 2012.

8. China Miéville, "Weird Fiction." Eds. Mark Bould et al. *The Routledge Companion to Science Fiction*. New York: Routledge, 2009.

9. House, Wes. "We Can't Ignore Lovecraft's White Supremacy." *Literary Hub*. September 16, 2017. https://lithub.com/we-cant-ignore-h-p-lovecrafts-white-supremacy/

10. Michel, Lincoln. "Victor LaValle Talks About Horror Fiction, Imaginative Illiteracy and Lovecraft's Complicated Legacy." *Electric Literature*. April 8, 2016. https://electricliterature.com/victor-lavalle-talks-about-horror-fiction-imaginative-illiteracy-and-lovecrafts-complicated/

11. LaValle, Victor. *The Ballad of Black Tom*. Tor.com Publishing, 2016.

12. *Lovecraft Country*. Dir. Misha Green. HBO, 2021. Based on the novel of the same name by Matt Ruff, HarperCollins, 2016.

13. Ruthanna, Emrys. *Winter Tide*. Tor.com Publishing, 2017.

14. Priest, Cherie. *Maplecroft*. Ace, 2014.

15. "The New Weird." *Wikipedia*. https://en.wikipedia.org/wiki/New_weird

16. "Constantine, Storm." *Science Fiction Encyclopedia*. January 10, 2021. https://sf-encyclopedia.com/entry/constantine_storm

17. "Bas Lag." *Bas-Las Fandom Wiki*. https://baslag.fandom.com/wiki/Bas-Lag_Wiki

18. Miéville, China. "The Condition of New Death." *Three Moments of an Explosion*. Del Rey, 2016.

19. Poe, Edgar Allan. "Masque of the Red Death." *Poe Museum*. https://poemuseum.org/the-masque-of-the-red-death/

20. As blurbed on the omnibus edition of Constantine's *Wraethu* books, Tom Doherty and Associations, 1993.

21. Michel, Lincoln. "The Grotesque Sublime." *Counter Craft*. March 30, 2022. https://countercraft.substack.com/p/the-grotesque-sublime?s=r

22. Jemisin, N.K. *The City We Became*. Orbit, 2021.

23. Link, Kelly. "Lull." *Magic for Beginners*. Random House, 2014.

24. Salesses, Matthew. *Craft in the Real World*. Catapult, 2021

25. Miéville, China. *The Scar*. Del Rey, 2004.

Chapter 14

1. Doyle, Sir Arthur Conan. *The Hound of the Baskervilles*. George Newness Ltd., 1902.

2. The SF Encyclopedia. "Urban Fantasy." https://sf-encyclopedia.com/fe/urban_fantasy

3. The SF Encyclopedia. "Contemporary Fantasy." https://sf-encyclopedia.com/fe/contemporary_fantasy

4. Elbir-Avirum, Hadas. *Fairy Tales of London: British Urban Fantasy 1840-Present*. Bloomsbury Academic, 2021.

5. Windling, Terri. "Charles De Lint: A Life of Stories." *Myth & Moor*. https://www.terriwindling.com/mythic-arts/charles-de-lint.html

6. Bull, Emma. *War for the Oaks*. Ace, 1987.

7. Bledsoe, Alex. "Emma Bull: Music and Magic." *Tor.com*. April 29, 2013. https://www.tor.com/2013/04/29/review-emma-bull-music-and-magic/

8. Jacqueline Carey is most known for her epic fantasy series that began with *Kushiel's Dart* (Tor 2001), but she also wrote an urban fantasy trilogy set in a fictional Michigan city that began with *Dark Currents* (Roc 2012).

9. Butcher, Jim. "Books: *Dresden Files*." https://www.jim-butcher.com/books/dresden

10. Liu, Marjorie. "Urban Fantasy: Hunter Kiss Series." http://marjoriemliu.com/novels/#uf.Jose Older, Daniel. "Works." http://danieljoseolder.net/books. MacMillan. "Authors: L.A. Banks." https://us.macmillan.com/author/labanks

11. Harris, Charlaine. "Sookie Stackhouse Series." https://charlaineharris.com/bibliographies/sookie-stackhouse/. Hamilton, Laurell K. "Book Series." https://www.laurellkhamilton.com/book-series/. Murphy, C.E. "Books." https://catiemurphy.com/books/#book_289. Briggs, Patricia. "Books." https://www.patriciabriggs.com/books/

12. *Grimm*. Created by Stephen Carpenter, Jim Kouf, and David Greenwalt. *NBC* 2011–17.

13. Butler, Octavia. *Fledgling*. Seven Stories Press, 2005.

14. Encyclopedia Britannica. "Hard Boiled Fiction." *Britannica.com*. https://www.britannica.com/art/hard-boiled-fiction

15. Chance, Karen. "Books." https://karenchance.com/books/

16. Encyclopedia Britannica. "Raymond Chandler." *Britannica.com*. https://www.britannica.com/biography/Raymond-Chandler

Chapter 15

1. Aldama, Frederick Luis. "Magical Realism." *The Routledge Companion to Latino/a Literature*. Eds. Suzanne Bost and Frances R. Aparicio, 334–41. Routledge, 2013.

2. Bowers, Maggie Ann. *Magic(al) Realism*. Routledge, 2004.

3. Straub, Peter. *The New Wave Fabulists: Conjunction 39*. Bard College, 2002.

4. Allman, Emma. "What Is Magical Realism?" *Book Riot*. February 8, 2018. https://bookriot.com/what-is-magical-realism/

5. Murakami, Haruki. "Super Frog Saves Tokyo." *After the Quake*. Vintage, 2003.

6. Sparks, Amber. "New Genres: Domestic Fabulism or Kansas with a Difference." *Electric Literature*. June 23, 2014. https://electricliterature.com/new-genres-domestic-fabulism-or-kansas-with-a-difference/

7. Peynado, Brenda. "Is Fabulism the New Sincerity?" *Literary Hub*. May 17, 2021. https://lithub.com/is-fabulism-the-new-sincerity/

8. Peynado, Brenda. "Thoughts and Prayers." *The Rock Eaters*. Penguin Books, 2021.

9. Hoffman, Alice. *Practical Magic*. Vintage, 1995.

10. Morrison, Toni. *Beloved*. Vintage, 2004.

11. Donaldson, Emrys. "The Albatrosses." *The Fairy Tale Review: Charcoal Issue*. Wayne State University Press, 2018. Quoted, referenced, and reproduced in the anthology with the permission of the author.

12. Márquez, Gabriel García. *One Hundred Years of Solitude*. HarperPerennial Modern Classics, 2006.

13. Hoffman, Alice. *Blackbird House*. Ballentine Readers Circle, 2005.

14. Bender, Aimee. *Willful Creatures*. Anchor, 2006.

15. Nagamatsu, Sequoia. "Rokurokubi." *Where We Go When All We Were is Gone*. Black Lawrence Press, 2016.

16. Link, Kelly. "Stone Animals." *Magic for Beginners*. Random House Trade Paperbacks, 2014.

17. Bernheimer, Kate. "Fairy Tale is Form, Form is Fairy Tale." *The Writer's Notebook*. Tin House Books, 2010.

18. Spitz, Ellen Handler. "The Irresistible Psychology of Fairy Tales." *The New Republic*. December 28, 2015. https://newrepublic.com/article/126582/irresistible-psychology-fairy-tales

Chapter 16

1. Anderson, Graham. *Fairy Tale in the Ancient World*. Routledge, 2000.

2. D'Aulnoy, Madame. "The Green Serpent." Surlalune Fairy Tales. https://www.surlalunefairytales.com/book.php?id=36&tale=886. For more on the way Beauty and the Beast has changed over time, check out Marina Warner's *From the Beast to the Blonde*. Farrar, Straus and Giroux, 1996.

3. BBC News. "Fairy Tale Origins Thousands of Years Old, Researchers Say." *BBC.com*. January 20, 2016. https://www.bbc.com/news/uk-35358487

4. Zipes, Jack. "How the Grimm Brothers Saved the Fairy Tale." *National Endowment of the Humanities*, April 2016 Issue. https://www.neh.gov/humanities/2015/marchapril/feature/how-the-grimm-brothers-saved-the-fairy-tale#:~:text=In%20the%201812%20tale%2C%20the,t%20shave%20or%20clean%20himself

5. Encyclopedia Britannica. "The Thousand and One Nights." *Brittanica.com*. https://www.britannica.com/topic/The-Thousand-and-One-Nights

6. Barker, Pat. *Silence of the Girls*. Penguin, 2019. Miller, Madeline. *The Song of Achilles*. Ecco, 2012.

7. See earlier references for Carter and Donoghue. Liu, Ken. *The Paper Menagerie and Other Stories*. Saga Press, 2016.

8. Kusher, Ellen. *Thomas the Rhymer*. Spectra, 2004. Howard, Kat. *Roses and Rot*. Saga Press, 2017. Oyeyemi, Helen. *Boy, Snow, Bird*. Riverhead Books, 2015.

9. Huang, S. L. *Burning Roses*. Tor.com, 2020. LaValle, Victor. *The Changeling*. One World, 2018. Moreno-Garcia, Silvia. *Gods of Jade and Shadow*. Del Rey, 2020. Okorafor, Nnedi. *Akata Witch*. Speak, 2017. Roanhorse, Rebecca. *Trail of Lightening*. Saga Press, 2018.

10. Warner, Marina. *Once Upon a Time: A Short History of Fairy Tale*. Oxford University Press, 2016.

11. Moreno-Garcia, Silvia, and Lavie Tidhar. "Faeries and Their Magical World Have Capitvated Us for Centuries." *Washington Post*. June 16, 2020. https://www.washingtonpost.com/entertainment/books/fairies-and-their-magical-worlds-have-captivated-us-for-centuries-here-are-some-of-the-books-that-did-it-best/2020/06/16/2f4c7a2c-aa51-11ea-a9d9-a81c1a491c52_story.html

12. Cho, Zen. *Sorcerer to the Crown*. Ace, 2016. Ng, Jeanette. *Under the Pendulum Sun*. Angry Robot, 2017. Brennan, Marie. *Midnight Never Come*. Titan Books, 2015. Donoghue, Keith. *The Stolen Child*. Anchor, 2007. Mirrlees, Hope. *Lud-in-the-Mists*. Collins, 1926. Plunkett, Edward (Lord Dunsany). *The King of Elfland's Daughter*. (1924). Del Rey, 1999. Heath Justice, Daniel. *The Way of Thorn and Thunder*. University of New Mexico Press, 2011. Stein, Garth. *Raven Stole the Moon*. Harper Paperback, 2010.

13. "The story of the youth who went forth to learn what fear was." *Brighton Film Archive: Third Reich Film Material.* https://screenarchive.brighton.ac.uk/detail/9322/

14. Berman House Blog. "The Creation of New Folktales: A Look into the Jewish Traditions of Goblins." https://www.behrmanhouse.com/blog/on-the-creation-of-new-folktales-a-look-into-the-jewish-traditions-in-goblins-of-knottingham

15. Pullen, Jennifer. "The Uncanny Way: Old Stories Make New Meanings." *Coral Covered Her Bones*: A Dissertation Presented to the faculty of the College of Arts & Sciences at Ohio University, 2017.

16. Atwood, Margaret. *The Penelopiad.* Canongate, 2006.

17. Ulmer, Jessie. "Red." *Corvid Queen.* Referenced, quoted, and reprinted in our anthology by permission of the author.

18. Gaiman, Neil, and Terry Pratchett. *Good Omens.* William Morrow, 2006.

Chapter 17

1. The Encyclopedia of Science Fiction. "Planetary Romance." *SF Encyclopedia.* https://sf-encyclopedia.com/entry/planetary_romance

2. "Darkover Series." *Wikipedia.* https://en.wikipedia.org/wiki/Darkover_series

3. Herbert, Frank. *Dune.* Chilton Books, 1965.

4. Yaszek, Lisa. *The Future is Female! 25 Classic Science Fiction Stories by Women, From Pulp Pioneers to Ursula K. Le Guin.* Library of America, 2018.

5. Shinn, Sharon. "Books." http://sharonshinn.net/books.shtml

6. Tepper, Sheri. S. *Singer from the Sea.* HarperCollins, 2010.

7. The Internet Speculative Fiction Database. "The Dragon Riders of Pern." *ISFDB.org.* http://www.isfdb.org/cgi-bin/pe.cgi?482

8. Muir, Tamsyn. *Gideon the Ninth.* Tor.com, 2019.

9. Anders, Charlie Jane. *All the Birds in the Sky.* Tor Books, 2017.

10. Mitchell, David. *Utopia Avenue.* Random House Trade Paperbacks, 2021.

11. Priest, Cherie. *Boneshaker.* Tor Books, 2009.

12. Murakami, Haruki. *Kafka on the Shore.* Knopf Doubleday, 2006.

13. Brockheimer, Kevin. *A Brief History of the Dead.* Vintage, 2007.

14. Lee, Fonda. *Jade City.* Orbit, 2018.

15. *Crouching Tiger Hidden Dragon.* Dir, Ang Lee. Columbia Pictures, 2000.

16. Lynch, Scott. *The Lies of Locke Lamora.* Del Rey, 2007.

17. Henry, Christina. *The Girl in Red.* Titan Books, 2019.

18. Bell, Matt. *Appleseed.* Custom House, 2021.

19. Michel, Lincoln. "The Long Messy Road to Publishing My Novel." *Counter Craft.* September 21, 2021. https://countercraft.substack.com/p/the-long-messy-road-to-publishing?s=r

INDEX

Page numbers: Notes are given as: [page number] n. [note number]

Index

Index